"THE ORDINARY DUTIES OF THE DAY": THE COLLECTED GRANDPA STORIES

Compiled by
MICHAEL P. RICCARDS
In collaboration with Cheryl A. Flagg

By the Author:
The Rose City Series:
A Hero of My Own Life: Living in Post-War America (CreateSpace, 2014)
Brief Encounters: The Memoirs of an Italian Grandpa (CreateSpace, 2016)
Plenary Indulgences (CreateSpace, 2017)
And the Earth Abideth (CreateSpace, 2018)
Great Trials and Petty Tribulations (CreateSpace, 2018)

Other volumes:
Woodrow Wilson as Commander in Chief (co-author) (McFarland Publishers, 2019)
Papal Greatness: The Ten Most Important Popes in the Catholic Church (CreateSpace, 2016)
Destiny's Consul: America's Ten Greatest Presidents (Rowman and Littlefield, 2012)
Faith and Leadership: The Papacy and the Roman Catholic Church (Lexington Books, 2012)
The College Board and American Higher Education (Farleigh Dickinson University Press, 2010)
The Myth of American Mis-education (Global Publications, 2004)
The Papacy and the End of Christendom: The Leadership Crises in the Church from 1500 to 1850 (Global Publications, 2002)
The Odes of DiMaggio: Sports, Myth, and Manhood in Contemporary America (Global Publications, 2001)
The Presidency and the Middle Kingdom: China, the United States and Executive Leadership (Madison Books, 2000)
Vicars of Christ: Faith, Leadership, and the Papacy in Modern Times (Crossroad Publishing, 1998)
Ferocious Engine of Democracy: The American Presidency 1789-1989 (Madison Books, 1995; second edition of volume 2, 2002)
A Republic if You Can Keep It: The Foundation of the American Presidency, 1700-1800 (Greenwood Press, 1987)
The Making of the American Citizenry: An Introduction to Political Socialization (Chandler Publishing, 1973)

The photograph on the front cover is of Raffaele and Luisa Finelli.

Portions of this book appeared in the author's *Tales and Times of an Italian Grandpa, Brief Encounters: The Memoirs of an Italian Grandpa, Plenary Indulgences, And the Earth Abideth Forever, and Great Trials and Tribulations*. The title is from John Henry Cardinal Newman's *Sermons*.

DEDICATION

MARGARET FINELLI RICCARDS
1917–2018
daughter, wife, and mother
who taught us gentleness in a harsh world

The Finelli Family, September 18, 1948

Grandma and Grandpa are in the second row, second and third on the left. The author's mother is in the flowered dress in the back. The little boy with big ears in the front row left is the author.

"Through his captivating 'Cantos', Dr. Michael Riccards introduces Grandpa's perspective on history, philosophy, pragmatism, morality, and humor. The old man masterfully preserves and promotes Italian cultural heritage while keeping the reader engaged.

The author's poetic prose presents Grandpa as the Italian 'Paterfamilias', who is instantly both *dulciter* and *firmiter* (sweet and firm). We all need this Grandpa in our lives."—

Cav. Dr. Gilda Battaglia Rorro Baldassari, Honorary Vice Consul for Italy, in Trenton, Emerita.

RAFFAELE FINELLI was born on March 21, 1884 in Rotondi, Italy, and died on May 25, 1969 in Madison, N.J. He married Luisa Perone on January 31, 1910. They came to the U.S. on February 22, 1910 on the ship *Celtic* of the White Star Line. They had nine children, not all of whom lived to maturity. Luisa was born in Benevento on November 4, 1889 and died on April 16, 1949.

Some people who have read these cantos or vignettes have asked if "Grandpa was real?" He is of course everyman, not just a relative doing unrelated chores in life. He was a working person who sought to make his way through the world as an honorable, tolerant, family-loving man. As to whether he was "real," yes, he was. He was my grandfather.

Everyman:
I pray you all give your audience,
And hear this matter with reverence,
By figure a moral play—
The Summoning of Everyman called it is,
That of our lives and ending shows
How transitory we be all day
This matter is wondrous precious,
But the indent of it is more gracious,
And sweet to bear away.
The story saith,—Man, in the beginning,
Look well, and take good heed to the ending.
Be you never so gay!

CONTENTS

ACKNOWLEDGMENTS

I am grateful to many people for anecdotes that are the basis for much of this collection, especially from Margaret Finelli Riccards. My wife, Barbara, has read these pages with her usual love and care, and I freely acknowledge the continuing editorial guidance of Cheryl A. Flagg, formerly Manager of Member Services, Council of Graduate Schools, Washington DC, and co-author with me of *Woodrow Wilson as Commander in Chief* and the forthcoming *Party Politics under FDR* . These stories were inspired by the Writing Seminar conducted by Rodney Richards, who so carefully commented on this work, and my fine colleagues over the last several years. The sketches were done by Robert Quinn.

The compiler is Michael P. Riccards, a former college president at three institutions of higher education and a public policy scholar for the College Board and the founding executive director of the Hall Institute. He is the author of several major books on the American presidency and the papacy as a management problem, and has written 24 verse plays, some of which have been produced.

SOME ITALIAN AMERICAN SLANG TERMS

Cafone: An uncouth person, lowlife (plural: *cafoni*)
Capisci: Understood
Coglioni: Testicles, balls
Fenucca: Gay person
Gabadost: Hard-headed, stubborn
Goombah: Close friend or associate
Medigan: American
Merda: Shit
Moulinyan: Crude name for African-Americans
Putana: Prostitute, slut
Sfacim: Bastard, son of a bitch
Stronzo: Turd, shit
Stunad: Stupid, in a fog

PREFACE

Dear Reader:

This collection is a series of vignettes, very short stories, on the life and experiences of my maternal grandfather. Readers have formed a deep attachment to Grandpa because he was a gentle, caring, hardworking, and honest man. Even in the 20th century, he was in many ways a child of the 19th century. It is also a series of stories on Italian and Italian American life with their principles, customs and anniversaries on display. With the death in 2018 of the author's mother, right after her 100th birthday, the last string of memory is lost from that family's romance.

The author is attempting to reconstruct and save the world of Italians in this country just as Philip Roth (also from New Jersey) and Frank McCourt recalled the worlds of Jewish and Irish life. The reasons that any of us keep those backgrounds alive is not to try to encapsulate those large ethnic groups as if they were tiny tribes to be examined. Novelists are not anthropologists.

But in the world we live in, American society is seized by political con men, financial sharpies, and even clergy who seem to have forgotten the spirit of the Deity they proclaim.

Librarians have asked if this volume is fiction, or biography, or history. The answer is yes, yes, yes. It is best to quote Ernest Hemingway's remark that he was "inventing from experience." These characters like Grandpa and his grandson are hopefully reliable alternatives to the harsh world we live in. The time will come when the nation's next generation or perhaps the one after that will grow weary of the current ethos and will look for alternatives. Perhaps these stories will provide the basis for such a decent re-examination.

The reader will rightly ask what is the creed that Grandpa lived by. He expressed it best when he was counseling a suicide-prone teenager:

> There are many fine men in Madison, more decent and more successful. I am just an old man who lives according to the tradizione, the old way of life. Tell the truth even if it hurts; give a man a handshake as your word; respect women and care for children; do one good deed a day; take care of the poor and the

maimed; acknowledge God even when He does bad things to you; enjoy the little things in life; promote friendships; treat strangers as friends; embrace the sun, fear the moon, await the change of the seasons, and smile every morning. Every day when I wake up I say, *Grazie a Dio sono vivo*. (Thank God I am alive.) There are many other codes that will make you more money, give you pretty girls to seduce, provide wealth, but in the end, life is measured by its simple triumphs, not by its world successes. Do well the ordinary duties of the day. For much passes away, except a man's reputation.

1. THE NEW WORLD

Grandpa came to this country with six relatives, all of whom lived in the same region east of Naples. In addition to their bloodlines, they shared one fate in common, each was not the eldest son in their family. And so for them only the army, the priesthood, or emigration was the answer to leaving the village or paese. Grandpa hated the army, even though his family liked to trace its roots back to the glorious "Red Shirts" who fought with the great Garibaldi in the nineteenth century to free Italy from the Bourbons and the papacy. He discounted the priesthood, probably as early as the advent of puberty. Emigration was the only recourse, and at the tender age of 16, he joined first with his father, and later with his paesani, in a great trans-Atlantic migration, crossing the ocean in boats meant more for animals, than for people.

As long as I knew him—even when he let me somewhat into his confidence—he never romanticized the "Old Country," as my sister likes to call it. He had been outside of his hometown several times before coming to America, and once on a brief excursion to Naples, Rome, and Florence. Apparently in Naples, he viewed the port region and the dangerously circuitous Amalfi Drive. In Rome, he claimed to have been unimpressed by the overly ornate St. Peter's Basilica, later arguing passionately with my mother that the money collected over the centuries to build the structure should have gone to the poor, especially the poor in the south of the country. However he respected the Sacred Steps outside the gates of St. John Lateran.

There on his knees, he crawled up the marble steps, allegedly brought from Jerusalem by St. Monica, the mother of Emperor Constantine, who insisted that Jesus Himself had staggered up those worn stones on his way to the Crucifixion. Grandpa and others saw the remnants of blood on the stones. For all his disdain of papal cant and parish priest hypocrisy, Grandpa loved the folk religion—the quiet ecstasy of Latin Catholicism and the black covered women who kept the faith for generations as far back as memory permitted.

It was in Florence that he suffered his greatest disappointment. There he was, he bitterly recalled seventy years later, a tall and modest structure—

1

R.M.S. CELTIC

almost like a polite re-creation. Deep in his heart, Grandpa expected more of Dante, more of the house of the imagination where the poet-chronicler of the agonies of Hell nourished from afar his love for the bedazzling Beatrice.

From the time he was sixteen until he reached full manhood, periodically he would go back to Italy, finally to woo and win a girl to be his wife. Grandma swore that when he came to her house, she ran off and hid in the flat-roofed barn, fearing this young man with his handlebar mustache, easy *medigan* money, and wing-tipped shoes that bore the imprint of his new homeland. Grandpa told a different tale: he liked what he saw, spoke with her father, and a deal was struck. As for her being in the barn, Grandpa simply said, "If she wanted it that way, to hell with her." Whichever tale is right, I do not know, but apparently, he must have prevailed, for she ended up being my grandmother, and she gave him nine children, three of whom never grew out of infancy.

Grandpa combined a jaunty sense of masculine command with an Old World patriarchalism. He was complex to the extent that even his daughters and sons never understood him. When he died, his daughters went dutifully through his last possessions. I tagged along and found a remarkable treasure. Next to his browning pictures of family life and his peculiar lithograph of Dante being led by Virgil into Hades, he had a serving tray with an imprinted picture displayed in the middle. My eyes brightened as I recognized a nude Marilyn Monroe, lying spread-eagle in the pose that made the centerfold of the first *Playboy* magazine in December 1953.

My God, what a treasure! But in a split second, homing in as if by radar, my Aunt Marie pulled the tray from my grasp and without missing a beat turned to my mother and pronounced that Grandpa, in his old age with failing vision, "probably mistook that picture for a Renaissance portrait." Even then I knew she was either lying or crazy. He was old and slowing down, but in that shell of a man still had beaten the heart of a normal male. Only in death could they deny his passion. The body that had entertained DiMaggio and seduced the Kennedy brothers had allure for him too.

In any case, tray or no tray, the great secret of his estate was "the book," and it was here that I knew more than Mama or Aunt Marie about the old man at his strangest. Apparently in a trip back to Italy, he purchased a book from a Neapolitan witch. She had released him from the persistent evil eye that he swore was given to him months ago in night school by an English teacher from Newark, New Jersey who had approached him in a blunt and forward way about the alleged prowess of Latin men. Grandpa explained her attraction thus, "She was divorced and had tasted the fruit of the forbidden tree," whatever that meant.

Leaving America on a ship, he was furiously stricken with a headache of incredible pain. When he arrived in Naples, the witch living in one of the city's many slums took him under her care, passed over his head a dish of cold water and dropped olive oil from her long painted fingers which spun around in dizzying circles. The dish told the truth—a woman of experienced evil with devilish powers had sought his soul. Luckily, his mind was on more pristine matters, and so once again storybook love would conquer all. The headache went away, the agitation lifted, and Grandpa passed a night he would never forget with the Neapolitan spell maker, a night only briefly divulged in bits and pieces to his grandson, while he savored the story when the sun had set and his daughters were off feeding their own families.

The witch told his future and predicted he would live to be 85, about the age at which he died. She also sold him a leather-covered black book, *The Book of Solomon*, with a cover embossed in gold Italian lettering. In that book were supposedly complicated phrases, codes, and numbered passages to the Bible that I could not translate into English. Out of his sight, one day, I took the book and tried to read it from the beginning. As best I could understand, it foretold the future, predicted great and terrible events, described character types to be wary of, unraveled the inscrutability of God's ways, and explained the promises of heaven and hell. But why was he so fascinated with the book, why he was so protective of it was a mystery. When he passed away no one ever found it.

It just vanished.

2. VERDI COMES TO TOWN

The greatest Italian composer of the century, Giuseppe Verdi, was traveling back from a vacation along the Adriatic Sea to the Naples opera house. He was riding in a regal coach with two horses, taking him through many picturesque back roads which would pass near the small town of Rotondi. The people there had heard about his trip and were delighted that he would be nearby. They wanted to welcome him, and although they did not have an opera house in that little town, they did have a full uniformed band.

Verdi was not just a composer, he was appointed a senator in the new unified Italy. During the period of Bourbon cruelties, his work had at the time been censored, but he was wily in avoiding the authorities. To symbolize his allegiance to the Italian Risorgimento, the revolution, he penned an opera called *Nabucco* which involved the famed chorus "*l'pensiero*," lamenting the captivity of the Hebrew slaves by the pharaoh. That tune became the unofficial anthem of the Risorgimento throughout the peninsula. Even his name became an anagram in Italian, **V**ittorio **E**manuele **r**e **d'I**talia *(*Long live Victorio Emmanuel, King of Italy). When the revolution was successful, as much as anything can be successful in Italy, Verdi became a national hero.

But national heroes have responsibilities, so he accepted the kind invitation to visit Rotondi and lead a parade through the center of town, stopping for a brief but sumptuous lunch. One of the onlookers was Grandpa, an aficionado of bands and music. Raffaele's family had no money left at the end of the month, so he never learned to play an instrument or even sing. Still he was going to the Giuseppe Verdi parade and was fated to walk at its end. His forebears had been allies of the patriots, and for a while hid the currency plates of the Risorgimento. The Spanish Bourbon governor learned of the treachery and tortured the members of the family by burning the soles of their feet. They still refused to tell the conquerors the fate of the plates, and the family became local heroes.

The very aged Maestro Verdi, armed with his top hat and weary at the end of a long journey, met the town celebrities, graciously bowed at their presence, and took from the bandleader the glorious baton, and he started to lead the band down a dusty main street to the town square. He, of course,

started with the chorus from *Nabucco*, which everybody knew, and all sang as they marched.

> Va, pensiero, sull' ali dorate;
> Va, ti posa sui clivi, sui colli,
> Ove olezzano tepide e molli,
> L'aure dolci del suolo natal!
> Del Giordano le rive salute,
> Di Sionne le torri atterrated.
> Oh, mia patria si bella e perduta!
> Oh, membranza si cara e fatal![1]

As they went past the local Catholic church, the parish priest was ordered by the bishop to turn his back on the Italian flag. It symbolized the new Italy,

---

[1] Fly, thought, on wings of gold,
Go settle upon the slopes and the hills
Where the sweet airs of our
Native soil smell soft and mild!
Great the banks of the river Jordan
And Zion's tumbled towers.
Oh my country, so lovely and lost!

the new Italian state, which had conquered the Papal States. But he was alone and Verdi was an anti-cleric anyhow.

In the plaza the people laid out tables of delicacies which the women had proudly made. "Viva Verdi," they cried, and he responded, "Viva l'Italia." At the luncheon the mayor casually told the story to the maestro of the bravery of the Finelli family. He pointed to his descendant, little Raffaele, who stood quietly over in the corner. As the party ended, Verdi rose with the baton and then stopped. He called the boy over and asked him to walk with him in the front, carrying the red, white and green flag of the republic. Raffaele was proudly now in front.

They returned by the same parade route, and Verdi struck up the Hebrew slaves' song once again, but he pointed to Raffaele and told him to carry high the Italian flag as they retraced the march. As they moved forward the maestro turned to Raffaele and said, "You have a good voice, and the mayor tells me you come from patriotic stock. What more could an Italian boy want?" Raffaele proudly marched by Verdi down the dirt road to his horses and elegant carriage. Once there the band continued to play tunes from *Il Trovatore* and *La Traviata* as Verdi took off his top hat and waved grandly. It was act five once again.

He heard them shouting, "Viva Verdi. Viva l'Italia," and was helped into the carriage and drove off. The band leader raised the baton Verdi had ceremoniously given back to him. They all marched home, Raffaele still carrying the Italian flag high, the red signifying of bravery, the white signifying purity of motive, the green signifying the beauty and hope of nature.

3. THE GREAT CARUSO

In the late nineteenth and early twentieth centuries the greatest tenor in the world was Enrico Caruso (1873-1921), a Neapolitan opera star who combined remarkable power and an extraordinary range. He appeared all over Europe and even in North Africa, celebrating the glories of classical opera and the new beautiful bel canto style. Grandpa loved opera, especially the patriotic Giuseppe Verdi's work, and he bought a hand-wound Victrola. On its moving table top he gently placed the 78 rpm single faced records that made Caruso one of the first singing celebrities.

In the early years of the new century, Grandpa put together a group from Madison of other Neapolitan born neighbors and set up a train trip on the Morris and Essex line to New York City to visit the old Metropolitan Opera built in 1883 at 39th and Broadway. By the time he finished, he and Grandma had some forty people from the parish who expressed an interest to go and see the great Caruso. The performance was set for Sunday, March 19, 1907, and the legendary tenor was cast as Canio in *Pagliacci*. Then they would eat at the inexpensive Lanza's Restaurant in the East Village. It would be an evening to remember, especially for people who rarely went to any event. As the day came closer, Grandpa was inundated by people in town, who couldn't understand Italian, but desperately wanted to see firsthand the great Caruso.

At the Madison train stop, the whole crew of opera fans and Caruso lovers mobbed the single railroad crossing and got on the moveable wicker seats. The group brought lunches, for two meals outside was just too expensive for most of them. But it did not matter, for they lived in anticipation of one of the most memorable events they could talk about for months after. Grandma was especially proud because Grandpa had taken the lead in this great excursion. They walked from Penn Station to the old Met, and Grandpa gave everyone a ticket. But as they moved inside the hall there was an awful sign in the foyer: Enrico Caruso is sick and will not sing today. The part of Canio will be played by Arturo Sefano. "Who? What happened?" Some wanted their money back immediately. What the hell, they had come to see Caruso not some understudy. Yet they had traveled so far on a Sunday, meaning that they could not simply go back.

In cold fury, Grandpa told them still to go in, and enjoy as best they could this fine opera. Stefano did a respectable job, but the refrain out of the audience was, "He is no Caruso!" And he wasn't.

After the performance, they took a fleet of cabs to the East Village to Lanza's Restaurant to eat a full Sunday dinner. The food was cheap, but it wasn't equal to the best of the women in the Madison ensemble. They began ordering and then eating, and out of the corner of his eye in a faraway table, Grandpa spotted, yup, the great Caruso. The tenor was joyfully eating and drinking, telling stories, and enjoying his favorite tales about his favorite subject—himself. Under his breath, Grandpa swore at the vain tenor, *sfacim*; he did not seem very sick to him. The waiter overheard him and asked what the problem was, for he was paid to make people happy. To Grandma's consternation, Grandpa told the whole tale of dedicated Caruso lovers coming all the way from rural New Jersey to hear Caruso, and then being pushed aside. The waiter said little, but he told the manager who in turn had the courage to really tell the grand tenor what was happening in the corner to his once sterling reputation. Especially troubled, Caruso asked him if those people spoke Napolitano, the dialect of the run-down urban neighborhoods where he had grown up.

Now Caruso was a truly great singer, but was consistently worried about his reputation, that it was all a hoax and he was a fool. *Was he the Pagliacci clown in real life?* he often wondered.

Caruso was dressed in a cutaway jacket with a huge handkerchief in his left pocket, French cuffs, a high collar, and a necktie with a pearl stickpin in it. He was partially balding and had dark full eyebrows. He was embarrassed by what these men and women might think of him, a real Italian hero to them. So he got up and walked over to Grandpa who he was told was the ringleader. He stuck out his strong right hand, and blurted out, "My name is Caruso. I am sorry you came to see me and I let you down. Sometimes my life gets so confused. Please accept my apologies and deep respect. Your name is?"

"Raffaele."

"And these are all your friends and I see your beautiful wife. You are a lucky man. I don't even have enough friends to fill one of these tables. Genova, here these are my new friends, they too are good Neapolitans. Put their dinners on my tab."

"No, you cannot do that," Grandpa protested.

"Yes, you are my neighbors. You remind me of my own family." They sat there smiling with their ill-fitting suits and long floral dresses up to their necks. "But I know you came to hear the Great Caruso sing, not eat and drink. Genova you know my favorites, play them in the usual order."

And then the powerful tenor's voice rocked the restaurant with old Neapolitan folk songs and opera classics. By the time he was done, he had sung: *O Solo Mio, Santa Lucia, Vesti la Giubba, Questa O Quella, Una Furtiva Lagrina, La donna e mobile*, and finally, *Ave Maria*.

The Madison audience and the whole restaurant applauded, hooted and shouted, "Viva Caruso," "God Bless the Great Caruso." And then the temperamental tenor came to an end to his performance.

He turned to Grandpa, "I know you all are from New Jersey. I go to Victor Recording Company in Camden to make my records. I invite all of you to come and be my guests. And now like the clown I must leave." He grabbed his cape, his cane, and his beautiful fedora and glided gracefully toward the door.

But he turned and gave Grandpa one of his caricatures of himself as a memento. It was better than an autograph, he judged.

Grandpa felt that he had given the Madison fans what they wanted only better, and Grandma was so proud as she kept the Caruso sketch next to her bosom.

A month later, Grandpa received a phone call from Caruso's agent. He was recording at the Old Trinity Church in Camden, a beautiful structure with great acoustics. He had saved a front row seat for Grandpa. Camden was a long way from Madison, but Grandpa went down. The agent remembered him and stuck him in a seat in the middle. After a magnificent recording session, Caruso brought Grandpa to his dressing room. "Ah, my friend, Raffaele, you honor me by coming here."

"You honor me by your kind invitation. I was sure you would forget."

"A man does not forget his friends or his paesani! Here I have made some of my best recordings, and my agent will give you copies of the last ten sessions. They are on the 78 rpms, only on one side. Some day they will be on both sides. Two Carusos for the price of one!"

So Grandpa carefully drove home and over the years he played the records over and over again. He played "Ave Maria" after one of his daughters died, and then after Grandma died. And when he was gone, his records were left with all his other toys of a long life. His sons inherited the apartment house, and anxious to sell it, they tossed out all the personal paraphernalia—the photos, the rosaries, and the 78 rpms discs. Only the sketch was not touched, for Grandma before her death quietly had given it to an old nun at St. Anna Villa who loved opera. Somewhere in the archives of that simple retirement home is a caricature of the Great Caruso, done by the Great Caruso.

4. DRIVING PUCCINI

We, you and I, forget that our grandparents were once young, in love, and had to deal with the trials and joys of life. In 1901, Grandpa again went back to Italy to take a bride. He very much wanted the innocent blonde girl in the Perone family in Benevento whom he had seen at church, like Dante saw Beatrice. They lived in a long, brownish stucco farmhouse, and she would stand on the balcony overlooking the fields and dream. The family had a reputation for taking care of the poor and infirmed of the region, and Luisa learned the arts of healing from the old women. Grandpa came from a family that was less well off, but he acquired from his family the same importance of helping the needy. Neighbors simply said both families were good people. Their children made a marvelous couple: from families that prized charity, gentleness, and good manners.

As related, Raffaele asked her father for her hand, but she ran away; she was reluctant to marry him and go off to a foreign country with a stranger. But she was convinced that she should obey her parents, so she had a wedding in the winter after the women in the family knitted a woolen wedding dress for her with a lace cape. They went to Capri for their honeymoon and on to the U.S after a long, upsetting boat ride.

Like most Italians, Grandpa listed his occupation as laborer. But his brother, Nick, became a chauffeur to the rich Americans living in the Madison area. He swore to Grandpa that this was the way to go, for Nick would do anything to make a fast and easy buck. Grandpa in the past had worked all day, and then at night attended class at Madison High School to learn the language and culture of the United States, his new home.

Grandpa read the newspaper, the *Newark Star Eagle,* for a nickel a day, and looked closely in the want ads. Then one day he saw a notice, "Wanted for week a chauffeur in New York City. Must speak Italian well. Call collect," and then listed a number.

Grandpa grabbed a dime off his dresser and went down to the drug store which had a pay phone. He called the number and got an Irish woman with a strong brogue who answered, "The Vanderbilts."

"I am calling about the ad in the paper for a chauffeur."

"Yes, please wait."

And then she put on the matron of the house, who in a cultured voice, answered, "Yes, I understand you are a certified chauffeur and speak Italian, is that so?"

"Yes, yes."

"Good, I want you to work for one week driving around a famed Italian composer who is being honored by the Metropolitan Opera House. I am on the board. I will pay you $1,000 for the week, and you can live in the servant quarters and eat there. We will, of course, take care of your laundry. Do you have a chauffeur's hat?"

"Oh, yes, where do you live?"

"We have several places; you will meet me and the maestro at the Vanderbilt Mansion on 1 West 57th Street. But you may know our place at Florham in Madison."

"Yes, of course, it is huge. I will arrive in New York City on Monday at 8 am. Is that fine?"

"Perfect, my man, Make sure you wear the cap Do not drive fast. I have a black Pierce Arrow."

Grandpa ran home and presented Grandma with his news—$1,000 for a week's work. "What a great country, Luisa! I must borrow from Nick the chauffeur cap."

She simply shared his delight but noted that this would be first time they were separated since they married. "I know, Luisa, but with that type of money we can buy a home for ourselves and a truck for my work."

So on Monday he went to Manhattan, and she prayed for his safety in that dangerous city. She went to 8 a.m. services every morning in his absence, praying for him and their marriage. The low Mass was said without any hymns, just in the old Tridentine Latin. On the right side of the main altar was an alcove dedicated to the Immaculate Heart of Mary. As she walked out of the church and down the hill, she said over and over again the prayer to St. Christopher for Grandpa in his travels:

> Dear St. Christopher
> Protect us today
> In all our travels
> Along the road's way
> Give your warning sign
> If danger is near
> So that we may stop
> While the path is clear.
> Be close at my side
> And direct us through,
> When the vision blurs

From out of the blue.
To my destined place,
Like you carried Christ
At close embrace. Amen.

Grandpa arrived at the Vanderbilt mansion, which occupied a whole stately block. He rang the chimes, and the Irish maid answered and escorted him in proudly. There in the parlor was Giacomo Puccini, the most famous conductor of the time. He politely rose, and introduced himself in Italian, speaking the dialect of Bologna. He was wrapped tight in his coat with a muffler, for he was always cold at home and abroad. Mrs. Grace Vanderbilt came into the parlor, pushed her poodle aside, and extended gracefully her hand to Grandpa. Then in Italian, she welcomed him and said how delighted she was to be able to set up Maestro Puccini with such a fine driver. She indicated that the Metropolitan Opera board, of which she was the major donor, had made Puccini a most generous offer to come and visit, and listen to his new opera, *The Girl of the Golden West*, or as the maestro called it, *La Fanciulla del West*. The Met premiere was in 1910, last year, and the opera takes place in Cloudy Mountain, California. The lead role is Dick Johnson, who was played by the great Caruso. For years Puccini and Caruso had been friends beginning when a young peasant boy arrived at Puccini's home in Lucca and asked if he could sing the role of Rodolfo in *Madame Butterfly*. Puccini was startled, but it was cold outside, and he wished to close the door, so he invited the tenor in. Being a gentleman he sat down and played the main aria from *La Boehme*, and Caruso sang. At the end, the composer inquired, "Who sent you to me…It must have been God." So they began their relationship. Mrs. Vanderbilt had heard the story a dozen times and loved it all the more. She then turned to Grandpa, "Tomorrow, you will drive both of them around Fifth Avenue. These two men like to window shop, and they may actually buy something!"

So the first day, Grandpa slowly drove Puccini around, and the maestro insisted on sitting in the front seat. He had nearly died in an automobile crash in Italy, so he wanted to see what the driver was doing. Puccini had badly broken his right leg in the crash and still had a limp. He enjoyed New York especially in the daylight at its finest, and once asked to see the poor houses of Little Italy along Mulberry Street where his compatriots struggled to make end meet and raise children.

The next day when he arrived, Grandpa went into the parlor, and there sprawled on a large sofa was the great Caruso. He was short, stocky, and dressed immaculately in a fine silk suit with a diamond pin placed through the center of his fine white shirt and tie. He jumped up and in the Neapolitan dialect welcomed the chauffeur as if he were a family member. He and Puccini were both delighted to be in each other's company and going shopping. Grandpa drove them down Fifth Avenue, and they stopped and went from one store to another. It was a fine example of what happened when poor boys get money and are let loose on the town. Caruso insisted that they stop at the St. Patrick's Cathedral on Fifth Avenue and look at the Neo-Gothic structure, rather different from the churches of their youth.

Caruso was hungry and desired to go to Del Pezzo's on 34th street, a familiar haunt for actors and singers of the day. He was so known and appreciated that the owner saved a table for him whenever he was in town. They even named a dish after him: "Tagliolini Enrico Caruso," spaghetti with chicken livers in oil and butter and chopped tomatoes. Caruso insisted that they go there for lunch, and invited Raffaele to join them as well. Puccini ordered chicken parmesan, Raffaele wanted veal parmesan, and Caruso insisted on his own dish with a side order of ziti with meat sauce. After a brief time talking, they were joined by David Belasco, the theater mogul who was training Met dancers to perform in the very different choreography of Puccini's *The Golden Girl*. He was himself an author and playwright and was concerned that the original book be honored. Then they were joined by Marziale Sisca, the owner of the Italian American paper, *La Follia*. After two hours, Caruso had finished two bottles of red wine from Lacryma Christi, near Naples. And Puccini weary with all the business talk, asked to go home. And so they did.

The next day, they began shopping near Times Square, and for lunch they went to Sherry's, the restaurant in the Metropolitan Opera building at 39th Street. The prices were high, but Caruso just signed the check to the board's account under Puccini's name. They were soon joined by the famed conductor Arturo Toscanini who led the opera orchestra and insisted that Puccini's notes be played as he wrote them. That respect made them lifelong friends; Caruso listened, believing that the score was meant to carry his enormous voice. Raffaele simply nodded and was impressed by the distinguished conductor's command of the music.

For the next several days, they went window shopping, and finally on Friday night, Raffaele finished up his duty to the praises of his fellow Italians. Grace Vanderbilt was highly delighted at her success in showing the town to the maestro, and she handed Raffaele ten one hundred bills. "I hope that I can call on you if I need your services, either here or in Madison." She had found out some way where he lived.

A delighted Raffaele went home on the train and met Grandma. He proudly showed her the money in crisp bills. They were going to purchase that apartment house he had seen from the railroad station. The $1,000 would be a respectable down payment for 81 Main Street, where he and Grandma would raise a family and live out their lives.

Six months later, a courier came from Western Union. Grandma hated Western Union; it usually meant a death in the family. But the letter was covered with a caricature of Grandpa, and she called him to look at it. He smiled it was one of the signature works of an idle Caruso. Inside, were two tickets to the Metropolitan Opera debut of a new opera, *Mona* by Horatio Parker, March 14, 1912. On the envelope was written in Italian script, "To our friend, from Caruso and Puccini, enjoy."

Grandpa was delighted, and perused the tickets and pronounced to his wife, "Ah, these must be Mrs. Vanderbilt's box in the Diamond Horseshoe, those are the best in the house, and they surround the second tier and stick out in front. Magnificent. God bless them all."

Grandma felt embarrassed, for she had no dress that would be appropriate for that evening, but Grandpa said that she was the beauty that would shine out. And so they went to the opera, and then after it, Grandpa took her to Del Pezzo on West 34th Street. When he walked in, the owner thought that Caruso had sent him, having seen them together before. So he gave him the tenor's reserved table and insisted that he himself would pick up the tab. Grandma was so proud, and she was overwhelmed. There, Grandpa started to hum the aria "*O Quanti occhi Fisi*" from *Madame Butterfly* which he heard Caruso sing in full throat to Puccini whenever they sat down to eat. He forgot the lyrics but remembered the music. Grandma blushed, and Grandpa ordered for both of them the wine that the great Caruso loved. "This is from Naples," he proclaimed.

They walked over to Penn Station and took the late train back to Madison. Grandpa and his wife sat in one seat facing home, and he took her hand in his. He never realized how small her hands were.

5. THE FRUITS OF WAR

During the Great War in late October 1917, the carnage revolted in the West around the battle of Caporetto on the Austrian-Italian frontier. The Austro-Hungarian armies, reinforced by Germans, ended up destroying the Second Italian Army, leaving the Italians' war effort in shambles. It was in that battle that the Germans used poison gas (chlorine and phosgene) which killed, maimed, and destroyed the lungs and bodies of thousands of men.

Grandpa's cousin, Bernardo, was a violinist with the local opera. He loved music more than anything in the world. He played within his limited scope, and it opened up his shyness to the sacred worlds of music. His moods changed with the compositions, and he lived in a world of joy and effusive expressions. He was a quiet, well-mannered young man who in 1916 was drafted and became a medic in the Second Army. And as he pulled a soldier at Caporetto to safety, he was hit by a puff of chemicals, and nearly died. He was brought to a field hospital and then to a major facility near the Alps.

For six months, on cold fall nights in Italy, he stayed bedridden, barely able to breathe at times and squinting at vague lights. He would go through cold sweats, and then become furiously hot. He tried not to moan, especially at night, but parts of his skin still had boils from the gas. One night, the young man lay looking at the lovely night, and a volunteer nurse came in. She gave him heavy doses of morphine to dull the pain and put him to sleep. Then she covered his face and chest with cold compresses, and he shook violently from the cold, so she tried to warm his body. And at one point in the darkness, she climbed into bed with him side by side to warm him up, and it was then that for both of them nature took its course. He had never felt that experience before: the softness, the tenderness, a union of two young lives. Two days later he was shipped home. The "great" Italian Second Army had no space for all its wounded, and so they moved him south to his family. He had no mother or father or wife, only his contentious older sister who lived on the farm. Bernardo was shipped to her in a nearly broken down train. Soon at home, she grew weary of caring for him, for he just sat in a chair staring out at the olive trees. Bernardo's sister was a woman of little sentiment, and she decided to write to her cousin Raffaele, who had made his

16

MICHAEL P. RICCARDS

way to America, the land of milk and honey. She had no shame and told him that it was his turn to shoulder the burden. She demanded Grandpa get a work visa for him, knowing of course that he could not work. Grandma came from a family that took the poor of the town into their home, a long tan colored dwelling situated in the middle of rich fields. She had grown up in a family of genuine personal philanthropy, and when Grandpa hesitantly proposed bringing Bernardo to the empty far bedroom, she simply agreed. Earlier, she had acquired a reputation for being a "healing woman," adept at folk remedies and traditional medicines in a section of Italy without many skilled physicians or nurses.

Grandpa applied for a worker's visa and met Bernardo in the Ellis Island pens. He quickly put a wide brim hat on him to hide his sickly face. Bernardo ended up at the apartment, sitting quietly in the back room day in and day out looking at the traffic on Main Street, and talking only to Grandma when she tried to deal with his eyes and sores. In the process, she learned that Bernardo loved one thing—his violin, long lost back in the chaos of Italy.

So that night she appealed to Grandpa, "You know I ask you for little, but I have one request."

"Of course, you know I will do anything for you, anything at all."

"I want you in your travels to find a violin for Bernardo."

"Why a violin?"

"He used to play. It gave him pleasure. We need something to help him. My cures are very limited with what he has."

"All right, I know Mrs. Gillette is giving away her late husband's possessions, and he had a violin and a flute."

So the next day, Grandpa arrived home with a violin and a flute, and thus Bernardo received from Grandma a used violin. He would tune it, and first ask Grandma each day if she would mind if he played. And she always said "No, of course not," and came to enjoy his music and turned off the Philco radio. Bernardo played and played, but he was still haunted by the demons of war, and the images of body parts, of dead children, of old men in lime pits. The doctor would give him moderate amounts of heroin to kill the worst manifestation of the pain, but two days later his insides throbbed again.

One evening Grandpa came to visit. He disliked going into the room and was happy to leave the care to Grandma. For the first time, Bernardo welcomed him warmly, and Grandpa sat down. Bernardo shyly asked if he could talk to him man to man. He told him in circumspect Italian of his liaison with the young volunteer nurse and described in vague words how beautiful the feelings were for such a woman—the only one in his life. Later he learned from his ill-tempered sister that the young woman who lived in the north of the country had given birth to a boy, his son, but Bernardo's sister refused to tell the mother his address or Bernardo her address. Because of his sister, he never knew about the son until he was in the United States.

The volunteer nurse was lost in the horrors of the war. He cursed his sister, and the next day he went into a near coma, and Grandpa, confused by the abruptness of it all, told no one anything, even Grandma.

When the doctor came again, Bernardo complained vociferously about the pain, and the doctor left several vials of morphine, but reminded him that with his limited eyesight, he should not fill the syringes. "Have someone do it for you," he warned. Bernardo nonchalantly agreed, but that night he drove all three vials into his stomach and died with the violin on his lap.

Grandpa and Grandma told no one how he died, for they wanted him buried in consecrated ground. Grandma simply argued, "He has suffered enough in his life. That was his hell."

A week later Grandma received a call from the lawyer, Volpe the fox. He needed to see her as soon as possible. "Oh, more trouble," she said to Grandpa. So they went up to Volpe's office above the drug store with the sign "Volpe and Volpe," except there was no second Volpe, he just like the sound of it.

Quickly he informed Grandma that Bernardo had left all he possessed to her in a will she did not even know existed. Grandpa was secretly delighted, for he had now a growing number of children, one of whom had contracted polio, and money was in short supply. But then Volpe announced that Bernardo had more assets than imagined. "He had a modest pension of 10,000 lira as a wounded veteran, but he had also the proceeds from the sale of the family farm to a German chemical company. With your sister's death, you are the sole heir. The estate is quite substantial."

Grandpa and Grandma walked home in silence and said little for days about their good fortune. Then two days later, after dinner, Grandpa was sitting on his porch smoking his best pipe. Grandma came over to see him and quietly said, "Dear, I have decided to give all of Bernardo's money to the unmarried mothers' home in Morristown run by the Sisters of Charity. They take good care of new mothers and their babies. Bernardo had no children, now he has many of them to care for."

"Do you mean all the money?"

"Yes, all of it."

Grandpa was tempted to tell her the whole story of Bernardo's secret life and love, but he kept the tale to himself as he had promised, for he was an honorable man.

And so, Grandpa just grunted, sucked on his pipe, and thought, *Easy come, easy go.*

6. THE THIRTEENTH CHILD

When in the 1920s, polio struck Grandpa's oldest child, the family resorted to endless doctors and finally a well-regarded masseuse from Berkeley Heights who used a variation of the Sister Kenny method of therapy. It took a long time and she was much in demand. While she and Grandma used physical massage combined with deep prayer, the pastor, Rev. John Lambert, came over to join and keep Grandpa company, and the situation slowly, very slowly, improved. Grandpa already held three jobs but needed more money to pay for the therapist. *That was*, he thought, *the only contribution a poor man could make in this herculean effort.*

He was at the end of his rope emotionally, and then one day he heard some Italian workers talking humorously of the legend of the Jersey Devil. Apparently, there was a rich merchant in Convent Station, near the nuns' residence, who wanted someone to lead him into the Pine Barrens near Burlington to track down this legendary monster since so many people claimed to have seen him. But the witnesses left with little evidence to back up the tale. Now Italians are a superstitious people, and Grandpa was not the least of them. But in the conversation, they laughingly remarked that the merchant would pay $1,500 to a traveling companion who knew the outdoors to go with him on his search. It was that offer that Grandpa was attracted to, and he carefully noted the name of the merchant and showed up the next day at his store in Morristown.

The owner was delighted and wanted to make sure Grandpa knew the details of the confusing tale. Over the years, starting in 1735, it was reported that Mother Leeds had 12 children already and cursed the thirteenth. The last child was incredibly ugly, sprouted horns from the top of its head, and had talon-like claws. He had red eyes, and changed into a long-shaped creature, like a hairy kangaroo with bat wings, and flew up the chimney stack. Years later, the publisher of almanacs and occult books, David Leeds, told the story and got into a nasty argument with the well-known rationalist Benjamin Franklin of Philadelphia. Leeds was a nominal Quaker, but they soon excommunicated him from their quiet midst.

Joseph Napoleon, the emperor's brother, who was living in Jersey, claimed he saw the devil traveling beyond his land. The war hero Commodore Stephen Decatur claimed he fired a cannon ball at the devil. The stories lived on into this century, and accounts of the Jersey Devil are still repeated.

Grandpa did not fully understand the story, but he signed up for the trip and moved slowly through the Pine Barrens toward Leedstown. Before he began, he prayed to St. Christopher, the patron of travelers:

> Grant me, O Lord, a steady hand and watchful eye that no one shall be hurt as I pass by.
> Shelter those dear Lord, who bear my company, from the evils of fire and all calamity.
> St. Christopher, patron of travelers, protect me and lead me safely to my destiny, Amen.

As they moved into the center of the Barrens, they saw some muted tracks and some bones, but nothing of use. Then one dim night with a quarter moon, they faced the White Steed whose hoofs matched the Jersey Devil's. They both saw a frightening looking monster that was a good 200 feet away. The merchant took out his new camera and took pictures for the record, but it jammed, and his pictures were ruined.

Still he sat down with Grandpa and sketched out what it was that they had seen including the White Steed, and he formed the footprints, but the mud was too soft to make a good cast in rainy Burlington County. Still, the merchant was delighted and at Bordentown he gave Grandpa $1,000—$500 less than they agreed on. He apologized but he had to use the remaining money to buy a new camera. Grandpa was angry for he needed the money for the therapist in the coming months.

But he had no choice, *for beggars cannot be choosy.* he lamented. He took the ten $100 bills and dropped the merchant off at St. Mary's cemetery where Daniel Leeds was supposed to be buried. The merchant had also made an appointment to read the parish records of the Leeds family, especially the siblings and, if possible, the 13th child. He walked over to the rector's residence.

Grandpa was glad to be rid of him, and in his old truck drove up the bumpy Jersey roads north to Madison. Thus he acquired enough money to pay the therapist for nearly a year. He was a man who had done a man's work. His son recovered, thanks to God and man, and went back to school. He was the only child of Grandpa's who went to college and became an engineer. The son acquired nearly a dozen patents and worked for Merck Pharmaceuticals. Grandpa though never told him of his experiences with the Jersey Devil, for his son was a man of science. Then one day, the old man saw that the County of Camden was offering a reward of $30,000 for the capture of the Jersey Devil which was to be caged and put on display for tourists. No one ever collected the money. Grandpa laughed and thought he was the only one who had ever made any money off the Jersey Devil.

7. ACCORDING TO THE ORDER OF MELCHIZEDEK

The worst war of modern times up to that point in history was the Great War which lasted from 1914 to 1918. Over 41 million people were killed or wounded. In addition the pandemic flu swept the world from 1917 to 1920 which took even more lives than the war did, some 50 million people. The eastern part of the United States was especially affected. One of Grandpa's children was struck with pneumonia and nearly died.

The St. Vincent parish played a major role in the borough. Despite the residual anti-Catholicism, the Sisters of Charity who taught school and provided nurses for hospitals, took over the care of massive numbers of patients and turned the old YMCA into a ward. The nuns arrived in the early hours in the Black Maria, a horse drawn stagecoach, which made trips of mercy back and forth every day and at night from the large residential convent of St. Elizabeth in Convent Station. When the war ended, the levels of anti-Catholicism in town markedly declined.

In the parish, the church was dependent on one extraordinarily gifted priest—a German American named John Lambert, who was pastor from 1913 to 1926 and was born in Philadelphia and educated in Brooklyn. He was a student at Seton Hall College before going to Brignole Sole in Genoa and the University of Innsbruck. In Genoa, Italy, the home of Christopher Columbus and the one time jail site of the remarkable Marco Polo, he learned Italian and respected the methodical culture of the industrious people and their commitment to the sea. He served most of his career in Hackensack, and when he was chosen to be pastor of St. Vincent, he was intimidated by the magnificence of the Norman Gothic church patterned on Christ Church at Oxford, and initially turned down the assignment.

He took an immediate interest in St. Vincent's Elementary School and added two wings to meet the demand for education he himself had created. To the outside community, especially his fellow clergymen, he was deeply respected and admired. He was, the bishop once said, a priest's priest.

He was also an amiable cleric, and stayed longer for confessions, visited the sick more frequently, tried to get employment for people in the 1920s, and said more Masses than he was really permitted to under Canon Law. Most charmingly, he walked the neighborhoods, stopping to talk with his co-religionists and strangers in their homes and stores.

Grandpa remembered him well, for he would drop by just to chat in Italian with no real purpose, like making small talk with your next door neighbor. Then when Grandpa's son Salvatore came down with the scourge of polio, Father Lambert would visit Grandpa and kneel down and pray with Grandma and the Swedish masseuse before they began physical therapy sessions. In the very depths of the family's despair, just before Christmas, he arrived with a crèche of the Nativity as a gift for the bedridden boy. The family never forgot the act of kindness.

In addition, the war and the flu epidemic left few able bodied men to dig graves for the coffins of the church's dead, and the ancient rite was truncated. It was difficult to dig a ditch in the cold Jersey winter soil, and people feared coming in contact with individuals felled by the influenza plague. To the surprise of parishioners, Father Lambert was seen outside after a funeral, digging grave sites as best he could.

The tremendous workload weakened his health and pneumonia struck Father Lambert, and he died like any other mortal man. Grandpa was terribly saddened over the loss to the parish and more importantly to his own family. He feared that there would be no one to bury their own priest, and he would die alone. He quickly got hold of the president of the Knights of Columbus and received a soft commitment from them to not only be at the Mass, but also to serve with him as pallbearers and go to the cemetery to inter the priest.

But much to Grandpa's surprise, large numbers of people of all religious beliefs showed up for the Mass given by the bishop for Father Lambert, showing once again that the good that men do, sometimes lives after them, at least for one generation. But few went on to the cemetery, avoiding the messy soil of what was called the "Priests' Circle." Luckily the Knights did show up in force, but the ground was frozen, and six elderly men were no match for the Jersey tundra.

And then down Noe Avenue came Johnny "Big Ben" Barone who worked for the public works department and conveniently without their knowledge borrowed a backhoe to rip open the ground. One could almost hear the gears when he gently and slowly drove over to the Priests' Circle and opened up the plot designated for the beloved pastor. The Knights of Columbus patrons placed the casket in the slot, and Johnny politely refilled the hole, with the pall bearers placing the huge number of flowers on top. Many people loved Lambert, but they feared coming in contact with diseased people, so they sent flowers to say something supportive. And in huge mountains, the arrangements sat there on top of what was supposed to be a modest grave representing a modest man.

The bishop jumped out of his black Buick limousine, gave a quick prayer in Latin, and reminded all, "He who believes in the Christ Jesus lives forever." And then he popped back in his car and left. It was cold outside.

Some of the faithful just stood and watched sadly—Father Lambert should have had some greater finale they thought. Then Gerry Gerro stepped out from the Knights of Columbus group. He had once been an aspiring singer in the New York City clubs imitating the early crooners. And he began to sing not a Catholic hymn, for he never went to church, but the Chorus of the Hebrew Slaves from Giuseppe Verdi's opera "*Nabucco*" (Nebuchednezza, 1842). The group picked up the familiar refrain, for everyone knew it—it was the patriotic song of the Italian Risorgimento, a sort of a Star Spangled Banner. The song was not sad or tortuous, but upbeat and loud, the sound of a free people.

Va, pensiero, sull'ali dorate;
Va, ti posa sui clivi, sui colli
Ove olezzano tepide e molli
L' aure dolci del suolo natal!
Del Giordano le rive saluta,
Di Sionne le torri atterrate.
Oh, mia patria si bella e perduta!
Oh, membranza si cara e fatal!

And then Gerro dropped back into English and repeated the first stanza:

Fly, thought, on wings of gold,
Go settle upon the slopes and the hills
Where the sweet airs of our
Native soil smell soft and mild!
Great the banks of the river Jordan
And Zion's tumbled towers.
Oh, my country, so lovely and lost!
Oh remembrance so dear yet unhappy!

And so that day, the Knight of Columbus buried a priest, above whose grave was a long tombstone for all the priests, which read "priests according to the order of Melchizedek." Grandpa did not know who he was, but figured he must have been a good priest, for why would they bury other priests here? As Grandma used to say, "Once a priest, always a priest."

8. THE 60th

In September 1927, Grandpa's friend Delgato gave him a New York Yankee ticket to see a baseball game on the last afternoon of the season. Delegato had gotten the ticket from his grandson, but frankly was afraid to ride the New York subways and sent it to Grandpa to pay in part for his losses incurred at a Friday night card game a month before. Grandpa knew nothing about baseball; when he saw it on the local playgrounds, he viewed it as a slow moving, graceless game, so different from soccer. But for some strange reason of adventure, he decided at the age of 43 to go by himself to the new Yankee Stadium. Previously the Yankees had shared the Polo Grounds with the Giants, and Colonel Jacob Ruppert built a stadium out of his own money. His funds came in part because of the increase in attendance since his acquisition of one player, George Herman Ruth, a pitcher and sometime fielder from the hapless Boston Red Sox. The owner of the Red Sox, Harry Frazee, then put the $100,000 he got for Ruth into a Broadway show, *No, No, Nanette*. Thus the curse of the Bambino went to a charming musical.

Grandpa had heard of the slugger, and he insisted on calling him Baby Ruth. And he knew the newspapers were ablaze with the possibility that Ruth might hit 60 home runs, breaking his own record of 59 in 1921. Grandpa knew that this was an important day and so he wanted to be a part of American history. He took the train into Manhattan and carefully followed the crowds wearing Yankee caps up to 168th Street.

As he rose out of the subway entrance, he saw in front of him the great American Coliseum, like in Rome, but in beautiful new blue which housed in those days some 62,000 people on a good day. Later the owners would expand it to nearly 70,000. His seat was in the high right field bleachers, rows and rows above the wall. The seats were comfortable, for in those days people had narrower behinds. This was the "house that Ruth built," fans proclaimed.

The entire stadium stood up and cheered as the Yankees took the field. In those days, the National Anthem was not sung at the beginning, so the game started immediately. The Yankees were playing the Washington Senators, with lefty fastballer Tom Zachary pitching. The fans came for one reason: to

see the Babe hit number 60, for the Yankees had already clinched the pennant as usual. Miller Higgins, the Yankee manager, scheduled Ruth in the number three spot, reserving the cleanup position for the incomparable Lou Gehrig who was having an incredible year himself with an average of .373, 47 home runs, and 178 RBIs.

The first time Ruth was up he was fanned on three fast balls. He had more home runs in baseball history, but he also had struck out more than anyone else in that same chronicle. The second time he was at bat he popped up, and ran with his spindly legs down the line to first base. But in the 8th inning, he drilled a fastball into the upper bleachers in right field and the stadium rocked with delight. The ball rose up off his quick thick bat and came down in the bleachers, in the cheap seats where Grandpa was seated. He was startled and he took off his old fedora to see the ball against the blue sky of New York. He did it for safety reasons, so he could see and not be hit. But the ball bounced three times, then over the grasping hands of the hysterical fans, and it fell like a lump in Grandpa's hat. He grabbed it and held it close to him. The stands cheered one of their own and patted him on the shoulders. What had happened?

Very quickly two of New York City's finest came and took him gently by the arms and carried him away. *What had he done now? Good God, he had left his citizenship papers home.* But they seemed honored to have him in their grasp and made their way into the New York Yankee dugout. He was to meet the Babe, they said. The game was soon over, and the delighted Yankees came in to celebrate the victory in the pennant race, especially to cheer on Ruth. He emerged grinning like a little kid and surrounded by a score of scribes. Ruth was tall, with a big belly, and spindly legs. "So, kid, you caught my 60th?" He called all men kids and all broads, well, broads. "Good for you. It was a great day for baseball, right? Look, that ball means a lot to me, and I would give you anything for it."

Grandpa quizzically looked, "It is yours, not mine. It just fell into my lap"

Ruth smiled nonchalantly, "Yeah, I get a lot of broads falling into my lap. But will you give me a number, money?"

Grandpa insisted, "No, it is yours alone," and he handed the scuffed ball to the slugger.

Ruth was confused, "God, you Italians are a strange people. I had a priest like you in St. Mary's when I was young. He made me into a ballplayer not a bum…oh well. I can't let you leave with nothing. The press will kill me for being a cheap bastard. How about taking a picture together, and I'll autograph it to…who?"

"To Raffaele."

"To Ralph, my best outfielder!" And then he turned to manager Miller Higgins and asked if Grandpa could stay and have champagne with them. But Higgins never answered, and Ruth said, "Of course you can. Here is the very first glass for you Ralphy, kid. And I am sorry about your hat, it got a little beat up, but you can have my Yankee cap. It is a little big, but I will autograph it too. The hat that the Bambino wore for number 60. Someday it will be worth a fortune."

And then he turned to his personal bat boy, "Make sure Ralphy has a limo to take him home, no subway for this guy. Where do you live?"

"Madison, New Jersey, west of Newark."

"Oh, near Newark. Yeah they gave me a banquet there in 1925. Good solid Yankee fans. That stupid Ty Cobb told people I was a black man because of my lips, it ain't true, but the Negro people turned out to see me. Hard working people, I wish they could afford to come to the stadium."

And so Grandpa arrived home only an hour and a half later. He tried to tell Grandma the story, but she was more impressed about the limo in front of her apartment house.

For many years the story circulated in the family, but no one could prove Grandpa was telling the truth, for he loved a good yarn and had left the cap in the limo. Then in 1995, his grandson met the bat boy who was then in his 80s at a conference on the topic of Babe Ruth hosted at Hofstra University. He got up the courage to ask the old man if he remembered the incident. "Yeah, the dago looked like Sacco-Vanzetti, a really nice and honest guy though. Babe sent him home in a limo that day and gave the ball to the Hall of Fame in Cooperstown. But he never knew the full name of the guy who caught it, so the Hall doesn't have an acknowledgement card. I told his story once before to a young newspaper man named Bob Quinn. I think he was going to write a story on it. Boy, that Quinn loved chewing tobacco like the Babe loved hot dogs. Did I ever tell you the story of when the Babe ate ten hot dogs before a game, and then couldn't play? Christ, was Miller Higgins pissed off at him that day. They called it the 'bellyache that shook the world.'"

9. FREEDOM TO CHOOSE

One cool afternoon, Grandpa was aimlessly sitting on a park bench in the center of town, across from the train station and the municipal hall where he had just paid his electric bill. He was looking at the dark clouds moving in, and wondering how soon rain would come. Then a high school girl sat next to him, whom he knew only in passing, Theresa Sandino, wearing the colors of Bailey-Ellard High School named after the relatives of the devout Mother Seton, who would be the first American-born saint. Theresa was sobbing uncontrollably, and Grandpa couldn't help but ask what was happening to her. She refused to talk, but then burst forward, "He said he loved me, but when I told him I was pregnant, he said he was married with a child and could not leave all that for me. I was just a toss in the hay, and not even a good one."

Grandpa didn't know what to say; he wished Grandma were here instead of him. For some reason people often will tell strangers what they will never tell their best friends. He tried to console her with meaningless expressions, which they both knew were meaningless, and then she said, "I am going today for an abortion."

Grandpa could not understand how a young Catholic girl soon would be in the hands of an abortionist. "Wait," he counseled, "think about this."

"I have and this is where I am at. If my parents find out, they would just wither up and die. And the nuns at the school will ban me forever as a murderer."

And then she went. Grandpa was rarely judgmental, on any matter, but he was clearly opposed to the idea of an abortion, for anyone for any reason. Some of his friends said it was because he was a narrow-minded Catholic, but it was more because of his love of babies.

As the years progressed, they would pass each other on the streets of the town and say nothing. Later, Theresa had two children, ages 7 and 5, and lived a normal life in Madison. One day as Grandpa was sweeping the sidewalk in front of his apartment building, Theresa saw him and deliberately came down the side of the street toward him. She said abruptly, "Last week my mother died. I have no parents or siblings left."

"I am sorry."

"So I need you to do a favor I have no right to ask. I want to put a tombstone in the church cemetery for my dead fetus. I can't think of her going to limbo." She used "her" since it seemed more vulnerable. Grandpa assured her that her baby was in heaven, but she refused to believe it. "I want you to have a tombstone with her first name, Catherine, and the date set in the Knoll of Innocents where other little babies lie in the St. Vincent Cemetery." Grandpa knew the cemetery caretaker and it was done. Several weeks later, he saw in the church bulletin a memorial Mass in honor of "Baby Catherine." He thought little about it and was glad that he could offer some consolation. But still after all these years, he was judgmental and almost harsh in his views of abortion.

Then Grandpa's wife in her early 40s, got pregnant, her last pregnancy, and it was a very difficult period for her. Finally at the hospital, a grim doctor approached a trembling Grandpa. "I am afraid we may have to make a choice, save your wife or the new baby."

Without a pause, Grandpa pronounced, "Save my wife." So it seemed that in the end he would sacrifice the infant, but through the miracles of modern medicine and much prayer that afternoon, they both lived and came home with him. Still, in his heart he knew he had made a choice, and whenever he saw his last son he was reminded of it. Every March on the anniversary of the abortion, Grandpa came up with flowers for the family, and he went also to Catherine's gravesite, there in the Knoll of the Innocents.

10. DEUS EX MACHINA

Few things are more demoralizing to a people than drought, for it seems as if the very gods are angry with their creatures. In the United States, the drought moved harshly across huge areas and created a dust bowl and massive migrations of poor people to the golden West. But in the 1930s, the curse of drought was also traveling along a streak from north of the New Jersey border down to the eastern panhandle of West Virginia.

Recognizing the doleful effects on the morale of the people in his state, the corrupt Jersey City Democratic boss, Frank Hague, decided to visit the man he had helped to elect in 1932, the patrician Franklin Delano Roosevelt. Roosevelt actually disliked Hague, but unlike the other urban bosses, Hague delivered huge pluralities for the new presidential candidate, and was simply satisfied with buckets of patronage and WPA jobs for his people. He could not care less about urban liberalism and the leftist philosophy of the New Deal.

When he came calling, which was rare, FDR made time to listen. This time Hague came to the point, "Boss, this drought is destroying the morale of the people of Jersey, and bad feelings are not good for incumbents as Hoover found out. New Jersey is by temperament a Republican state, and I fear for 1936. Frankly, I am not sure how many dead people I can call up to vote for the party's ticket, that is, for you."

Roosevelt as usual nodded but said little. Then he reasoned, "Frank, rain is the key, plain old-fashioned rain."

Hague was a bit annoyed by the condensation. "We can't control rain, but we can surely bring hope to the people in this mean summer time. That is what you do best, boss, and I want you to go into the northern Republican counties and help me offset the margins. I am worried about '36; you are a great president, but you are a damned controversial one too."

Roosevelt was in no mood for an argument, and besides he rarely disagreed with people to their face. "Okay, Frank, set it up with Jim Farley. On to Jersey."

"I cannot be with you there, boss, those counties hate me and the Hudson machine."

"Fine, as long as they don't end up hating me," FDR chuckled.

Jim Farley, the head of the Democrat party, needed a large rural place in Morris County where FDR could meet masses of people and shake some hands from his open Lincoln convertible, "the Sunshine Special." Farley came to choose the two estates in Madison owned by Geraldine Rockefeller Dodge, who operated huge tracts of land, and employed hundreds of Italian immigrants, especially to grow roses. Thus as noted the tiny borough was called, "the Rose City." Being a Rockefeller, she detested FDR and at a cocktail party on Park Avenue in Manhattan, she called him "a traitor to his class." Roosevelt probably was, but Farley had FDR's wealthy mother, Sara, who traveled easily in the circles of the hereditary rich, approached the Dodge matron. Geraldine was quick to relay her views to Sara, but Sara responded abruptly, "My dear, your Grandfather John D. hated our cousin Theodore Roosevelt, but your family and the Morgans made more money afterwards than before. Besides I just cannot see my telling Mrs. Vanderbilt, who just adores my Franklin, that you would shun the president of these United States!"

So Mrs. Dodge gave in, and in late June let FDR make a major appearance at her two huge estates. Grandpa saw the event announced in the *Newark Star Eagle*, and he decided to go and see FDR in person. He had once seen his cousin in the back of a campaign train in Madison. Teddy was short, stocky, powerfully built, but had a remarkably high pitched voice. And during the gubernatorial campaign of 1910 in Jersey, he had also seen, on the back of another train, Woodrow Wilson of Princeton University campaigning for his first elective office. Dr. Wilson was tall, thin, and talked to the people as if they were smart, and people responded gratefully by giving him a sweeping victory.

But many said FDR was even more magnetic, and the old man had heard him on the radio in the early Depression when he explained the banking crisis. So Grandpa got up early, drove his pickup truck to the estates, where all the guards were Italian laborers, who let him park next to the pathway Roosevelt would follow. What struck Grandpa was how many people, even workers, wore their Sunday best to the event, out of deep respect for the office and the popular incumbent.

Like clockwork, FDR arrived in his Lincoln, waving his old fedora, jauntily holding in his mouth an up-tilted cigarette holder, and sporting his pince-nez glasses. Applauses and cheers went up, especially from the workers, and Grandpa watched as FDR's broad face lit up as he viewed the people he governed. He sat in the leather back seat, with a blanket over his shriveled legs even in the heat and twisted his huge torso with his large shoulders around, to greet the cheers. He insisted on stopping, nodding, and talking to the people, wishing them a good day as the merciless sun beat down on all of them. One old lady said it was like talking to your next door neighbor. Then the car made a stop right in front of Grandpa, and FDR grabbed his hand and remarked, "My good friend, we are wearing the same type of hat. I love these fedoras. I have five of them."

Grandpa responded reverently, "I love this one too, Mr. President."

Roosevelt continued on though, "How are things going?"

"Not good, the drought is killing us, nothing grows."

"I know, I too am a farmer and raise apples at Hyde Park. It is dry there also, and the crop is awful."

"I wish you could bring rain with you," Grandpa kidded.

"I have many New Deal programs, my friend, but only God brings the rain. Let us both as Christian gentlemen pray more."

"Indeed, Mr. President. Thank you."

And FDR moved on, and at the next stop, he pushed himself uncomfortably over the top of the door to shake hands with a kid on crutches. "It is okay, they get easier to use, son, it will be easier. Don't fear."

The vehicle moved on through the immigrant workmen who were paid little by Mrs. Dodge. Actually they said she loved her dogs more than her workers. And FDR knew that, as he knew his class. He was old money, they were nouveau riche. Cousin Teddy had told him the difference years ago. After a few words, he left the estate, he turned around and raised his fedora again, and Grandpa thought it was for him, as did thousands of others. As his car was pulling out of the long driveway, there was Mrs. Dodge in her old stately black Packard, who graciously came out of the car to say hello to the president of the United States. FDR gave her a huge smile and hug and thanked her for letting him "use her estates." She was totally honored, and as he left for Morristown, he remembered what Mama had said about him being a "traitor to his class." *Indeed, I am Geraldine, indeed,* he mused. And when she was asked why she, a woman, came out of her car, she observed, "Well, I had to, he is a cripple you know."

At home that evening, Grandpa kept thinking about the sight of his smile, the thickness of his right hand, and the steely but friendly eyes. He was a rich man, but loved the people, he concluded. That night he watched as the heavens opened up and it began to drizzle and then for the next two days it rained slowly but steadily, the best type for crops. As he watched from his porch door, he grabbed a cigarillo, and put it in his mouth tilted upwards, and grabbed his old fedora and put it on. He looked in the mirror, and just laughed.

Democrats insisted that FDR had brought the rain with him, that it was a blessed moment when he came to the heart of the Republican north counties. That of course was nonsense, but across the nation, the voters in November responded favorably as FDR won re-election by the greatest majority in modern history. He carried New Jersey, made inroads in the northern counties, and most surprisingly even Grandpa, for the first time in his life, voted for a Democrat, just FDR, none of the others. When one of his sons expressed surprise that Grandpa did not stay with the Republicans as always, he answered that he "had never met Alf Landon, but FDR I had talked to."

11. POPE LEO XIII

Grandpa was in many ways a traditional Italian male who had little use for college education for women, including his daughters. He opposed them going to college, refused to pay, and was proud of his view that the normal way of things was that they marry and have children. Deep down he would have preferred if his daughters stayed home with him for their natural lives, for he enjoyed the company of families and was not enthused about their spouses. But the collapse of the male economy in the Depression, and the varied opportunities opening up by the dearth of men during the war, led women to challenge their own roles in society.

One of his daughters, Margaret—named after the Queen Consort of Italy—was to move toward a profession, and the only ones that seemed acceptable then were either teaching or nursing. She also wanted to join the Army Nurses Corps or the Navy Nurses Corps, but as noted her mother had heard that the women who ended up in the services were girls of loose virtue, *putanas*. Thus that option abruptly slammed shut on her. Teaching was out of the question since it required college and was blocked by Grandpa's traditional attitudes. So she chose nursing, or it chose her. In those days, nursing training was often conducted out of hospitals not colleges, and they could train women according to their institutional needs.

Margaret decided to apply to the program at Overlook Hospital in nearby Summit. A bright teenager. she appeared with a file containing her high grades and sparkling letters of recommendations. The program director was a prim and proper, tall lady who thought that personal charm was a weakness. The mundane interview went well, then the supervisor looked at her last name, noted that it ended with a vowel, and for some reason, she decided to inquire, "Are you an EYEtalian?"

Margaret simply responded, "Yes, my father came to the United States in 1898."

"Oh, I guess he has had enough time to become civilized." Margaret was shocked and then offended, and when she left Overlook, she knew that that place was not where she wanted to learn and to work.

She arrived home, and there in the kitchen was Grandma who excitedly asked her how she did, knowing of her daughter's records and hard work ethic. Margaret upset, blurted out the closing remarks, and Grandma became disturbed and tried not to relay the story right away to Grandpa. He had known anti-Italian hatreds over his long time in the United States. Instead she insisted that her daughter walk up to the church and talk to the monsignor.

The monsignor was the vicar general of the diocese, and twice would be offered the bishopric which he declined in order to stay in Madison. He served on the board of Seton Hall College and attended every home basketball game religiously. He was a graduate of the famed North American College, a center in Rome known then as a breeding ground for men who went on to become bishops and cardinals. His network was powerful, broad and lasting. He spoke Italian fluently and told his people he was speaking to them in the Neapolitan dialect so they could understand him, not in the tongue of Dante. They loved him and he them.

Margaret approached him somewhat timidly although they had known each other for years. Hearing out her story, the monsignor went to the rectory phone and called someone, and then he immediately left with Margaret in his car to Elizabeth, N.J. There was the imposing hospital of St. Elizabeth, lying in the middle of the industrial heartland. They walked into the supervisor's office, where he was treated with all the deference he deserved. The nun listened to the Overlook story and went on to recruit Margaret for their program. In some ways it was stronger since the hospital served more of the poor, immigrants, and industrial areas. Then the monsignor interrupted and told the nun that he had a file with Margaret's sterling grades and references. "Oh no, we accept your word that she is appropriate for this Catholic hospital. She will begin in the class of August 1." And that was that. The monsignor gave his blessing to the efficient nun, and he and Margaret went home. She was to be a nurse. Later at 19, she was put in charge of the kinetic Emergency Room, and she excelled, and of course the monsignor heard all the stories. It was another triumph for him.

As time passed, she left the hospital for industrial nursing, met a boy, and got serious. She wanted to be married by the monsignor who had played such a wonderful role in her life. She appeared at his door, walked inside the damp, dark rectory, talked about being at St. Elizabeth, and how well it reflected on the Church, and then she broached the question. At 25, it was time to get married, and she wanted to do so in her beloved home church, St. Vincent. But the monsignor had given his curates a promise that he would stop doing marriages but let "the boys do them." How could he say yes to her, when he denied her sister? He was sorry and so was she.

At home, she told the family the outcome, and Grandpa listened intently, for he had learned about the Overlook incident and was unforgiving.

The next day he quietly grabbed a bottle of his finest wine and went up to the church. He rang the doorbell, and the monsignor appeared, and smiled. He respected the stoic family Grandpa and Grandma had raised, and he always enjoyed a real chance to converse in Italian to keep up his language skills. Grandpa gave his finest wine to the priest, promising him it was the first squeezing of the grapes and sat down to share a drink. But he had not come to exchange pleasantries. They got to talking of late nineteenth century Italy, and Grandpa subtly remarked that as a boy he had seen the aged, stooped Pope Leo XIII, who had electrified the Church with his letter, *Rerum Novarum,* a pro-labor charter that put the Church for once on the right side of history. The monsignor excited, insisted that he too had met Leo and laughed at how he looked like the French atheist Voltaire. He went on and on about Leo and how one man changed the Church. He noted that at Mass in the Vatican once the pope had passed out and recovering said he had a vision of St. Michael defending the Church against the wiles of the devil. That was why they said a prayer at the end of Mass in those days to St. Michael, the vigorous Archangel.

Grandpa had not heard that story, but he agreed as if he were a Dominican theologian and remarked that the people in Naples loved the aristocratic pope, and the love of the people is the greatest gift in leading the Church or a government. Monsignor gamely agreed.

"It is like here monsignor; the people love you so much. They need you to tell them the Gospel, baptize their children, marry their daughters, and bury their dead. With you beside them, they see God standing with them."

The monsignor understood the gist of the message and eventually accepted Grandpa's compromise. The monsignor would perform the actual service, but his boys would give the long-winded Cana conference instruction. They parted on good graces.

As for Grandpa, when he came home from visiting the monsignor, he simply said that the monsignor was going to be the celebrant. Margaret was startled. "What did you say to him?"

"We talked of Italy. He loved it there."

"Yes, yes, but what did you say that changed him around?"

"Well he is a big admirer of Pope Leo XIII, and I told him how impressed I was as a very young boy seeing him."

"Did you ever see Pope Leo? Have you ever spoken to Pope Leo?"

"No, he was an old man by then, a prisoner by his choice in the Vatican."

"Well you did not even know the pope, and yet you made the monsignor think you did!"

"Pope Leo is the pope of the working man. And who is more of a working man than I am. Yesterday he did a good deed. I will pray to St. Michael the Archangel on his behalf."

Margaret and her fiancé went to Cana and a new harsher priest insisted on noting that her fiancé had not been confirmed, rarely went to Mass, and the marriage would be doomed to failure.

But it lasted for nearly fifty years, produced two college educated children, and as Margaret aged all her siblings passed away until approaching age 100 she stood like a single strong oak in a hardy field.

12. HINDENBURG DISASTER

The Great Depression was a long-lasting, terrible experience for the people of the United States. No group, except the blacks, suffered more than women, and young women leaving high school had nowhere to go. Some of them ended up in minor clerical jobs, social work, teaching, or nursing—the caring professions that of course were then and still are low paying positions. To go into teaching positions, though, the candidates had to graduate from college and be certified. That was a special impediment for Italian-American girls, for at that time their fathers thought that higher education was a waste of money—their daughters were meant to get married and bear children. Then their men would support them.

And so, it began that at age 18 Margaret was a first-year nurse in training, caring for the poor, the afflicted, and the mentally challenged. Then at the incredible age of 19, she was made the chief of the Emergency Room. When the monsignor heard of the lightening quick promotion, he prayed to the Sacred Heart for her, and after the 6 a.m. Sunday mass he saluted Grandma and Grandpa for the types of children they raised for the good of the Church. Nothing made Italians parents feel prouder than praise for their children. Grandpa quietly wondered to himself if he should have sent her to a local college after all.

Hospitals in industrial areas know the challenges of catastrophes, and young nursing students had little time for initiation. They learned by doing and then learned more. But then the worst happened. On May 6, 1937, a German passenger airship, the LZ 129 *Hindenburg*, caught fire in midair and was destroyed trying to connect to the mooring at the Naval Air Station in Lakewood, New Jersey.

The radio stations, led by announcer Herbert Morrison, immediately picked up the catastrophe, and hospitals from around Lakewood were put into action to rush to the site. Even though St. Elizabeth's was almost a half an hour away, it had a good ER room and experience in dealing with chemical burns and industrial accidents. Sister Agatha ran into the ER, grabbed the nurses and shoved them into all the ambulances they had available, and threw in clean surgical outfits. She was clear to the young supervisor, "Stop at no red lights, bring the living and the dead back, and above all do not throw water on them or apply ointments. Use the surgical gowns without lint as blankets. Use your own ornamental blue capes as blankets if you need to."

When the St. Elizabeth contingent arrived, the Naval Base was in chaos. Of the 97 people on board (36 passengers and 61 crewmen), 35 died—most in the hull. The *Hindenburg* was still in flames when they arrived, bodies were lying in pieces and survivors and onlookers alike were in despair, and other ambulances greeted St. Elizabeth's with relief.

People walked around dazed, crying for their loved ones, and later giving up the ghost. But the well-disciplined nurses from a Catholic hospital did what they were told to do, and probably saved more people than expected. It was almost into the night, and they used the van headlights to light up the naval grounds. The military medics gave way to the nurses, for they had never seen a blimp or this type of carnage. Everyone said this was the transportation wave of the future. With that fire and pictures of the crash, the airship age was abruptly ended. The disaster of the fire and the fall lasted an incredible 35 seconds or so.

The majority of the casualties was from the hull, while others jumped to their death. The nurses from St. Elizabeth's grabbed as many as they could, but bodies were lined up as they made their way back to the hospital's burn unit. One of the patients in the head ambulance was Werner Franz, the 19-year-old cabin boy, He was putting away dishes when the pipe above him broke, and the cold water shocked him back to the ugly reality round him. He ran one way and then another to get out of the blimp. The officers were jumping out of the doorways, and Werner ran after them. He tumbled to the ground, and there the head nurse from the ER grabbed him as he was in a daze and put him firmly in the ambulance. He had no major burns they could see, and he just sat and watched for hours the agonies of the wounded and dying. Like all young people, he had once believed that he was immortal, but now he knew better.

What he lacked in burns, he made up in trauma, and he shivered next to the head ER nurse on the bumpy way to the hospital. The nurses were greeted by a cadre of Sisters of Charity nuns, recruited from the local Catholic schools. How they got there so quickly was unclear. It was said later that it was Boss Frank Hague of Jersey City's machine's finest hour. He provided the transportation. They were told to cover the patients loosely with non-stick bandages, not to wash them in water, prevent shock by raising the patient with his feet 12 inches above his heart, and cover the person with a blanket or even a cloak. The beautiful blue capes of nurses covered many of the bodies, dead and alive.

With the much-publicized events, the ER rooms filled up with priests giving the last rites. As vicar general of the diocese, the monsignor drove in from Madison and administered Extreme Unction, the sacrament of the dying, not even knowing the faith of the victims. To him it did not matter, God's mercy was for everyone. He had never seen such carnage—it was like a war without bullets.

The monsignor looked for his parishioner and was watching her confidently directing her colleagues and insisting on both efficiency and compassion. Werner was still in a state of near shock, and she personally wheeled him into a private room. He moaned and went into delirium, as if he had been struck by an artillery shell.

That night when the living patients were comforted, and the dead respectfully carried away to nearby funeral homes, she was able to return to Werner's room, and looked him over. It was then they both realized they were nearly the same age.

No one had cared for Werner, for there were no wounds they could see. He was filthy, covered with dirt, segments of rubber, and smelling of smoke and burnt flesh. Near him had been a severed head of a woman, just rolling around, and he seemed to be screaming at her that night.

The nurse immediately began to wash his body. He was a handsome blond, young man, with strong stomach muscles and no real hair on his body. He seemed to have a quick smile, but he was solemn that night. She slowly washed his body and could not help but be impressed. As she worked her way down his chest, she slowly pulled off his trousers that were ripped to shreds. She recognized that like most gentiles of that time he was uncircumcised, and she had to give special care to washing the creases of his genitals. As she moved her washcloth over and over him, he seemed to smile, and she made believe that she did not see what she was doing. She turned him over carefully and washed his back and buttocks, and then covered him with a surgical gown.

He seemed to enjoy all of it and pleaded to sit up. She conceded, and he asked if she would join him in the corner chair. She agreed figuring that he was still suffering from the effects of the explosion. He started to talk slowly in good English with a slight German accent. He wondered aloud why he was saved, and others had died. She said it was just God's will, but he answered back that there is no loving God, look at the tragedy. He believed only in human effort, and the rest were fairy tales. She disagreed, and he smartly remarked, "What are you, a Catholic or something?"

"Yes, I am."

"You can believe if you wish, all I know I am alive here, and around me were the dead and the maimed. Show me your God."

"Be grateful, Werner, be grateful," and he stopped when she tenderly used his first name. She took her washcloth and wiped his eyes again, but he moved over and kissed her suddenly. She had never been kissed before, and she pulled away. But he went on kissing her. They continued and finally stopped.

"Is there anything I can get you from the hospital?"

"Yes, if I am going to be here, I would like to have an American English novel to read and learn your language better. I can speak it but not read it. How long am I to be here?"

"Well, it was just to be a day or two, but the doctors think you are suffering from the effects of shell shock like in the Great War, and they want to watch you closely. Maybe a week. I will see if I can go next door and get something for you to read. It is only three a.m. now." And then he moved over and kissed her again, and she let him.

The next morning she went to the Old Curiosity Shop around the corner and asked the proprietor for an American volume that would be easy for a foreigner to read. He confidently gave her Ernest Hemingway's *A Farewell to Arms*. It was a powerful and erotic romance of a young nurse falling in love with a cynical American wounded in battle in Italy.

She brought it back to Werner, and at night they would read it while the rest of the ward was asleep. Then one night, the supervisor saw them alone and insisted that he was strong enough to leave tomorrow.

Sadly, the next day his nurse walked him to the entrance, and they slowly kissed goodbye. He mounted a cab and went to the Deutsche Zeppelin-Reedier in New York City to see what his next assignment was. But they did not want a Hindenburg survivor in their office, and he was sent off to a branch office in Los Angeles. He worked there, learned accounting, and then in early December 1941, the führer declared war on the United States. Roosevelt responded that all Germans in the US were enemy aliens and put them in relocation camps inland. Werner practiced his English on his American guards and worked in the office as an accountant. They left him alone since he was useful, and Americans hated detail work.

When the war ended, he worked at a variety of West Coast plants, and then headed to Albuquerque, New Mexico where he met Paul Allen who with Bill Gates was creating a new information technology company. Allen liked Werner and used him frequently. Werner never married or even dated, Microsoft became his whole world, and Allen rewarded him with shares of stock. He stayed there from 1975 through his 75th year and finally retired a very rich man. Werner got weary of taking care of himself and entered a very luxurious assisted living complex. During most of the days he followed the market and calculated his real wealth. He was the only person there who had the *Wall Street Journal* and *Barron's* delivered to him personally. He had assets of almost half a billion dollars, and he donated $100,000 to the New York Goethe Institut, so Americans would not think all Germans had been Nazis. Then he took the rest and wrote Gates that he wished to join the group of wealthy men who gave their final bequest to Bill and Melinda's foundation, especially to curtail the ravages of disease in Africa among the babies there.

At age 94, he died.

Across the continent, the nurse he once loved, married, had two children and lived a conventional peaceful life. She too entered an assisted living home and died right after her 100th birthday. Ironically, she died in Overlook Hospital which had been so anti-Italian when she first applied to them. That year the co-chair of their foundation was an Italian. Before her afternoon wake, her son and his wife went over to see what possessions of hers they should honor. She had a rosary given by her son and blessed by St. John Paul II, a book of prayers from the Divine Mercy Shrine in Massachusetts, and a faded green book. The son opened up the book, which was a first edition of Hemingway's *A Farewell to Arms*. In it was inscribed, "The world breaks everyone, and afterwards some are strong at the broken places. Love, Werner."

13. THE FOOTBALL WEDDING

Over her long years in America, Grandma received no letters or packages from her family in Benevento. In part the problem was that she could barely read, for the Italian Risorgimento had failed southern Italy, especially by not providing education for women. When the mailman arrived and formally handed her a tissue paper letter stamped Benevento, Italia with her name on it, she was startled and then excited.

She ran up the flight of stairs to the first floor apartment, and handed the letter to Grandpa and proudly announced, "See, Raffaele, mail for me!" He looked up and saw the missive and began to delicately open it. He read,

"My dear cousin Luisa, I am so happy to write to you and hope all is well in America. We are doing fine and still observe the Lady Of Mount Carmel feast in July that you so loved. We wish Raffaele and the children God's good wishes. I write to you to inform you that one of our relatives, Arturo Perone, is traveling to America. He is a high-ranking member of the Mussolini government in this province, and he is going on speaking engagements. I ask that for the New York-New Jersey part of that trip you please put him up at your house for a while. It is a good sign of the loyalty of the Perones for one of their own. I so miss you and our days as young girls. Alas, we have now become our mothers. Love, Jena."

Grandma was delighted to be asked to host her cousin Arturo and turned to Grandpa for his concurrence. He just nodded, but quietly under his breath he murmured, "*fascista.*" Grandpa hated the thug Mussolini.

Arturo arrived on time by ship, and Grandma wore her finest dress. She embraced him with her usual warmth, and Grandpa formally welcomed him to America. The next night, she made the Perone family dish—cheese ravioli. The key to preparing the dish is roll the pasta thin enough to fill with ricotta cheese and yet not so thin it would break in the boiling water. Arturo loved her dish and insisted that she cooked better than anyone back in Benevento. She praised her own mother for teaching her the correct ways.

That very weekend, one of her children was getting married at St. Vincent

Martyr Church in Madison, and the family rented out the Forum Club hall for the reception. The women had divided up the cooking chores, for each had a specialty they were most proud of. And the early morning before the two p.m. mass, the women folk arrived at Grandma's to stuff torpedo rolls with ham, prosciutto, salami, roast beef, cheese, and sausage. Then they carefully put them in waxed sandwich bags and into boxes with a sticker labeling each with its contents.

Guests would soon be given the torpedo rolls of their choice, and they would be frequently thrown across the room, "Hey, Cupie, cappicola," "Hey Frank, salami and cheese." The sandwiches would fly like small torpedoes as they floated in the air, thus the expression used by Italian Americans, "football weddings." On the right of the hall long boards had been laid out on wooden sawhorses with tablecloths, and on them were the feast of the faire presented by the women. On one end were Italian bows covered in honey, and on the other end were piles of Italian sugar cookies. No one went home hungry.

At the Forum Club, Grandma took Arturo by the hand and introduced him to each member of the families, proudly saying, "He is a Perone." He insisted on wearing his fascist uniform: leather black gloves, black coat with a wide belt cutting across his chest, and long boots with a braided cap. Italians loved uniforms and nobody more so than Mussolini.

Grandpa just watched him as he made his way around the large crowd. He moved like the experienced politician he was. Italians are a warm people, but they are also a suspicious people, and Grandpa disliked the fascists and their agents.

In only a couple of weeks, Arturo had arranged for a speaking event in Madison and the environs employing the names at the wedding to talk about the advent of fascism in the ongoing Spanish Civil War. General Francisco Franco, using the banners of the Catholic Church, fought against the provisional government, and brutally cut his way through his nation.

Arturo had commanded quite a large crowd that night, and even Grandpa went with his grandson. After Arturo began an effusive testimonial to his *Il Duce* for the great progress he had accomplished in Italy, and his glorious triumph in bringing civilization to Abyssinia and Libya, Grandpa thought to himself, *Fought against poor men with spears.* Grandpa quietly listened but shook his head at the word "civilization." Then Arturo shifted rhetoric gears—he told of the heroic activities of the 400,000 Italian "volunteers" fighting in Spain on Franco's side. It was a union of fascists, protecting the Church from the communists and fellow travelers, including the American Abraham Lincoln Brigade.

Then he told his audience that they must use their influence to keep the American Neutrality Act in place, despite the activities of that "Jew President, Franklin D. Roosevelt who favored the communists." Grandpa suddenly found himself greatly annoyed at this foreign agent of Mussolini criticizing America's president. At question time, he rose up slowly and said, "I want to thank my wife's cousin for coming here to talk. But my hospitality knows boundaries. Arturo, I have met President Roosevelt, talked to President Roosevelt, and as a Republican I voted in 1936 for him. I don't know if he is Jewish, I thought he was Dutch. But we in Southern Italy are such a mixture, I can't believe it matters in this short life. If my president wishes to oppose Franco, I must believe he knows why. And how can you praise Mussolini for sending in 400,000 Italian boys and not allow America to send in guns and planes?"

Arturo pleaded for the U.S. to remain neutral, but then undermined himself by asking the group for money to support Franco's crusades. He reminded the Catholic Italians that even the pope respected Mussolini and signed a treaty in 1929 with him. But one priest there remarked that Mussolini imperiled the Church and persecuted the Italian Catholic Youth groups. "He is an atheist, he is not a Catholic, nor is his baptized ally Hitler. They are wolves in wolves clothing." Arturo defended Mussolini as he was paid to do, but some of the audience was berating fascism and regarded Pope Pius XI as a boob librarian.

The meeting lasted over two hours, and then split up into chaos. Arturo walked away with nothing, and was furious, especially at Grandpa.

The next morning he told poor Grandma that he had to move on to Boston to talk to other groups and gallantly thanked her for her hospitality. He said nothing to Grandpa. He called a cab for 81 Main Street to take him to the Newark Airport to go to Boston.

Grandma was a bit confused, but she knew that a man's work is his work. She then asked Grandpa if she could dictate a letter to her cousin saying what a fine man Arturo was, and how she even brought him to a wedding of the families.

Arturo was uncommonly successful in his trips and ended up going to Argentina to woo the Italian population there. He met a young ambitious military officer who was named Juan Peron. Arturo convinced him he was a relative of the clan in Benevento, and he had previously gone to the Italian Military Academy in Turin to study strategy under Mussolini. In less than a year, he acquired all that knowledge, and went back to become part of the Argentinian government.

Eventually Juan Peron (who dropped the e) married a loose-living radio actress named Eva Duarte, and they gained power in the troubled state of Argentina. Grandpa kept track of Arturo, and then of the rise of Juan Peron. When Evita died prematurely in 1952, she was at the height of her incredible popularity. The Peronists petitioned the Vatican to have her declared a saint. The pope, then Pius XII, simply laid the request aside.

And that is how close we Perones came to sainthood.

14. ITALIAN INTERNMENT

Grandpa who could write in beautiful traditional Italian script corresponded with only a few friends in Italy. He seemed to feel that he had to cut off most of his ties when the terrible wars came. He hated the upstart Mussolini and saw him as another tinhorn despot with whom his land had been so bedeviled. The only exception was a long correspondence he had kept up with Francesco Finelli, a distant cousin to whom he wrote frequently. Francesco lived with his parents, selling used clothes to make a living in the city, and working side-by-side with them.

One day he had met an aged immigrant who like about one-half of Italian emigrants had come back from the United States, returning home to finish out their lives. The old man had played the violin for a small orchestra in Philadelphia and enjoyed his years in the public eye. But at seventy-five he returned home and would play only for himself. When he met Francesco, he was looking for a Prince Albert overcoat which Francesco happened to have. But the old man was short on funds and suddenly promised that he would teach Francesco how to play the violin, and on his death, he would bequeath the beautiful polished instrument to the young man. Francesco agreed.

The old man turned out to be a better teacher than a performer, and Francesco blossomed as a solo violinist. He soon played with a local orchestra, and everyone revered the quiet beauty of his strings. The violin was not in fact a wooden box, but it seemed to be a voice able to move people's hearts. He played not only Italian favorites, but Mozart and even Chopin.

Then in the meatgrinder brutality of World War I, this gentle soul was called up to serve in the dubious Italian army. As they were being mauled at the awful battles in the Alps, the army officials took notice of him, looked at the slim and kind Francesco, and put him in the ambulance corps. There he was surrounded by the terrible casualties created by the stupid pompous commanders of the Italian army. One bright afternoon, when the Italians were being overwhelmed again by the Austrians at Caporetto, Francesco did all he could to help carry the wounded and the dead to the next ambulance. The bodies were piled up six in an ambulance, half of them had already gone to meet their Maker. These Italians were not good soldiers but were simply the weary young descendants of the once famous spirit of centurions of so long ago. Now they were victims of the mechanized designs of the once Great War. There are no heroes in an artillery battle.

During one incident a shell broke apart and splintered the legs and arms of ambulance members. Francesco fortunately was shielded from the shrapnel by a large tire and was saved from further harm. Heroically he grabbed a wounded fellow ambulance man and dragged him for what seemed an endless distance to safety. His leg was ripped to pieces; Francesco pushed him into the vehicle and helped load him on as they rode down the bumpy road to a field hospital. There he would care for the wounded man who was very grateful. It was so easy to be left out of the triage of medical cases.

Once in the hospital, they struck up a friendship in broken Italian and English. Francesco told of his ambitions to be a concert violinist, and the wounded soldier spelled out his dreams of being the world's greatest novelist. He was the twenty-year-old Ernest Hemingway.

In several weeks' time, Hemingway was moved to a real hospital, where he fell in love with his nurse, and she became the subject of his great work, *A Farewell to Arms*. That war ended. The Italians won, being on the Allied side. But the weak and wounded went by broken-down trains to their homes, and Francesco went back to his violin.

All of this he told Grandpa, and Grandpa wrote him of a position listed in the *New York Daily News* for a concert violinist for a new group forming at the famed Carnegie Hall in New York City. Francesco wrote a long hand-written letter to them, and it took years for them to come up with the funding. When they did, it was finally due to the new rich who had lived off the blood proceeds of Mr. Wilson's war. In his letter Francesco related to Grandpa the story of his bravery in saving a man named Hemingway. He asked if he had ever become an American writer. Of course Hemingway had reached such real heights and was known even to Grandpa. He gave Francesco his address, Charles Scribner's Sons, the publishing company on Madison Avenue in New York, New York. Sometime later a letter from Francesco made its way to Paris, and Hemingway quickly responded. He remembered so well what had happened, and he treated his old colleague respectfully. He invited Francesco to join him for the running of the bulls in Pamplona, Spain. He sent a translation in Italian of his novel, *The Sun Also Rises* with his letter. Francesco was not terribly athletic and said he was busy with his violin and his modest engagements.

But Hemingway proved to serve as a good reference in America, and he was true to his word. Soon Francesco was invited to Carnegie Hall for a month, and his parents were so proud. At the New York docks he was greeted by Grandpa and Grandma who immediately made him feel at home.

They set up a room at the end of their apartment, and he could easily take the local train to Carnegie Hall in New York City. He loved the building and adored its magnificent sounds and echoes. At home he entertained the grandparents and their guests, night after night, way past midnight, and on the weekends, they created a local band that entertained overnight in front of Grandpa's beloved garden.

Then one night there was a knock at the door. Grandpa opened it and there stood a grim Tommy O'Brien, now a policeman who had been a playmate with Grandpa's children years ago. "I'm sorry, Mr. Finelli, I am here under orders from the president of the United States to arrest a member of your family."

"But Tommy, it is me, Raffaele. You know all my people for years. What does the president know?"

"Yes sir, but you have an enemy alien here."

"What is that?"

"An illegal Italian who is not a citizen, a Francesco Finelli."

"Francesco is a violinist in New York City."

"No, right after Pearl Harbor, Mussolini declared war on the United States, and all Italian citizens are now under suspicion. Francesco Finelli is a member of the Italian veterans' group, a subversive organization, *Ex Combationi*."

"What? They raise money for widows of soldiers killed in the Great War. Those soldiers were America's allies."

Then Francesco having heard his name walked in the kitchen. "You, Francesco Finelli, are being detained and questioned for your membership in a subversive Italian organization."

Grandpa grabbed Francesco's arm and said, "Don't worry. We'll help. Where will he go? Where will he be?"

"Right now we are taking him to the courthouse in Morristown, then it's anyone's guess where a commission of three military men and two civilians will take him."

Francesco looked confused. "Raffaele, what did I do?"

"Nothing, we will find a way to end this infamy."

Francesco left with only the clothes on his back and his violin. Grandma gave him a bag full of groceries, and he was handcuffed and led away. She asked Grandpa, "If they can do that to him, can they do that also to us?" Grandpa simply nodded. It was a frightening interlude.

Francesco was shipped to a relocation camp in Gloucester County, New Jersey, with no one even knowing that he was interrogated for an hour about his support of the Italian widows' association. He was a veteran and helped raise money for the widows and children left in the wake of the war. That his interrogators never really understood, and he didn't understand them. He was not a politician, and it was the professional politicians and bankers who ran the new Italy. He never knew Mussolini or fascism, or why the pope made a treaty with Mussolini. That was not his life.

When he was interrogated, they wanted to know which he loved more: Italy or America? He didn't understand the question, even in broken Italian. "I love it here in America. I love Carnegie Hall, but I am a born Italian." He was charged with being an enemy alien, incarcerated and then shipped all the way to Missoula, Montana where he remained in an internment camp for Italians. They said the president of the United States approved all this. Hundreds of Italian citizens were held like rats in a maze. They tried to learn each other's dialects and were bored in the hours they spent doing nothing day-after-day. Others got jobs in local industries or helped fight forest fires. Some raised gardens by the Quonset huts just to keep themselves occupied. They ironically called it Camp Bella Vista. After three months. Francesco started playing his violin at night, and he attracted an appreciative audience which included some other Italians who also had carried their own instruments with them. The American soldiers enjoyed the show, for they were as bored as the inmates. One evening a beefy American sergeant found a broken-down piano in an old hut and added it to the group and changed the very nature of their repertoire.

They began to do selections from Verdi and Puccini, and one night sang in Italian the chorus of the Hebrew slaves from *Nabucco*—ironically a song of liberation. All this Grandpa and Grandma never heard about.

Finally Grandpa wrote to Ernest Hemingway at Scribners and explained the weird situation about the man who had saved his life. Could the recognized author help Francesco? Surprisingly, Max Perkins, his agent, quickly passed the letter on to Hemingway, and he typed a personal letter to Secretary of War Henry Stimson whom he had met at a party in Georgetown, asking for mercy for Francesco.

Three months later, the administration was having serious reservations about incarcerating Italians like they had the Japanese. People complained that the restrictions even fell on the legendary baseball player Joe DiMaggio's father in San Francisco bay. Roosevelt feared the loss of Italian votes in the East in states that the Democrats needed for election, and he asked Stimson to rewrite the Italian restrictions. In 1944, on Columbus Day, Stimson grandly ended the Italian incarceration just in time for FDR's re-election.

Soon a thinner Francesco and his violin made their way back to Newark airport. There he was greeted by his family with cheers and delicacies. They wanted him to come home, but he was a changed man.

He thanked them profusely, but said he was leaving in an hour on a trip back to Italy. "Why? Francesco please let us show you the real America," pleaded Grandma.

But with tears of gratitude, he responded, "I am only a small gentle man. You Americans wish to be the new Rome, to rule the world. To rule the world, you must become wolves, and I am a simple sheep and must go home." He walked down the ramp and crossed over to the bus to take him to a ship back to Italy.

He never wrote anyone again in America, but from relatives Grandpa heard that he got married, had a boy who hated music, and bought a little farm near Rotondi. There he sat outside under a fig tree with his wind-up victrola, playing Maria Callas in *La Traviata*, closing his eyes while they played together at Carnegie Hall.

Further reading:

"Italian Americans and World War II Detention Camps" from Gilda Rorro Baldassari, The New Jersey Italian and Italian Heritage Commission.

Steven Fox, *Unknown Internment: An Oral History of the Relocation of Italian Americans during World War II*, Boston: Twayne Publishers, 1990.

Lawrence Di Stasi, *Una Storia Segreta*, Berkeley: Hayday Books, 2001.

15. VICTORY GARDENS

More than just about anything else, Grandpa hated war, and the rise of Mussolini and the Fascists was to him a detestable course. In his early years in power, Il Duce was praised even by Winston Churchill and Franklin Roosevelt as a great inspiration. He was the role model for Hitler, who later became the senior partner in their perverse relationship. Grandpa had never been deceived. Italy was full of sawdust dictators; Mussolini was only the latest.

When the Second World War came, Grandpa worried about the virulent anti-Italian sentiment that reminded him of the groundswell of the Sacco and Vanzetti trial after the Great War. He and his fellow Italian-Americans were disloyal "dagos", "wops", and "guineas", lap dogs of Hitler. In FDR's famous anti-Italian chant, Italy had stuck the dagger into the back of its neighbor (France)—furthering the Mafia stereotype in the U.S.

Somehow, he wanted to do something to show his personal loyalty besides flying the American flag above his apartment house. One of his sons was drafted into the Coast Guard and was stationed off the North Carolina coast; a second son was rejected for an undescended testicle. What that had to do with firing a rifle, Grandpa did not understand. Two of his girls wanted to join the WAVES or the WACs, but Grandma scotched the idea when some of her friends remarked that army girls were *putanas*. So they did not join, but instead worked in the war effort at home—at Purolator Air Filters and the Picktinny Arsenal in Morris County. Rosie the Riveter had come of age in the family, and across America women would never be the same.

Grandpa wished that he too could do something, besides as Voltaire said, "to tend in life one's garden." But like all people, he did what he did best. One of the lawns he mowed belonged to a Mrs. Sanford who lived on Green Village Road, and whose husband had taught Latin at the high school for over a generation. After he died, she had terrible diabetic complications and had to have both feet amputated. One day longingly looking at her back lawn, she asked Grandpa if he would like to turn it into a garden of flowers and tomatoes. He jumped at the idea and created a Garden of Eden bigger than his own. Each time he would come, he would pick up the old lady and physically carry her outside to see the budding garden, and then he would bring her back in the house.

He had a deep respect for old people, especially those incapacitated, and once in a while he would stop at the ice cream parlor and buy her a sundae. And together they would inspect the gardens. One day as he was watering the large garden patch, a very proper middle-aged woman came in and introduced herself. She was the Madison chair of the Homefront Victory Auxiliary that supported the war effort by planting victory gardens all over the borough. She dressed as if she were soaked with money and told him that her group had been watching his successes and compared them to their own poor anemic efforts. Would he be willing to help the auxiliary and instruct them how to grow fruits and vegetables since the president of the United States had promised tons of vegetables and fruits to the British and Russians under the Lend Lease Act? FDR had done it as a way of stressing Allied solidarity, and he was probably right to do so. But they had little fare for their home use and their extended parties.

Grandpa looked at her at first and thought, *these Americans are so willing to ship their sons abroad, but not their fruits.* But in a war effort activity, and being Italian, he could not say no. So he asked her to come with her group in three days, and they could begin class one. He held it in Mrs. Sanford's backyard to her immense enjoyment, for now she was doing her part for the war effort. Over fifty Madison doyens took lessons on planting, nursery techniques, and harvesting plants and even flowers. And at the last class, he gave each of them gratis fine seeds from his own collection. They were delighted, and as Nature opened up her bounty, they even passed a resolution of appreciation, and the auxiliary placed a story in the *Madison Eagle,* which noted in passing that he was born near Naples, ITALY.

That was his contribution, modest but at least one that showed where his loyalties lay. One afternoon, one of his nephews, Nicholas, visited him. He arrived dressed in full Marine Corps uniform, and he came over to show Grandpa his beautiful garb. Nobody does it better than the Corps. Then at the end of the visit, he quietly said to Grandpa that he did not think he would live to come back. He was 19. Grandpa tried to reassure him that the war was nearly over in Europe and would soon be over in the Pacific. Nick had been assigned to the division that would eventually take Iwo Jima. He was in the first group that hit the beaches and was ripped apart by Japanese machine gun nests. For two days he lay dying, and then passed away as the Corps moved on to victory; captured in the first picture were three of his companions raising the American flag on that miserable island. They all died later in combat.

When Grandma brought her husband the terrible news of Nick's death, he shook first with grief and then with anger. He took his aluminum chair and threw it with all his aged force into the tomato plants, cutting a swath in the middle of them. That was so unlike him that even Grandma was frightened.

Several years later he was watching a television documentary about World War II and suddenly realized no one in the family knew where Nick was buried. Was it in Iwo Jima, in the Pacific, or in Arlington Cemetery? So the next day, he grabbed one of his grandsons, and said that no one knew where Nick was buried. He had to find out. The grandson protested, "Grandpa that was years ago, halfway around the world."

"Yes, but he is somewhere. You're a smart boy, find him. Yes!"

"Yes, sir."

For two weeks no one could unearth a clue; someone even insisted that in John Wayne's film on Iwo Jima, the great Duke at one point, asked, "Where is Nickie?" "That was our relative," they insisted. So everyone watched the film twice, but there was no such dialogue.

Then one day it struck his grandson that nobody's better at keeping track of Marines than the Marines, and so he wrote to the chief archivist of the Corps. Two weeks later, the archivist sent Nick's death certificate and a book on the famed battle. Nick was wounded immediately, died two days later, and received a variety of citations for bravery, including the Purple Heart. Then the certificate listed his cemetery and even his plot number. It was a small Armed Forces cemetery in South Jersey off the Garden State Parkway.

The grandson gave Grandpa the information, and he promised that he would name his newest pansy after him. He took the certificate, and proudly visited Nick's brother and sister. But at the door when he told her his information, she cursed him and the crippled president who had sent her brother to his death at 19, and she added that the country was now even buying toys from Japan. "Go away, let us forget," and she slammed the door in his face.

He was totally shocked, and at home he ruminated about Nick's burial place. This was not a question of war, or even of honor, but of family, *la famiglia*. He went to his go-to-guy, Alphonso, who had himself been a Marine in peace time. To get along with his drill sergeant at Camp Lejeune, after each leave he would bring back some of Grandpa's finest wine, and thus stayed in the sergeant's good graces. Grandpa knew what he was doing, but he figured Alphonso needed any help he could get. He ended being a retired corporal.

Grandpa was unusually blunt that morning with Alphonso, "We know where Nick is."

"He's dead, Grandpa."

"I know that. We want to honor his grave."

"We don't know even where he is buried. He was chewed up by the Japs."

"Yes, we do," and he triumphantly pulled out the archivist papers.

"I want you and some of your Marine buddies to go in your old uniforms to visit the grave and put these flowers on it. We must remember the dead.

Even if you all are too fat and cannot close the uniforms, wear them anyhow. I do not want you guys in jeans and Yankee tee-shirts. Don't look like Madison *cafoni. Capisci?*"

So Alphonso true to his word rounded up two carloads of out of shape full-dressed Marines and the grandson, and drove down the Parkway, and there in the resting grounds of the Armed Forces, they found Nicholas' remains under a granite slab, "1926–1945. d. Iwo Jima." Alphonso placed the flowers on the stone, and said the Lord's Prayer, since it was the only religious prayer he knew. But one of his buddies pulled out a tarnished brass trumpet and dolefully played taps, and another cried out "Semper Fi," the Corps slogan, "Always faithful."

That night, they gave Grandpa a full report, and he gratefully acknowledged their fine work. Even when he heard of the spontaneous burst of taps, he stoically just gripped his chair, and said nothing. Then he murmured, "And it is for such reasons that boys go to war they know they will never return from, and old men plant trees they will never sit under."

He nodded, got up, and walked into the densest part of his garden, took off his old battered fedora, and wept alone.

16. MEMORARE

In Benevento, Luisa was known as the most devout girl in the parish, deeply dedicated to the Virgin Mary. A group of girls created a 4' x 6' banner of Our Lady of Mount Carmel surrounded in blue with a gold band which they brought out for a three day novena starting on July16. In Italian there was inscribed "*La solidarieta della nostra signora di Mount Carmel.*" They gave everyone a brown scapular which, if one wore at the time of death, meant the Virgin would assume their soul into heaven. Although the feast day was a custom created by St. Simon Stock in the Holy Land in the Middle Ages, it was acknowledged especially in the Latin countries, and nowhere were the devotions greater than around Naples.

When Luisa got married to Grandpa, she took the banner rolled up in brown paper with her to Madison, and there a group of profoundly dedicated women celebrated the feast. In the third year, Luisa observed the Mass drew over 100 women who showed up at the church in homage. She was a quiet, gentle, hospitable woman who some insisted had the healing powers. And as long as people remembered, her daughter and then her granddaughters took care of the observance. When the Madison Historical Society wished to encase the banner in a glass enclosure, they refused, preferring to keep it deep in a closet at home.

Luisa inculcated the feast day into her whole family, and each wore a brown scapular, even when practicing baseball. Then one day, she was standing on her back porch and saw as clearly as a September morning, a young, beautiful woman with light brown hair dressed in a white gown with a blue cloak over her shoulders walking through Grandpa's garden. She stopped and smiled at his large ripe tomatoes, then smelled his mint collection with joy, and paused to pray at the rose bush he had planted in memory of his oldest daughter who died at 26. Grandma watched in sudden awe, and wanted to cry out, but she couldn't. And then the image slowly faded out. That night she told Grandpa what she had seen, and he just paused in deep silence.

Together they cultivated three separate gardens: one in the backyard, one in the lot next to them, and then one in the center of town. Grandpa wanted her also to run the grocery store on the ground floor of his apartment house and make sandwiches for the working men who came in before noon. But he concluded she gave away more free torpedo sandwiches to the poor than she sold in a given day. Once he said to her, "Can't you at least cut the cappicola a little thinner?" She also had a reputation as a person who could deal with minor cuts and abrasions, and some men stopped in to have her treat those, and soon mothers did the same for their young children.

She placed some of her younger children in the backroom of the store, where they mostly read Nancy Drew mysteries and the Childhood of Famous Americans series. Once a week she took the kids to the Madison Free Public Library, built by a philanthropist who imitated Andrew Carnegie. He also built a money-generating building across the street which provided revenues for the library. Then the library bought a little house across from the main library, and provided books, small green chairs and tables, and pictures for very young readers. *Nothing is greater than a free library,* thought Grandma, even though she could not really read very well herself. That was one of the broken legacies of southern Italy after the so-called Revolution. Nearly every small town in New Jersey had a library.

She hired a young woman to keep an eye on the kids while she worked the gardens and the store. The nanny was about 18-years-old, finishing up high school and in love with the little ones. Grandma totally trusted her and treated her as one of her own. She even went to her wedding at St. Vincent's, and held a reception for her and her husband, Enrico, who was a writer for the *Star Ledger.* Then one day she came in shaken as if she had been in a car accident. Grandma, extremely sensitive to moods, inquired what was the matter. Lilly claimed that she had fallen against the apartment wall one night. Grandma looked at her and remarked, "And my dear, what really happened?"

"Enrico came home drunk from work at the newspaper, very angry at how he was being treated, and he pushed me so hard against the wall, I passed out."

Grandma was shocked but said nothing. Then the next weekend, Enrico hit her and gave her a black eye. When she told Grandma the full story, she was horrified. Lilly was not to be a punching bag; they were just newlyweds. That night she told Grandpa, and he said nothing. She persisted, "How can a man treat his wife like that?

Grandpa just looked up and said, "You do not expect me to get involved. Besides Enrico is a good guy."

"How good can he be if whenever he gets drunk, he beats his wife? Is that a man's idea of marriage and love, Raffaele? "

"I cannot do anything, Luisa, don't ask me to."

Two weeks later, Lilly dragged herself in and Grandma thought she was not going to make it through the harsh day. She had spent the weekend in the hospital in Morristown. In the middle of the afternoon, Grandma went up to see the monsignor and explained the situation.

"We only allow annulments, and she doesn't have a reason for such a step. I cannot grant or even support an annulment. We don't believe in divorce as you know. She just must live with it, and pray he changes."

"We should separate them and pray he converts, monsignor."

"Now you know our beliefs, Luisa, she surely knew him when she married him. Unless he would not have children, there is little I can do."

"Who wants to have children with an *animale*?" Luisa answered back irreverently to the priest.

He was startled because people in those days, especially women, didn't talk to priests in that tone of voice. "I am sorry, but that is our religion. And you best remember that if you encourage her to get a divorce, you too will sin grievously. Think of your soul, Luisa, you are a good woman, but it only takes one mistake and you are damned to the eternal fires."

So she went back to the store, and for several weeks she saw the same pattern of violence, and finally Luisa gave her an address of a woman's shelter in Morristown, and the name of an attorney in Madison, Frank Volpe, who handled divorces and just about any other matter.

After months of abuses, the newlyweds separated and eventually got divorced. The church immediately cut her off and denied her the sacraments. All the women's groups avoided her: the Solidarity, the Altar Society, and the Daughters of the Virgin Mary.

She would take the PS 70 bus from Madison to her new job at Morristown Memorial Hospital and struck up a friendship with the bus driver. They socialized, then dated, and finally decided to get married. The monsignor refused to preside over the marriage. Sadly, he said, it violated canon law.

She then arranged that they were to be married in the beautiful town hall. Lilly invited Luisa, and that day she laid out her purple dress with a white neck piece and began to get dressed. Grandpa came in and asked where she was going. She told him straight out, she was going to Lilly's wedding at town hall. Grandpa was startled, she was so obedient and devout in the faith. "If you do that, they can excommunicate you, Luisa. You don't want that to happen. Maybe they will even declare our marriage invalid."

Luisa scarcely looked at him, "Fine, you take care of the five children."

The city mayor pronounced the vows according to the regulations of the state, and none of her family came, including her mother and sisters. Only Luisa came. After it was over Lilly went up and thanked Luisa for being there.

"I know it was not easy for you. I wish others had come."

"Maybe, Lilly, they will someday."

Luisa left, walked down the slippery marble steps, and past the dirty leaf piles near the street entrance. She forgot her gloves, put her hands in her coat, and started reciting her favorite prayer to the Blessed Virgin Mary, "*Memorare, O pilissima Virgo Maria, none sees adytum...*" Then she stopped and started saying the prayer out loud in English. Perhaps it was time for a new language in the new land:

Remember, O most gracious Virgin Mary
That never was it known that anyone who fled to your protection
implored you help or sought your intercession,
    Was left unaided.

Inspired with this confidence,
I fly to you, O Virgin of virgins, my Mother:
To you do I come, before you I stand, sinful and sorrowful.

O Mother of the word Incarnate,
Despise not my petitions,
But in your mercy hear and answer me.
Amen

Surely the Virgin understood. She too had been a mother, she too had known pain, she too knew forgiveness. And then she arrived at 82 Main Street.

17. A GAY VENTURE

Once at Sunday dinner, the whole family gathered around for a sit down event. The usual was there: minestrone soup, salad, lasagna with meatballs, crispy bread, and eggplant rotini. Later cakes and pies and espresso appeared. It was standard fare, but this time the conversation became unexpectedly erudite. "Which is the greatest freedom the American people have," asked cousin Carmine to start the ball rolling.

The answers followed quickly from different sides of the weighed-down table: freedom meant, of course, freedom of religion, the freedom to a speedy and fair trial by jury, the right to bear arms, the freedom to petition and assemble. Grandpa said little, until he was reminded that he had lived in America the longest, and which freedom was the most important to him.

Slowly he remarked that in terms of freedom of religion, God made some people atheists, so who cared? The trial by jury had become ignored in the incarceration of Japanese for no reason. Freedom of speech—did it extend to the Sacco-Vanzetti case? No, the greatest freedom is "to be just left alone in America, left alone by the government and by your neighbors." It was a solitary philosophy of individual liberty, but that was his view—just to be left alone.

Then two weeks later, a group of neighbors, led by Frank Volpe called "the fox" by other lawyers, pounded on Grandpa's front door. He was augmented by two other men: Genarro Tardino, an old friend of Grandpa's, and Father Joseph Tedesco who was a young curate at the local Catholic Church. Volpe had a petition he wanted Grandpa to sign.

It concerned Johnny Romano's hire at the German meat market, and it demanded that he be fired immediately, and kicked out of the tiny room he lived in off Green Village Road. Grandpa was confused and asked what the reason for such a move was, jobs were tight as it was, and he knew Johnny to be a nice, pleasant boy who would become a fine young man.

"He is, Ralph, a homosexualist, a faggot, a *fenucca*," cried Volpe.

"I have never once seen or heard of a problem. He is a good boy."

"Now, sure, but he is lying in wait to attack our children, and we all know your strong views about protecting the family. He must be driven out of town before he strikes," Volpe insisted.

"Has he done anything anywhere? Are any people complaining to you?"

"No, but it is coming soon. People know you because of your Victory Garden article in the newspaper, and we need your name on this petition. It will give us credibility," Volpe gratuitously explained.

"But you don't need me. People will make up their minds by what they see."

Grandma listened quietly from the door well of the other room. She knew that once they questioned his commitment to the family, that they had raised his anger. *Men are such fools,* she thought.

The young priest, Father Tedesco chimed in, "But it is a violation of Church law, sodomy is the evil one's sex. The Church says those people are disordered in their appetites."

The old man was becoming agitated, "What have I done to you that you would think I would sign this? I came over on the *Celtic* with some of you or your fathers to Ellis Island. Now you come to my home with this. It is disrespect, especially in front of my wife." Then he paused, "Now if you let me make one change I will sign. Drop Johnny's name and write into it all Italian people."

"What? We are not the homos, he is. I just built a new gazebo in the park for the children out of my own money," remarked Volpe.

"I just built a stone fence at the playground to safeguard the children," pronounced Tardino.

Volpe would not stop, "We know what you did to protect Alesandro's frail daughter, accused your own cousin. Remember what happened to Cirlingo when a family found out that he raped their young daughter. They hunted him down and hung him, and no jury would dare convict them. What did you say then, Raffaele?"

"I did not even know about it till much later. What are we *fascista* the way you want to act?"

"Mussolini and the Fascists were good for Italy," the priest chimed in.

"Maybe he was good to the Church, but not to the people who refused to be *fascista*. Remember how we felt with Sacco and Vanzetti, are we to be hoodlums too?" Then he abruptly looked at them and said, "You disrespect me by coming here." As they left, Grandpa turned to Father Tedesco, "Tell the monsignor that you need to go to confession, not those hardheads, *gabadosts*."

As they walked down the fourteen steps to the street, he remarked, "*Stronzo*." Grandpa approached Grandma and asked simply, "You need anything at the pig store," the common name for the German butcher since he had a gigantic pig on top of the roof.

Grandpa walked up to the German meat store and ordered two pork chops, a pound of imported Polish ham, and some chopped meat. He was greeted by a smiling Johnny, but before he finished Grandpa told him that a group was trying to run him out of town. Johnny had known about it, and blushed. Grandpa did not ask; Grandpa did not care. He had moved to this borough forty years ago, and he was not sure what the homosexuals did that so upset people.

But during the week, Grandma, who had better rumor mills than the men, heard that Mr. Heinz was firing Johnny; he was German and did not want any trouble. So on her own, Grandma told the old man that she just could not take care of her growing family, manage three gardens over the borough, and operate the deli that they had in the right store in the front of the apartment complex. So Grandma would need help, and Grandpa hired Johnny, probably knowing what she was hinting at.

John was a great catch. People liked him as he liked them. They appreciated the good attention he gave them daily. And sales went up 25% immediately. After four years, he decided to live in Greenwich Village and study art history at NYU. He and Grandpa had parted friends, and every Christmas they would receive from John and his new companion, an architect, a nice Renaissance card for the holiday. Then one year they went to London and adopted a black baby who loved to smile and was now on their Christmas card. In the note with the card, Johnny had written that the baby had been baptized, and was an Episcopalian.

18. ST. ANTHONY OF PADUA

Antoinette de Grazia was a quiet, innocent, loving woman who married Andrew Gagglione, a truck driver and loyal member of the Teamsters Union. They were deeply in love all their married lives and had two grown children who lived in Chatham and nearby Florham Park. Antoinette was a modest woman and even during sex she controlled herself, fearing that she would somehow cross the line into sin. When in confession Father Patch told her not to worry, she still was reluctant. Her husband had accumulated enough seniority so that he could drive just within the state and be home every night for a late dinner. At sixty-five he retired, and spent his days outside reading *Il Progresso* and drinking a little wine, enjoying the kiss of the sun.

All they had left was boredom and grandchildren. Antoinette stayed mainly in the kitchen baking Italian cookies with pinoli nuts for those grandchildren, so they remembered the traditions. On off days, she worked with the Sodality Women dedicated to preparing the altar linens. After twenty-five years, her colleagues gave her a small statue of St. Anthony of Padua, her favorite saint and the patron of the town her parents had come from.

Then one day, she went to arouse her sleeping husband, and found him dead. She became hysterical, called the police, and they came and confirmed the death. Her children wanted her to live with one of them, but she gallantly refused. All her things were in her home, each of all her memories saturated every piece of knickknack and article of clothes. Suddenly she began to board up her windows and also the back door. No one could get in, and she put four bolt locks on the front door.

The New Jersey National Guard tried but could not enter. She was totally sealed off from the world. She thought, *Now the devil would never be able to come in and get my soul. He could not get in to bring death to me like Andrew who loved the outdoors.*

Her children and grandchildren came and knocked on the door, but she refused to answer. Father Patch came one day and knocked on the door, but she feared it was the devil in disguise. She had packed food and canned goods, but using them day after day, she began to run out.

Now Grandpa had heard the strange story of her self-incarceration, and he wondered how long she could last in that house running out of food. So he brought her produce, beef, and even carried loaves of French bread, for what is an Italian without bread? He would simply leave it at the door, and when he came back the next day, it was gone with his note asking if she wanted anything else. Often, he went down the narrow back stairs to his cellar and got some canned tomatoes, pears, peaches and olives, and left them also at her door. He noticed once that, in the red mailbox, the letters began to pile up and included what looked like bills from the utility companies. He knew he couldn't open them, for it was against the law, so he brought the letters up to the Dodge Municipal Building and explained the situation to the utilities' representatives. They couldn't care less, and ripped their own mail open, and informed him that Antoinette was in arrears, and they were shutting off her water and electric in two weeks' time. *She would wither up,* the old man thought. So he made out two checks and paid the bills and asked that in the future they be forwarded to him. He never said anything to her family who should have known this would happen. He also held a collection of pension checks from the generous Teamsters and from Social Security which he did not open.

So on it continued, as Antoinette led a lonely battle against letting death into her life. Grandpa continued providing food for her, and each day or so it was accompanied with his note. Her children did not visit anymore, and neither did Father Patch. They thought they were honoring her wishes, or they just stopped caring. Grandpa had a more measured view: she was scared, afraid of the devil, terrorized by death, and still in deep mourning for the only man she ever loved. Then one day he came back and saw the food he had left was still there. The next day the same. He called her children, and they contacted the fire department which came over and axed though the locks on the door. She was dead, sitting quietly in her husband's favorite chair, with a prayer book of St. Anthony of Padua on her lap. She had in it an index card which read, "Gift for Raffaele." And so the firemen had the body removed; the house was like an oven, she probably expired due to heat suffocation since no air could get in.

One of the firemen was kind enough to give Grandpa the prayer book. Grandpa was deeply moved by the gift from the fireman, Joe Fushetti, whom he had known for years. Then he looked at the calendar which St. Vincent Church had given out from Burroughs Funeral Home. It was good business. It had Renaissance portraits of Mary and baby Jesus, and he looked at the previous days' boxes. Antoinette had died on the feast day of St. Anthony of Padua, June 13, the very day the saint died centuries ago. Grandpa turned to the fireman, "You see, Joe, she didn't die in the powers of the devil, but in the arms of her favorite patron saint." Then he gave Joe the basket of food he had prepared for Antoinette for the last day, and Joe took it with dignity and walked down the front stairs. Behind him, he heard Grandpa say simply, "Waste not, want not."

19. FACTS OF LIFE

He was totally exhausted and slowly climbed up the back porch steps. Grandpa's brother had promised on their mother's grave that he would help him today, but once again he never showed up. Probably he had fallen under the spell of his only mistress, cheap wine. So the old man was left with six lawns to cut in the afternoon, on top of the eight furnaces to take care of in the early morning. He determinedly made his way to the apartment, and there was only Grandma making dinner for him. The children were either grown up and gone or this week the younger ones were at the church's sleepover camp. They were mercifully alone.

He briefly nodded to Grandma and then just sat down. She was in a cheery mood, equal to his own weary spirit. She poured him some wine, and gracefully placed some cream soda in it. This evening he would prefer plain old fashioned water to refresh his bones. Somebody had told him that we are 90% water in our bodies, and he felt he needed its strength above all else. Grandma was making a quick meat sauce with linguine, some crispy bread, and a salad.

"Where is everybody?"

"They all have other things to do. You only have me tonight."

"A most pleasant fate."

Grandma went on relating to him the latest gossip. "Did you know that Volpe the lawyer is going to Italy for two weeks to see his family?"

"The conquering hero returns. Why would he spend his money on that?"

Grandma reminisced, "It might be nice to go back, let's have a second honeymoon in Capri."

"I'd rather drive up to St. Anne De Beaupre in Montreal."

"Did you know Louise is pregnant again?"

"Three children in three years, they are busy people."

"Indeed, she is overwhelmed with the two she has."

Trying to change the subject, Grandpa asked, "How are your three gardens doing? The one up town is not blossoming as well as the others. I think it needs more water, and that is hard to connect up there. The others look good."

"I made the sauce with your tomatoes."

"Ah, good."

It was typical married plain talk, events going nowhere, and then Grandma sat down with two plates of pasta and two salads.

She continued, "I hear that the priest at Cana class has told Elizabeth and Joseph that they are too young to get married."

"What do you mean, too young."

"They should wait a while. She's only just turned 17 and he is 20. The priest feels they are just too young."

"The Virgin Mary was 15. You were young too."

Grandma reminded him, "I was 21, and there is a great difference in a woman's life between those ages. You are still a girl becoming a woman. What is the rush to get married?"

But Grandpa countered, "Joseph is determined to marry her, as soon as possible. He needs a woman he told me, and he is afraid that if he waits, she will date other men."

"Maybe she should. She needs to see other men and become more mature."

Still he tried, "But he seems to be in love."

Grandma proclaimed, "Love is not enough. She needs to be older. Women are so dependent on a man; they must be careful not to make a mistake. In our old country, the whole family watched over the marriage, judged the family he came from, and got to know his real reputation in the streets."

Grandpa defensively insisted, "He is a good boy, a hard worker, he takes any job to make money and saves for her. He says he is deeply in love. They don't *have* to get married, do they?"

"Oh no, her mother is very careful, like a hawk. Maybe you could tell Joseph that marriage is more than romance, that life is hard, and a family is much work."

Grandpa flatly declared, "I can't go to a young man and tell him to hold off his love for a while. I should mind my own business."

"She deserves a right to grow up. She is only a girl. Her mother is a widow with four daughters and wants to marry them off one by one quickly."

"One down and three to go. When is the wedding?"

"In September."

"We had better mind our own business. No one told us when to get married."

"But you and I were older, and our families made the match."

Grandpa fell back on his chair and concluded, "So you tell me all the time…. It was a good match, " Grandpa muttered, but she said nothing more on the topic.

And so Elizabeth and Joseph got married. Soon they had two female children, one right after another. The locals called them, "Irish twins," babies born within ten months of each other. Joseph worked harder and harder to give his wife whatever she wanted in the world: a new house, fine clothes for the girls, and even one Christmas a fur coat for Elizabeth. She turned in his modest engagement ring for a huge stone, and Joe worked harder and harder for he was young and strong.

But rumors were rift that she was a flirt in town, especially when he was working long hours. She wanted more and more, and he could not say no, but then she complained that he was never home to entertain her. He was hearing in oblique ways that she was being seen all around town, and her mother was watching the kids more often. Grandma said she "wanted to be wooed again." Grandma, of course heard the rumors before Grandpa, for he was away from the house and alone all day. Grandma briefly told him the stories, but he said little.

Then one summer's day he was trying to figure out why he could not grow better boxwoods, and he went over to a rural estate owned by the Vanderbilts which had magnificent boxwoods marching up the driveway.

One area was particularly isolated, and he stopped and cut some plantings, hoping that a good bloodline could be transplanted to his anemic crop. Then he saw through the foliage a Buick convertible around the bend, and in the back seat was a couple naked and rutting like two young sheep, going at it passionately and with a healthy vigor. The car belonged to a salesman who sold encyclopedias whom the old man knew since Grandpa was buying one volume a week from him. The salesman was under Elizabeth, while she squealed with delight; she had the volume Q of the encyclopedia stuck between the cheeks of her tight ass. The whole back seat was full of boxes marked "Q", for that was that month's letter.

Grandpa quietly retreated home. But before he came in for dinner, he stopped at the ice cream store and didn't buy a half gallon, but instead purchased a box of candies with a plastic bow on it. It was a Whitman sampler with two layers of assorted flavors. He climbed the front stairs, not the back ones, and then without comment presented the sampler to Grandma as she opened the door to the kitchen. She was delighted and startled and was grateful after all these years that he was still capable of surprising kindnesses. When he went to wash up, she wondered, *What has he done wrong now?*

Later when the encyclopedia salesman came to sell Grandpa the next volume, it was volume Q, and the old man said he would rather skip that letter in the alphabet. When his kids complained that the set went from the letter P to R, he observed that there were too few entries under Q to deserve buying it.

20. ZIO ALFONSO

"God from afar looks graciously upon a gentle master." – Aeschylus, *Agamemnon*

Grandpa had five living children and a score of grandchildren, but still he lived alone. Often he just left his kitchen door open, leading out to the hallway, and would welcome people who just dropped by. One could, for better or worse, smell his cooking, and hear him singing his favorite aria, Mozart's "*La Donna è Mobile*," ("the woman is fickle"). One day in fact he was cooking meat sauce when a homeless man arrived quietly at his open door. Grandpa invited him in to share a spaghetti dinner and told him to sit down and have a little vino, and then he started talking to the dazed man.

It turned out he was a homeless veteran whose wife had died of tuberculosis and he had no money for a hospital or doctor's visit. For some reason he went on and on about his combat experiences and how when he came back with all his medals and ribbons of distinction, Madisonians didn't recognize him. He did some odd jobs in town, but he was frequently out of work, out of food, and homeless.

Grandpa knew he was in a bad way and gave him some of his decent older clothes and a pair of shoes, and called the head of the YMCA, Johnny Tessararo, whose father Grandpa played cards with until the old man died. He got the homeless man a room, and Johnny mentioned that the YMCA needed a night watchman and porter, and suddenly the homeless man had a salary, a room, and a real job. He was overwhelmed and thanked Grandpa profusely. He finished his spaghetti and walked to the nearby YMCA, for there is no better welfare program than a job with dignity.

It was not an isolated incident, but the most telling was the continuing need for assistance for his hapless brother. One more time, Grandpa was slowly frying sausages and peppers in tomato sauce. He waited for it to slowly cook and began re-reading *The Book of Solomon*, a volume of predictions and codes, gospels and spiritual advice. It was bound in a shiny black leather cover; he bought it in Naples years ago when he was a young man. Grandpa was a bit frightened with its visions and kept it under lock and key in the top drawer of his mahogany dresser. The gypsy who sold it to him called it at times the *Book of Solomon*, naming it after the great king with 900 wives who had built the magnificent temple in Jerusalem.

In the front door walked his youngest brother, Alfonso, whom Grandpa had encouraged originally to come to America. He was a loser back in Rotondi, and Grandpa figured the New World would be a new chance for him. While Alfonso was the youngest in the Finelli family, the family genealogists could find no record of his birth. Was he simply a stray neighborhood child or just a victim of bad nineteenth century Italian recordkeeping?

He married a shrewish girl who, of course, became a shrewish wife, and they both traveled on to the United States. Grandpa found him a job as a laborer on the Dodge estates, but Alfonso was not impressed by serving the wealthy. "What do these people have that I don't have? We walk on two feet, are born of a woman, and die alone."

He then became a chauffeur for the rich families in Madison, but he was too faithful a member of the Brotherhood of the Grape. Several mornings he was so hungover that he slept past his pick-up times, and finally lost his clients. Josephine, his beloved, screeched at him until he could stand it no longer. He went to St. Vincent rectory and talked of the need for a Catholic divorce which the clergy call an annulment, but the monsignor told him that since he had been married for ten years and had four children, it would be very difficult selling that to the diocesan review committee.

He then ambled down the hill and ended up at Grandpa's. As usual, the old man welcomed him in for lunch and laid out a sausage and pepper sandwich on a torpedo roll. But first Al wanted vino—straight. "You got anything stronger, Raffaele?"

"Ah, you don't need that stuff, Al. Drink the vino and make sure you cut it with a little cream soda like I do."

"Cream soda? *Merda*!"

"Yes, Alexander the Great cut his wine."

"Yes, and he died at thirty-two!"

"Here open up the roll," and he poured in sausage and peppers. Grandpa asked him, "How are you doing?"

"Awful. I am divorcing Josephine. I saw the monsignor."

"You people divorce every month."

"I will never go back."

"What of the children, Alfonso?"

"They are on their own. They came out of her loins."

"What is the problem?"

"She is a shrew, a bitch, a ball-busting curse."

"How much of your problem, Alfonso, is due to alcohol?"

"Sure, I do love the stuff. You know that I always did."

Grandpa looked away; quietly he put away the *Book of Solomon* and picked up the *Newark Star Ledger*. "Let's see if we can find you a job."

"I am tired of being poor in a town of the rich men. I will serve no man."

Grandpa ignored him and said, "You can live in the back room, but you must work with me. You can mow lawns with me." So Alfonso went off in the morning with Grandpa. He was partially in an alcoholic haze.

Grandpa took the two lawns out in the back and sent Al off to the front lawn. Al pushed and shoved, and he worked for a straight hour and was already weary. Grandpa had so tightened the screws that the blades were closer and gave a nicer clip to the lawn, but Al finally got a screwdriver and loosened the two screws on either side to relax the blade cuts. Now it was fairly comfortable. He murmured to himself, "Raffaele screws the bolts tighter than a bull's ass."

But he resented Grandpa after a few weeks and wanted to be on his own, he said. Grandpa called the supervisor whom he knew at Graystone Mental Hospital and got him a job as a gardener. Al knew nothing about plants, but the hospital used so many Italian laborers that the supervisors didn't even keep track of them.

One afternoon he went to the unmarked entrance on the right side which was a darkened auditorium. The inmates were watching a movie. That day it was "Gilda" starring Rita Hayworth and Glenn Ford. Alfonso was mesmerized by Hayworth, her beautiful long hair, her magnificent face, her long shapely legs, singing "Put the Blame on Mame, Boys." She was electrifying, sensuous, and every man in the darkened auditorium lived inside his own fantasies. Alfonso was a partner in the commission of that passion.

"This is what a woman should look like. Good God, why didn't you give me a woman like her?" Murmurs turned to hoots as she provocatively bent over. "Why does that nearly worthless man attract her so? I would love her forever. What does he have that I don't? In the films the hero cannot be a small, runtish, dark WOP with calloused hands. We smell of garlic and sweat. She wouldn't even pass me by. Wouldn't even want to hold my hand, wouldn't even give me a quick kiss. This is an angel meant for God. But he's no god and neither am I." He sat then until the end. His supervisor found him in the last row and summarily fired him. Without any money, he moved back into his little Cape Cod on Main Street, right across from the shopping center, at the very beginnings of the town where the welcoming sign said, "Madison, the Rose City." After a year, Josephine got some female illness, took to her bed permanently, and remembered over and over again the death of their oldest son Nicky, a marine who died at age nineteen at Iwo Jima. Alfonso drank more heavily, lost other jobs, and went to work part time across the street at the A&P in the vegetable department. At night he was able to take the ripe vegetables and fruit home and sell them across the street at his stand in front of his Cape Cod. He would also visit Grandpa's garden and pick some of his best vegetables and mix them together with his own. He made a fair living selling produce and lived in remorse over his feelings, his loses that life dealt to him. He would frequent Grandpa's shed and pilfer gallons of wine and lived his life as almost a recluse.

When his brother Raffaele died, he suddenly looked down at his casket and said, "This is the end of an era." And indeed for him it was. All his brother had done was now over, and nobody stepped up to fill the void. Josephine lit candles to her son's memory long ago, and the rest of the family stopped coming.

Two years later Alfonso also passed away, and as Aunt Marie walked by his open gravesite, she pronounced gently, "He was a sad lonely man."

Fate had demanded that all are born alone and die alone. But it is tragic in the short span of years we have to live alone.

21. THE SECOND COMING

Billy Joe Thompson was born in Norman, Oklahoma from a casual liaison between an aluminum pots and pans salesman and a dusky waitress who worked in a back road diner. The salesman would travel over the byways of the Sooner State, and, as an incentive to buy his wares, he gave each woman a copy of the New Testament which he had gotten in bulk free from the Gideons. After a while he noticed that the Bible was better received by the usually lonely country women than the pots, so he became a traveling minister preaching the word of God from tents and also selling bottles of special elixir to take away life's aches and pains. Since the elixir was 65% proof it seemed to work divine wonders.

By the time he reached adulthood, Billy Joe decided to attend a Bible seminary where he met Oral Roberts in Tulsa. Oral was not only a good and honorable preacher, but he also was a faith healer, curing people like Jesus did in the Gospels. Billy Joe graduated and started his own tent revivals, but he was chased out of Oklahoma by county sheriffs who demanded a cut of his gate and collections. He refused out of principle, and left for more northern climes, ending up in Virginia. But those people were already attached to their own evangelical faiths, and he had few parishioners.

So he decided to bring the Good News further north where he had heard that people rarely believed in God. He wanted to be somewhat closer to the place of Mammon, New York City, so he settled in New Jersey, and lo and behold he ended up in Madison on the railroad line to New York. The Reverend Billy Joe rented first a store front on Madison Avenue, and became instantly successfully; in a year's time he took over the old Elks Club auditorium when they moved to Main Street. They had a large bronze elk on the front lawn, and the preacher replaced it with a blinking neon sign, "Jesus Saves," which drove the neighbors crazy. He did well in attracting audiences and his congregation increased by leaps and bounds.

But as he pushed the word of the Lord Christ, he wanted more and more to be like Him—to be a true healer, to cure the crippled and lame, to give the blind sight, and the deaf hearing. He felt so strongly that he quietly went and hired three lowlifes from Irvington, N.J. to whom he would give canes and crutches and then they would come to Madison and be cured following his service. Other people with lesser ailments showed up and, by the power of their weak minds or strong faith, claimed to be cured, whatever that meant.

The Reverend Billy Joe began to believe his own illusions, and one Sunday he screamed that Jesus Christ was returning to earth on July 1, at noon. He would appear walking down the center of Madison's Main Street, providing salvation to all true believers that He once spoke of. The whole town was aflame that Jesus was returning, and that he would be in Madison, not in Jerusalem or Rome.

The Catholic pastor denounced the holy rumor from the pulpit; Jesus was not coming, and if He reappears the Catholic Church would know first. But large contingents of Italian Catholics planned to turn out, and the pastor noticed a marked increase in the number of confessions on Monday evenings and Saturday afternoons. Grandma and the children of course heard the story and planned to lean out of their windows to see the Savior's return. Friends of Grandma called and asked if they could please show up and see the vision from her windows, and she of course said yes. She insisted however that she had to make eggplant parmesan with rotini for the guests.

Grandpa meanwhile thought the whole excitement was nonsense. And he sarcastically asked Grandma why, if this was the Second Coming and the end of the world, would people need to eat afterwards, but she insisted on being a good hostess.

When July 1 came, Grandpa went to the 7 a.m. Mass and prayed in front of the statue of the Blessed Virgin Mary. It was a strange mystical statue, and the eyes of the Virgin seemed to follow you as you walked by her. No one knew why. Grandpa compared it to the smile of the Mona Lisa which he had seen in prints. He quietly prayed to her for protection in a hostile world, and went home saying nothing to anyone.

At a few minutes before noon, Grandpa was in his backyard garden, and his driveway was beginning to fill up with strange cars. They could not even walk to see Jesus. They had to take their new Oldsmobiles and old trucks to Main Street. As noon soon approached, Grandma and the kids leaned out of the windows to see the sight, and the apartment was packed with friends and friends of friends.

At two minutes before twelve, the excitement was palpable, and at noon all looked at the street which for once had been cleaned by the borough. But Jesus didn't come walking. Then at 12:05 he did not come, or at 12:15. He just did not walk down Main Street. In his garden Grandpa kept on working as people faded way. Grandma, not to be outdone, served her eggplant to the apartment dwellers. Later the Reverend Billy Joe said he had miscalculated the date; Jesus was coming next year at that time. The preacher was holding a special prayer service to welcome the true believers and thank Jesus for giving us more time to repent. People in his church began talking in grunts and groans, and he compared it to Pentecost when the Holy Spirit gave the faithful the gift of tongues to preach the gospel all over the world.

The next morning Grandpa again went to the 7 a.m. Mass, and stopped at the Virgin's statue. He thanked her for not allowing the end of the world yet, for he had a lot of living to do. In two years, the preacher left Madison and began a popular radio show, *Jesus Saves*, in which he told people to place the part of their body aching them close to their radio and feel the heat on top of the box. That was, he insisted, the healing power of Jesus entering them.

22. THE KLAN

Geographically part of New Jersey is below the Mason-Dixon Line, the historic division of North and South. In the two Lincoln elections New Jersey did not go to the Republicans in either. After the war, the state elected as its governor George McClellan, the Union general who opposed the Emancipation Proclamation. Anti-black sentiment grew in the state as the great black migration to the North took place before and after World War I.

One of the consequences was the re-emergence in the country of the Ku Klux Klan, a self-proclaimed white supremacy, anti-black, anti-Catholic, anti-Jewish, anti-immigration collection of hooded hooligans who were sworn to purify the nation. They paraded and circulated materials mainly in the Midwest, but soon came to south Jersey.

On July 4, Madison was having its annual Independence Day parade, and down Main Street came the full stream of floats, bands, veterans from the wars, the drum and bugle corps of the Knights of Columbus, the Elks, the Masons, the daughters of black AME church, and fire engines. Grandpa loved parades and since it was coming down Main Street, he put out a lawn chair in front of his apartment house and smoked his pipe as the demonstrations went by. The engines were usually at the end of the parade, but suddenly he heard people starting to boo. There were eight Ku Klux Klan men carrying a banner "Purify America." They marched down the street, as if they belonged, as if they were locals. One hooded man passed out broadsheets saying, "The Klan has come to Madison." It argued that Madison had too high a ratio of Negroes, Catholics, and immigrants and needed to rectify the percentage. The Klan was there to help.

Grandpa read the circular, and as they came by, they had a stuffed shirt and pants with a black head and noose around it. It reminded him of the terrible stories he had heard as a boy of the mass lynching of Italians in New Orleans in 1891. "These are the same type of people," he murmured, "now they are here in town."

Three weeks later, he was looking at his prized garden one night, and through the cherry trees he saw a sudden fire burst up in the form of a flaming cross. It was on the grounds of Pearson's Lane right where he had planted a garden of pansies and boxwoods for the inhabitants. He ran out of his backyard, pushed through the rusty fence and saw eight men in white hoods, cheering and shoveling wood chips on the cross "Go home niggers, back to the southland, mammy." And then they laughed, climbed into the two rusty trucks, and left. The families in Pearson's Lane looked out their windows in fright. Grandpa just stood alone near the charred cross, as it burst into his pansies and set the boxwoods up in flames. Finally the people came out, dazed and frightened, for this was not what happened in this quiet town. Off on the side of the cross was a stuffed shirt and pants hung by the neck off the cross.

Grandpa had worked long and hard on that garden. It was originally his idea. He became angry and then cold furious. A little black five-year-old, Jeffrey, came up to him, with tears rolling down his round checks, "Pop-pop, they have burnt our garden, why? Why?"

The old man grabbed the little boy's hand in his own coarse brown hand. He let go the boy's little hand, and simply responded, "Because in this life, some people cannot stand to see beauty."

"But it is gone, Pop-pop."

"Nature is never defeated; you and I will rebuild it to be more beautiful than before." He walked over and kicked the cross which cracked open like the gates of hell. It was Dante's Inferno without Virgil to guide him. The boxwoods fired up and then consumed themselves, like evil does eventually.

The next day he went to see Joe Pearson who was pacing in his office, furious that anyone would dare deface his property. "Come in Ralph, did you see what those redneck bastards did to my land, my very land."

"Yes, Joe, and you know they will be back. They will come again."

"You think so? I wonder when."

"That is what I wanted to ask you. You know a lot of people in this town who talk a lot. For $20 and a free drink, men give away their birthright."

"Yeah, I've got to get the next date of an attack. I'll give each of my black boys a gun to kill the bastards."

"No, no, that is best way to get them in trouble."

"Yeah, you're right. Let me handle that part, Ralph. What do you want by the way?"

"Of course, I was shocked at what they did to your property. You are such an important man, any one of us could be next. We need to spite them, and rebuild the garden they destroyed."

"What garden?"

"The Pearson garden, the very spot where they burnt that awful cross."

"Lousy godless bastards. What do you want?"

"A ton of fine topsoil delivered as soon as possible. No one is going to destroy the Pearson park!"

"Exactly, the lousy cowardly commies. I will send over a ton tomorrow. Let's make it as before. Then we will set the trap."

"No guns."

"Oh no, I was just mouthing off. Who the hell wants to arm a bunch of darkies anyhow?"

Grandpa went off to see Reverend Ernest Lyons of the Bethel AME church and talked about the terrible attack on many of his parishioners. He told the preacher that in the middle of this attack, they planted a cross as a symbol of hatred. They needed to replace it with a large crucifix of Jesus, a symbol of love and redemption. Did the good preacher have any old crosses in the church basement? In fact he did, the church was remodeled last year, and some parishioners complained that the hanging Jesus was too graphic, so he had a more modest one of the Resurrection take its place.

Then the preacher gazed away, "Didn't they realize that before the Resurrection there had to be the Crucifixion."

Grandpa nodded, "You and your people can put it in the same spot in the middle of the garden on private property where it will be safe forever."

So the preacher had two strong men accompany him, take the crucifix out of the basement and bring it to Pearson's Lane the next day just as the ton of dirt was arriving. In the back of Grandpa's truck were flats of pansies and rows of young boxwoods. When the dirt was laid out, the preacher insisted on giving a prayer to Jesus to keep harmless these fine people and this great neighborhood garden. So the crucifix stood tall surrounded by young pansies and early style boxwoods, as little Jeffrey walked around watering carefully each plant with half a container of water which was all he could carry at one time at his age. It was a rather edifying site. Dr. Shapiro, a conservative Jew, sent a check for a white picket fence around the garden.

A week later the Ku Klan Khan in all its heroic grandeur arrived in two rusty pickup trucks with another cross drenched with gasoline. Whooping and howling, they jumped out of the truck, except for an older member, the local imperial Kleagle, who slid out of the front passenger seat. As they moved toward the new garden, the doors of the Pearson apartments all opened and out came a dozen black men all wearing Brooklyn Dodger shirts with the number 42 on each of them. They were carrying real baseball bats, 36 ounces, and surprised the hooded crew. From across the street, six young men came running out of the railroad station. Grandpa, looking over the fence, recognized them as young Irish and Italian men from the Knights of Columbus. Together the Klansmen were surrounded, beaten, and then stripped of their elegant white robes. The first to go were the pointed hoods, and lo and behold the imperial Kleagle was the town dentist, Dr. Edward Coop. He was always complaining he never got paid for the work he did on Negroes.

The Knights of Columbus tied up the Klansmen, stripped of their robes, except for the dentist whom they stripped totally. It is funny how one's private parts shrink when in danger.

Grandpa quietly watched over the fence, and went back inside, for the action was over. The next day, he went up for a postmortem with Joe Pearson who was in his office with his feet up on his cluttered desk, smoking a big cigar.

"Hey, Ralph, a little rioting going on in your backyard I hear."

"Yes, there is no more Klan in Madison. "

"Nope, you know neighbors must stick together. It is like when we fought the Japs after Pearl Harbor. You did a nice job on that garden, although the cross was a bit much. I am not much of a believer in any of that stuff, but it still looks nice. Where did you get the money for the fence?"

"Dr. Shapiro sent me a check."

"That cheap Jew sent you a check for a garden with a cross in it? Damn. Just as I said we all stick together. Besides after the blacks, the Jews are next for those redneck bastards. Did you know they said they were going to throw a firebomb into your back garages?"

"My garages, why?"

"Yup, they said you were too close to the black boys, especially with those gardens."

"I am glad that someone found out when they were coming. By the way, Joe, why were all the men in the Lane wearing Brooklyn Dodger T-shirts with Number 42 on them?"

"Hell, Ralph, you got to read the sports pages. That is the number of slippery Jackie Robinson; the blacks love that streaking boy. I must admit he is good."

"Now where did they get those baseball bats from?"

"Who knows, those blacks steal like crazy. By the way, there are three left in the corner there, take one. Just put it in your garden as a good luck charm."

Grandpa took one, it had a good feeling to it, and it said, "Louisville Slugger." He then asked, "Where did the Knights of Columbus find out about that meeting?"

"Oh, Fred O'Reilly is the president and I called him and told him that the next stop of the Klan was to burn the convent that night."

"Was that truth?"

"Who the hell knows with those rednecks? They've done it before."

"The Madison police were right on time."

"Yea, it shows what a tidy contribution to the PBA can do."

"You had it all figured out."

"Here before you leave, Ralph, take this."

He threw him a jersey with the number 42 on it.[22]

"Now, leave me alone, I need to make some money. Had some unexpected expenses."

Then Grandpa went home, but he went around the corner, past the movies and looked at the garden. There was little Jeffrey playing on his tricycle. His family called him Jeffrey since they wanted him to fit into the larger world. He saw Grandpa and came running up, "Pop-pop, this is more beautiful than the old one."

"Yes, you did a good job, Jeffrey."

Then the little boy remarked unexpectedly, "My mother said you are a saint unknown to the world."

Grandpa got serious, "No, no, I am just an old man trying to even scores before it is too late. When are you going to school?"

"In September, I will be in kindergarten, but it is only for a half day, but that is okay." Grandpa gave him the jersey as a gift. "But I am too small for this."

"Don't worry someday you will be big enough to wear it."

Then they parted. In September Jeffrey went to public school, and his teacher asked the pupils to draw a picture of the best person they knew outside of their family. Jeffrey drew a picture of a man with an oval head, a tuff of gray hair, and a small mustache. Mrs. Anderson was surprised, he was white. "Jeffrey, who is that man?"

"He helped me make a garden in Pearson's Lane near my home. You should come and see it, Mrs. Anderson. He is a nice man."

23. GRAZIO A DIO

Grandma died on April 15, 1949, two days before Easter Sunday. The family held her wake in the living room, and then she was buried according to the traditional rites of the Roman Catholic Church. Grandpa was in deep mourning and roamed through the apartment with a sense of loss and hurt. He had loved her from the first moment he saw her in her church near Benevento and made as much money as he could in the United States to prove to her father that he was a rich *medigan*, which he really was not.

The times in the United States were not easy ones as Grandma recorded. They lost two infants and a twenty-six year-old daughter, Grandpa's favorite. Death seemed to overshadow their fine and stable marriage, although change was always ready to show its ugly features.

Grandpa was deeply in love with her. What her feelings were is difficult to say for it was a *masciade*, that is an arranged marriage. They lived in Madison, New Jersey their entire adult lives and made that small town their universe.

Grandma died of a rare neurological ailment of the brain. She was only fifty-nine. Her family had a good record of longevity—she did not.

For weeks going into months, Grandpa was sober and melancholy, walking around the flat, almost lost, looking for her. But she was not to be found.

He stopped going to church, even blaming God for taking away his beloved. They should have been married many more years. He stopped praying and put her old Bible aside, having no use for it. Grandma barely could read or write, but she knew certain Psalm verses as her favorites.

After six months to the day, he went into the bathroom and in the mirror was a handprint in powder. How did it get there, he wondered? No one used the bath but him. The handprint was a small hand, almost like his wife's size. The rug that he had laid down in the room was pushed over to one side. Who did that?

He quietly took out a piece of paper and drew over the handprint so that he could have a record of the print. It was all so strange.

He sat down to have a quick breakfast and there was Grandma's Bible, open to her favorite passage: "Yea though I go through the valley of death, I will fear no evil, for thou art with me." Grandpa felt eerie since the Bible usually was inside the second room's mahogany closet chest. Did he place it here? Why didn't he remember that? That afternoon he visited the local fortuneteller, a Neapolitan witch lady who had a reputation for good predictions. She asked him if he was suffering from the evil eye, *il malocchio*. She grabbed a bowl of water, said the doxology over it, and then dropped oil drops. "In the name of the Father, the Son, and the Holy Ghost, bless this good man. Oh Almighty God bless him. Bless him Blessed Virgin. Take away the curse of the devil and his agents of the evil eye." She and Grandpa looked at the water, and the oil drops were totally dissipated. He was not suffering from the evil eye. His pain was deeper and more profound than *il malocchio*.

He came home and rushed into the bathroom again. The palm print was still on the mirror. He loudly called for his daughter upstairs and showed her the print. She was startled and noticed that in the print the ring was on the pinky finger, not on the ring finger. "It is just like Mama's. She had arthritis in the end and couldn't get the ring over her knuckle and put it on the smallest finger," the daughter said. "This is the print from Mama's hand!"

Grandpa just stared at it, as in a daze, and he told her of the rug and the opened Bible. He felt a sense of wonder and awe and a sense of deep sorrow and loss. His daughter counseled him to visit the monsignor, long a family friend, despite Grandpa's recent apostacy.

He pondered her advice and decided to drive up to the rectory in his new Ford green pickup truck. He quietly walked, noticed the flowers that he himself had planted a year ago, and rang the doorbell. The old monsignor himself appeared, as if expecting Grandpa sooner or later. "Hah! Ah Raffaele. *Vieni qui.*" Grandpa timidly walked into the foyer. "It's been a long time since we've talked."

"Yes, not since my wife died."

"Have you forgiven God yet?"

"Probably not, monsignor."

"I understand it. I hear that all the time from other people."

"Monsignor, I have come on a strange errand. My Luisa has been dead six months, and I have seen strange signs that she is still with me."

"Like what?"

"On my bathroom mirror, a white palm print, her size, with a wedding ring only on the smallest finger she had. Then a rug that moves in the doorway, the one that I had tacked down. And in my kitchen is her Bible, open to her favorite Psalm."

The monsignor had known Grandpa for years, and he was convinced of his sobriety and good judgment. *What was he leading toward*, he wondered.

"Can it be, monsignor, that she is in some sense alive and with me?"

The monsignor thought for a while. "Of course Luisa is with you. She will be with you until the last day."

"Ah, will I see her in heaven and be rejoined with her? I hear that at the last judgment we will be united again with our spouses and family and friends. People say that at the resurrection of the body we will appear to each other as we were in early thirties. Is that so or is it an old lady's tale, monsignor?"

"The love we feel on earth is not a heavenly emotion. For the love of God so overwhelms all feelings that we are only attracted to Him, our creator. Our love on earth is but a slight mirror reflection of His enormous light. For God is love itself. God is mercy itself. The love you feel on earth is God transmitted through the people that we love so much here."

Grandpa quietly responded, "So I will never see my one love ever again?"

"Your love of her is enduring, and the enormous love is embraced in the enormous love of God. She is a part of the God of love."

Grandpa said, "Like Beatrice and Dante in *Paradiso*?"

"Yes, like their true love. Coming up Raffaele will be Laetare Sunday, one of the two times a priest wears pink. Not black, not green or white, but a pinkish-purple lavender. This time I will offer up the Mass for Luisa and your true love. Will you come?"

"That is very fine, monsignor. I am so proud of even being mentioned from the pulpit of my own church." And so Grandpa went home. The image on the mirror was barely visible, and he read again Psalm 23, "Yea though I walk through the valley of death, I will fear no evil, for Thou art with me."

On Laetare Sunday he went to Mass, received communion, and prayed for his wife's soul. The pink color was like her, bright and sparkly and pleasant. From that day he would rise up and say in his earliest morning, "Thank God, I am alive today."

24. JURY DUTY

As Grandpa opened the long official envelope from the clerk of Morris County, he was surprised to be notified that he had been summoned to jury duty. In all the years he had been an American citizen, he had never been called for jury duty, and he was sort of proud of the honor. He was to present himself at the county courthouse on March 1 at 9 a.m. The courthouse had three trials that day, and there was little parking, so the clerk's office had set up a shuttle bus that would go to the train station and then to the intersection of the #70 Public Service Transit bus.

The night before March 1 arrived, he set two alarm clocks by his bed just to make sure he was up early and didn't miss the train. In fact he got up even earlier and walked to the nearby train station across from the movie theater and near Pearson's Lane. He climbed up the stone stairs and held on to the pipe banister as he wore his favorite warm gloves. The train coming west was on time and he soon arrived in Morristown. Indeed there was the shuttle to take prospective jurors to the courthouse, and he and four other people boarded it.

The courthouse was a bit dilapidated, but inside the signs to the jury bullpen were clear. The room was a large auditorium that sat about 300 people on uncomfortable metal chairs. He was one of the first in the room so he sat up front because his hearing was going. Once assembled, the clerk informed the jurors that there were three trials that they were going to work on, establishing a jury for each today.

Each jury would have a pool of 15 jurors and alternates, and if a person was not chosen for one trial, he would get preferential treatment for the next one. The clerk in mechanical language thanked the prospective jurors for their commitment to American democracy and to the judicial system—a constitutional guarantee. In a great flourish, he reminded the group these were the rights American boys had fought and died for just a few years before. Grandpa was especially moved by the appeal to patriotism.

Each member of the group was given a numbered ticket, and the clerk pulled the numbers out of a fishbowl, just like the government had done for the draft during the war. When the clerk began calling names, Grandpa was number 3, a surprise to a man who rarely won anything. The first thirty including him marched off to Room 101 and took an oath to tell the truth. Lawyers on each side had the right to challenge a juror, and in rare cases to announce that he or she would use the preemptory challenge to exclude any person without giving a reason.

The first case involved a wife beating dispute. The attorney for the defense, John O'Reilly, was an NYU law graduate who looked like he was 12 years old; he asked Grandpa if he ever struck his wife. Indignantly, he answered, "Never, never we were deeply in love." O'Reilly thought to himself, *This guy is a liar, I never met a dago who didn't knock his wife and kids around.* He asked that Grandpa be dismissed without cause. *What have I done wrong?* Grandpa wondered.

In the second case, Grandpa arrived as they were quizzing the jurors, and he recognized the lawyer for the plaintiff as Joseph Russo from the Falcone legal factory. He asked Grandpa slyly, "You look like a working man. Have you ever used a power saw to cut lumber?" His client had lost two fingers in an accident with the saw.

Grandpa responded simply, "Yes, I certainly have many times, but you have to be careful with the saw."

The attorney was arguing a negligence case against the company, and prudence was exactly the virtue he did not want stressed. He turned to the judge and said, "This person is a distinguished working man, but may have had too much experience to be empaneled and may inadvertently sway the rest of the jury." The argument made no sense, but the judge let it ride, and Grandpa ended up in the room for the third case, involving a numbers runner who was stupid enough to try to entice an undercover agent to use his services while they were both in a newspaper store. The numbers runner had seen the man trying to buy a copy of the racing form, and he figured he had a mark. Bad intuition, bad choice. It was too flagrant, so they were going to make an example of him. Imagine, gambling in Jersey!

The state's attorney asked Grandpa on examination if he was a heavy bettor and played the numbers. He responded that he did not gamble and did not even play bingo at the church. The attorney looked at him with his squint eye and thought, *Damn dagoes, never tell the truth. What Italian does not gamble?— come on.* And so Grandpa was again dismissed on a peremptory challenge and was back in the auditorium. Soon the clerk came in and announced that the juries had been empaneled and their services were no longer needed. Once again American democracy depended on volunteers like them, even though they did not end up serving. Exit back to the shuttle.

Grandpa felt he had let someone down, somehow, but he couldn't figure out who or why. "Another day in my life lost," he mumbled. The shuttle let some passengers out, and the train going east was far down the track. Grandpa and a few others waited on the cold platform, and then boarded.

The train was an ugly Army green color, with wicker seats which were the type that could be pulled in either direction. Grandpa sat alone, deep in his thoughts about the jury system.

A man with a beautiful cashmere coat and long hair and a neatly trimmed beard occupied the seat in front of him, a wealthy businessman thought Grandpa. He must have made his money quickly, for he looked only in his early 30s. Then in struggled a lean African-American man with no shirt on, Army fatigue pants, and soiled boots. On his left arm was a tattoo, celebrating the Marine Corps with its motto "*Semper Fi*,"—Always faithful.

It was so cold that March day that Grandpa could not imagine how anyone could go around shirtless and not freeze to death. Grandpa had an overcoat, scarf, hat and fine gloves on and was still chilled. The conductor quickly saw the man and zeroed in on him, demanding a ticket which he knew the traveler would not have. He told him he was going to be kicked off at the next stop. But Grandpa had purchased two tickets, in case he lost one, for he was a prudent man. He leaned over into the aisle, and quietly said, "Here this ticket is for him."

The conductor was clearly annoyed, took the ticket, and murmured, "Damn lowlife on this train."

The traveler looked up at Grandpa and seemed dazed. Then as the train rolled into the Convent Station stop, the man in front of Grandpa took off his beautiful overcoat and wrapped it around the poorly clad man, and he put his hat on him as well, and vanished quickly. The traveler looked up and tears rolled down his cheeks. Grandpa gazed out the windows, but he could not see his face or find him on the platform. He just vanished.

As the train moved toward Madison, the poor traveler wrapped the fine coat around him and proudly took the hat on his lap. At the Madison stop, Grandpa got up and impulsively gave his finest gloves to the man, and then pressed in his left hand a $20 bill. All the traveler could feel was the sharp edge of the bill and the rough hand of a working man. Grandpa exited from the front, and through the window, he saw the traveler trying on the gloves and covering over the tears on his face.

As Grandpa went slowly down the icy stone steps, he instinctively reached for the frigidly cold iron banister. It was like when dumb kids put their tongues on metal surfaces in the dead of winter. Grandpa walked down unassisted. At the bottom of the stairs, he pushed his hands into his coat pockets, and began to walk home. But then a black Buick stopped. It was the monsignor on his way from the church to Overlook Hospital to make some sick calls. "Do you want a ride Raffaele? It is too cold to walk, and I am going down Main Street." Grandpa jumped in the car, and immediately felt the mercy of the heater blowing on them. "What are you doing out on a day like this?"

"I had jury duty in Morristown."

"Oh, I had that last year until they saw my Roman collar!" Then Grandpa told him for some reason the story of the naked man and the benevolent stranger. The monsignor partly didn't believe him, "Oh, you are a great storyteller, Raffaele. I may use the tale in my homily this Sunday."

Then Grandpa pondered, "Is that not what Jesus said— if you have two coats, give one to the poor. This businessman gave the only one he had with him to the poor, how much greater was his gift?"

"Yes, yes indeed, you are right."

As Grandpa was telling the story, he was rubbing his hands to increase the circulation. "You know Raffaele, you need a good pair of gloves."

"Yes, yes I do." And he got out of the Buick, thanked the monsignor, and heard the priest say, "Remember me in your prayers."

25. REMEMBRANCES

The merry month of May was a gardener's favorite time of the year. On the rickety wooden porch Grandpa had set out a collection of young flowers, new seedlings, and a greenhouse for plants meant for the gravesite of Grandma who had died two years ago in 1949. Somehow just bringing the flowers to the cemetery seemed like a memorial to his wife, a way of silently talking to her about the world she had slipped off from.

He would almost go crazy sometimes thinking of her in a box resting in a concrete sleeve, imprisoned in the cold and then in the humid summer. He was an old-time Catholic and was committed to believe in the comforting religious tenets. Yet still he wondered if it all was a mere fantasy, and if we are like the pansies he planted: with a blossoming, a steady growth, a pretty explosion of colors, and a rotting away forever in the fall. He had seen too much evil to be complacent about the triumph of good, and too much of earth not to believe all was transient, for a gardener seems to lose immortality.

For his trip up to the cemetery on Noe Avenue, he decided to take his oldest granddaughter, Louise, who worked at Rexall's Drug Store all day. She too knew and loved Grandma and was especially fascinated by her curative powers using herbs and roots. So they climbed into his 1949 green Ford pickup and drove slowly to St. Vincent Martyr cemetery. Since they were one of the first families to buy a plot there, they had their choice of where to spend eternity. Grandpa chose flat, dry land near the entrance gate. It probably did not matter, he judged, but there they would all be together.

They took the rusty tools and the plats of flowers and placed them on the gravesite, and Grandpa looked aimlessly up the hill and noticed Joseph Carnato, long widowed, who was planting a single lily. One could see him dressed in his brown high boots and sable-edged vest. In his dim mind he saw angels playing hooky and drinking in front of the bar on Fairmont Avenue. He took his wife Angela in his arms and waltzed and then fox-trotted, and she was his once-upon-a time true love. Neighbors said he was an old mysterious guy giving music lessons, coming in with his violin, the veneer of civilization in a world that was harsh and brutish. Once he was fleet of foot, weighed down with only a sparkling wit, enjoying the lightening in his wife eyes. Oh, Angelica. He grabbed his hickory cane and bowed formally to her stone.

Grandpa finished his own work, and in gratitude offered to take Louise to lunch at Rocco's. They arrived in the back lot, and the youngest son in the family greeted Grandpa with a respectful salute. They sat down, and surprisingly he saw Joe in the far end.

He was sitting in the darkest corner table, holding hands with Clarisa, a pretty young Irish lass who worked at Woolworth's at the cosmetic counter. Joe no longer seemed as frail as before, looking like an old vagrant on the edges of civilization. His hands were expressive, he was laughing as she giggled, and this was how he spent his time nowadays.

26. PAPA AND GUNS

Like many people living in rural Italy, Grandpa had grown up with guns, usually as a protection against wolves and vermin. He would, if necessary, fire a weapon, but never loved to hunt, for he hated killing living things. When he emigrated to the U.S., he packed the hunting gun in his suitcase, which was never opened by the authorities on Ellis Island. It did not matter, for the agents believed in the sanctity of the Second Amendment.

At his first apartment, he placed the rifle and the ammunition in the corner of the main bedroom, but when kids began to come, he placed the rifle in the cellar on top of a shelf, and in a separate area he put the case of shells in the back of the coal bin. He always preached the dangers of guns to his children, the girls could not care less, but one of his sons—the oldest— was a curious fellow, and he shipped $25 to a local dealer and got a shiny pistol which he continually took apart and put back together again.

One day, Salvatore was giving the gun a good cleaning, and he reassembled it too quickly. Leaving one shell in the cylinder, he pointed the gun down toward his foot and absent-mindedly fired. A bullet ripped the boot apart, and he felt a terrible pain by the big toe. He screamed so loudly that everybody in the apartment house heard it. "Oh, Jesus Christ, I have shot myself. Oh, God it is so bloody."

Grandpa ran out to the porch and yelled for his daughter Margaret, a registered nurse, "Do something." She had covered the ER in St. Elizabeth's Catholic Hospital, where weekend shootings were a way of life. She ran down the creaky wooden stairs, ordered her inquisitive son to get some bandages for the bloody wound, and the son stupidly came back with three Band-Aids in hand. She scorned his efforts and took his shirt and made an expert tourniquet. By that time the ambulance that Grandpa had called came, and the doctor noted with admiration the expert job she had done, saving Salvatore's foot. They took him down the stairs to the vehicle and to the hospital. So he recovered, and Grandpa in a fit of anger took his gun, dismantled it and threw it in three different green garbage bags. He did not know what to do with the ammunition, so he opened up the box that had Italian lettering on it and threw it away. He grabbed the random bullets and put them in a plastic bag from the A&P and brought them to the police station saying he found them in the back of his beloved garden.

In 1932, Grandpa had taken Grandma to see the film *A Farewell to Arms* with Gary Cooper and Helen Hayes. It was the story of a wounded army officer who is sent to an Italian hospital after the battle of Caporetto and is nursed by a beautiful aide with whom he falls in love; she becomes pregnant by the liaison. It was the story of Bernardo, his relative who had ended up living in Madison and was cared for by Grandma, and eventually took his own life.

Twenty years later, Barnes & Noble announced that the great novelist Ernest Hemingway was autographing copies of his newest book, *The Old Man and the Sea*. Grandpa did not like to drive in highway traffic, especially on Route 22, but he wanted a signed copy of the new book. Waiting two hours in line, he saw Hemingway lumber out of the limousine. He looked tired, disheveled, and disoriented—somewhat like Bernardo did. When he finally met "Papa" Hemingway, he remarked that he enjoyed *A Farewell to Arms,* that it was a true story in his family. Hemingway stopped signing and he quizzically looked up. "It was?"

"Yes my cousin was in the ambulance corps at the battle of Caporetto."

Hemingway responded with pride, "So was I, I was in the ambulance corps and was wounded. I wonder if I ever worked by him." Then Hemingway respectfully signed the book, and handed it to Grandpa saying, "May God bless your cousin's soul in peace."

Grandpa put *The Old Man and the Sea* by his picture of Giuseppe Garibaldi, a true warrior in the Italian Risorgimento. He tried to read it, and although the words of Hemingway were simple, his construction was complicated and beyond Grandpa's ability to enjoy it. Several years later, he decided to ask his granddaughter, Diana, to read it to him at night. She liked to read, and he would pay her a two dollar bill every night she read. It was a short novel and it was easy for her to get through.

The work was the story of a proud, old Cuban fisherman who would sail out with a young boy to seek the great fish of his life. Soon the boy left him, but Santiago continued to fish for it was his life's work. As he sailed, he constantly asked himself what would the "great DiMaggio do," for Cuba was baseball country. At one point, Grandpa told his granddaughter that he once had ice cream with the "great DiMaggio" at a Dairy Queen roadside stand in southern New Jersey. But Diana was not impressed for she did not even know who he was.

In the end the Old Man captures the fish and talks of his resolution. Grandpa asked, what did the word "resolution" mean? Diana simply said it was a determination to do what you start in life. She left, and Grandpa thought about the meaning of the word. He hoped it would characterize his life, especially as he got older. *Ah*, he philosophized, *it is a great life if you don't weaken.* The old man never wanted to weaken, but some days life just seemed so difficult that it almost overwhelmed him.

But he did love the novel.

One day he read in the *Newark Star Ledger* that Ernest Hemingway, Nobel laureate and Pulitzer Prize winner, had died. He had put a shotgun in his mouth one early morning while his wife slept and pulled the trigger. *God, how could he do that to his wife?* Then he wondered, *What happened to resolution, what happened to being tough in life?* But Grandpa read on—this suicide came in a family with a long history of suicide. He couldn't help it; the killing instinct was in his blood, in his poor family's depressed soul. Yes, he couldn't help it. And the column went on, "Hemingway is best remembered for his remark, 'Courage is grace under pressure.'"

27. REAL SANTA CLAUS

As Christmas was coming, Aunt Marie took charge of the family gathering since she was the best cook and also had the largest house. She and her husband owned a stately white Victorian with pronounced gables and a wrap-around porch on a huge piece of property. She had married her first cousin, much to the chagrin of her family and the local Catholic pastor. But when she threatened to run away at 15 to get married, both forces declared defeat. Her husband was short of stature, but big of heart, and they lived happily. Marie claimed that in times of stress she saw from the kitchen window the Virgin Mother in the garden, so her husband put a porcelain bathtub standing up on one end with a statue of the Immaculate Heart of Mary in it and surrounded it with sharp rocks making it a veritable grotto. It was a sight to behold even if one did not believe.

For Christmas all the women in the family chipped in with their specialties. The table featured spaghetti marinara, fine pasta e fagioli, eggplant parmesan, baked ziti, Virginia ham, yams, fried potatoes and assorted cakes, ices and candies. Aunt Marie had decided that her husband should play Santa Claus, and she bought him a suit and tailored it to size and trimmed the beard. The little kids loved him, the middle kids were unsure, and the older kids were cynical about the very existence of the man. But Santa gave everyone nuggets wrapped with M&Ms and cheerfully wished them all "Merry Christmas." He even tweaked Grandpa's nose and pronounced, "*Buon Natale.*"

The food laying at the table was a feast to behold. *How lucky we are, compared to the poor people of Africa and Asia,* Grandpa unexpectedly thought. *Thank God, Italy and America had such fine farms, we never knew drought and famine.* The house seemed at times to have a hundred rooms, and after dinner a weary Grandpa vanished into a small study and sat in the easy chair where a copy of the Christmas day *Newark Star Ledger* was open. It was unusually thin, and full of little real information, but he still began to read it for something is always better than nothing.

After several minutes alone, his peace was interrupted by his three littlest grandchildren: Anna who was 5; Louis 6; Jenny 7. They came in together almost on a mission to ask him a simple question, for they trusted the old man who was honest and forthright to even the little people.

Jenny spoke first, "Grandpa, is there really a Santa Claus?"

He was hoping that he would not be the person to deal with the issue; it was worse than the facts of life talk. He preferred that the women handle those matters.

"Why, you just saw him."

Jenny replied, "He was short, the one we saw in front of Kresge yesterday was tall."

"Well sometimes Santa lets his elves dress up for him."

Louis plaintively said, "Kids at school say that there is no Santa Claus, has never been a Santa Claus. Is that true?"

Little Anna chimed in, "Oh, no, no Santa Claus. What a terrible Christmas this will be."

The old man gathered them close, "Look, a long time ago, east of Sicily, there was a country now called Turkey which had a famous Catholic bishop. He was loved by all and was a good man with a long beard and a pointed hat. Girls who wanted to get married had to give the husband-to-be's family some money. But many girls' families were too poor to come up with the money. So at night this good man would walk around in his robes and throw into the barely open windows bags of money so they could get married, and he usually did that on Christmas Eve. The bishop was a saint, and people still call him Saint Nicholas."

Jenny interrupted him, "But what does that have to do with us Grandpa?"

"Well, he like all people died, and his place was taken all over the world by other men and women who on Christmas leave presents for children everywhere. You can say now that there is not one St. Nick, but many St. Nicks, and what they do is called the 'spirit of Christmas.' We all show our love for baby Jesus, and much of the world celebrates the spirit of Christmas, even those who do not know the Christ story. We send each other gifts and we give to the poor. In Italian towns, people bring baskets of fruits and candy to the front door of the poorest, and then some even leave toys for the children in the house, and much happiness arrives. See that, honey, is the spirit of Christmas—giving not receiving, loving not worrying."

"But who gives it to us, Pop-pop," asked Anna.

"Each family has Santa. The best Santas are your mommies. They cook the meals, they wrap the presents, they send out Christmas cards to friends who live far away, they set the table with special care, and they bring to us the spirit of Christmas."

Then Louis cried, "But what if you have no momma, like you Grandpa?"

The old man looked quietly down and then assured him, "I go to a kind person's house like Aunt Marie, or I stay home thinking of what Christmas was like with Grandma and the children years ago. I have memories that fill me with that spirit and love."

Then he reached into his pocket and came out with three envelopes, each having a $2.00 bill with Thomas Jefferson's portrait on it. He gave each of the little kids an envelope saying, "These come from Santa to you all."

And they left happy, but then Anna turned around, "Are you kidding us, Pop-pop?"

He smiled and picked up the *Star Ledger* again. *It is too hard being a grandfather nowadays. How did I suddenly get so old? I can remember my own grandfather just yesterday...*

28. THE SEXTON

Grandpa fervently believed in marriage, totally and completely, and for everyone. One day he explained to me the need for different types of trees to be near each other in order to cross-pollinate. It was, I guess, his idea of introducing his naive grandson to the birds and the bees…in a real sense. He had spawned a large family, and he once offhandedly remarked that he wanted to have more children, but Grandma demurred as she nearly died from the last one.

He aided and abetted marriages, especially for his daughters, even though he admitted that some of them married urban boobs. Still, they all married Italian-Americans and nominal Catholics. To his surprise one of his sons remained unmarried. Grandpa began to fear that he was either a "homosexualist" or was going to be a priest. But Dominic was neither, he was just shy and rarely dated. To supplement his meager income, he worked at night at the local theatre which once had been a vaudeville house, featuring the likes of Eddie Cantor in blackface, Burns and Allen, Sarah Bernhardt, and to everyone's delight the master of them all—Al Jolson, also in blackface. America was very different then.

White people sat in the main auditorium, and blacks sat in the upper balcony, called inelegantly "nigger heaven" by some of the town residents. Grandpa was not much for the movies, but Grandma was, and she would take her second son Dominic with her. It was with him that she saw a remarkable sight—the Great Jolson in *The Jazz Singer*. It was the first talkie most Italian people in town had ever seen, and they insisted that the voices they heard were hidden behind the curtain. But soon they realized it was a brave new world they were viewing.

Dominic finally took a job as an usher at the movie house, and five nights and on weekends he guided people down the sticky rug to their seats, sometimes for a double feature and a news reel. Several times a week, he began to escort three young women about his age to their seats on the left, and after a month or so, mustering all his courage, he struck up a conversation with one.

They got to talking about films, about the Hollywood pantheon of actors and actresses, and who was their favorite. In their own starless lives, they related to the luminous Gable, Grant, Crawford, Gilbert, Stanwyck, and of course Bogie.

Soon fantasy gave way to thin reality, and they got married under the grape boughs of Grandpa's ripe gardens. The lazy bees buzzed around the pile of pressed grapes in the back, and a three piece local band played Neapolitan love songs. And for the first time, all saw Grandpa and Grandma gracefully dance the tarantella. Grandpa truly had a great evening, and when all left, he sat on his aluminum chair in his garden covered overhead by his fig tree and inhaling the smell of mint. He had exchanged his dress suit for his old corduroy shirt and his stained fedora. He leaned over to Grandma, "This was a tough one to get married, Mama, but it is done, and as you wished according to the rites of the church and your pastor."

"No," Grandma said slyly, "the first was the hardest."

"Yes, Marie," Grandpa agreed. Marie was the oldest child who at 15 years of age had stubbornly decided to marry her first cousin, a 4'9" artist and housepainter. The Catholic Church opposed the unions of first cousins, but Marie insisted that she would run away with him without benefit of the sacraments. A horrified pastor used his friends in the Vatican, and the cousins were granted a dispensation, got married, bred four children, and lived happily ever after. Grandpa had vigorously opposed the union, and as he observed, "You can never trust the Church to be hardass when you need it." He never respected Pope Pius XI, since he had made a treaty with the Fascist thug Mussolini in 1929.

As for Dominic and his bride, they honeymooned in Niagara Falls, a far cry from Capri where he and Grandma had gone. But after five days, the phone rang, and Dominic was pleading with Grandpa that they come home early. The old man asked if anything was wrong. "No..."

"But if you come home early then people will talk. Finish up the two weeks. Goodbye."

Grandpa was a bit embarrassed to tell Grandma about the conversation, so he did what most men of his and our time do—he kept quiet, hoping that time would heal all wounds. And trees would eventually blossom.

The newlyweds came home, set up house in a third floor apartment above his parents and quietly lived there. They rarely socialized except with the two sisters of the wife, and Dominic proved to be a model employee for the Erie Lackawanna railroad. He also was willing to work overtime, to come in on holidays, and on religious days.

In five years, they had no children, and Grandpa was wondering at times if they even consummated the marriage when he remembered the phone call. But it was inappropriate even to talk to his son on the matter. Those were deep divisions, especially between generations. Children learned about sex in the street, and the information as expected was often unreliable.

The family had close ties with a branch that lived near Albany, New York and which was also devoted to the feast of Our Lady of Mount Carmel, an Italian happening with all the trimmings. It had food, religion, banners, endless fireworks and happy unruly children. That year Domenic wanted to go to the festival, but his wife as usual was vigorously opposed to making the long trip. This was in a period before the federal interstate system opened up the whole boring Albany area to travel.

Dominic was growing restive, tired of being angry with his wife and weary of seeing his harpy sisters-in-law and his self-satisfied mother-in-law. After all she had finally found a husband for one of Macbeth's three witches. So on a Thursday he climbed in his Chevy and drove up the harsh roads. It was indeed a long trip, longer than it should have been as Dominic dithered along. Long trips permit long reflections, and he reviewed his life, and the nature of happiness in a chronicle of limited days and frightening nights.

Off a side road was a farmer who sold peaches, which Dominic loved. He passed the farm, and there was a small but interestingly attractive Catholic Church—the St. Francis of Assisi's mission. He stopped on the gravel parking lot, and walked into the warm, sparkling nave.

He prayed in front of the crucifix, sidestepped to the side altar dedicated to St. Francis of Assisi and across to the other side with a statue of St. Clare. He stepped to the back pamphlet rack and quickly read a study of St. Francis and his teachings. The saint started by fixing up old run down churches and living a life of sacrifice and dedication.

Suddenly Dominic saw his life perfectly through the blessed life of Francis, but this is not the 13th century he calmly reflected. *How does one live now? Who do I talk to every day? Can we seriously cut off all ties to one's parents? Friends? Co-workers? It is too huge a jump in one's life. How did you do it? Giving up a future, a mother and father, and loves? But what love do I have now?*

He sat there quietly and looked blankly at the crucified Jesus above the marble altar. How brutal did the palms look... He left, and there on the right door was a notice to the parishioners. "Wanted church sexton. Room and board and $40 a month provided. See pastor inside."

Days passed to weeks to months and even years and Dominic had vanished. No one had seen him at Erie Lackawanna, at the relatives in Albany, or at home. After six months his dedicated wife began wearing black, and she mourned the loss of her beloved. They said a funeral Mass in absentia for him, and the family placed a stone in the ground with his Christian name and his dates.

Grandma was heartbroken, and six years later she died slowly. On her death bed, she looked around and her son was not there, and she expired in tears of despair and deep, deep sorrow.

Grandpa had hurt even more, and he could barely deal with either tragedy. After several years by himself, but surrounded by other sons and daughters, he was still so lonely and depressed, and he seemed at times to move aimlessly around in a fog. That summer, he asked a grandson to drive him to the feast day of Mount Carmel outside Albany. He had not been in that area for many years, not being much enthralled by their gauche festivals of Italian Christianity.

Every other member of the family intensely disliked driving with Grandpa for he insisted on stopping wherever there was a fruit stand or a flower display he liked. But he went with Alphonso, who as usual lost his way back to the main road from one such stand, and they ended up across the road from the St. Francis mission and cemetery. Grandpa had his reservations about the world-wide Church, but he enjoyed looking at stained glass windows, especially when the sun was high. Alphonso dutifully pulled over to the foot of St. Francis. The old man jumped out of the car and entered the church, sitting at first in the very back of the nave. He admiringly examined the window showing St. Francis taking the angry wolf by the paw, a scourge who had plagued the local village. St. Francis talked to the wolf sympathetically and reached an agreement—the wolf would be given food every morning, and in return he would be the protector of children and defenseless animals. Francis was portrayed as blessing the wolf—a triumph of good over evil.

Grandpa ambled outside, and there to his surprise he saw a familiar silhouette—the sexton. Good God, it was an aged Dominic. He screamed out to the sexton's bent-over figure. In near horror, Dominic, covered with dirt and the dust of marble chips, looked up.

"It is you, truly you, my son? What are you doing here? We have looked for years for you. Your mother, your wife have cried out. Their faces were creased with streams of tears. The court has declared you legally dead after seven years. The monsignor has already buried you. Come, come back with me. Why aren't you talking? Is it a stroke?"

Dominic at first feared the old man's wrath and said nothing. He searched around for words, "How is Mama?"

"She died in 1949, and you were not even there," Grandpa said bitterly, "She died of some brain ailment, and you were not even at her bedside. May God forgive the prodigal son."

"Ah, Mama...I did not know."

"Of course you didn't, who the hell knew you were even alive. What are you doing here? What is wrong with you? Come get in the car."

Grandpa could barely control himself, but Dominic did not move. "Papa, listen I won't go back, especially after all these years. I won't go back to a loveless marriage, to living quietly on your third floor, to a meaningless job, I won't go back to HER! Would you have lived with Mama in a loveless marriage, papa?"

And the old man began to sob deeply, and Dom began to cry also. "I never realized it was that bad," Grandpa said. "I was too busy with a large family. We all have problems in marriage, we did...."

"But papa, no love, no love." And the old man said nothing in response. Then he looked at the small cemetery that seemed almost manicured. Blankly he remarked, "You have done a good job here, Dominic, A job worthy of the souls of the dead."

"I also take care of the church; the parishioners are so poor and dirty."

"How much do you make?"

"Room, board, and $40 a month. It is more than enough, and the farmers bring us vegetables, and fruits, and even bread. It is a good life. And I know God is blessing me."

After a sense of delay, Grandpa insisted, "If God is blessing you, who am I to curse you? Goodbye, my son."

"Say nothing to anyone, papa, please. "

"Who do I talk to closely now that Mama is gone?"

They awkwardly embraced, and Grandpa slowly got into the car, and Alphonso drove away.

Grandpa was quiet, and then they arrived in Albany and the relations' house. The bottom floor was a mini-supermarket. At night they cleared out the meat bin and served some slightly old and very tough cuts to the distinguished guests. Grandpa pushed the pieces around and ate just the overcooked pasta.

That night he took Aunt Dolores out into the moonlight. She was a slight, dour woman—so typical of the older brand of Italian widows. But she was also the younger sister of Grandma, and her husband had recently died. Grandpa got down to business—would she marry him? She thought a little and said no. She was committed to living in Albany with her two daughters, and he was committed to staying home with his family. Also she knew he was trying to re-live his youth with Grandma, and she did not want to be a mirror image of her happier sister. Besides she never liked his calm, almost stately airs. Her late husband was what the kids called a "cut up," a man given to practical jokes and alcohol. So the evening ended, as it began without even a whimper. Grandpa probably did not want her to say yes anyhow, but he was lonely, and at times she gave off a spark or two that reminded him of Grandma, but only a little bit. In this rough life though a little bit is better than nothing.

In the early morning, he grabbed Alphonso and said, "Let's go home," and neither said anything all the way down the road. At one point, Alphonso asked if he wanted to stop and buy fresh tomatoes. The old man abruptly responded, "No, we've got better tomatoes back home, the Jersey tomato is better."

At home, Grandpa profusely thanked Alphonso, and sent him back to his mother with a jug of fine wine. It was one of the few presents he had that meant anything. Alphonso did not know the difference between Grandpa's wine and Manischewitz.

Now the old man had a secret to deal with, one more personal than his old *Book of Solomon*. Should he tell the non-widow of Dominic, but she was the very reason the boy left. *Shit to her,* he muttered. *If she could not keep him happy before, why would she change now after all these years?* Besides she still lived on the third floor rent free. She never offered him a cup of coffee or a slice of cake. *I bet she gives her sisters a good meal...on Dom's pension.*

And as he got worked up, he went to his garden, picked six pansies and put them in a nearly empty tomato can. A month later he handed me a sealed letter, "On the day I die, you open the letter and call the number and tell the sexton of my passing."

"Who is it, Grandpa?"

"Never mind, you will know the fruit, by the tree, son."

Some years later he was having a heavy lunch at his youngest son's house and was surrounded by several small grandchildren playing. And he quietly slumped over and died.

I quickly heard the awful news, and obediently opened the letter. I saw an Albany number; I recognized the prefix. I called St. Francis Assisi Mission and Cemetery and I asked for the sexton, and firmly told him, "Grandpa has died, and the three day viewing will begin on Wednesday, the Mass is to be on Friday." Suddenly the receiver went dead. I never spoke to the other party.

And then on Friday at St. Vincent Martyr Church Grandpa was laid to rest, covered by a bed of pansies that he so loved. All eyes in the old Norman Gothic Church turned to the front row. There on the left side entrance emerged Dominic steadfastly moving in with his siblings, and in the pew behind was his once wife and her sisters. He wore a nice suit, an Arrow shirt, and a black tie. As the Mass progressed along, the priest reflected on Grandpa's integrity and compassion and then he burst out, "He who lives in Christ Jesus will never die." Dominic was the only person to say "Amen," "so be it" in Hebrew.

After the Mass, the interment was next to Grandma, and a repast, that the old man provided money for, occurred before we all disbanded. But at home, I was startled to learn Dominic went up to his old third floor apartment where his "widow" lived all these years and reclaimed his life. He lived with her until they both passed on. She said he had had amnesia. For a few summers he tilled the old man's garden; in the winter he read over and over again St. Augustine's *Confessions*. Both Augustine and Grandpa had reached out from the grave.

29. AN UNSPEAKABLE CRIME

Central to his life was the sanctity of the family, not just as a vague principle, but as a way of dealing with people. Grandpa had come to the New World with several cousins, "paesani," and they formed a tight bond in America. One of his closest friends was his second cousin, Alesandro, who lived not far from him. Alesandro had a very docile wife and a young daughter about ten or eleven. One day a delighted Grandpa decided to share some of his burgeoning tomato crop with his cousin and brought over a bushel to his house on North Street, the Italian section of Madison.

When he drove up, he saw the daughter, Alicia, run out of the house sobbing intensely and headed toward the tree-covered section of the property. Grandpa left the truck and carried the tomatoes over to her, and asked "What's wrong, my child?" She cried "Nothing, nothing," and so he left, for he had four daughters, and girls loved to cry. Alesandro was delighted to receive the old man's gift, and they chatted only for a short time since Grandpa had other deliveries he wanted to make. Nothing tasted better than vegetables from one's own home garden, he always insisted.

Two weeks later, he again came up to see Alesandro to give him some of his mint, and in the yard under the big bush was a sobbing Alicia. Again Grandpa went over and asked, "Can I be of help?" She bluntly responded, "No, leave me alone, you will get me in even more trouble." But as he looked down, he could not miss seeing that her panties were pulled up tightly and there was a red spot in the middle. He left, entered the house, and found his cousin who was startled and was pulling up his trousers in the living room. He wanted to play bocce with Grandpa in the backyard, but the old man insisted that he had errands to run.

Grandpa drove home more slowly than usual. He saw what he saw, a wounded girl. Like most of us, he really knew little about sex, but he had a truckload of children and grandchildren. When he arrived home, his oldest daughter came with a magnificent lasagna and presented it to him. He thanked her profusely, and she told him, "Eat it while it is hot."

But he resisted, "I don't feel too good. I am sick to my stomach and shaky in the legs. Maybe it is just the sun. It is so hot in New Jersey this time of year; you would think you were in Libya with the Italian army."

But when she left, he put the Pyrex tray in the refrigerator, and began to think more clearly. He loved his cousin, but he saw what he saw. He took a shower and tried to wash not the dirt off his hands, but the feelings of disgust he lived with. He watched television, but his mind was elsewhere. So both weary and alert, he went to sleep but could not forget what he had seen. He tossed and turned and thought, *No man has a right to tell another man how to run his house. Where was Alesandro's wife if there were some problem? Didn't the neighbors see what I had seen? No man has a right to tell another man how to run his own house.* He believed that principle with his whole being. He finally dozed off but woke up in a cold sweat with the dream of young Alicia crying and desperately holding her hands out to him. All he could see was the blood spot.

For three nights, he was upset, and even stopped going to work. He uncharacteristically grabbed Grandma's Bible and started thumbing through it. He used the index for the first time to find what he wanted in it. The next day, he knew that he could not let it pass. He could not talk to his family about such behavior; he insisted that priests not being married would not understand, and all he could think was that it was a sickness of the body that required a doctor's advice, but deep down he knew it was a sickness of the spirit. So he went to see Dr. Miro H. Shapiro who was the family physician and who cared for Grandma in her last hours. Shapiro was not a very good physician, and he had begun to practice just when the miracle drug penicillin was introduced. So whatever people had, he gave them penicillin. If they were healthy, it did not matter; if they were sick, the drug seemed to work for most people, or they thought it did. Grandpa had avoided doctors, but other members of his family swore by Shapiro.

He went in and Dr. Shapiro greeted him with a hearty, "Haven't seen you in a long time, my friend." Grandpa felt like someone had just walked on his grave, but he got down to business. Shapiro was not a great physician, but he knew what Grandpa was talking about fairly quickly despite his oblique and convoluted presentation. He told the old man, "This is a matter for the government. I insist that you report the incidents to the child services unit of the borough of Madison." In both Italy and America, the Italians rightly distrusted the government and most other institutions except the family. Grandpa wanted Shapiro to call the bureau, but the doctor was too smart to get involved in Italian disputes, especially among family members. These people were so clannish he thought.

Grandpa walked up the hill to the Borough Hall. It was a beautiful Doric temple built by Italian workmen and financed by Mrs. Dodge who named it after her son who died in a car crash near Paris at the age of 22. He was her only heir. The hall was immaculate, the marble sparkled, and the walkways were protected by a black plastic carpet. Grandpa looked up at the directory to see where the child services unit was and found it on the second floor. He entered the office, and said, "I want to speak to someone in charge." He got an elderly woman who listened to his tale. She would have dismissed such talk as the ramblings of an old Italian coot, but since the newspaper's story on Grandpa and the Victory Gardens he was a minor celebrity in Madison, and she could not simply show him out. She promised to pass on his report, and the office did the typical bureaucratic response, it pushed it to the county public attorney in the Morristown office.

Grandpa left, looked at the woman, and insisted that all this be done quickly, for he had wasted three days in his own mind's meanderings. She promised she would, but she knew that it would be headed to the dead letter file in the prosecutor's office. But the prosecutor was a young Irish kid who had just graduated from Fordham Law School and wanted to make a quick reputation and run for public office. He saw in the report a highly visible case and moved on it.

Two days later, Grandpa got a call asking him if he would testify against his own cousin if necessary. He coolly responded that he would, but when confronted with the accusations Alesandro broke down and admitted that he had indeed sexually molested his own child. The judge eventually gave him a year in the Rahway State Penitentiary, and he was let out after six months for something called "good behavior." As soon as he got out, he attacked Grandpa as a traitor, a spy, a government agent, and a man who allowed Alesandro's daughter to be put in an orphanage. Actually Alicia ended up in a nice foster home, and Alesandro had only his wife left at home. But the idea of turning in your cousin, your *cugino*, your friend, your *paesano*, tasted sour to many Italians in town.

Even his daughter criticized him, "How could do that to your favorite cousin? You have destroyed his life. You get yourself in these controversies and you don't let go. Let people take care of their own children. You have to be more careful, papa."

He looked back and simply said, "It was an abominable act, abominable to God and man."

But his daughter was right in one sense. He noticed that when he was in town, at the hardware store or the A&P men, even old acquaintances looked the other way as if they were studying the tangerines. But the women would look him in the eye in almost a plaintive way, piercing his mind and reaching into his soul. At his weekly card game, his goombahs criticized his getting the government involved with Italian families, and how what Alesandro did was misunderstood, you know how hysterical girls are. The old man listened and pushed himself away from the table. They thought he had left, but he came back with the Bible he had been reading. He opened it up to where the Mass card was, a card featuring St. Joseph, the patron of good fathers. And in the Gospel of Mark, he read, "And Jesus said that anyone who causes scandal among the children, it would be better that he put a large millstone around his neck and cast himself into the sea." Then Grandpa observed, "The judge gave Alesandro a year in Rahway; Jesus would have been much harder on him. He committed an act that is so bad that even God cannot forgive him. Which of you men would let your children and grandchildren play at his house? It is an abomination, an abomination. You talk of Italian pride and unity, do we have to have this sick man in charge of children, even his own? Think before you answer." No one answered.

He once saw Alicia who was living a normal life with her adoptive parents, or as normal as could be expected. She simply walked by him not saying a word. She was embarrassed. Later, she got married to a lineman from PSE&G, and they had two daughters. The first was called Louise, not a very chic name then. But the old gossips on North Street told Grandpa's daughter that Alicia named her first born after Grandpa's beloved late wife, Luisa.

Louise later went on to become a pediatric surgeon specializing in cleft palates for the young. But by then Grandpa had long since died. As Shakespeare observed, and so it is that "golden lads and girls all must as chimney sweepers come to dust."

30. THE CIRCUS CLOWN

The whole county was abuzz. Ringling Brothers and Barnum & Bailey Circus was coming to town! Actually it was a rehearsal for New York City's Madison Square Garden debut. The circus would try out new acts, plan new carnival feats, and increase the bill of crowd-pleasing happenings. Being shrewd managers, the circus owners set up the tent and stalls for northern New Jersey and nearby New York City residents willing to drive out to the fields of Florham Park.

Posters were all around Madison and surrounding towns, and Grandpa looked at the one on Main Street in front of his apartment building. It featured the dates, the Florham Park site and a magnificent elephant head. The elephant looked like the one he saw in school that Hannibal drove across the Alps when he invaded Rome. Grandpa wanted to go, but nobody he knew shared his curiosity or the patience to fight the traffic and the people on the narrow, single lane road out there.

A day later, the new doctor in town, John Adams, whom Grandpa had kindly invited to a family dinner, stopped him in the drug store where he was buying a newspaper, and asked if he would like to go to the circus with him, his wife, and his seven-year-old son. There was room for one more in his Chevy. So Grandpa was on his way to the circus.

He was surprised to learn from the doctor that the Ringling Brothers management had a profit sharing arrangement with the popular singing cowboy, Gene Autry, who would lead the procession into the tent arena, on his famed horse Champion while he belted out his theme song "I'm Back in the Saddle Again."

Outside the tents were all sorts of games of chance and supposed skill. The circus performers divided the world into two types of people: cons and marks, and they were shrewd men ready to take the happy suckers. The games were usually fixed, but no one admitted that. The first night a young accountant consistently hit the wheel, able to call the numbers with unnatural regularity. He walked away with more prizes than he and his wife could carry, but later that night he went back and told the pitchman how he could calculate the final number by looking at the arch of his hand as it twisted the wheel. For one occasion the con man got out conned. Grandpa knew the accountant and delighted in the story when he heard it.

Once there, he enjoyed himself, winning some minor prizes which he gave to the boy. He figured it cost him $5.00 to pick up prizes that cost the circus 30 cents to buy. But fun is fun. Grandpa had a sweet tooth and he enjoyed cotton candy, caramel covered apples, and sweetened popcorn, and so did the little boy who followed him. Finally the family went into the big top and planted themselves in the front row of general admissions on bench seats that had been rented from an old out-of-use school. The seats were uncomfortable, but who cared?

The barker came out and welcomed the crowd to the "greatest show on earth," their slogan which might be applied to life itself. He had a fine top hat and a red coat that reached down to his mid thighs and asked them to cheer for the fine people who made up the circus family. So they did again and again. Even Grandpa cheered in his own way.

Out from the back, the procession of clowns, ballerinas, weightlifters, high wire artists, elephants, tigers, and decorated horses came prancing in. The clowns roamed all over the field and tweaked the noses of little children. The doctor's son was anxious and said to Grandpa, "I am a little afraid of clowns."

"Don't worry they are just like us except dressed to look silly."

At the final part of the show, the singing cowboy, Gene Autry, was sitting high as the recognized Champion came galloping in. Autry was dressed in a beautiful white hat with black trim, a sparkling vest and strong manly chaps down to the tops of his brown boots. He had a broad face, and he lit up when he waved to the children. He had four strong spotlights focused on him which came together when he pulled Champion up into the air. Grandpa thought he was looking at him directly. What was he doing there?

He paraded around, and the chestnut colored Champion pranced, lifting his powerful hoofs higher than usual. But then one of the clowns ran randomly toward Autry and caught a hoof in his head. The crowd grasped as he fell to the ground. Autry was horrified as he pulled Champion over to the other side of the ring. The accident took place right in front of the Adamses, and the doctor grabbed Grandpa by the arm to come with him. As he reached the clown, he ordered Grandpa to resuscitate him, a procedure he only seen in firehouse drills. The doctor screamed, "Push hard up and down on his chest here. I will breathe with you and try and get him back." So they did that for what seemed countless minutes. As circus figures surrounded them, the great Autry came over wishing he could do something, anything. Finally the clown revived and was taken off the arena field to the mindless applause of the crowd. Grandpa was shaking and the doctor had red and white face paint all over his lips.

On the way back home in the car the boy sat with Grandpa, and remarked, "I am no longer afraid of clowns. When I saw him hurt, I realized that he was just like me when I fall. I will never be afraid again." Then he looked at Grandpa approvingly, "You are a hero, you saved his life."

Grandpa quietly responded, "Oh no, it was your father who is the hero. I just did what he told me. He gave the clown the breath of life." The doctor and his wife in the front seat were quiet, but deeply proud of his remarks. Every man wants to be a hero in front of his son.

The boy then said, "You know I memorized Gene Autry's Code for Cowboys, it is on television all the time. Do you want to hear it?" And without any answer, he began to recite the ten principles of a good cowboy:

1. The cowboy must never shoot first, hit a smaller man, or take unfair advantage.
2. He must never go back on his word, or a trust confided in him.
3. He must always tell the truth.
4. He must be gentle with children, the elderly and animals.
5. He must not advocate or possess racially or religiously intolerant ideas.
6. He must help people in distress.
7. He must be a good worker.
8. He must keep himself clean in thought, speech, action and personal habits.
9. He must respect women, parents, and his nation's laws.
10. The cowboy must be a patriot.

Grandpa smiled as he went through them, and then finally said, "That code of life is good for more than just cowboys."

31. PARROTS IN PARADISE
(for Maria)

Grandpa was sitting at the head of the table, a nominal honor for the dinner the aunts put together for the weekend of Our Lady of Mount Carmel. That feast day was celebrated usually in July by Neapolitan families who emigrated to the United States. It was followed by a parade, a Mass, fireworks, and entertainment booths that occupied the church's parking lot. Our family, as long as any of us remembered, was in charge of the Mount Carmel banner, a blue satin image of the Virgin surrounded by gold fringe. As it began to get worn, the matrons of the family refused the very generous offer of the Madison Historical Society to place it under glass to preserve it.

Grandpa was rather quiet that day, thinking of better times with Mama, and when these adults were his young children. On the table was the usual: baked ziti, chicken parmesan, meatballs and sausage, salads, crispy bread, and assorted displays of desserts. It was a family of diabetics who loved starches and sweets. Luckily though, Grandpa had to say nothing, for his oldest child, whom he called Salvatore, and the others called "Sadie," was explaining his latest findings on the family genealogy. He had traced back the roots of the clan to the eighteenth century, and even found that one had married a Ben Franklin, whatever that meant. But today, he was explaining that the family just didn't end up on the east coast of the United States, but had gone to Australia, Canada, Argentina, and even nearby Cuba. He was proposing that the family send ambassadors to each family branch and then report back. For some reason, the idea caught on like wildfire, especially when he told the diners that Grandma's family, the Perones, was related to the Argentine dictator, Juan Peron, the husband of the elegant Evita.

He felt that Grandpa should go to Cuba to represent the family; Grandpa rarely went out of New Jersey or nearby New York City, so he was very hesitant, but when everybody seemed enthusiastic about the other areas, he consented. He was going to Cuba.

Cuba in those days was ruled by a corrupt dictatorship that invited in the Mafia to run its new casinos. It was a dirty marriage of convenience. But Grandpa did not know that, and instead concentrated on writing to the

Cuban branch inviting himself as coming on behalf of the family. His letter was immediately answered in Italian, so he knew they had more memories than his own children of the language and culture.

When he arrived, he was greeted at the Havana Airport by a huge crowd of people who hailed him as if he were a celebrity. They hugged and kissed him, took his decrepit luggage, and grabbed him by the arm to go to their cars. He was surprised that they spoke not only Spanish but also Italian and English, and he had no problem understanding his fellow countrymen.

At home, they took him to the best room in what was a hacienda, and then insisted on introducing him to every member of the household, and to the extended cousins who drove from Havana to pay their respects. It was a long, elegant house with a huge sunroom that had in the midst of it a caged parrot. Grandpa had only once before seen a parrot, and that was in Naples when the bird, perched on the shoulder of the great clown Punchinello, did a routine with the comic. This parrot was apparently the special pet of a little girl of six or so with big beautiful brown eyes and a quick smile. The parrot was less impressed, and kept on calling the old man, "Tonto" which meant idiot.

Night after night they would have splendid dinners, a mix of Cuban food and traditional Italian fare. During the days, the kids went to school, for their parents wanted them to make something of themselves, and the parents went to work. He was a doctor, and she was a manager of a nearby hotel, so Grandpa often ended up alone in the beautiful house. One day the doctor took him to see the town plaza with the stunning church dedicated to the patron saint of Cuba, St. Lazarus, the friend of Jesus who was raised from the dead and later became a bishop in the new faith. It was a magnificent structure built from hard rock and was imbedded with jewels inside the rocks. In the church was a statue of Lazarus, and on a side altar a statue of their other patron, Saint Barbara, who was wrapped in a red sheet, her color. Grandpa had never heard of either of them, but the Cubans effortlessly mixed the Yoruba customs with the traditional Roman Latin rite. So much seemed strange. There was though much more singing and even dancing at the Masses, very different from St. Vincent Martyr in New Jersey where most of the old people fingered their rosaries while the priest mumbled along.

One day, the old man went to church by himself and saw a fairly young American dressed only in cut off fatigues and Marine Corps boots. He was planting flowers around the whole church, an activity that Grandpa was no stranger to. He went up to him and praised his choice of plants, and then inquired where he was from. "Minnesota, but via the Marine Corps in Korea."

Apparently, this well-built man had finished his service in the war years ago but was still affected by its horrors. To remind him of the beauty of life, he planted flowers wherever he went. He was in Cuba with a buddy in the

Corps who invited him to join his rich family outside Havana. He came and began to plant flowers at the house, and then asked permission to begin a flower garden around the church. Grandpa also instinctively dropped down and helped him plant.

The veteran was reciting a well-known Cuban poem by Nicholas Guillen,

When I see and touch
Myself, Juan with Nothing more yesterday
And today Juan with Everything,
And yet today,
I turn my eyes, I look,
I see and touch
And wonder how it could be.

The young man told Grandpa the stories of his terrible times at Seoul, Inchon, and Pusan. He hated the war they drafted him for, and saw no glory in killing, or in the mud trenches where one rarely saw beauty of any type. He was kept on he said by the memories of flowers back home and of spring times when the sun kissed the land and implanted flowers and trees.

After a week, he vanished. Grandpa heard that he had just gone back to the States.

But Grandpa kept the gardens rich and visited the church to pray to saints he never heard of. Then one day he came back to the doctor's house, and he gave the parrot several seeds, nuts and pieces of fruit, which the parrot loved. He began calling grandpa "Tio" and was spouting about the need to find the "tesoro." Grandpa did not know what he was babbling about, until little Maria told him that he was constantly talking about a tesoro or treasure buried near the old cemetery. The next afternoon, Grandpa went into the sunroom, dropped more seeds and nuts, but held up the fruit chips. "Where, parrot, is the tesoro? Where near the cementerio?"

The nasty bird called him a "tonto," fool, again, and then said out of nowhere, "Tonto, under the biggest tree."

Grandpa dropped the fruit, ran for a shovel, and went to the cemetery, and there far away was a huge tree with a big hump at its base. He absentmindedly started shoveling and after a foot and a half of dirt he found a rusty box. Grandpa pulled the handle, and it was so old it just came off in his hand. He shoveled around the box and pulled the whole thing up. Inside were sacks of old Spanish gold pieces, worth a small fortune even back then.

Grandpa recovered the box and wondered what type of bags he needed to carry them. He had come all the way to Cuba to become rich! That night though some rebels burnt the church of Saint Lazarus and the whole steeple with the cross of dying Jesus was consumed. The community was devastated and the pastor, an old Capuchin, told the people that they did not have the money in the parish to fix it. It would be best to close their old church.

Grandpa heard the wailing and crying that day at Mass, and he felt guilty. God had not made him to be a rich man; he knew that in his heart. So he talked to the Capuchin and took him to the old tree and said that there was enough gold to fix the church and even build a school for the young where they could learn their letters and also their faith. The priest called it a good deed in a naughty world.

The next Sunday, the Capuchin informed the people that a prophet from a foreign land had given him the money to fix the church and to build a school as well. The faithful prayed before the statue of St. Barbara, and Grandpa just watched silently.

He had to get home after three weeks, and he was leaving the next day. As he said goodbye to his new family, he stopped by the parrot's cage, and said "Adios." The patriot looked at him cross eyed, and responded, "Tio Tonto," Uncle fool.

32. JOLTIN' JOE

One could not go too far for good humus, for rich, elegant soil was the basic ingredient of nature's bounty. Grandpa would roam over the barely paved byways of New Jersey, for though it was a heavily urban state it had vast areas of farms and fields. One lazy summer afternoon in the dog days of August, he was traveling in his decrepit Ford truck to pick up a full load. As he slowly moved on, he saw an isolated Dairy Queen ice cream stand in the middle of nowhere. There wasn't even a telephone line to connect it to the main telephone company in the region.

Grandpa loved ice cream of any type, and he decided to treat himself to a full-sized sundae with nuts and whipped cream, and sat down at the covered, but rusted, outside table. As he settled in, a large black Lincoln pulled up. Out stepped a tall, trim, graying man who looked like a United States senator. He went in to get some ice cream, and as he waited, five people ran up and timidly asked him for his autograph. The stranger was surprised at where they came from, but reticently signed their pieces of scrap paper.

Grandpa realized then that the attraction was the former baseball player for the New York Yankees, Joe DiMaggio, the hero of his children and even his older grandchildren. DiMaggio walked to Grandpa's table and politely asked if he could sit and enjoy the shade. "Sure, please do so. You bring quite a group with you!"

"They are everywhere. How the hell they came here is beyond me…Do you know who I am?"

"Yes, you are DiMaggio, the baseball player. My kids have followed you for years, especially after 1941."

"Yes, the year of the streak. Do you know why I sat here? You look exactly like my father, he was a fisherman, a great fisherman—are you from Sicily too?"

"No, I am from the Naples region, a gardener. See the lettering on my truck."

DiMaggio was a man of few words, but that day the old man seemed to bring out the conversation he rarely shared with anyone. It was infrequent for him to even say "hello" to strangers at autograph shows. But recently he had divorced his second wife and needed some human company that was not in his pay. "You know, my father had three sons, none of them enjoyed fishing. We all became baseball players, me, Dom, and Vince."

"I have three boys also, and they cannot tell the difference between a mushroom and a cherry tree."

DiMaggio, a man of little humor, started to laugh at the remark, and then quietly revealed in embarrassment, "I have one son, and he lives in a trailer near a garbage dump. I sent him to the finest schools, the most expensive ones, and he lives in a garbage dump, the son of the great DiMaggio."

"Boys go in different directions; girls are more likely to stay near home. I saw your wife in a movie I was taken to by one of my daughters. She is very beautiful."

"No, that is my second wife."

"You had two wives?"

"Yeah, the first one lasted four years. This second one with Marilyn lasted all of nine months. I just could not sit and watch other men look at her ass and boobs every night and twice on Sundays."

"She is very beautiful."

"Yes, she is but that is not enough. My other wife was also beautiful, and an actress too. My parents were married over forty years. How about you?"

"My wife died early, when she was sixty. We were married less than forty years. I miss her every day, especially at night."

DiMaggio had said more to the old man than he usually said in a month. "They had so little and yet so much. I have more money than God, three houses, men who never let me pick up a tab, and women who throw their hotel keys at me in casinos, and I have a publicist which I never had when I played, and a good shrewd accountant. I have to ask what they want from me: money, banquet appearances, autographs, and dinners with their divorced friends."

"Sounds like a good life."

"You think so…. I am still unhappy."

"Unhappy. You are a hero to boys. You know even heroes have heroes: Napoleon had Julius Caesar; Caesar had Alexander the Great; Alexander had Homer's Achilles. In the end, the heroes go back beyond records, back to myths. They say that you are the greatest baseball player of all time. Even greater than the Baby Ruth. Be happy."

"No, I am not greater than the Babe, but yes, I had a hero too, Lou Gehrig—he was quiet, serious, consistent, and above all excellent."

"I know little about baseball, In Italy we played what you call soccer on fields, on the sides of a hill, in the town squares. All the world plays soccer except here."

"It is a great game, someday the soccer world will have its own Babe. But the most important thing is to play it well, better than any other boys. Once at the end of my career, I was asked why I still tried so hard. I said honestly, 'Somewhere in the stands is a kid who has never seen DiMaggio play before.'"

The old man nodded, "Each man is the master of his own measurements." Then DiMaggio quieted down, and the old man stopped as well. Joe got up, took the left-over ice cream cups and napkins, and bussed them to the nearby barrel. He simply nodded at Grandpa and walked away. The old man ventured, "Hey Joe, want an old man's advice?"

"Yeah, go ahead, even Ty Cobb gives me advice."

"Go back to your wife, the second one. You had a life after baseball, and she will after the movies. And the two of you will have love and marriage in the quiet years."

"Pop… you want my autograph?"

"No, now I can tell people we met one afternoon in the sun under an umbrella, eating ice cream."

33. PADRE PIO

One sunny humid New Jersey afternoon, I decided to visit Grandpa and went instinctively to his backyard garden. There he sat quietly reading from the major Italian newspaper *Il Progresso*, the most popular Italian American newspaper available at the drug store. I entered, and remarked, "Hey, what are you reading?"

"Ah, just the paper, you never get the truth from these guys. Here, have a seat near me." And then in a rare expansive move, he began as if to tell a fascinating story:

"Do you know of Padre Pio? Of course, you do. You went to a Catholic school. Well, I bet you don't know, I was born at the same time and also in southern Italy. He ended up living in San Giovanni Rotondo, and I lived across the peninsula in Rotondi. Our friendship started out in the strangest beginning."

"Strange, in what way?" I inquired.

He knew he had my attention.

"Many years ago, my grandparents died almost together. Grandma was a kind, religious woman, who early one morning was crossing the new railroad tracks and was hit and killed by a speeding train. The train had just come though that area, and people were not used to its rush through the calm fields. And my grandpa was so affected by her sudden death, he cried and moaned for weeks, and a month later he too died. The local doctor said he was in good health but died of heartbreak. His heart just stopped beating, as one night he dreamt of his true love.

"So several times a year, the whole family would go to the great cathedral in Benevento, the regional capital city in the area. Once it had been a separate kingdom, a duchy it was called. It used to be called '*Malvento*,' the bad wind city. But then the Romans won a big battle off the coast, and renamed it '*Benevento*,' the good wind. Such is the power of conquerors. For hundreds of years it was allied with the popes, especially with the corrupt Alexander VI, the Borgia pope. A church was built into the wall guarding the inner city, and it was beautiful.

"So we would go there and pray for the souls of grandma and her beloved grandpa, a sad story of love. I would go with the adults, and one day I met a boy about my age. His name was Francisco Forgione. His parents could not read or write, and mainly farmed the land in Pietrelcina Campania. I came to know him well, and we frequently talked of growing up Italian. He was a slight, sickly boy with the most piercing eyes, deeply religious like his parents, but did not go much to school because he was sick. We had schools in those days that taught the letters, not much else, but they were better than no schools at all."

"What was he interested in, if he could not really read?"

"He loved to talk of the saints, and told me that he would see Jesus, the Virgin, and his guardian angel. Could I see them also? 'No.' He was sure that everybody saw them. He would ask if when I went to the great cathedral I could get him prayer cards for his wall, and I did so. I never told him I had to pay for them, since it made him so happy.

"As we grew older, we became closer, and he told me that he was going to become a Capuchin, you call them Franciscans. But when he applied, they rejected him, for he could not read well. His father shared his dream and went to America to make money quickly to afford a tutor for the boy. I never knew why the Franciscans rejected him, because the monks around St. Francis of Assisi were not intelligent either. But after 600 years, I guess they changed. Finally, the boy was enrolled as a Capuchin, and was given the name, 'Padre Pio'—in honor of one of the very early saintly popes.

"Meanwhile I had left for America, coming back finally to take a bride. We wrote each other frequently, and I told him of the New World that his father also knew, and he related to me his strange, new devout life. His health was poor as usual. He rarely slept or ate, and he often fainted saying Mass. When he prayed, he experienced a vision, and at times his fellow friars said he flew above the ground. Strange, isn't it, but so many people saw it.

"For a while as a priest, he said Mass at his home church and stayed with his parents. He was deemed unfit for military service during the terrible Great War. Then he wrote me, that one day at Mass he began to get the wounds of Christ."

"You mean the stigmata?"

"Yes, on his hands and feet and in the side, like Jesus. He even had marks on his brow. He wrote that he feared these things, wondering if they were the works of the devil. For the devil even tempted Jesus on the cliffs, did he not? Padre Pio feared these signs which so scared him, and he prayed they would pass away. He did not understand how he could be seen at two or three places far apart at the same time."

"Transverberation?"

"Whatever it is called, he was seen by good people in very different places. How could this be possible, he wrote me. Over the years the Holy See had officials who charged that he was involved with women on the side, and his life was totally restricted in the beginning of his time in the monastery. The poor fellow never knew a woman in his whole life, but his mother.

"In confession, he could read immediately the hearts of people. Once he told me of a man who just walked in, knelt down, and the padre said, 'Give up your whore and go back to your wife before you come back to seek forgiveness.' Another rich man came to visit in confession, and the padre said, 'Stop cheating the peasants on your land, give them back 25% of the produce you enjoy. It is easier for a camel to go through a needle's eye than for a wealthy man to go to heaven.'

"One day my family in Italy wrote me a letter, asking if I could help a lady get an appointment to visit my old friend, Padre Pio, and help her young granddaughter from Sicily who was blind from birth. She had no eyeballs at all. My family knew this grandmother well. I never wrote him asking for favors, but I did this time. He took the poor girl into his cell, and after his prayers were over, the grandmother impatiently sneered at him, 'She still cannot see.' And Padre Pio said to her deliberately, 'She now sees, and if you open up your heart to God you too will see another way.' And so it happened.

"I wrote him once and asked what advice he could give to the world, what words to live by. He wrote me back simply, 'Pray, Hope, and Don't Worry.' Good advice from a good friend. For years, I sent him prayer cards from America, so he could build up his collection. Once I wrote to him, 'Someday boys will be collecting Mass cards with you on them.' But he never answered my last letter, he was too sick at the time, and even the Holy See changed its view of Padre Pio of Pietrelcina, as thousands came to visit my friend, every day."

34. A JAPANESE GARDEN

Outside the boundaries of Madison, N.J., there was an expansive lumber yard and hardware store which had taken up that spot for some thirty years. Grandpa frequented the lumber yard and knew the proprietor, Carl Jamieson, fairly well. Jamieson was a quiet, and at times morose, person whose wife had died in childbirth and left him a daughter, Maria, to raise as best he could. He sent her to St. Vincent Martyr School, Bayley-Ellard Catholic High School, and Drew University in town.

While an undergraduate she met a boy she fell in love with and was going to marry him within the year. The boy was from Hiroshima, Japan, and had been brought over to the United States with his grandfather, Akita Kawabata—brother of the greatest novelist in Japan who later won the Nobel Prize for Literature in 1968. Carl had no real family in the United States, and plaintively asked Grandpa if he would come to the ceremony and then to the reception at the Bottle Hill Tavern where the Marquis de Lafayette once stayed in 1824. Carl told Grandpa that he would be greatly honored if he came, but candidly remarked that the groom had been sponsored by the United Methodist Church on Madison Avenue to come to Drew and adopted its version of weary Protestantism. The couple would be married not at St. Vincent's, but at the Methodist church in town.

Grandpa just shrugged and insisted that the couple had a right to choose their own ceremony. Then Carl added in passing, "Raffaele, this boy is a Jap."

"A what?"

"A Jap, Japanese. I know your family lost a nephew on Iwo Jima in 1945."

"Yes, but that was ten years ago. The war is over, Carl."

And so on the wedding day, Grandpa wore his good suit and paisley tie to the United Methodist Church on Madison Avenue with its yellow and gold paned glass windows and maple wood front altar. The ceremony was different from the Catholic Mass and vows, but still the couple seemed so in love that it was infectious. The old man thought back to his marriage in Italy, and then to this honeymoon on the Isle of Capri.

At the reception, Carl went out of his way to introduce Akita Kawabata to Grandpa, and in broken English the two older gentlemen got to know each other. Grandpa learned that the boy, David, was Akita's favorite grandchild, and on August 5, 1945, David and Akita traveled in the morning to meet his brother and introduce his grandson at the place the author lived and worked in Osaka. On August 6, the United States dropped the first atomic bomb, and then dropped a second one on Nagasaki. Over 140,000 people were killed—mostly civilians. Six days later, the emperor announced the unconditional surrender of the Japanese empire to the Allies.

Only luck and fate had saved the grandfather from the horrors of Hiroshima. The Jesuit residence and the Methodist retreat house were spared for some reason. The Methodists tried to send some young survivors over to the United States, and David Kawabata became a student at Drew University where he entered into the mathematics department. He lived at home with his grandfather who read Japanese novels all day and waited anxiously for his grandson to come home. He had been pleased when he fell in love with a pleasant American girl, and together they visited Carl for his permission to marry. The Kawabatas were embarrassed for they were poor and had no dowry, just love, to give the bride's family.

Carl had in his mind a picture of crazed Japanese fighters in John Wayne movies, especially those who in a "day of infamy" bombed Pearl Harbor. But he came to accept David and his grandfather in part since Maria loved David so much, and he did not wish to alienate her.

Grandpa watched with some hesitation the whole strange new family, for he too had residual feelings about the Japanese. The Bottle Hill Tavern saved the side porch for the wedding and had a rock band for the entertainment. Their selections were not Grandpa's choices, but the next generation surely loved the early fathers of rock and roll. Maria waited though for a slow waltz and, since it was ladies' choice, she held out her hand for Grandpa to come and dance.

As they moved slowly, she thank him so much for coming. Apparently, some old family friends had refused to go to a wedding of a "Jap," and she regarded Grandpa as even more of an old world gentleman. Then she asked if he would like to know Mr. Kawabata better, for he had been a gardener for the new Buddhist shrine in Hiroshima. After the bombing, the city was a huge collection of cursed ashes, and the Buddha in the center of the blast, made of bronze, simply melted down there, like butter under the hot sun.

Grandpa rarely said no to anyone and promised her he would go over during the reception to strike up a conversation with the elderly Kawabata. Maria sat at first between them and got the dialogue going. Finally Grandpa graciously remarked, "I understand that you are a gardener in your homeland."

The Japanese gentleman nodded slowly and then said, "If you ever see the remains of Hiroshima, there is a domed structure left standing. It is called Genbaku Dome. I was the master gardener at the Shukkei-en Gardens."

Grandpa just listened, and then remarked, "You know I have been asked to create a garden at Drew University outside the main library. How would you like to work with me? We can split the fee."

"Oh no, not necessary, but I would love to work with you. When, sir, do we start?"

"We will start the next week when the university is on vacation." Then Grandpa went on, "I am planting boxwoods at the walkways of the library, and then three layers of flowers. Each will bloom at different parts of the spring and summer seasons."

Mr. Kawabata nodded and smiled, "I like that, constant life, that is why I became a gardener."

"So you will join me?"

"I will have it all worked out!"

Grandpa realized that he had presented him with a finished plan. "How about you designing a Japanese garden on the long side of the library? That area is totally bare."

"Yes, I could plan, if you wish, a true Japanese garden."

Grandpa liked the idea, and so in one week they met at the university and began their labors. First, Mr. Kawabata helped Grandpa lay out the boxwoods which seemed so English to the Japanese man. But then Grandpa added his favorite flowers—pansies. And he added perennials then for the future from seed packets. He was planting for the generations beyond his own.

At lunch they sat down on a bench. Grandpa opened his sausage and pepper sandwich which had been bought from the Madison Deli, and Mr. Kawabata opened his plastic box of vegetables and rice, and started eating with chopsticks, skillfully wielding them as he had since he was a young boy.

He then said, "I understand you lost a boy at Iwo Jima. I am sorry. It was a most terrible battle."

Grandpa thought for a while and matter-of-factly responded, "Yes, he was my nephew, only 19, never knew a woman's love, and chose the Marines. You know, it is said that the Marines are proud that they never leave any soldier behind, but their officers just threw young men into their meat grinder battles in the Pacific. Five men at Iwo Jima held up the flag, and it made all the newspapers. The corps did not mention how many ever came home. Only later did they even admit that the second picture was posed... Sorry to bring all this up."

Mr. Kawabata nodded, "I wish to express regrets for all of this to you and your honorable family. After Hiroshima and Nagasaki, the emperor admitted to us that he was not divine at all, not so good, after he led us into this war."

"You were from Hiroshima. May I ask why you were not at home on August 6th?"

"I had taken my grandson, David, to the sacred golden temple in Kyoto that day and was to join my brother in Osaka later. The temple is so beautiful there, the haze welcomed us to the golden structure. Because of that I missed the bombing, and when we came home nothing was left standing. People were scarred and were vomiting until they died. The Methodists funded David to go to college, one of their own. Our neighbors were all dead, and people even had their buttons imprinted on their skin and the skin peeled off. 140,000 people died. The Methodist and Jesuit rectories were not touched. In agony, they sent my grandson here and asked that I go with him since I no longer had anyone. Do you know, Raffaele, what flowers came back first at the dome site? Oleanders, I wonder why."

Grandpa responded, "Oleanders are the most poisonous of houseplants. Perhaps only poison can emerge from poison. You and I are gardeners. We live not to deal with the terrible facts of war, but to plant and respect life. I am glad you are here."

"Thank you."

Grandpa then remarked, "I like the plans for *our* Japanese garden."

"Ah so, it looks like this. First we must find flat rocks for the floor and a pipe with running water will cover the floor over here. The flowing water will go back into the bowl, and it will return in a circular way. There will be a high rock by the wall, and Japanese maples in each corner. A bench will sit in the middle of it, yes? Then I would like to place a Buddha statue—even though they are Methodist. I am not getting the tailored look as you do. This nature is providing a place of contemplation."

"It will be perfect, let us begin."

And so in a long weeks' time, they worked together on this strange garden that seemed so out of place on an American campus, and yet gave the students a sense of peace and tranquility. When the men finished, they sat on the bench together, admiring the waterfalls they had connected, and looked with different feelings at Buddha. Grandpa wondered if he was in heaven with Jesus.

Later in the early fall, Mr. Kawabata was invited by his grandson's wife to address an assembly in the auditorium of Madison High School. All the students were reading John Hersey's *Hiroshima* which detailed the experiences of six people who survived the awful blast. He was so proud to speak at an American school and invited his only friend, Grandpa. His grandson's wife introduced him to the restless students, and he quietly began, "Thank you. I am from Hiroshima, and on August 6, my grandson and I were away. When we came back there was only destruction and chaos. People were walking numb, and the armed forces did not know what to do. We have never experienced an atomic bomb before."

But as he went on, there was a stirring and one of the boys with a DA haircut got up and said, "Tell them about the Bataan Death March." And then a second insisted he tell them about the attack on Pearl Harbor.

Mr. Kawabata froze, and suddenly Grandpa jumped up, "Bataan, Pearl Harbor. Boy, I know your name and because you play football, you are not excused from good manners."

The student, Tommy Gero, responded, "You should be quiet at our school assembly, old man."

Then Grandpa became coldly angry. "You listen to me, Mr. Gero. I have known Coach Monica for many years, and he is not going to take well to one of his players insulting people. You will never play in the Suburban Conference again." And suddenly Gero plopped back into his seat.

Maria had Mr. Kawabata rushed off the stage and outside the auditorium. Grandpa came up and said, "Come, let us go. I want to sit in our gardens alone." He drove his pickup to Drew, and they enjoyed their gardens.

Finally an embarrassed Mr. Kawabata insisted, "It is too soon to talk of the war, too early. Too much hurt for all of us. I just thought I could be a link between foreigners and hope." Then he pulled out a paper with the Hiroshima prayer on it.

God our Father, we acknowledge the terrible responsibility of the knowledge of good and evil. We have not always chosen well. We acknowledge that the hearts of human beings are tainted by sin, that we do not see clearly or love purely, and that we are sometimes misled by fear, hatred and despair.

Grandpa nodded, and said, "We must get that on a bronze plaque and place it on the stone wall for the next generation."

Mr. Kawabata was proud of the idea, but then he observed, "Where can we find a person to make such a plaque?"

Grandpa soothingly observed, "My friend, I am Italian. We all know a person who knows a person.

35. THE BOARDWALK

Grandpa was not an enthusiastic beach goer, and rarely did he visit the decadent, dirty Jersey shore, especially as he got older. He once said it was a neon imitation of the Bay of Naples. But one day, some of his grandchildren came and begged him to go with them to Asbury Park. He had a tough time saying no, and so he went with them in two cars packed full of the next generation. They did not want to pay the tolls, so they had to go through a hodgepodge of old roads to the Mecca of the working class, Asbury Park by the sea.

When they arrived, all clamored in delight and said that they would meet at the strong glass dome in the middle of the boardwalk, and each asked Grandpa to come with them, but he said that he would rather walk the full boardwalk, and he had not brought a bathing suit anyhow. He did not even own one. He sat on one of those benches that moves both ways, and watched the people go by, young girls wearing little to cover their private parts, and boys who spent all winter lifting weights to look like Charles Atlas. *They haven't changed much,* he thought.

As he watched the sea waves gracefully break in, he began to become mesmerized by the movement; they seemed to cover him over even though he was so far away. His mind drifted to melancholy memories, for the sea reminded him of the Isle of Capri where he had honeymooned with Grandma.

It was in winter, she was dressed in a white woolen bridal gown with a long train, and the women in the families had expertly made the garment for her. They went to Capri…and then his mind rebelled. *Basta. Enough.*

He watched in front of him a group of fundamentalist Christians, placing a large plastic mold in the sand. When they took it off, it was a sad portrait of the crucifixion of Christ. Grandpa was a bit taken back. It was so out of place, but Asbury Park did seem at times like Golgotha.

He became hazy, and walked to a sausage and pepper stand, but the sandwich was stale and the meat greasy. *You have to prick through the skins before you cook it, what is the matter with these guys?* He moved down to get a piece of pizza, but it was mushy and had little mozzarella on the ends. *Not a good feast,* he thought.

As he walked the boardwalk, he saw an old time gypsy who read fortunes, like the one he had met in Naples. He had a strange fascination for them, wondered how long they could go on and on. He walked into the dirty tent and paid $5.00 to a woman with long blue nails and piecing black eyes, dressed in plastic beads and scarfs. She smiled knowingly and asked him some preliminary questions to get the lay of the land. He had done this before and was deliberately noncommittal. She grabbed the palm of his right hand and began. "You are a real man, who works for a living. Your line here shows you will have a long life, until your 80s. You are a happy man, but there are lines of unhappiness here. You lost your wife young, and some children—a young daughter in her 20s, I see."

"It is true, yes," Grandpa remarked.

"You are a good man, but you are surrounded by devils. They haunt you; you must make peace with the devils. Do not worry about God. Here for another $10, I can give you spiritual energy to put your body in shape to pacify the devils. It is worth it. They are strong, stronger than God Himself. You look here, you see the devil's work. The whole beach is full of devils. Give me $10 now!"

The old man was upset at the whole sour tenor of the reading, and he quickly got up and began to run out of the tent. She screamed after him, "I curse you. I curse you in the name of Satan, the prince of devils." Later he realized that she had stolen his Timex watch off his wrist.

That night he went home quietly, thanked his grandchildren for the fine day and locked the doors behind him. The sun, the rhythms of the water, and the glaring heat made him tired, and so he dozed off in his old clothes.

In the middle of the night, he engaged in the dreams of the troubled. He was visited by a sharp looking *medigan* who approached him as if he knew him over the years. "My friend, how are you? We have not talked much, and you are getting old. I know that in your deepest heart you are saddened, and I am here to take all that feeling away. I will take the sorrows away, for sorrows are unfulfilled desires. If you shake my hand and pledge your loyalty, I will stay with you forever. I will bring you beautiful women. It has been a long time since you felt that flesh. I will give you more money than you can spend in two lifetimes. I will make you a major power. You Italians call it 'respect'. You will be everyman's master, and they will love it. All the delights of the world will be yours. First, we will get rid of that truck of yours and get you a new Oldsmobile 98. Come here and shake my hand, we have a deal?"

Grandpa woke up in a sweat, and then turned cold, and jumped up. He could not understand what had happened. He went to his *Book of Solomon* and looked under "Dreams." His dream was called a "vision," and it said that such visions were a man's true wishes.

No, that can't be so. He showered to take the sweat off him, but the dream stayed in his mind. For two more nights, he saw the *medigan* and each time he upped the ante, finally promising him immortality.

Uncertain what to do, the old man tried to work harder and harder, but the work was not enjoyable, it was a curse laid on Adam. Finally out of despair, he could think of nothing to counter it. One night at cards, his friends laughed at his story, and one said he deserved much good fortune. Another insisted God had struck him down so often because of his pride, the devil was now taking God's place. Still a third said the dream wishes went back to his boyhood.

Finally on a Sunday afternoon, he went up to the monsignor who was delighted to talk to a person in Italian. Grandpa told the full story to an increasingly somber priest. "You see why the Church tells you to avoid fortunetellers, they're pathways to Satan and hell."

"What do I do?"

The monsignor gave him a vial of holy water from the shrine of Our Lady of Fatima, the Virgin who before had appeared to the three shepherd children in Portugal. "Take this water, and sprinkle it all over your apartment, especially the bedroom. The devils will stay at bay."

"That is good for my rooms, but what of me? It is me they want, every night"

"Yes, it is, yes."

The monsignor reached to his neck and took off a gold chain with a tiny medal on it. "This it is the Miraculous Medal of Mary. In 1954 Pope Pius XII gave me this in an audience, the medal marks the feast of the glorious Assumption of Mary into heaven, body and soul. He who wears this medal will go immediately to heaven on his death. Here, I give it you."

"No, no I can't take it. It is from the pope and it is for you alone."

"I can get another one whenever I want, I know Pius well; he made me a monsignor of the highest rank, a protonotary apostolic, and he will send me another."

So Grandpa walked out with a Miraculous Medal. At home he sprinkled the holy water, and that night he slept like the proverbial innocent baby. He wore the Medal at once, at work, at night, in the shower, and when he was buried, they left the Medal on him as if it were a part of him. Meanwhile the gypsy, who had so tormented him, had her tent burn down on the boardwalk, and the city health authority put in its place a pay toilet.

36. AN UNLIKELY HERO

In the early summer evenings, Grandpa, who had no air conditioners and only one small kitchen fan, would go for a walk. Frequently he followed the streets up to the sounds of kids playing baseball in the rundown park on King's Road near the center of town. He did not understand the game, but he loved to see the active, energetic boys wearing specialized T-shirts playing for the regulation seven innings. He thought it was a peculiar game, sometimes only two or three people played consistently, whereas in soccer everybody seemed to be engaged. But baseball was the American pastime, and he was now an American.

On several days he saw one team wearing shirts advertising Mantone's Garage, and another the Pearson's Moving Company. Frequently sitting in the front row of the splintery stands was a boy with thick glasses and a slight limp who would ride his big, bulky Schwinn bike, while everyone else had theirs with gears and brakes on the handlebars. Finally one night he casually asked the boy, Joey Gallo, if he wanted to play too. He said yes, but the coach said he wasn't able to make the team, so he would just watch and cheer for both sides. "You see, I am what the other kids call me, behind my back, a retard."

"What is that?" Grandpa responded, although he knew, and just did not want the kid to think that all people used that nasty expression.

"I am a slow learner and don't remember the signs well. My mom says I am not slow but just careful."

"Oh well, you should play anyhow." Night after night he was there, enthusiastic, but not playing. Finally, Grandpa decided to see if he could help. His daughters complained he did not know when to mind his own business. He talked to his old friend Jumping Danny Wilson and asked if he could teach the boy some principles. Danny politely answered that basketball was his game and some boxing. But Grandpa flattered him, "You are a great athlete, and you can do easily what you learned in all sports. Give him a try?"

Jumping Danny promised to do so, and he worked with Gallo in the afternoon and on the weekends, teaching him the fundamentals: hitting, running, and catching, He would throw the ball to him at varying speeds, get him to square off and bunt, and block a hot ball. Then he told Gallo to go to the public library and get the famed textbook on hitting by the immortal Ted Williams. The boy could not read the language too well, but he looked intently at the pictures of the great slugger swinging. Then he approached the coach, who sort of brushed him off again.

Grandpa watched the conversation that night, and decided that Drew Cleary needed a little push, and he went to see Sam Mantone at the garage just across the street from him. Mantone had known Grandpa for years, and he was friendly with his youngest son who once worked for him. Grandpa told him the story and noted the last game of the season was coming up. Could he, as a major sponsor for years, talk to the coach and get him to play Gallo in at least the very last game? Mantone simply said he would, and he picked up the phone immediately and called in a favor,

Grandpa then went to see Joe Pearson in his office which as usual had no secretary and only the boss sitting behind a pile of papers. "Oh, Jesus H. Christ, Ralph, What do you want? I have had a bad winter quarter, so forget about getting money from me. What is it now? Another illegal to hire?"

"No, no, I just want you to do a good deed which the whole town will know about."

"How much, Ralph?"

"Not a penny. There is a boy who is slow but who wants desperately to play Little League. Can you call Drew Cleary and get him on the team at the last game? All the town is talking about the kid,"

"Who is talking?"

"Well Sam Mantone who also gives money to the League is talking it up."

"I hate that bastard. All I have to do is call Cleary and put the arm on him?"

"That is all and the whole town will know!"

"Look, I only give money to the League because I don't have to give then to the United Way. I can't stand those old biddies who want me to give my money to town lowlifes."

"Did you see the beautiful playground we built in your honor for the Pearson Lane children?"

"Yes, you did a great job—at least it didn't say Pearson Memorial Park. Those little darkie kids look so cute running around; it's when they get old that they are a pain in my ass."

"Ok, thanks, please call Drew, Joe."

The last game of the season came, and Joey Gallo got a Pearson Movers T-shirt and a Mantone cap and ended up playing right field, the elephant burial ground for lousy players. He was so excited and luckily no balls were hit to right, so he just punched continuously his newly oiled glove. It had Jimmy Pearsall's name on it, the Red Sox who ended up in a mental hospital and was the subject of a movie, *Fear Strikes Out.*

But at bat, Joey was still weak even though he was last in the lineup. The first time he popped up to the catcher—foul out. The second time he struck out on three pitches. Finally at the end of the game, the bottom of the seventh to the coach's chagrin, Joey was up with three men on base, and the team was behind by two runs. The first pitch was a strike on the corner, the second pitch was a low ball in the dirt which he struck at. And then for the third pitch, the cocky pitcher threw a fast ball down the middle of the plate. Joey Gallo swung with all his might from his heels and closed his eyes. He hit the ball on the sweet spot, above the trademark, and the ball traveled over the heads of the third baseman and the left fielder who was playing too close.

The Pearson team screamed, "Go, go, Gallo, go."

All three runners scored, and Joey took off his glasses and rounded second, ready to slide—yes slide—into third. But he didn't have to, for it was a standup triple, and his team won the game 5-3. Some purists said the score was really 4–3, but in any case, Joe's team won. The kids gathered around him and pounded Joey on the back, proclaiming that he was the MVP in the championship. Jimmy had his glasses in his left hand and stood tall and erect on the bag as he watched his parents wildly cheering and that old Italian guy applauding. The coach, Drew Cleary, gave him the ball as a souvenir, and he held it close in his pocket on the way home. That year the Little League had a banquet and invited Phil Rizzuto of the New York Yankees. As he went to sign the ball from the game, Gallo asked, "Mr. Rizzuto who is the greatest player you have ever seen?"

"Joe D, of course," he answered.

The next fall, Joey tried to be an altar boy, but he could not master the Latin. The monsignor though gave him the altar boy prayer book, from the St. John Berchmans Sanctuary Society, and told him to recite the responses every day.

At 14, he contracted tracheal bronchitis and quickly died. Under his pillow, the family found the St John's prayer book and an autographed baseball wrapped in Saran Wrap. At the wake, the whole team showed up, and so did Joe Pearson. Grandpa looked at the boy and thought, *This is a great life if you don't weaken.* So at dusk in the summer, a boy had stood up strong and tall on third base and played like the hero he was deep inside.

37. HARASSMENT

Of all the young women in Grandpa's extended family the most beautiful was Sophia. She was elegant, pleasant with a full figure and a quick smile. After graduating from St. Elizabeth College, she got an internship and then a permanent job as a co-producer for Stanley Goldstein's television show on the RKO Network. She was truly blessed and proud to be working for a real television personality who also spun off his own personal industry that sold tee shirts, mugs, and popular history books which often ended up on the *New York Times Book Review* list. On television he was a Republican pundit who knew everything about insider politics; he was a consultant for the RKO network on planning strategies to get Emmy and Academy Awards for its movies and shows. He was also an inveterate womanizer.

One day, Sophia came in his office with the producer's schedule, and he moved over to the door and locked it; he grabbed her breast and slipped his hand under her shirt to teach the girl the extent of his desires. She was startled, scared, and pulled away. As she left, he warned that she was "ruining a great career."

The next day, she was so afraid that she took several sick days and avoided telling her conservative parents what had happened. Instead she went to her Grandpa and laid out the full story. He was nearly speechless. He tried to explore her options. He told her to go to the police, and to the Manhattan District Attorney, but women had done that before and received short shrift.

Her boss was a heavy contributor to Republican candidates and the national party, and his boss was a total tool of the Democratic party. Charges never seemed to make their way up the legal chain of command. Grandpa consoled her, but he did not know what to do with the whole episode. Sophia told him how RKO had settled with abused women for millions of dollars, the last one for $5 million dollars. That was more money than Grandpa knew even existed. Still as they explored this option, she repeated the choice, and told him it seemed in vain, and she left with a sense of gratitude for his time and a powerful let down.

As she left his apartment on 81 Main Street, she turned not right to New

York City, but left up Main Street to North Street. Then she went down the road to visit Don Archibald Gallo, the retired mob boss and a former associate of his goombahs, the Gallo brothers. As she arrived at his modest Cape Cod house, he was sitting as usual in his aluminum chair reading Dante's *Inferno*. She pulled up and called out, "Don Gallo, may I have some of your time?"

He laughed at the lovely girl and responded, "Of course, I am surprised that your self-righteous grandfather would let you come and visit me."

"He doesn't know; I come on my own on a very personal matter."

And then she told him the whole sordid story; when she came to the amount of the settlement, he was flabbergasted—that was more money than the mob made in a month of Sundays. She was so sweet and innocent; he could not see her defiled by a Hollywood-type pig. "Yes, I see him on television at night. You can see he is a sneak and a hypocrite. He calls it 'truth,' but it is all spin."

"I don't know what to do. The last woman to complain was paid off and hasn't been able to find a job since, Don Gallo."

"Yes, he has that power, you cannot do that." Then he sat for a long moment, and fingered through his Dante, and finally asked, "What are you going to do for the foreseeable future?"

"I have taken a week's sick days,"

"Smart girl, but you must come back. What is your boss doing?"

"Well, he is going to a Broadway musical opening and is taking his date, the star of the show, to the Waldorf Astoria, probably for the evening and beyond.

"Of course, where is the show opening?"

"At the St. James Theater on 44th Street."

"Yes, I know it I well, it has very narrow streets. Take a few more days off, and let me ponder the matter, my dear."

And then on Saturday night after the show, a long stretch limousine arrived at the St. James on 44th Street. Two bulky men with black gloves jumped out and roughly grabbed Goldstein. He at first thought it was his limo. But they pushed him into the back and left the startled starlet by the sidewalk. One of the men looked at her and said, "Tonight you are lucky."

Stanley vanished for over a long week and was found disoriented in Staten Island in a doggy park near the waterfront. His jaw had been broken three times, and the doctors could barely put it together. He could only talk in muffled sounds. His television show was cancelled, and his associates were no longer impressed with his sage advice on the Emmy and Academy awards.

A year later, Don Gallo was sitting on the lawn chair and got a perfumed envelope, not exactly his fare. It was an invitation to Sophia's marriage to a *medigan* lawyer from New York City. She wanted to be married in her home church, St. Vincent Martyr in Madison, N.J., and her husband could not care less. Don Gallo had not gone to church since his wife died and had not been invited to a wedding for as long as he could remember.

He proudly bought a new suit and arrived at the church, quietly sitting in the back on the bride's side. But suddenly her brother grabbed him by the elbow. *What have I done to be insulted,* he thought. No, he was in fact being taken up to the first row and sat next to a startled Grandpa. The old man said little, but just nodded, *How did I get put here, next to a Mafioso?*

She came down the aisle in virgin pure white and was given away to her proud fiancé. After the marriage, to everyone's surprise Don Gallo was invited to the reception. He said little and when the bride came around, he dropped a substantial check in the jeweled purse. And then as the dancing began again, she came over and asked him to engage with her in the tarantella. He had not danced since Maria had died, and he was delighted to move with her across the polished floor. He had a night that lasted forever.

Then thirteen months later, he received another invitation, this time to the baptism of Sophia's new son, also to be held at St. Vincent's. He was to be called Philip after his father, and Archibald after only Sophia knew.

In the old church with its Norman architecture in the Christ Church style at Oxford, he sat down and watched the entrance of the participants into the church. The baby was quiet as the monsignor touched him with salt and with oil. As he poured the holy water of the first sacrament, he and the godparents were asked if in his name they rejected, "Satan and all his wiles," and they did so.

Don Gallo watched carefully and thought, *It is good that the Church will have the baby avoid Satan and all his sins, but in this world, it is necessary sometimes to traffic with evil so innocence can prevail.*

38. THE LAST CURSE

Of all the many men Grandpa worked with in his long years as a chauffeur and then a gardener, none had won his heart more than Giuseppe Caruso. He was startlingly handsome and built like Michelangelo's David. He was witty, talkative, and exuded a sense of quiet charm.

When it was July in Jersey, he would take off his guinea t-shirt, and work even harder semi-naked. In the Madison apartment complex on Main Street, women of all ages would come to the windows to look at his elegant physique. But he had a habit of swearing profusely in both languages, and that continuous stream of obscenities was offensive to adults, especially older women.

His parents had died in a terrible head-on collision late one night on Route 22. He was an orphan who came to regard Grandpa almost as a father. Over the years Giuseppe fell in love with a beautiful girl he met at Madison High School, and she fell under his spell. Her parents owned the historic Bottle Hill Tavern, and several times Giuseppe had dinner there with Carlotta. Her father's response was always the same, "Sweetheart, you can do better, "*Tu puoi fare di meglio.*"

The affair went nowhere.

One noon day, Grandpa and Giuseppe sat under a huge maple tree, for the elms had all been destroyed in New Jersey. The boy suddenly got serious. He told Grandpa his whole sad tale of woe, and the old man knew the problem, but at first said nothing, for it was not his place to give advice. Giuseppe pleaded, "When I go over to see her, I dress impeccably, clean shaven, and freshly showered. She gets excited, but her father is cold as ice."

Grandpa tried to show some consolation, "I know Mario, her father. He is a good man, even though he is from Rome, but like all of us fathers we worry about our daughters. If I had my way, none of their husbands are worthy of my girls."

But Giuseppe continued, "I love her, what can I do? You surely know that feeling."

The old man hesitated and finally said, "Let me tell you an old Neapolitan folk story. For it is from such tales, that we draw wisdom."

"Once upon a time, there was a poor farmer outside of Benevento who died and left his legacy divided in three—an equal portion for each son. After a decent period of mourning, the sons realized that the sums were too small to do much with. The oldest son, Pieto, finally said, 'I will go to town and take my share and increase it so that I come back a rich man.' They bid him farewell and off he went, finally finding a good job at the rectory of a visiting priest. The condition for his employment was that if he would avoid cursing or taking the Lord's name in vain, then at the end of the he would win week double his wages. Pieto agreed and went to lay down a long road of crushed rock leading to the church. At noon he would get lunch, and at night he would also get dinner from the two attractive housekeepers who serviced the rectory. By midday he waited for the lunch he was promised, but the food never came. He returned to the house that night in a huff and swore at the girls. The priest confiscated his money, and Giovanni left a failure.

"He told his brothers that his cursing had cost him his future, but his brother Fiore decided to return to the rectory, using a different last name, and seeking out the same job. So off he went, and the priest would pay him double his wages if he could work all day and avoid using the Lord's name in vain. He did that until he realized that he too was not getting any food or drink at noon. He returned to the rectory and was furious, cursing the priest for his faithlessness. He used a long string of profanities that only Neapolitans know. And so he also lost his money.

"Then at home he told his brothers that he too had been duped, but the youngest son, Piolo, a lightweight fellow, but a very intelligent boy decided to try for himself. He waited several days, and then went to see the priest. The clergyman thought, *There must be a bumper crop of cafones this summer in Benevento.*

"And Piolo went to work, planting trees between the rectory and the landowner in the next field. He left the rectory though, quietly filling up his pockets with cheese, bread and sausages. He worked through the noon hour, but soon he was thirsty, and saw on the horizon a small peasant's hut. He walked over, and said he brought good wishes from the priest, and the peasants were so delighted they shared a bottle of fine wine that they had just made.

"At night he went to the rectory and cast a cold eye at the priest's comely housekeepers. He controlled his tongue and asked the priest what he had to do the next day. But the priest told him that he had to visit the cathedral at Benevento, the one cut into the side of a mountain, and visit the bishop. If Piolo joined him and avoided any profanities, that bet would be tripled. Would he agree?

"Piolo did indeed, and the next morning off they went up the road. But the road was a muddy pit, and the priest feared that his shoes would be ruined. 'Go back to the rectory and get my overshoes.'

"Piolo ran off and told the ladies that the priest commanded him to squeeze their ample breasts for good luck. They looked at him incredulously, and then he screamed out the window, 'Do both, your reverend?'

"'Yes, yes, let's go.' And Piolo squeezed most artfully, and then grabbed the overshoes. When they came back to the household that night, the young women felt humiliated, and swore at the priest in the most profane way. The priest responded in kind for he had grown up in the neighborhood. Piolo stayed in the background, and then stepped forward to take all the money due him. A year later, he got married, and made a small fortune when he opened a used clothing store in Benevento."

Grandpa stopped talking, and Giuseppe understood all too clearly his patron's disguised advice. Two weeks later, he left Grandpa's employ, ran away with Carlotta to Las Vegas and found the only priest who would marry them without all the banns of matrimony. His name was Reverend Max Oliva, and of course he was a Jesuit.

When the couple came home, they told her parents of their good fortune. Mario was quietly furious, but he realized that it was better to bend than break, and besides it was a Catholic ceremony. Nowadays one is lucky if one's child even gets married formally. Mario only insisted that he be allowed to give a giant reception at the Bottle Hill, and they of course agreed. The next morning he took Carlotta to the finest gown maker in town and insisted that she have a white wedding dress and that the part over her stomach be skintight. He had lived in that town long enough to know that busy bodies at St. Vincent's parish would draw all sorts of conclusions from the swift nuptial.

At his reception, alcohol flowed like the waters of the great Passaic River in Paterson, and he spared no cost in shipping from Italy the most beloved delicacies he could find. At the reception, Giuseppe had no family, so he put Grandpa at the head table. The bride asked the old man to dance with her right after the first song, and he loved watching her lithe moments, for he was old but not dead.

Thirteen months later, the couple had a baby boy, whom they named Mario, as is the tradition in Italian families. Meanwhile Giuseppe had gone off to study to be a medical assistant at Morristown Memorial Hospital. There he was known for his gentlemanly ways, and easy manners in dealing with even the most difficult sick person. To Father O'Hara, Mario called him a *perfetto gentiluomo*.

39. THE RAKE

Every Friday night, Grandpa and three of his oldest friends, Delgado, Pasquale, and the Nuzo man, as we called him, met to drink and play cards. It was a game with a lot of noise, the endless slapping down of cards, and the slow raising of interminable betting of small sums which lasted until one or two in the morning. They took the freshly pressed wine—often little more than sweetened grapefruit juice—and mixed it with cream soda.

Grandpa disliked drunks, which probably explained why he was a bit aloof from Delgado, and he did not understand how the Europeans (by which he meant the Irish and English) could drink whiskey and rye straight day after day. He reminded whoever would listen that Alexander the Great would also cut his wine, and that he went on to conquer the world at the age of 32.

His favorite though was the Nuzo man, a tall, neatly dressed individual who was born to wear suspenders and always possessed a bowler hat and a smile. Every weekday Nuzo went to the cemetery with a lunch bag and a lawn chair to talk to his wife who was buried there. He asked her advice, talked about their ungrateful children, and reminisced. When the sun started to go down, he folded up his chair and went home. His daughter, Cecilia, wanted him committed to a mental institution, but in all other ways he was sane. When she accused him of being unbalanced, he simply replied, "Visiting Mama is better than watching the soap operas every day." No jury of his peers would have bothered him.

Every Friday afternoon, he would walk down from North Street, past the cemetery, and by the sky blue-colored Knights of Columbus Hall to Frank's Meat Market. As he walked, he saluted every man and tipped his hat to every lady. He was very Old Italy. He doffed his hat at elderly ladies, dressed in proverbial black, young marrieds usually bloated with an expected child, and even little girls like my sister.

That weekly ritual of Old World conversation and card playing continued for years and years, and even now after the death of all of them, one can still feel their presence when the evening at the end of the week comes. They seemed to celebrate their passage together, their modest successes in this strange land, and their brotherhood of the grape which moved on through time. But one evening the game ended with an unusually bitter conflict. They would fight about many things, all of them so inconsequential they dissolved the next morning. This time though my Grandpa was accusing Nuzo of theft—not stupidity or credulity, but outright theft. Nuzo angrily denied it, and on and on it escalated, with the two others trying at first to ignore them, and then taking sides.

Grandpa insisted that he had loaned Nuzo a rake, his best one, and it had never been returned over the winter. Now he was short his favorite rake. Nuzo swore on the grave of his saintly wife he had returned it and told Grandpa to look in his own tool shed, "that shithouse," as he called it. Somehow Grandpa took that as an insult to his family and accused Nuzo of having thieving tendencies like his father in Italy. Nuzo countered by characterizing Grandpa's father as a penny-pinching money lender and a despoiler of honest widows. Then Nuzo stepped over the line of a fair fight. He accused Grandpa of having stolen the girl he wanted to be his wife, the girl who had run away to the barn to avoid him with his *medigan* money and ways.

The onlookers could not believe it. He was talking about Grandma. Had they been lovers? Had they at least held hands in the haystacks in the barn? Grandpa was never a very physical, let alone a violent man, but he moved menacingly toward his once friend. And Nuzo, as sweet at the gods' nectar, was ready for battle. Luckily the two were quickly separated, but in one night, a life of friendship was shattered.

A month later, Nuzo broke his hip in the cemetery and went to the hospital where he contracted pneumonia, the friend of the old. His daughter, suddenly became solicitous, insisted on the full range of high tech machines to keep him breathing. But he resisted, asking only to die, as he put it, like "a noble man." She persisted and for a month he lingered, imploring her and his parish priest to let him die with dignity, to be with God and his beloved wife. The priest sided with his daughter since she headed up both the Sodality Mothers and the Altar Society. The next day Nuzo summoned up all his strength and courage, lifted his frail body out of bed, and locked the door. He pulled out all the plugs near him, including the television, featuring reruns of *I Love Lucy*. Buzzers went off, nurses tried to force their way in, but when they did, he was finishing up an act of contrition, dying as he lived in the bosom of Holy Mother Church.

Only his daughters told Grandpa of Nuzo's manner of death and of the funeral Mass that was to be said Monday morning. At first, he stayed silent and then he vacantly asked no one in particular, "Did Nuzo mention where he had put the rake?" The next day he worked in the garden earlier than usual and watched dispassionately as the rest of the family all walked up to church.

As the end of the fall, as winter approached, the trees became stick skeletons and the flowers turned to mulch. Grandpa gave one of his grandsons a $2.00 bill (he was the only person we knew who still had any) to clean up the tool shed. And, yes, there in the corner behind the burlap bag pile had fallen the much-disputed rake. The grandson pulled it out and ran to him in glee: he had found the lost treasure.

But he did not know, as all came to know, that the rake was not wanted now. Grandpa took it quietly, laid it by the pear tree and went on working. Later that evening he seemed to regain his composure and with his resurrection, he explained the sudden appearance of his long lost rake. What likely happened was that Nuzo on his death bed asked the Almighty for forgiveness, and all that stood in the way was the sin of theft. So in a vision, his daughter had been told of his crime and was instructed by the spirit of her father to return the rake. Grandpa insisted that this was true, and he was going to confront the daughter, in a gentle way, to admit her complicity. But he never did, and the rake stayed outside all winter, getting rusted and being covered several times by snow and ice.

Then in the last year of his life, Grandpa asked his same grandson to walk with him and carry a lawn chair he had just bought at Kresge. He gathered up a large bouquet of pansies, lovingly placing them in a brown bag. They walked up the hill, past Frank's meat market and the Knights of Columbus hall. As they approached the cemetery, he asked for the chair, gave the boy some quarters, and told him to return in an hour to that spot.

Slowly, as if every bone had begun to ache, he walked up the slope past the mausoleums and the common family markers. First Grandpa went over to the grave of Nuzo and placed some of the pansies on the headstone. He seemed so lost, so out of place as if energy were moving from his withered hand through the flowers to the grave site itself. And then he went on, over to the far right where years ago he had buried Grandma and three children. There too he placed a bouquet of pansies, the first I can remember, on those graves. He opened up the lawn chair and uneasily settled in. One could hear him talking again in a loud whisper, at first noises without words. He was not speaking English, or the dialect of Italian they used. The language was a mysterious stream of words, perhaps just the language of young lovers. As he knelt down on the grave and plucked the weeds, he cursed the church sextons for their negligence of that final resting place.

40. THE NEW COUNTY FAIR

Sometime in the winter, the Morris County Board of Freeholders decided to showcase its county fair, so that it matched what was going on in the neighboring parts of the state of New Jersey. They began to put real money into the three day event in August and made a concerted attempt to attract younger people to what was seen as an old fogey gathering. Whatever was the tone, Grandpa loved fairs, especially ones that focused on agricultural products. People got awards for the largest tomato, the biggest cucumber, the sweetest Jersey corn. He did not enter the contests, but he liked to see who won. He also enjoyed watching the children on the rides, especially the bumper cars where the very young would recklessly crash into one another. It was good training for Jersey driving. He tried to convince one of his children or grandchildren to go to the County Fair with him, but even Alphonso said he was not interested. So Grandpa went by himself, driving his usual 25 miles per hour in the dusk. Once there he got a senior citizen discount, which put him in a good mood, and went over to the stands to eat. He gobbled a stromboli and then had an Italian ice. *It was so sweet it probably causes diabetes,* he thought.

Across the fields, he heard music being played—it was Gerry Gerro singing selections from Verdi, and Grandpa naturally gravitated to the seats. The average age of the audience there was probably 100 years old and was predominantly old line Italian. He sat down and enjoyed Gerry who seemed in good form, though he forgot at time the lyrics from several arias in *La Traviata.*

The next presentation was very different. It was a thin young boy with a huge amount of hair who had played at the Mississippi-Alabama County Fair and Dairy Show in September 1956 and got rave reviews from hip critics. So the board had brought him in to win over the young. He had played to good crowds, and teenage girls especially loved his very movements and the animal sounds of his music. Grandpa was at first startled by what he saw, and watched with some bemusement the screaming of girls and the annoyance of their boyfriends. With a strong voice and sloppy diction, he sang old time gospel, unknown Negro songs, and country and western all in one session.

Oddly enough, Grandpa came to enjoy the sheer energy of the artist and the electricity that passed through the crowd around him. *Even an old man can learn,* he mused, and he stayed and listened intently, for this was not what he had grown up on. When he left, he felt invigorated and enjoyed the ride back home.

Then the second night he was back again, by himself, and headed past the food stands and the rides, and went to the first show of the new young singer. He sat in the front row, and once again he drank in the novel music that somehow he felt he had no right to enjoy at his age. It was more than the old blues or western tunes, something new was happening. Grandpa came back two hours later to listen again—not to Gerry Gerro, but to this new singer with the undulating hips. When the session was done, the young man placed his guitar down, and dropped gracefully off the stage and walked over to Grandpa.

Politely he said, "Sir, I saw you last night and twice tonight. Is this really your type of music?"

Grandpa responded effortlessly, "No, I know Verdi and Puccini, and the songs of Italian working men, but you are very different. Still I like it. But why do these girls scream so when you move?"

"When I first began, I was awfully nervous, so I would raise my leg up and down inside my baggy pants. The girls apparently thought it was sexy, so I kept it a part of the act."

The younger singer was embarrassed, but still wanted to keep up the conversation and avoid the milling teenage girls. "I am a working man too like your people, I am actually a truck driver. But in Mississippi I play a little guitar and listen to the sounds of church people—white and Negro. Does that shock you?"

"No, not really. You have a strong voice and a good sound. Perhaps you should try other sorts of music."

"What types of songs do your working men sing? Where are you from anyhow?"

"Naples, they sing of love as you do, and loneliness as you do. But not in a cowboy western sound. That is western, right? We have no cowboys in Naples."

Ignoring the question, the young tall singer asked Grandpa to hum him one of their songs, and Grandpa a bit self-conscious reached into his bag of tricks and sang, "O sole mio," written back in 1898.

"I don't know the language, but I like the beat. Does the singer before me know it?"

"Of course, Gerry knows it like a baby knows his mother."

"Come back tomorrow, and I will see if I can learn the tune and add my own words. This is how music will be made from now on. No more borders, no more barriers, sir."

Grandpa laughed and promised to come back. Maybe he should have given him "*Vesti la Giubba*" from *Pagliacci,* but this virile singer did not seem like a tragic clown who would ever lose a woman.

True to his word, Grandpa came back, and this time brought Alphonso to drive him. They sat down and after Gerry finished "*Largo al factotum*" from the *Barber of Seville* he then introduced the audience to this young singer who would follow him with a new version of "*O sole mio.*" Rather astutely, the young singer had asked Gerry to sing first a stanza in the familiar Italian, and then he began, 'It's now or never, Come hold me tight, Kiss me my darling, be mine tonight..." The audience was confused; the old timers did not know why the regular words were not good enough, and the teenagers did not know why their singer was doing such old stuff.

But it was remarkable, people were singing along in two different languages, and enjoying the old/new tune. Here was a Southern rhythm and blues singer of Negro songs reaching over to Italian favorites. Grandpa proudly nodded as the young man reached the high notes effortlessly and speeded up the beat. Alphonso looked at Grandpa, "What the hell is he doing to '*O sole mio*'?" Then Grandpa went up and firmly shook the young man's hand with a great flourish. The teenagers could not figure out who he was, and the old Italians wanted to find out how their Raffaele knew some kid from Mississippi. Italians don't live there.

In 1959, the singer taped the song, and it immediately hit the top ten popular music charts. Grandpa would hear it on the radio and on juke boxes in rundown pizzerias. In a strange way, Grandpa felt he had reached across the generations at least once in his life, and now made history, for music is the universal language.

41. JURY OF ONE'S PEERS

When Grandpa got the afternoon mail, he saw a letter from the Morris County clerk's office—it was a notice to appear at the Morristown county seat for jury duty. He had gotten a similar notice before, and he had ended up in the jury room and was disqualified for three different trials, for reasons he thought were anti-Italian prejudice. He felt humiliated and was finally glad to go home, but the county had experienced a crime wave, and all the defendants demanded a jury trial, rather than a simple bench trial.

One case had caught the public's attention. An eight-year-old girl, Anna De Luca, who went to St. Vincent Martyr Elementary school, was playing in front of the neighborhood Acme Market trying to brush up on her hopscotch. All her friends had gone to camp and some to sleep overs, but her father could not support sending her away and did not want her to be over at strangers' houses. So she entertained herself. Having such a charming personality, she rarely felt lonely or put out. One day a wizened-looking guy, in a white paneled truck, called her over, grabbed her, tied her to the front seat, and drove off with her screaming and frightened. Outside Madison's boundaries, he raped her, but she escaped, and noticed his name on a license wrapped in a plastic tube on his driving column.

When her father, Salvatore, found her hours later, she was sobbing uncontrollably as he tried unsuccessfully to comfort her. Finally with a sense of personal guilt, she told him what happened, and remembering the license related his name. Her father, who was a widower, took her home and swore to her and God that it would never happen again. Then he drove her to Overlook Hospital, where they were kind and healing. Her father, Salvatore De Luca, watched her very closely after the assault, and then one night he took her to Aunt Rosa's so they could go together to see the latest Disney movie. Anna loved Disney's animated films. Then her father went home without her and emerged from his cellar with a long hunting knife. He had carefully tracked down the assailant from what he knew of the license and figured the pervert to be a creature of habit. He saw the white paneled truck one night, and the rapist sitting there, picking his nose, and waiting for his next prey.

Salvatore went up to the truck, and with one fell swoop pulled the driver out, saw the license, and plunged the knife into his heart and then he cut off his gonads. It was not in his judgment true retribution, for the loss of innocence can never be repaid. Then he wiped off the knife and dropped it by the dead body.

Within two weeks the county police force had solved the crime, and the aggressive prosecutor, Thomas O'Brien, a graduate in the bottom quarter of Fordham Law School, figured he would take on the case himself. When the day of the jury selection process came, Grandpa took the #70 Public Service bus, rather than the train, to the courthouse building and was punctual as he had been years ago. But this time with the overflow of jurors and cases, the senior judge took a more active role in the jury selection.

He walked in wearing his robes of authority, had the jurors sit down, and Grandpa ended up Number 3. He wore his only suit and tie, since he thought that that was the dress code. Others came in wearing tee shirts, ripped jeans and sneakers. He had figured that there would be a long waiting time like before, so he looked for a copy of the *Newark Star Ledger*, but it was sold out, and all that was left was the *The New York Times* and the *Wall Street Journal*. Grandpa had no stocks, so he bought the *Times*.

The judge explained the cases before them that day, including the prominent trial, *The State of New Jersey v. Salvatore De Luca* for murder in the first degree, that is, he had committed premeditated murder. But he refused to plead so the judge, as was the custom, entered "Not Guilty" for him. Overall, he was most concerned about this trial, which he was personally going to preside over, and he asked the first twenty people if they knew the defendant, and if they had ever heard of the case. Grandpa had neither and he was suddenly on the panel. The judge moved swiftly, avoiding the usual voir dire process, and asked the lawyers if they had any objections to any of the 12 people and the 2 alternatives he had chosen. They did not, so he led them to the main courtroom, and left the other judges to deal with the lesser cases.

In the jury box, Grandpa sat in the front row, attentive but quiet. Both lawyers and the judge thought the case was cut and dry. De Luca had killed the alleged rapist, and he would end up with a 30 year sentence in Rahway Prison.

The state judge then looked at the jury, stressed the gravity of the case, and needing a foreman, he chose Grandpa. Grandpa remembered that they did not even want him several years ago. The judge told Mr. Finelli that he and the other jurors could take no notes or discuss the case.

It was August, which in New Jersey is like being in Manila in the summer. The old building was not air-conditioned, and they brought in three loud fans. The jurors complained about the sounds and asked that the fans be turned off. They obviously were taking the case seriously. When the trial began, the prosecutor was Thomas O'Brien and for the defense was a pompous Andrew Falconi. Falconi was appointed pro bono by the court; he was a Seton Hall Law School graduate and was not exactly Perry Mason. But the case was seen by most observers as a slam dunk. The question was how long De Luca would rot in jail.

O'Brien began by calling the Madison police chief to the stand, "You are the chief of police and have been on the force for twenty years?"

"Yes, sir."

"And you were the officer who worked the De Luca and the Langone cases?"

"Yes, sir."

"Please tell me how you were able to track down Langone in the first place."

"He had served in the Army, and we compared his fingerprints to the sample from the rape kit. We found a perfect match."

"From that you concluded he was the rapist, and you were going to pick him up?"

"Yes, and then we received a phone call from a neighbor reporting a male in a white van who had been mutilated."

"Mutilated. How?"

"He was stabbed in his heart, and his genitals were cut off."

"Cut off?"

"Yup, like a capon."

Falconi said nothing and others offered no objections to the graphic description.

"Who arrested Mr. De Luca, and did he deny the crime?"

"He said nothing, and to this day he has not talked at all."

"How did you know it was he who killed Langone?"

"It was fingerprints again. He left his full palm print on the handle of the bloody knife which he dropped by the corpse. It fit his print perfectly."

"Thank, you, your witness."

Falconi rose up slowly, "Would it surprise you if I told you that the defendant has not even talked to me yet? The court and I entered a plea of not guilty."

"No, he has been in a daze, I think."

"Tell me, chief, you have been a fine athlete at Madison High School, and later a Marine, and I know you have seen men in various stages of undress. Would you say that Mr. Langone was left with testicles bigger than most men?"

O'Brien finally jumped up, "Your honor, who cares if the rapist was hung or not?"

But Falconi shot back, "This man is on trial for his life. I need a little room for questioning." The judge simply concurred.

"What is your answer?"

"I only saw the remains, but yes, he was a big hombre, counselor."

"And you have seen the rape kit: the eight-year-old girl, was she small?"

"Yes, she is a tiny thing."

"Thank you." And then the case continued with the usual evidence. The pictures of Langone's body, the knife, the white paneled truck, the matching fingerprints, the rape kit. Falconi was surprised at the latter. They used a rape kit on an eight-year-old girl.

O'Brien had concluded the case, arguing that the sullen, silent De Luca had committed premeditated murder. Falconi had no evidence for the defense. Then he shifted gears quickly. He brought in a nun who taught the girl at St. Vincent's to give testimony. She was an old crusty Sister of Charity who lived in Convent Station. With no smile on her lips, she was being asked to tell the jury about little Anna De Luca.

O'Brien vigorously objected that the girl was not on trial, her father was, but Falconi successfully argued that knowing her was important to understanding him. The judge concurred since he did not want to expose the girl to any part of the trial, and he chose to let in the nun's full testimony. Besides, he didn't like contradicting a nun who had been his 8th grade teacher years ago.

"Sister, thank you. Please tell us a little about this girl. Is she a troublesome or weird girl? Is she a boisterous child?"

"Oh, Jesus, Mary, and Joseph, no, she is the best child I have taught in over thirty years. She is sensitive, very nice to new children, and without prejudice. This year we named her the girl who crowned the statue of Our Lady on the feast of the Assumption—a major religious holiday for our parish."

"You would not say that she was wild?"

"Of course not, what a ludicrous idea, Andrew." She had taught Falconi in the 4th grade.

"Okay, thanks, for your time."

"No questions, Mr. Prosecutor?"

"No questions, sister." And she left in a flurry past the jury and out the front mahogany doors.

"I would like to call to the stand nurse Andrea Lewis of Overlook Hospital."

"I object your honor. It is obvious that Mr. Falconi is subtly laying the groundwork for a trial based on the rape not on the murder. What he is asking the jury is to engage in jury nullification."

The judge grew flustered and highly annoyed, "Mr. Prosecutor, that is exactly what I did not want brought out. Now I have to explain to the jury the whole notion of jury nullification."

O'Brien was embarrassed, and Falconi simply looked at his polished fingernails.

"Ladies and gentlemen of the jury, jury nullification is a discredited theory that the jury has a right to overlook the evidence and come back with a verdict that is based not on the law, but on their own preferences. You are a sworn jury and are only to take into account the facts of law and evidence, and we will instruct you at end of the trial. Now, Mr. O'Brien since you raised the issue of this rape kit, we have a right to hear from the nurse who tended the rape victim. Mr. Falconi continue."

The nurse appeared wearing a starched white uniform and the traditional pitched hat. She was what you expected a total professional from the past to look like.

"Now, Nurse Lewis, you took care of this young girl when her father brought her in?"

"Yes, he said little, but we got from the girl what happened."

"What did the rape kit show?"

"She had been raped and the assailant did not wear a condom."

"He did not even wear a condom… Delicately, can you tell me the state of the girl's private parts?"

"There is nothing delicate about it, Mr. Falconi. She was ripped apart down there. She will need reconstructive surgery at a later date. Her thighs were covered with blood, and she was in a state of near hysteria."

"In your professional judgment have you ever seen such a case?"

"No, we get rapes, but not of such a young girl. My heavens, she was just a tiny girl."

"Were the police there?"

"Yes, soon the chief came and avoided looking if he could. I have known him for years. He is a modest man. She wanted her mother's medal, which we found on the floor."

"Thank you, Ms. Lewis. I'll let you get back to your important work."

"No questions from the prosecution."

And that was it, the judge informed the jury that this case involved first degree murder, not rape. And it was a verdict based on evidence and the law. Grandpa slowly led the jury into a windowless cement block room, and they started to discuss the case, and soon people began to fall off to go to the bathroom.

Grandpa stopped the march of old men with prostate problems and menopausal women of all ages. "Let's stop, take a break, go to the bathroom, have a coke and water and then we can all settle down in our seats."

Inevitably, he established his authority. Then he sat at the head of the table.

He began finally, "Ladies and gentlemen of the jury, we face a case of murder. Salvatore De Luca is charged with killing Frank Langone after he raped his daughter. The judge says the case is based on the evidence."

Grandpa started, "I want to get from you, with your permission, some initial secret ballot on how we are leaning." The paper ballot was a surprise 6-6, a divided jury on the basic question of guilt.

Grandpa stopped the discussion and then said, "Let's go over the evidence. Mr. Jefferson will summarize the prosecutor's case." Herbert Jefferson was a local Prudential agent whom most of the people in the area knew, and he made a strong case showing that there was no doubt—reasonable or otherwise. The evidence was clear and convincing, he proclaimed. Jefferson was Grandpa's Pru agent, and he had known him for years. He was an honest but limited man who played by the rules as he saw them…or so Grandpa thought.

Grandpa then turned to Elizabeth Esposito, a 59-year-old woman who ran a small grocery story on Main Street from seven in the morning to eight at night. Her husband had died recently, and she had no children. She managed the store on her own. Esposito reported the evidence but moved beyond the murder. She described the abuse of the young girl, and at one point she started to cry, "Oh, God help the little girl. Such infamy." Then she turned to Grandpa who had known her for half a century, "Oh, Ralph, she has to have reconstructive surgery down there; who is going to reconstruct her mind and her soul?"

Grandpa started to stop her, "Please Elizabeth, just give the defense," but then Phil Scoti, the longtime butcher on North Street spoke out.

"No, no, she's right. I would kill Lagone and grind him into hamburger. We are indeed bound by evidence, but we twelve are the humanity in this case. If you just wanted a legal opinion, let the judge do it. No, we are the conscience of the community, can we dare to send him to jail?"

Grandpa then recognized the assistant pastor of the Lutheran Reformed Church, who had been quiet the whole time. "We are not lawyers but are simply a check on the system. Did he do it or not? I am afraid in the eyes of the law and God, he did."

Phil snapped back, "Then let God judge him. I cannot see sending a man to jail who did what I would do. Which of you parents or grandparents would not take up that knife?"

A long silence ensued. They were waiting for Grandpa to give a judgment. He spoke at first very slowly: "It is obvious that De Luca killed Langone in the most gruesome way. And he almost enjoyed it. But the rape was so brutal, she's so pure and young. I too was shocked by his size and the need for reconstructive surgery. She will live with that crime every day. The question, my friends, is simple: do we tell the judge that the evidence shows he is clearly guilty of murder or do we say that in the eyes of this jury he is justifiably innocent? Which do you want"

The emboldened minister insisted that this really was jury nullification. Phil assured him that he didn't care, he felt good about this exception. For eight hours they addressed the questions:

What law takes precedent, the law of man or the law of revenge?

If we forgive this murder, what about the next murder the jury can overlook?

If a jury can overlook this one crime, when can it overlook the next, and the next?

If we argue against applying the rule of law, then what good is the system of law?

They wanted to know the difference between the code of natural law and criminal law. Most didn't even know what "natural law" meant.

Suppose the murderer killed the wrong rapist?

Little kids exaggerate.

Didn't the judge seem to indicate that the verdict should be guilty?

Could they get in trouble for a different verdict?

On and on the debate went, going over the same terrain many times, and not coming to a conclusion. Finally Grandpa said: "Friends, you know it is time to make a hard decision, that is why we are here. I appreciate the sanctity of the law. I know what it is like to live in a country ruled by thieves and mobs. But in America, we have only the law which we must prize, for we too are Americans. But the decisions of men must be seen sometimes as above the law of God. We say, minister, 'Thou shall not kill,' but we send our boys off to war to protect us. Our law must account for circumstances, for real life, for harsh experiences, for the right for a father to be a man.

"I don't know De Luca, as a friend or otherwise. But I do not want him behind bars. And when I see his daughter skipping rope I will smile and say hello. And I will ask her how her father's doing. That is one man's opinion, one man's vote, now I need for you all to give me a show of hands to report to the judge. Those in favor of innocence raise your right-hand, those in favor of guilty your left-hand." And so it came to pass that twelve different types of people disobeyed the judge and the laws and voted innocent. Grandpa then said, "How shall I report this?"

Jefferson volunteered, "I'll help you with the verdict statement, Ralph."

The bailiff called the court to order and the judge in the nuances of feudal English law asked the jury foreman, "And how say ye, freeholders?"

And Grandpa read the following: "We the jury of the county of Morris unanimously find the defendant—Salvatore De Luca—innocent. We wish the judge to know we do not believe in jury nullification but believe in justice and in extenuating circumstances."

O'Brien jumped up and asked that the jury be polled, and each person offered, "Innocent." Falconi was delighted; De Luca remained sullen. The judge thanked the jury for its time and then uncharacteristically added, "and your obvious thoughtfulness."

The spectators and jurors filed out quietly. Grandpa shook hands with each fellow juror and was the last to leave the courtroom, grabbing his *New York Times*. Then he went up to the bailiff and asked why he had been chosen foreman, and the officer answered, "Easy, Ralph, you are the only one who came in a suit and tie. To the judge you respected the system, and when he saw you with a copy of the *New York Times*, not the *Post* or the *Daily News*, he thought you were an intelligent man not just a working stiff."

Grandpa just nodded.

There was a newspaper man from the *Newark Star Ledger* at the exit, and he stopped Grandpa and asked how the jury could overcome the evidence, and then sharply charged, "Was it because there were so many EYEtalians on the jury, a people who believe in revenge?"

Grandpa looked up at him and calmly responded, "No, it because there were so many fathers and mothers on the jury."

42. THE SPONSOR

In the early afternoon, Grandpa was standing in front of his apartment house, looking aimlessly across the street. Directly in front was the Solano Chicken Market, Mantone's Garage, and down the street was Burrough's Funeral Home, always open for business, the vulture "*l'avvoltoio.*" Grandpa noted once that the centers of Chatham, Summit, Springfield, and Madison all looked alike, and he wondered if all small town America was the same. Down the hill came the mail carrier, a pleasant loquacious Jimmy Fitzpatrick who greeted Grandpa with a novel remark, "Hey, Ralph, got an important letter from Italy for you. Maybe they want to draft you."

The old man was startled and looked at the tissue paper letter with its Napoli, Italia stamp on it. He carefully opened it up, and there was a letter from Rotondi, which was his hometown, from a person he had known as a youngster. It was Franco Serapi, who lived in what the Italians would have called Grandpa's "*paese.*"

With his careful handwriting, he started off praising Grandpa for his personal courage in moving to America at such a young age and making his fortune in the New World. He insisted that matters were getting worse in Campania, "the drought, high taxes, endless corruption, extremist politicians." He begged Grandpa to serve as his sponsor, so he could make his way to America. Frankly, Grandpa never cared for him; he was an impostor, a fake, a lecher from the time that he had pubic hair. But he was still from the same *paese*, and Grandpa had never said no before to a request for being a sponsor. The Italians had created a great chain of immigration that extended not only to America, but also to Argentina, Canada, and even Australia.

Being sympathetic to everybody's problems, Grandpa agreed, and in three months with his old green Ford pickup, he was in the parking lot across from Ellis Island waiting for the ferry. Franco greeted him with the same bravado the old man remembered, and he went back to Madison where Grandpa let him stay in the very last room of his apartment. Grandpa expected that he'd begin working with him, but Franco disliked physical work as much as a bat dislikes light.

He told Grandpa that he had been studying English intensively before he came over on "the cattle boat" as it was called, and he wanted to get some office job in Madison since he was after all bilingual.

He informed his friend that he wished to be a real estate agent, selling homes to Italians and Italian Americans, bringing to them the very definition of the American dream. Grandpa was tolerant and introduced him to Jimmy Cante, head of the Madison Realty Company.

They got along well, Franco was fairly successful, and the next year he decided to go back and take a bride, just as Grandpa had done. He courted and married a virgin brunette, Anna, whom he had seen at church on a Sunday. Under strict supervision, they courted and married, and left for a honeymoon in Rome, and then took a cruise ship to America.

Franco dressed in fancy used clothes, and Anna's family thought he was a rich *medigan*, and he furthered the polite illusion. In Madison, he promised all to his lovely young bride, who was just beginning to understand what it really meant to be married to this guy. Franco's male buddies figured he would finally settle down, raise a family, and stop being the town lecher.

He sold real estate; Anna ran a small delicatessen with her two children in the back. She worked at the store from 7 a.m. to 8 p.m. every day, including Sunday, often missing Mass. Franco got bored selling just real estate to *cafoni*, as he said, and he was too used to Anna's tight body at night. He took up his old habits—prowling. One of his favorite habits was to attend weddings. He'd figure out where the reception was held and zero in on a maid of honor because for some reason those events made them more receptive. Since he was also working every Friday night at the Madison Motor Inn as a clerk, he had an easy spot to bring his hungry conquests. He even tried working the Italian funerals, but the women there were too old, too cranky, and covered in macabre black. For years they would wear widow's weeds, and he was too young and vibrant for sharing in their misery. Besides old people smell. Elder women smell like overly ripe strawberries.

He also sought companionship the old-fashioned way—he paid for it at a cat house in nearby Morristown. Franco especially liked a hooker named Big Rose, but she got pregnant by him or by somebody else, and he helpfully reminded her about an abortionist running a back-alley office in Chatham. Franco did not believe in using condoms because he said it was like "a man wearing a raincoat in the shower."

The word of all this got back to the male laborers who spread it around among themselves, saying what an asshole he was. And of course, the part about the abortion made it to the pastor. After one wedding, he pulled Franco aside and chastised him for his part in any abortion activities. Franco, of course, denied it, but he didn't care—he didn't believe in God anyhow. Abortion was just a modern convenience for a mistake.

One of the male construction workers spread the word about Franco after having had too much vino at dinner with his wife, who in turn told other wives and still others. It seemed everybody but Grandma and poor Anna knew what the story was. The women decided to talk honestly with Anna for women must stick together in a macho world. They approached Anna as a friendly group saying, "We must tell you your husband is cheating on you with *putanas* in Morristown."

Anna quietly took in the unsavory news. "Yes, I have known it for quite a time, but as long as he comes home to me and, more importantly, my children, I don't care what is going on." The women just looked at each other quizzically and filed out of the delicatessen.

Franco continued his paid conquests. He took up with another hooker, Florence, but after six months with the active vixen, he realized that he had contracted something…down there. He learned from Dr. Felepa that it was an incurable form of syphilis, and it would only get worse. Antibiotics were still in their infancy. Offhandedly, Felepa said to him, "You unfortunately have the same incurable disease that Nietzsche, the philosopher, had at the end of his life."

Franco said to him, "Who the hell is Nietzsche?" And Felepa told him bluntly that he had only a few months before his body would be totally poisoned. First, he would go insane, and then he would be dependent on everyone for his food and basic needs.

He was devastated. What had he done! Had the priest put the evil eye on him? Priests can do that, you know, and then he simply resigned himself to the thought that in the end he would be with his beloved wife watching over him. He didn't tell her of his disease; he was cool but still affectionate. At least he would die in the arms of his beloved, not with some *putana*. That is the way God wanted it, he speculated in a sudden burst of hazy belief. A month later, Anna was cutting capicola for a sandwich for a construction worker. She grabbed her chest and fell over and died of a massive heart attack in front of her own children. The worker called the ambulance corps, but she was dead before they even arrived. When Franco heard, he couldn't deal with it, screaming hysterically, "Who is going to take care of me now? Who, oh God, who?"

At the funeral he told Grandpa the whole story from the very beginning, and then angrily turned and said, "It's your fault, Raffaele. If you hadn't sponsored me to come to America, I wouldn't be in these straits." Grandpa looked at him quizzically, and just simply sat down to say a rosary for Anna's pure soul.

As Franco rapidly deteriorated, the mental authorities just put him in a padded cell in Greystone to protect him and others. He would swear in two languages, denouncing the pain that he was suffering from syphilis-afflicted dementia. One day he started banging his head on the padded bars cursing, "You son of a bitch. I am a good man, a loyal *medigan*, a good father to my children and must get back to them. I need to stop this craziness. The doctor told me that I had what a German philosopher called Nietzsche died of. I went to the library the next day to find out who he was and how he died. He was the man who first proclaimed, 'God is dead.' I never said that. I never believed that. His mind turned to mush like mine is now. What became a simple sexual encounter with some American *putana*—I never even paid her the last time. Oh God, I am a good man, am I not? Oh Anna, tell God I am good. I was never a Nietzsche. God have mercy, save me." And he kept on banging his head against the bars, until he lost consciousness, and then mortality.

They laid him out formally at Burroughs of course, and Grandpa and Grandma went to pay their respects. Only the two children and an aunt were there.

As they began to amble back up the hill to home, his daughter commented to Grandpa, "It is so sad that Anna wasn't there in his final moments. They loved each other so."

And Grandpa looked away from her and observed, "Yes, it was sad."

43. SAN FRANCISCO, HERE I COME

The Knights of Columbus of St. Vincent Martyr parish decided to go whole hog in celebrating the feast of Our Lady of Mount Carmel, a three day fest that Grandpa's family was especially devoted to since they had possession of the pale blue ornate banner of the Virgin used in the parade. He drove up to the festival, and enjoyed watching people eating the Italian delicacies, kids throwing darts at balloons to win prizes, and the older people smiling and remembering when they marched as youngsters in the procession in front of the Benevento cathedral. They even had a raffle with two grand prizes: a garish Olds 88 and a free round trip to San Francisco. Grandpa bought five tickets for the trip since there was no way he was going to drive a bloated car with fins on it. He knew he would never win, since he never had won a raffle in his life. God in His wisdom had decided that he was not to be a rich man, and the only thing he could acquire would be by his own hard work.

His arthritis was beginning to hurt so he left early; anyway, he wanted to be home to watch *Gunsmoke*, which came on at 10 pm. He especially enjoyed the marshal who was 6'7", only wounded but never killed a miscreant, and would clear out a crowd with one punch to the jaw of the troublemaker. One of his friends told Grandpa that in the earliest days of the show, Kitty ran the bar and was a procurer of girls for the rooms upstairs. But as the years passed, she was more proper, ran a clean business, turned the rooms into apartments for travelers, and became Marshal Dillon's love interest. Grandpa did not remember that part of the story, but he was glad that the marshal had found true love.

At the end of the night, he was getting ready for bed when the phone rang. He hated when the phone rang after dark since it was always bad news. But this time, it was Geraldo Esposito. "Mr. Finelli, you won the trip to San Francisco." He was amazed for he had never expected to win anything. He was just glad to have cannoli at the festival.

Two weeks later, he made plans to visit San Francisco and see his granddaughter, Susan, who was high up in the Ghirardelli Chocolate Company which made such magnificent chocolates. She was unmarried, but Grandpa could not figure out why. She was not unattractive, he once said to his daughters. Susan was delighted that he was coming out and made plans to show him her great city by the bay, for people claimed it had seven hills just like Rome.

She greeted him with great affection, and the first full day took him to see the chocolate center which was housed in an old factory, totally redone into a real chocolate emporium. Grandpa had a sweet tooth, and after she gave him endless samples, she promised she would send a huge box of various chocolates to him in Madison.

They then visited the city, and Grandpa was pleased at the beautiful pastels that colored the houses on the hills. He was surprised that the houses were so close together and had no room for gardens. Susan also proudly took the old man to the Bank of America, which was originally founded by an Italian immigrant, Amedeo Giannini, who turned the modest saving and loan association to a major force in the city. During the terrible earthquake of 1906, Giannini had stood in front of the modest bank and loaned money to the city's inhabitants without collateral, trusting them with only a handshake. When the city recovered, he became a hero to them all. Grandpa liked that story for it was one in which an Italian had traveled across the continent to bring his skill and his way of life to the end of the New World.

The third day, Susan had an important meeting at work which she could not get out of, and she gave Grandpa a handful of tokens and told him he could take the trolleys all over the city and see what the different neighborhoods looked like. He went first to the Golden Gate Bridge and marveled at the architectural beauty of the structure, "what a great creature is man." He then hopped on the trolleys and went into the Italian area, took the bus where he got off at the City Lights Bookstore which had opened in 1953. Everyone said that the Beat movement had been spawned there, and while he did not know who the Beats were, he still figured he wanted to see the place. It was devoted to poetry, and was owned by Lawrence Ferlinghetti, the great poet who was indicted on obscenity for printing Allen Ginsburg poem, "Howl."

A large crowd was seated in the vestibule and Grandpa came in and sat by the door. He was not a learned man, but in his youth had been exposed to the poetry of Petrarch, a friend of Dante. Ginsburg acknowledged Ferlinghetti's contribution to the great Beat movement, including Jack Kerouac's *On the Road,* and the verses of Gregory Corso, neither of whom Grandpa knew. Then Ginsburg read from his famed poem, "Howl", "I saw the best minds of my generation destroyed by madness, starving, hysterical, naked, dragging themselves through the negro streets at dawn looking for an angry fix." It was very sad. Then he sparked up and told the crowd that he had just finished a poem to his gay lover, Peter Orlovsky, and he read a long stanza about their homoerotic relationship. Six older ladies got up and walked out. They thought modern poetry was Robert Frost and T. S. Eliot...*In the rooms the women come and go, talking of Michelangelo.* Grandpa left with them, not in protest, but because he wanted to ride the trolleys more.

He was to meet Susan at the Joe DiMaggio Italian Chophouse restaurant at 610 Union Street; the restaurant specialized in steaks and was owned by the brothers and sisters of the great Yankee player. At dinner Grandpa told Susan about meeting the slugger at an ice cream stand in south Jersey in 1955, but she did not seem to believe him. She had seen DiMaggio walking around San Francisco since he lived there and grew up as a boy near that very section.

After several more days, Grandpa said goodbye to his successful granddaughter who seemed to be doing so well even though she was not married and left the city by the bay. She dropped him off at the airport, and he checked in to go back to Newark on United.

He had had a delightful time and was so proud that some Italians had come all the way across the continent. He wondered if those western Italians were of a hardier breed than those who stayed in New Jersey and Rhode Island. As he stood in line to get on, he noticed a tall man dressed in a dark wool blazer and gray pants, behind him in line. He turned around and there he was, DiMaggio, a bit grayer and more stooped but still looking like a U.S. senator. The celebrity immediately recognized the old man, "Pop, do I know you? Do you remember me?"

"Of course I remember the Great DiMaggio; we once had ice cream together, but no one believes me."

Joe laughed and acknowledged, "Yes, of course. I remember you. And I want you to know that I took your final advice. Do you remember?"

"Yes, yes, I do. I was sorry later to be so forward."

"You told me to go home and marry Marilyn and live a good life together. She and Arthur Miller are through. I am going to propose to her, and I am certain she will marry me again."

The old man was pleased, but in front of him was a terrible ruckus. A confused and troubled mother was trying to calm her mother down and hold on to her 7-year-old. "Mom, you have to go to the end gate, way down there. Please go ahead. I can't take you there. Our plane is leaving soon, and Emily can't walk that fast there and back."

But the older lady was obstinate, saying then she was not going, period. The conversation became shrill, and finally DiMaggio looked at the mother and said quietly, "You know you can leave Emily with me. We will be just fine; I have three granddaughters nearly her age. Would you like to stay here with me, Emily?" The girl smiled and nodded, and her mother could not say to no to a great celebrity, one whom everybody in the airport knew and trusted. So off the child's mother ran with her troubled mother in tow.

"You know I am going back east to sign 1941 bats, to symbolize my best year when I hit in 56 consecutive games."

Grandpa responded, "Yes I remember. The record that will never be broken."

"No, they are all meant to be broken. I just don't want to live to see it. Anyhow, I am taking half the bats and putting them in a bank vault; they will be the legacy for my granddaughters. By then they will be worth a small fortune, and the rest I will sell and live off the proceeds. Emily, do you want one of my bats?"

She smiled and nodded, and DiMaggio reached into his coat and took out a pen and paper and wrote down her address. Meanwhile the plane started boarding, and Grandpa was afraid that DiMaggio would miss the plane. *Maybe I should stay with the man and the little girl.* But reading his mind, DiMaggio remarked, "Look, you had better go or you will miss the plane. I will wait with Emily, as I promised. Besides you need to get back and go to work. I am simply going to the Waldorf to sign bats tomorrow. Not exactly tough work!"

"Goodbye, Mr. DiMaggio."

"No, no, Joe. Watch for the wedding on television, you made it possible."

So Grandpa boarded the plane watching as DiMaggio was telling Emily about the dolls his granddaughters loved best. Grandpa hated flying, sat in the window seat, closed his eyes, and began to doze off. Then after ten minutes, he thought he was in flight, and looked down at the ground and remarked, *How small people look down there, they look like ants.* Then he realized they were ants; the plane hadn't taken off.

Back home, he found a huge box of Ghirardelli chocolates on the porch. Susan had kept her promise. What a nice girl. He put out the chocolates for all to eat when they visited him. Then one afternoon, Delgado came to see him and sadly told him he heard on the radio that Marilyn Monroe had died of a drug overdose. Grandpa at first could not believe it, and then he felt such remorse for poor Joe.

For twenty years, DiMaggio sent six red roses three times a week from the Parisian Florist Shop to her crypt at the Corridor of Memories, and then for some reason he abruptly stopped. Why, no one ever knew.

44. THE SECRETS OF FATIMA

He still could not resist mentioning to me at least some forecasts in his secret book. One day he asked me blankly what I knew about the three secrets of Fatima. Of course, all of us in Catholic school had heard that the Blessed Virgin herself had given three secrets to the shepherd children in Portugal—two of them were already known: a vision of hell and the terrible destruction of World War II. The third secret was written down by the only one of the children still alive, a Carmelite nun, who sent it to the pope to be released. The pope, the amiable John XXIII, uncharacteristically suppressed it, and Sister Lucia, bound to obedience and silence, refused to contradict his judgment.

I waited as Grandpa calmly opened up the *Book of Solomon*, whose secrecy I had violated in the past. There it said, according to him, that great and terrible tribulations were in store all over the world. He read the predictions that the Angel of Destruction would come and prepare the ways for the Last Judgment. Before the end, the Anti-Christ would assume the chair of St. Peter and bring about the destruction of the papacy and the division of the Roman Church.

So that was the reason John XXIII refused to release the news. It appeared to tell of the demise of the very office he held. Did he, I wondered, this good man, fear that in opening up the Church he had let the Anti-Christ in? Did he fear he was, without realizing it, the Anti-Christ himself? Good Pope John?

I didn't ask Grandpa those questions since he had at best a lover's quarrel with the Church. For a while he had stopped going to Mass, somehow blaming God for Grandma's premature and harsh death. Part of Grandpa was pagan, Latin pagan. When the priest at her funeral droned on about his wife's immortality with God, Grandpa eyes lit up with a burning coal ferocity that I had never seen before. He murmured out quietly as if to challenge the Almighty Himself, "*Se esiste*," "If He exists?" God and the priest never answered, and Grandpa quietly hung his head until the final benediction.

Still Grandpa made somewhat of a peace with the church of the saints.

Like the women and me, he fell under the spell of the cult of the Madonna, the pure love of the Blessed Virgin. And at times, he spoke directly to the carpenter, St. Joseph. It was a good and fitting choice. He spoke father to father, workman to workman—praying a special intercession for Joseph's steadfastness and strength, to a man who taught a boy (mortal or God) how to plane a board or draw a plumb line with a simple string.

I never really asked Grandpa what his beliefs were, but I was still fascinated by the third secret of Fatima. Grandpa claimed he knew more than anyone else about the Fatima revelations, and dismissed my questions by telling me to write poor Sister Lucia, the Carmelite nun, which I never did. Later I told Sister Agatha at St. Vincent Martyr Elementary School what Grandpa had told me, and she slapped my face twice and warned I must pray for his sinful soul. When I relayed to Mom the whole story one night after my Wednesday bath when I was feeling strange and quiet, she told me Grandpa was getting old, and Sister Agatha really was concerned with my salvation. Somehow, I believed Grandpa though.

Several weeks later, I decided to confront Grandpa directly with Sister Agatha's challenge and went into the garden where in a classical sense he sat under his fig tree and vines. Actually though he was pruning the fig tree which he bent over and laid down for the winter. At the same time, he was mixing a hybrid of pansies, his favorite flower. I don't know if he had read Mendel, but he must have known almost intuitively the laws of mutations and cross breeding. He looked lovingly at his fruit trees, remarking how every season the female and male trees had to be within breeding distance of each other—almost like pining adolescents. He created his own grape bower, tolerated the honeybees that tended to sting the rest of us, and rested in the shade as God did on the proverbial seventh day.

I called to him, as he was on his knees, joined him, and told him the story of Sister Agatha. At first, he displayed a stoic sense of calm, but then he whispered a curse that I think remarkably implied that Sister Agatha was not a virgin and in fact sold her favors for liras. Then in a furor, he promised to tell me his fearful dream from last night, referring to the *Book of Solomon*, reciting from memory in clear English:

And there in the desert grew up as out of nowhere,
Four riders mounted on the horses of Disease, Melancholy,
Famine, and the largest, Death. The fourth of these was
A great steed, the head of which looked like a huge skeleton.
The forces of lightness and darkness did battle, a war more
Enveloping than any before even the last one here on earth,
God Himself was wounded, and all his favorite champions,
Including St. Michael, were brought low.
Women could not conceive, men grew impotent.

Food was scarce, days were too hot
For travel, and nights too cold to sleep.
All of nature was hostile to man.
Libraries went up in flame,
Schools crumbled crushing children,
And babes roamed the roads
Crying for their mothers and dying of thirst.

As he described the awful visions of his dreams, Grandpa seemed to become almost motionless and then in a quick reflex he kicked his chair, sending his newspaper sprawling into the garden. I looked over and read as best I could the headlines in Italian in *Il Progresso*. A sudden chill went through me even as the sun reached down. The very plights he foresaw were stories of that day.

He seemed to notice my fear, and stopped, stood up, and cursed *Il Progresso*. It was, he proclaimed, a cheap rag—a tool of a reactionary Italian family who had once celebrated Mussolini. Then he went on to tell me once again his views about the thug Mussolini, whom he detested. He was alright, Grandpa judged, when he was alone—he drained the swamps which even the ancient Romans neglected, civilized the Africans, made the trains run on time. But then he met that "mad Hun"—Grandpa's shorthand for Hitler and all Germans he had ever disliked. Soon Mussolini went crazy, and so the Communists caught him, and hung him by his heels in the front of a gas station, and then people spit on their Il Duce. His wife was a saint, Grandpa concluded; his boy was a good jazz musician in Milan. And so it ended, and I never asked about Fatima or Mussolini again.

45. THERAPIES

As long as I knew him, Grandpa distrusted three types of people: priests, insurance agents, and doctors. In his mind, all of them dealt with death, and the ones he detested the most were doctors. How far those feelings went back I do not know. I do know that when my mother was a newborn infant, the terrible influenza plague of 1918 swept across Europe and then the eastern United States. More people died that winter of the flu and pneumonia than in the Great War. When my grandmother brought the local doctor to see her sickly daughter, he quickly concluded, "The best that could be done is to keep her quiet and let her die in peace." My grandmother, in a rare display of anger, chased him out of the kitchen with a butcher knife, put the baby near the warm oven and watched over her day and night for nearly two weeks. Mom obviously lived, and Grandpa came away with a deeper appreciation for Grandma's care than for the doctor's advice. In his long life, he was to bury other infant children not as fortunate, experience the loss of a young daughter and watch helplessly as another daughter died at 45 of the tests done to diagnose what turned out to be a benign brain tumor.

When I was older, I once remarked to him that Thomas Jefferson also hated doctors, and he concluded that whenever three doctors gathered vultures would begin circling overhead. Grandpa nodded; the great president was right. The healthy had no need for doctors; the sick never seemed to benefit from them. It was better to nurse oneself, he concluded and so twice a year he flushed his system with baking soda and fluids like he was cleaning out a set of rusty pipes.

It was during this time, in the later years of his life, that he came to do full battle with the medical establishment in one of the most poignant episodes I can remember. In the winter of 1957, my cousin Carmelita had her first and only child. Carmelita's parents had both died, and at a fairly young age she married Rocco Petrazini, a construction worker whom she met at a CYO dance at the St. Vincent Martyr auditorium. She fell in love with him at first glance, seeing in him attributes that none of the rest of us could discover with a Geiger counter. She found him virile, vivacious, and commanding; we agreed he was boorish, crude and wearisome. But Carmelita was a pleasant girl who loved life and saw facets of beauty and excitement everywhere. What a wonderful mother she would make.

But that was not what happened. The pregnancy was followed by a terribly difficult labor, an unexpected Caesarian, and a severe period of depression. In those days, people had come to know of "post-partum" let down, but being Italian, in their own way, they were remarkably unsympathetic to their own daughters. One just shook it off, stopped that damn nonsense, and got back to work. Mothers would come over to teach their daughters the care and feeding of infants, and they would set up bassinettes, diaper tables and cribs on the first day, for it was bad luck to anticipate the baby's safe arrival in any way. So much of the color scheme ended up white or yellow, for blue or pink expressed a choice already.

Carmelita though did not come home, sinking instead into a very deep depression, communicating with no one except her husband whom she greeted with loud screams of inarticulate rage. After a week of this, he allowed her to be put in the Oak Ridge Nursing Home, a residential facility for the mentally ill. The baby was passed each week from one aunt to another until Carmelita "got well"—whatever that meant and whenever that would occur. No one told my grandfather what was happening. It was something they called "complications."

Three times the old man climbed up the hill to Oak Ridge to visit her, each time being turned away by the staff, and each time bringing back his flowers. At first, he was confused, then hurt, and then angry. He could not imagine how any doctor—he regarded any male in white up there as a physician—could deny his granddaughter the chance to see him, especially since her parents were dead and her husband seemed to have vanished. Then one day he casually asked me to tell him what was my cousin's problem. Frankly I had assumed that he knew what I had heard in my easy eavesdropping: that Carmelita was sad, refused to talk to anyone, did not recognize any of her relations, knew nothing about the baby, and was undergoing shock treatments.

He listened intently to all I spouted off about, and then asked what those treatments were. Being a know it all, I told him in gruesome detail how they strapped electrodes on her head, tied her down, and sent electricity to shock her out of her depression. He visibly shuddered, gripped the arms of his kitchen chair, and seemed upset, stopping only when he saw the reaction on my face.

And this is the story I later heard from various people: Minutes later he was hurrying up Main Street to the center of town and ended up in the offices of Andrew Falcone, attorney at law, a son of a friend of Grandpa's from year one. The old man, agitated, had simply walked by Falcone's secretaries, saying he wanted "to see the boy," and caught him alone in his law library working up some papers for another sleazy divorce case that the

Falcones were so known for in town. In rapid staccato Italian, Grandpa explained the situation, and demanded that Falcone come with him to the hospital immediately, before they could harm her again. Falcone resisted until Grandpa sat down and wrote out a generous check, grabbed him by the sleeve, and they made their way to Oak Ridge.

There, Falcone was his obnoxious best: he charged the hospital with false imprisonment and violation of Carmelita's civil rights under federal statute and the constitution of the sovereign state of New Jersey. When the sanitarium officials insisted that they had Rocco's consent, Falcone pronounced that Rocco had vanished, and that Grandpa was Carmelita's nearest blood relative. He started talking about negligence suits, insurance problems, and liability. Knowing that they were dealing with one of the greatest ambulance chasers in the Western world, the sanitorium officials turned their patient over to Grandpa.

I saw her that night sitting motionless, drawn, and ghostly white in his parlor. Grandpa was standing by her, holding her hand, patting her head, and quietly talking, talking, talking. For the next two weeks, he stayed home taking care of her, and bitterly ignored the demands of his daughters that he return her to the sanitarium. It was clear that he was horrified by the whole scene, especially by the shock therapy which only confirmed his view of doctors. All that was barbaric to him, so cruel that he still wavered between anger and sympathy whenever he remembered. My mother was positively furious when she found out I had told him about the twice weekly therapy, but I did not care, for I figured that whatever Grandpa did could not be any worse or any crueler.

But it was apparent that his regime of Italian food and tender loving care was not bringing Carmelita out of her isolated world either. Grandpa surely tried. He took her for walks, first in his beloved garden and then in the park, while he praised the beauties of Nature and Nature's God. He prayed for her in ways I was sure were alien to his skeptical nature, but his words went unanswered, and as one day melted into another, Carmelita looked blanker, more depressed, and more hopeless. Maybe she belonged in Oak Ridge with the doctors; maybe theirs was the only therapy that could bring her back to life.

I felt sad for both of them—surely for her, but also for him as he fought so heroically and so alone against a secret enemy that was threatening his family and the peace he valued. Nothing worked and the apartment had a death rattle about it, day and night, and I found myself staying away. Finally a month into this, Grandpa had reached out and found Rocco who was living alone in a cheap apartment in Chatham. He demanded Rocco come over, cleaned up and fully dressed. Not by coincidence, that was also the week that my mother was watching the baby, who was now over two months old. She brought the infant to Grandpa's apartment and had him sit on her lap in the kitchen with Rocco blankly looking on. Then Grandpa let Carmelita in, all dressed up, and still looking like she was *stunad*. He sat her between this strange baby and a spruced up Rocco and began talking. He introduced the baby in an almost formal way, complementing Rocco on his care for him, and reminding Carmelita that any infant needed both parents. Then surprisingly, he admonished Carmelita that she was supposed to be breast feeding the baby, but because she had not gone home, the baby had to live off thin canned milk which explained why the infant looked slight. "See him, look at that poor fellow!"

Grandpa got up to serve some Italian cakes and coffee, almost nonchalantly as a good host would. Mom jumped up to help, but he shushed her down and continued. He talked of Grandma and their children, going through each and everyone, including those who had died. Mom was close to tears, Rocco seemed confused, and Carmelita was as blank as the day she came out of the sanitarium.

The baby began to get restless through the whole talk, and Grandpa asked me to hold his bottle up since it was "too heavy for such a small fellow." I did as he ordered, but the infant was not pacified. He cried and fussed, and Mom began to move towards him, but Grandpa cut her off. His therapy had failed, his care was for naught, and all that was left was Oak Ridge if Carmelita were lucky.

And then, almost as if on impulse, Grandpa began to open Carmelita's blouse and placed the baby in her arms, resting his face on her left breast. We were all a bit taken back by the suddenness of his action, especially in that regard, for he was in so many ways a discrete and Victorian man. But the infant latched on as if by design and began feeding time. Carmelita held him close, did not move, and yet still seemed blank. We were quiet, the baby began to fall asleep, and Grandpa for reasons unclear to me started to stack and wash the very dishes he had just put out. He emptied the uneaten cakes in the trash and washed the coffee pot while Rocco and Mom were still sipping their first cup. Then almost lost in his world, he asked Rocco and Carmelita to take the baby home, and the three of them left without a word or a nod. Grandpa sat down and reminded Mom and me once again of the story of how Grandma had saved her life in the epidemic of 1918. With an edge to his voice, he looked at Mom and remarked how Grandma knew of the stupidities of those doctors. And then with more tenderness, he stared away from us toward the back door, looking out at his garden and grape bower and wondered how she would have handled all this.

Carmelita grew better, took fine care of her baby, and stayed a wife to Rocco through good times and bad. She never recovered her sense of sweet abandon that we remembered in what seemed a thousand years ago. Yet she was normal by the conventional definition, functioned well, eventually got a job at Merck Pharmaceuticals, and lived a quiet life. To this day though she avoids driving by Oak Ridge, choosing the longer route down Shunpike Road. I read a while ago, after Grandpa's death, that electric shock had been generally replaced with some drug therapy which doctors quoted in the article had found to be "more efficacious."

46. NOE'S POND

As a boy in Italy, Grandpa loved to fish by himself in a well-stocked lake near his hometown. He would dreamily recall the verses of Petrarch written to his love, Laura. His teacher was partial to the famed poet's language, for with the immortal Dante, Petrarch was among the first great practitioners of the new Italian language. He recited Petrarch in sonnet 227 which his teacher loved. The oral tradition was important in a culture with few schoolbooks.

> Breeze blows that blond curling hair
> Stirring it, and being softly stirred in turn,
> Scattering that sweet gold about, then
> Gathering it, in a lovely knot of curls again.

> (*Aura che quelle chiome bionde et crespe*
> *Cercondi et movi, et se' mossa da loro,*
> *Soavamente, el spargi quel dolce oro,*
> *Et poi 'l raccogli, e' n bei: nodi il rincrepe.*)

Ah, Laura…

When he reached the age of 16, his father informed him that the two of them must travel briefly to the eastern United States and make some money to send home to the family. Uneasy at that stage of his life, Grandpa still went, and they roomed together at a rundown men's boarding house on North Street in Madison, New Jersey. They and their fellow immigrants worked for a belligerent, huge, angry, ruddy Irishman who generally hated "wops," as he called them. One of the tasks assigned to that work team was cutting pieces of ice for use under iceboxes in houses. Refrigerators had not yet been invented for the masses. Grandpa and his father cut ice blocks on Noe's Pond. But after five months of harassment and abuse, the Irish boss got into a fist fight with Grandpa, and soon he and his father went back home. Then three years later at 19, Grandpa came back to the United States, and stayed again in Madison, but this time worked in the huge rose greenhouses to cultivate those august flowers. The city actually embraced its nickname, "the Rose City," which it still holds today. Grandpa went on to other jobs: chauffeur, caretaker of the houses of the rich, and finally landscape gardener. In his own eyes, he had embraced the American dream. But even as an old man, he still loved fishing, and would go back to Noe's Pond, now part of a country club for the local rich, where the workers knew him and left him alone. One cold winter morning, he carefully sidestepped the ice's thin layers and sat on the pond to begin fishing.

On his right, he saw a heavy set woman ice skating, moving probably too close to the weakest spots. Suddenly she crashed through the ice and ended up in the lake, unable to climb out up to the surface. Grandpa could not swim, and he ran around looking for some object that he could use to float. He found a partially hidden Packard tire behind a tree. He abruptly grabbed it and dragged it out skillfully, walking gently out on the ice to throw it to the woman. She reached for it and pulled herself up to the ice edge where he anxiously waited for her in the dismal cold. He patiently carried her to the shore, and she seemed to have passed out. Quickly he noted that she was pregnant, and barely breathing. He had put his lips on few people except Grandma, but God forgive him, there was no choice. He gave her mouth to mouth resuscitation the way he had seen it done before.

She did not respond at first, but then she spit up water into his face, and regained consciousness. He supported her, and with their wet clothes dragging them down, he pushed her into his Ford pickup and headed for nearby Overlook Hospital. He drove as fast as he could, in his case 25 miles per hour, and pulled up almost triumphantly to the emergency entrance of the hospital. The orderlies moved quickly to change her clothes and take care of her and her fetus.

When the nurses asked her what she was doing on the ice, she told them that in her youth she had been an award-winning ice skater, and she just wanted to feel once more the pleasure of movement. It was a crazy thing to do, she admitted.

Grandpa parked the truck in the hospital garage and went in dripping wet. The nurses gave him an old doctor's uniform to wear in place of his wet clothes, and he patiently waited outside the ER. After several hours of confusion and professional care, a doctor came out and told the old man that the woman and the child were fine. And he also noted that the family had come already; they knew the woman from her husband who was a wealthy New York City broker who served on the hospital board. The doctor was secretly delighted at his colleagues' flawless responses, and he gingerly crowed.

In the hospital room, a single of course, were the husband, their two children, a priest, and their lawyer. When Grandpa walked in with his dripping boots and hospital uniform, the patient smiled and said, "So you too have joined the hospital!" Her husband looked admiringly and took Grandpa aside. He remarked how incredible was his courage and offered him a very, very generous reward in municipal bonds. Grandpa simply responded, "No, I did what anyone would do." The husband insisted, "No, most people would have walked away or called the police and watched her drown."

Grandpa just concluded, "People are not like that."

Then he nodded at the wife and wished her "and her baby to come well." He left for home, muttering, "I wished I could swim." When the lady had her baby three months later, she surprised her family by naming the baby "Ralph" after Grandpa. She found out his name and his address and sent him a card acknowledging the birth and who the little one was named after.

Her family thought that she must have named him after a rich uncle, not an Italian gardener. So it was Ralph von Cleveland III, who lived off Shunpike Road in the Hickory Tree section of Madison where the young Theodore Roosevelt used to summer.

Every Christmas Grandpa mailed the boy the same gift he gave each of his many grandchildren—a $2 bill with Thomas Jefferson's image in the center of the envelope. No one knew how he got such bills, since most people thought the U.S. Treasury had stopped printing them.

A decade later, Grandpa passed away, and was buried according to the new Catholic rites under the Vatican II rubric. He hated the new Mass, saying that with all the jumping up and down, and shaking hands with people who had a cold, he felt like a holy roller. But the Mass went on, and the young scrubbed altar boy at the service was a student from the Catholic school, Ralph von Cleveland III. In his right pants pocket, he had a $2 bill.

47. MEETING DR. EINSTEIN

The *Madison Eagle* story about Grandpa and the Victory Gardens had given him a modicum of publicity. He became in the local eyes a "master" gardener, a sobriquet he generally felt uncomfortable with. But one of the people who read the column was James Stafford III, an investment banker at Lehman Brothers and a member of the governing Board of Trustees at his alma mater, Princeton University. He was the chairman of the committee on buildings and grounds for a campus that took great pride in its elegant appearance.

But there was a persistent problem at the university which had added a wing to its beloved Firestone Library. The front strip of land would not nourish flowers as it once did. The university had a masterful buildings and grounds crew, but they were bewildered by the problem. So Stafford took matters into his own hands and decided to bring in Grandpa as a consultant to restore the campus site. Grandpa did not really know what a "consultant" was, and he could not see himself driving down the byways of Princeton for weeks in his green Ford pickup truck. But Stafford presented him with a very generous stipend and offered him a driver and car to make the trip. With that money, Grandpa could finally afford to pay for a new furnace which his apartment house desperately needed, and he was a bit enticed by being invited to the great university. So he agreed.

The first area he examined was the soil, and it had been thoroughly picked through for pieces of construction limestone, and the crew planted over it all types of flowers. None of them seemed to flourish in that spot. Grandpa stripped back the soil, looked at the mix of the ground site, and was enthralled by the beautiful surrounding Gothic buildings. As he moved back though, he felt behind him a stooped old man with wild bushy hair and a mustache, watching him and overlooking the job. He simply nodded, and then walked on as he had chosen so many days before.

One of the buildings and ground staff came up to Grandpa later, "Do you know who was watching you?"

"No."

"That was Dr. Albert Einstein who lives and works in town. Einstein is said to be the smartest man in the world."

"What work does this smartest man in the world do?" Grandpa asked.

"He thinks. He is paid to think, to think about the universe, about light and how things move above the earth. I don't fully understand it all. But I have seen his name and have watched him walking around."

"Does he teach here?"

"Oh, the students would never learn from him, and even the professors can't understand him."

The next day, Einstein came walking by again, stopping in front of the library and re-examining it since it rained the night before. At noontime, Grandpa sat on the nearby bench, opened up his lunch box, took out a cold sausage and pepper sandwich and a thermos of water. The white haired man quickly sat next to Grandpa. "Well, what are you going to do with the problem strip? I would just throw white rocks on it and forget about living things."

"I don't know quite yet. Maybe I should listen to your advice. I think I know you. You are called the smartest man in the world, they say."

Einstein laughed, "If I am the smartest man why can't I figure out the world. How does it fit together...? I can't even figure out why flowers will not grow here.... You are from Italy?"

"Yes, near Naples."

"I am from Switzerland, your neighbor over the Alps! Previously I lived in Germany, but even before the Nazis, some university professors called my work 'Jew physics,' and booed me at conferences in my own homeland. At least here people leave me alone. It is good except for those unfortunate Japanese Americans in internment camps."

Grandpa nodded, and responded, "Some camps also included Italian and German Americans. There was a family camp called Crystal City in Texas. Even in Madison, I was questioned by the local town police, by boys who knew me for forty years, who played with my children, who were friends with my nephew who died in Iwo Jima. They wanted secret information on other Italian Americans, as if we became spies in the past year. But we did not go through what the Japanese did, all for no reason."

"I did not know; you and your people should sue the government."

"No, my people are too ashamed and embarrassed. They just want to forget it and celebrate their sons in uniform."

"You should sue, sue!"

Grandpa changed the conversation abruptly, "So, you can see the stars and other places in the skies?"

"I don't actually see them; I can write their dimensions on paper. Now others use telescopes to find out if I am right. So far, I am, but I do not know how it holds together. You, of course, believe in the traditional Catholic God, a Creator."

"I don't know how traditional it is, but I do believe in God. In the mornings, I say '*Grazie a Dios sono vivo.*' Thanks be to God for letting me live another day."

"We should all do that, even if we don't believe," Einstein interjected.

Grandpa soon ran out of conversation, and then walked toward the flowerpots and kicked the dirt. There he saw the black roots of the pansies as they rotted. He had seen this before even in his own garden. The crew had covered over some lime chips, but neglected the soil's need for iron, important for plants as for people. That was why these pansies had black root rot disease. Later he had all the dirt taken out by the crew and replaced with good new soil from the farms around Princeton. He directed them to put in young fully formed pansies. The university people love the change.

Dr. Einstein watched in amazement, "You are a genius, my friend."

"No, you are the genius, I am just a gardener."

"I study the skies, you study nature. "

"I see the bounty of nature all around me. The soil is as beautiful as the sky to me. What do you see in the world around you?'

The great man solemnly pulled out a letter he was sending to his daughter Lieserl. "Listen to this, my friend: I tell her that when I proposed the theory of relativity, few understood me. But now I also believe in an extremely powerful force that science has not found an explanation for. It is the force that governs all others, it is universal LOVE. Scientists, especially me, have looked for a unified theory, but they forgot love is light, love is gravity, love unfolds and reveals. For love, we live and we die. Love is God and God is love. This force explains everything and gives meaning to life. Now I must change my famed equation and say that the energy to heal the world is from love, squared by light. Love has no limits."

Grandpa was an unlearned man and did not understand the expressions of relativity, gravity, and the need for a universal theory. But he politely nodded and wished the great man well. When he got into his car, one of the crew stopped him and asked what Einstein said to him. The old man simply concluded, "He is so smart. I don't know exactly what he said, but he talked of the power of love, and he seemed happy to leave that to his daughter."

Compiler's note: This letter was in the possession of Hebrew University of Jerusalem and was sold in 2015.

48. EVIL

One morning, Grandpa was a little late in getting started, and he sat down for a modest breakfast—dark coffee, biscotti, and a piece of fruit. Suddenly he heard the town's whining alert from the fire department go off throughout the borough. He rushed to the windows on Main Street, and there he saw young men running to their trucks and cars, abandoning their shops and businesses for volunteer fire department duty. Gerald Solano across the street came out of the chicken market and screamed, "The Church is on fire." There were a dozen churches in the borough, but to most people it meant St. Vincent Martyr Church on Green Village Road.

Grandpa got in his truck and followed them, for though he was too old to have a role, he was surely inquisitive. As he approached, the flames lapped out of the steeple, and rows of uniformed children were marching out in twos. Apparently, the nuns, who usually got attention by pressing plastic clappers, had always demanded perfect obedience from the children in the past, and this time it paid off. The altar boys left by the left side door after being sent out by Father Stephen Patch who for some reason insisted on finishing the Mass. Soon hefty timbers fell on the pews and the impressive chandelier came crashing down on the communion rail.

The volunteers put out the fire, but in the process did damage to much of the sacred insides of the church. Still the main destruction from the fire and the water was the steeple that had first gone up in flames and was later covered with tarps. The local Presbyterian Church offered its fine building for Sunday Mass for the local Catholic population. But the pastor, while grateful, held Mass for two years in the school gymnasium.

The costs for rebuilding were over $250,000—a high sum for that time and a real drain on a parish that operated a tuition free parochial school. The major question was how did this happen? The chief of police, a St. Vincent graduate, brought in the state police, and in turn they asked for assistance from the local FBI office in Newark.

Immediately during the fire and for a week after, the chief smartly had pictures taken—not of the wounded church, but of the spectators who came to look at it. Grandpa was in several of them. But the chief believed that the fire was suspicious, not simply faulty wiring as some postulated. He looked at more pictures and tried to find common figures in those shots. In four of them he found Johnny De Soto, a public works employee, a young man whose parents had died together in a terrible car crash on Route 22. He frequented some local watering holes and cheap pizza places, but always alone. He had once applied for a gun permit, but the police turned it down, saying he did not have a business or handle cash. The chief had De Soto brought into his conference room and said directly, "Look, you son of a bitch, we know you burned the church."

De Soto vigorously denied it. But after the chief worked him over with a few well-placed shots to the belly, he began to melt under the withering examination. "I demand a lawyer."

"There are no lawyers this week in Jersey, they are all at a bar association convention at Atlantic City."

"I don't even go to that church, why would I want to burn it down?"

The chief started slapping his young face back and forth until De Soto cried out, "Yes, yes, I did it, and I am happy I did."

The chief looked quietly into his eyes, "Why would you burn a church?"

"Because I want to show everyone in town there is no God. And I knew that at 8 a.m. it would be full of children, and I wanted to see burning, crying children, hear their anguish, smell their flesh, and let them see that God is a fool. God is dead, ain't you heard, chief?"

The chief just wrote down all he said and handed it to Johnny for his signature without emotion. "Any remorse, Johnny?"

"Yes, I'm sorry those little bastards got out safely, each and every one of them. Goddamn nuns. "

At home Grandpa was upset at the destruction of a church built by generations of Italians with little money to spare. Grandpa had planted all the flower boxes around it. Now they were covered with ash.

That troubling night he watched his black and white Dumont 12 inch television. It was situated in a huge piece of furniture, but it was still an impressive sight. He watched on it some of his favorite programs: *Perry Mason* and *Gunsmoke*, although they were not on that night. Instead he watched a history of the Nazi concentration camps, a gruesome topic, which confused and fascinated him.

What especially got to him was that the Nazis accumulated shoes of the victims, and there was one pile which had tiny shoes belonging to young children. That image more than any other stayed with him, except for the wrought iron German slogan over the entrance, "*Arbeit macht frei,*" "Work will make you free." They never understood the dignity of work; for them it was punishment and death.

Two weeks after the fire, the fire chief and the chief of police decided to have an open public meeting with the parishioners to explain what they knew. With the pastor looking on quietly, they went through stage by stage the skillful search, careful interrogation, and the final confession of one of the borough's own. The people were shocked. The Italians could not conceive how one of their sons would hurt the church where his parents were married and he himself was baptized. It was, they screamed, "*contra natura*," a crime against the laws of nature.

The younger yuppies, who were buying up homes so they could be nearer to commute to New York City on the railroad, argued that his action was due to the fact he was poor, alienated, and cut off from society. Why hadn't the church and the borough officials noted that before and helped? He was a victim of his environment. That was the reason for his actions.

Then the fire chief quietly reminded them that De Soto had given his motive himself—he wished to see the children—their children—burn alive.

Grandpa rarely spoke at such meetings. He was not educated like the Falcones or Volpe the fox. But for some reason, it all came together, and he rose up and spoke:

"I have listened carefully to what has been said. I knew John's parents and they were good Catholics who fasted during Advent as well as Lent, who gave their boy an education, offered to send him to the university up here, but he couldn't get in. They used all their friendships to get him a job in public works and waited for the day they would have grandchildren. Such is the cycle of life.

"But the boy is a bad seed, he chose to be alone and then to hate being alone. The chief tells us he wanted to burn children to death. Oh, Johnny, you can burn down our church, but we will rebuild it. But our children, Oh God, may He have mercy on your soul. But then you cry out that God is dead. I say He is not.

"Johnny was not poor or neglected or suffering from mental illness, as our new parishioners say. He was simply evil, for in this time there are two forces: good and evil. I know, for I too have fought the Devil. I was one who did not believe in evil. Is it simply, as you say, mental illness? No, it is evil, the Devil lives. I am a child of this 20th century and have seen his handiwork in all its destruction. Why is it Johnny says God is dead, but not the Devil is dead? For he knew the truth."

And then he abruptly sat down and applause rang out to his embarrassment. He left quickly at the end while the discussion continued and degenerated as it usually does.

At home, he was exhausted, and his back hurt him, and then there was a knock at the door. It was Isaac across the hall. He had heard about the church and gave Grandpa an ice cream roll from the Bottle Hill Tavern kitchen.

Grandpa gratefully cut two huge slices of the cake, and the two of them savored it—one of the few treats of old age. Grandpa told Isaac the whole story of the meeting, and as his neighbor looked so sad, Grandpa stopped. Then Isaac asked if he ever had heard the story of the rabbi who went home after the war to his temple in Warsaw. There in the rubble, in the near darkness was an old crumpled man. The rabbi recognized him, "Yahweh, why are you lying here in the corner?" And He answered, "I am sick, sick until death of the human race I created."' Grandpa simply nodded, and then said aimlessly, "little shoes."

Isaac countered that he had once visited Auschwitz and saw a tiny buttercup in the rocky road, creeping up between the rocks. He took it and put it in his passport. He still had it.

"Why did you do that?"

"Because I needed to show that the good forces of life go on."

Months later, work on the church continued. The old Italians who knew stone cutting and mural painting volunteered to help the contractors, and the young men learned much from the old timers. The women of the parish crocheted lace for altar coverings to replace the ones ripped apart and burnt in the fire. And Grandpa went to the flower beds and replanted the flowers as before, but added a statue of the Infant of Prague, baby Jesus. In life, one does what one does best, and so on that day he reaffirmed the good. But somehow it did not seem enough to him. The evil that men do is so huge, so long-lasting, so frequent, and the good accomplished by men seems so modest.

49. THE BULLY

Grandpa's grandson, Marcus, could easily walk from St. Vincent Martyr Elementary School to his parents' apartment on Main Street. He was a quiet fourth grader who was studious, but not a great student. He was a bit shy but sensitive to the slights of the world. For some reason he had incurred the hatred of a town bully, Barry Cramer, who made a career out of harassing him on the short trip home. Cramer was what the nuns called a "public school boy," a nominal Catholic kid who went to the nearby public school. Whenever he saw Marcus, he screamed his promise that someday he would beat the stuffing out of him. The pleasure for him was making Marcus's life frighteningly uncertain. It was a great source of joy for unkempt Barry.

Every afternoon he would seek him out and confront Marcus as if that were the day of reckoning. And then he would arrogantly walk away, mission accomplished. Marcus tried going home two different ways, but once he reached Main Street, he could see Cramer waiting, waiting, waiting. In the afternoon Marcus would run toward home and end up panting as he reached the backyard. This had happened several times, and Grandpa said nothing, believing that his grandchildren were the responsibility of his children and should be spared another level of adult supervision. But this time, he asked what was spooking Marcus so. Totally frazzled, he related all, and admitted that he never told his parents for they would think he was a coward or a sissy.

The old man just stared at him and told him that later he should come back to the warehouse where he kept his tools and his gallons of wine. Then Grandpa went across the back fence and visited his friend, Danny Wilson. Everyone knew Wilson was a famous high school basketball player, but in his youth he was also a contender for the middleweight championship in boxing in New Jersey. He knew Tony "Two Ton" Galento of Orange who had almost knocked out the great Joe Louis in 1939. Later Danny taught boxing to youngsters at the Madison Boys Club. Grandpa explained the situation, and Danny promised to meet with the boy at the warehouse after work the next day. Then he told Grandpa to use his name and go to the local boxing ring and ask to borrow two sets of old boxing gloves, one size large, and a boxing bag.

Grandpa did so early in the morning, even neglecting to water his garden that day. The grizzled-looking attendant with a woolen cap resting on the top of his head sarcastically said to the old man, "So, who you gonna challenge—the champ—old timer? Remember your timing." Grandpa came home and attached the top of the chain that held the boxing bag, and it dropped to about five feet. Grandpa aimlessly looked at it and gave it a random punch with his bare fist, and it bounced back toward his face.

When early evening came, Grandpa, Marcus, and finally Danny Wilson showed up, and Grandpa explained Danny's background to his grandson, which Marcus only knew because of his basketball records at the high school. Danny took Marcus in hand, showed him how to move his legs, how to cover his face from the opponent's blows, and then how to throw different types of punches. He showed Marcus how to use the bag to increase his range and how to dodge and weave. They did that for three nights in a row, as Grandpa sat on a pile of burlap bags watching the lessons. After all these years, Danny was still in some ways lithe and agile, and Marcus began imitating his easy ways each night.

Finally a week or so later, Marcus was on his way home from school, walking by the Municipal Building across from the vest pocket park with the drinking fountain. Out from behind a maple tree jumped the Cramer kid who started, "Hey faggot, this is your day, you little St. Vincent fairy." He moved increasingly close toward Marcus, with his hands up, and his rotten teeth showing. Then for Marcus, this was the time. He wheeled back and aimed his closed fist at Cramer's face. He missed his face, but he hit him squarely in the center of his shoulder joint. Cramer fell back, grabbed his arm and started crying loudly. All of sudden a haggard-looking woman appeared from nowhere and denounced Marcus, "You bully boy. How could you hit my son for no reason? I'll go across the street and get the police. Come here son, away from that bully."

Cramer went away with his mother and whimpered along as they went up the hill. Marcus felt taller and stronger than before. Once in the backyard, he told Grandpa who was trimming a cherry tree what had happened. The old man smiled and said, "He will not bother you again, that is the way with bullies. I want you to go and thank Mr. Wilson and give him a gallon of my best wine."

So Marcus made his way to Pearson's Lane and rang the doorbell. Danny appeared with a grin and listened to Marcus's proud tale. He nodded and then took the gallon graciously, and philosophically observed, "Your grandfather is a great man. He is beloved here for what he has done for the neighborhood and has carefully taken care of people; most people don't know everything he has done for many others as well. But because he is so good himself, he sometimes forgets that to deal with some people, you have to keep your right up. If you don't, the bullies will rule the world, and we would all be speaking German. Keep your right up, son."

50. SEMPER FI
To: Nick

Marcus parked his Ford Fairlane in Grandpa's driveway, jumped out and walked down the black macadam path toward the garden. The driveway lay on one side of Grandpa's apartment home, on the other side was a cyclone fence that separated his land from his son's auto body repair shop. Marcus called for Grandpa, and saw him bent over, weeding the little rosebush planted in memory of his second daughter, his favorite, who had died at 26 of some female disease Grandpa still did not understand.

Marcus called to him, and Grandpa proudly responded, "*Vieni qui,*" and he then opened the two aluminum chairs he had and placed them overlooking the tomato plants. "How are you Marcus? How is college?"

"It is fine, fine Grandpa. I see you have gotten a contract to work on some of the public playgrounds in Madison. Big job, huh?"

"Yes, it is a fine contract."

"I was wondering if you needed some help?"

"You and I working together, that would be fine. It is hard work, my son."

"No, I was thinking more of a friend, the Joey Esposito kid. You know his parents on Springfield Avenue."

"Yes, but the son is a favored war hero and he is decorated and respected. Surely his parents will not want him to work as my assistant. Besides, doesn't the government find such men jobs?'

"He has nothing else, Grandpa, except for a Korean wife he brought back home."

"But surely the government takes care of them: they give them education, mortgages and free medical care." Grandpa went quiet, and then said to Marcus, "Tell him I would be proud to be with him. Have him meet me here, Monday at 7 a.m. How did you meet him?"

When Monday morning came, Joey arrived at 6:30 a.m., ready to get going. Grandpa treated him with respect, and they drove to the Castle Playground at 66 Shunpike Road off Green Village Road to begin a day's labor. In the hot sun, Joey took off his tee shirt, but not his gloves. His muscled body bore scars from shrapnel, and his back had the lines of lash marks. In Korea, he had been trained as a sniper, able to take the highest ground and pick off Korean sentries. He was an unerring shot, and he was careful to safeguard the children who looked like little Korean Communists below.

Then one afternoon, he was captured by a North Korean patrol, and shipped off to a prison camp run by the Communist Chinese. They enjoyed their trophy captive and whipped him with leather thongs and put on him a U.S. general's hat. He refused to communicate with them, even to ask for water. Then one, day, the interpreter pushed tiny slits of bamboo shoots under his finger and foot nails. The nails turned black bloody, and he refused to scream in pain. His interrogators laughed, and a translator told him that the next night they would drive a piece of bamboo into his penis tip. They genuinely enjoyed the art of torture. They wanted him though to first think over and over again of his fate, for the anticipation of pain made the real thing even worse.

But early in the morning he heard American B-52 bombers shelling the area around the camp, and very soon a battalion of Marines arrived, and liberated the camp. Semper Fi. They brought the Communists together and hung them upside down alive, and let the sun do its duty.

Joey was flown off to a U.S. hospital in Tokyo for treatment. The physical pain passed, but he was overwhelmed with night terrors. They put him in a ward that dealt with his nightmares by giving him heavy pain killers. For three weeks he was nursed full time by a Korean aide, the dispenser of drugs and then one night love.

The Corps transported him home first class as a much decorated hero. His parents were proud of him but avoided speaking to his so-called wife. He barely lived off his GI pension, and only got a two room apartment on North Street because the renter had a boy in the Corps also. Joey applied to the Veteran's Hospital in East Orange, one of the worst facilities in the system. They had him wait for three months, and then said he had old-fashioned "shell shock," and time would heal all wounds. It is simply a matter of patience, they insisted. He would fit in sooner or later. But as he and his wife knew, three in the morning was hell on wheels.

Grandpa would bring water and a spare sub of sausage and peppers, but Joey preferred to just sit under large maple trees and read the beautiful lyrics of Edna St. Vincent Millay, whom he had studied in college. He could sometimes read aloud, and Grandpa could hear him say:

> Long had I lain thus, craving death,
> When quietly the earth beneath
> Gave way, and inch by inch, so great
> At last had grown the crushing weight,

Into the earth I sank till I
Full six feet underground did lie,
And sank no more,—there is no weight
Can follow here, however great.
From off my breast I felt it roll,
And as it went my tortured soul
Burst forth and fled in such a gust
That all about me swirled the dust.

Grandpa wasn't sure that he understood all the words, but he loved the sound of the words. It was like Dante. Then one afternoon Joey inquired, "I understand you lost a nephew in the Marine Corps?"

"Yes, he died in the first wave that hit the beaches at Iwo Jima," Grandpa sadly related, "He was only 19. He is buried in southern New Jersey in a veteran's cemetery near the coast."

"Do you ever wonder why I always wear gloves?"

"No, it is hard work. I figured you did not want to cut your hands."

Joey then told him the story of his torture and pulled off the gloves to show him his horrendous black-blooded fingers. He concluded, "My toenails are like that too. They were going to put bamboo shoots up my cock, but then the Marines overran the camp."

Grandpa shuttered as he looked at the fingers and thought of driving bamboo shoots inside of himself. "I'm sorry."

"It is what it is. At least the Marines didn't leave me. Leave no man behind."

"Yes, in the case of my nephew, they returned the remains of his body, but he lost his spirit that day on that man-forsaken island. Even his parents refused to look at the remains. Only God knows him."

"I left my God in the prison camp with the gooks."

Grandpa quietly walked away, and then turned around, "But you are a real hero, the government should take care of you."

"That was yesterday, new men come in to take our place and are chewed up, and we are told to melt in and man up."

"What does your wife say?"

"She is going to divorce me and move back to Tokyo."

"Oh no, no more tragedy, my dear Joey. Please come next Sunday over to my daughter's house on Green Avenue, we are having the whole family over for brunch, and I want them to meet a genuine hero in the service of his country. "

"Thank you, Mr. Finelli, but I'd rather be at home when I am not working. My wife sees little enough of me. I am not much for socializing since Korea."

"As you wish." Joey worked for a month for Grandpa, was well paid for his efforts, and then stopped showing up. A week later, Grandpa heard that he was looking for some easy cash, and he had tried to hold up Rose City Liquors, using his old service revolver, supposedly a souvenir. But he was soon caught and arrested. For some reason the Morris County prosecutor fast tracked the trial.

Then to his surprise, Grandpa was subpoenaed to be a character witness for Joey. Marcus had refused to get involved. Joey's attorney was a public defender with one year experience, and he had nobody else but Grandpa. Grandpa of course put on his only suit, wore an Arrow white shirt, and a striped tie he had for funerals, and took the #70 bus to the Morristown Court house.

He took the stand early. He was asked what he knew of the boy, and he told them all—his fine family, his seriousness as an altar boy, his time in college, his war record, his decorations for bravery and valor, and how he had worked hard for him for a month. He told also of his marital troubles, and of night terrors that Joey had related to him.

But then Grandpa, not known for his public speaking said to the judge whom he had been acquainted with for years, "Please, your honor, you know I am a working man, but as an American living in this great nation, I wish to speak. He left a good family, and we taught him to kill. He was rewarded for his patriotism, for fighting for his country in a war no one wanted. And when he came home, we did not even provide him with a modest job, and so his wife left him alone in a dirty two room apartment. She did nothing. But he continued on, and despite his service, he grew too weary and robbed a liquor store for quick cash with a gun with no bullets in it. He did everything right, and yet, your honor, he came out wrong. That should not be. It should not be. We need a new story. America needs a new story. Put him back in my care, let me be responsible for him. We will live together, eat together, and he can room in my apartment."

The judge looked sadly at him, and Grandpa was dismissed without the prosecutor being given any chance to cross-examine. Joey just smiled weakly as Grandpa left. The jury was quick in its verdict. It found him guilty, and the judge sent him to jail for sentencing next week.

The guards took him out of the courtroom, down the polished hallway, opened the elevator door, and he quickly stepped in. But there was no floor, and he tumbled down the shaft, and then the car followed crushing him to death.

Later Grandpa heard of his fate and was in deep mourning. Marcus came over and told him the full story, and then surprisingly gave the old man the copy of Millay's poems. Grandpa couldn't really read them, but Marcus said, "You know she was a vixen, Grandpa."

"Vixen."

"A *putana*, sort of."

"Oh."
"Listen to her description of life:"

My candle burns at both ends,
It will not last the night,
But ah, my foes, and ah, my friends—
It gives a lovely light!"

Grandpa listened, and for the first time he started to hear his own laughter, "What a vixen she was, Marcus."

51. O'SOSTEA—THE SYSTEM

Grandpa had gotten a major contract to help clean up the Madison Parks in time for the Fourth of July. Although it was a lot of work, he had loved the Fourth ever since he came to America. He bought a small flag and hung it out on the back porch, and he would read the Declaration of Independence on that day out of respect for his new country.

One day he was outside trying to figure out how to recement the sidewalks in front of the apartment house. Jersey was so terrible in the winter and then so hot in the summer that the cement cracks just opened and closed, leaving spaces that were dangerously uneven for walkers. While he was looking at the mess, he was approached by Gerardo Antonucci an old acquaintance who had come over with him on the boat, the *Celtic*. They were not close friends but good acquaintances over the years, stopping often to talk of the weather and the family.

"Raffaele, *come stai?*"

"I am good and you, my friend?"

"I am fine, but the aches and pains are fighting my good humor. I have come to ask you for your advice."

Grandpa loved to give advice. It was a sign of respect, and also it was free.

"My grandson Frederico graduated last week from Madison High School. And now he has nothing to do. He is not very bright, and so he cannot go to college. I even tried to pay them extra for tutoring assistance, but he was rejected by Drew and Fairleigh Dickinson. His mother cried all week. He has no skills and cannot make a living like we did—an honest living with his hands."

"I know the problem. The smartest people in my family are the girls, and I am hoping they marry some rich men, not some yucca head. How did our wives raise such boys who now believe they are princes?"

"So true, Raffaele, so true. I want him to work hard, and was wondering with your new contracts, if you could use a hardworking boy with a strong back as a helper. I will pay you money on the side to take him but don't tell him. Please, my friend."

Now Grandpa was not very good at saying no, so he nodded and told him to have his son at the apartment on Friday. Gerardo was so grateful, that he thanked Grandpa over and over again in two languages.

When they met, Gerardo was right—the kid was not too swift, but he had a pleasant personality and one could live with that. They began working on the grounds of the schools, and they looked beautiful when the job was done. Then one day, Grandpa was relaxing and heard a loud intimidating knock on the door. He opened it and saw a tall, thin, young man with a black shirt with French cuffs, and a Luger in his hand. He pushed Grandpa over to the edge of the sink and said authoritatively, "Listen to me, we're the new Camorra in this area and we are hunting for talent. We have decided to take into our system, the Antonucci kid. He will be a runner for us. He will move narcotics from Canada through Providence to North Carolina. He will be seen as a furniture man from Asheville. We will surely pay him more than you will. If you get in the way, this is what you will get." And he put the gun into the old man's mouth.

Grandpa did not move. But for some reason, he demanded, "Get out of my house."

The old man was fearful, but he insisted on saying, "You Mafioso. You have given us a bad name for a hundred years. There are twenty-six million Italians in this country, only 6,000 are Mafioso. Yet it is you that get all the television and movies. You defame us all."

"Shut up or you will join your beloved wife. Say nothing to the boy. Just fire him so he will work for us."

Grandpa knew that Lucky Luciano had friends in Madison, and that District Attorney Thomas Dewey had chased him out of New York City, but the Roosevelt administration had worked with him in the last war to counter Mussolini in southern Italy. Suddenly the murderer was a patriot! Then as he continued his reign of terror, they sent him back to Naples. "What an infamy," the old man once had said to his wife.

The hood vanished, and a shaken Grandpa sat down not sure what to. He was not a man of violence, but he knew that he was not going to throw this young naïve boy to the wolves. He sat and thought, and then went into the bedroom where he had a statue of the greatest warrior in history, St. Michael the Archangel. St Michael had headed up the good angels who raised an army to support Almighty God and cast Lucifer, the most powerful archangel, into the bowels of hell. Stories tell us that St. Michael barely beat the forces of evil, but in the end, he became the patron saint of warriors of decency and vigor.

He took the statute and put it on his oil clothed table and prayed to him in the old prayers of Pope Leo XIII.

Sancta Michael Archangel,

Defende nos in proello, olio
Contra neguitiam et insidias diabolic esto. prasidium
Impart ill Dues, suppliesces deprecamur

Saint Michael Archangel,
Defend us in battle
Be our protection against the wickedness and snares of the devil
May God rebuke him, we humbly pray…

There he looked at the plaster of Paris statue originally done as a model in 1636 by Guido Reni in Rome. It was a telling of St Michael with his sword in one hand and his foot on the head of the devil, which Grandpa swore looked just like what he had experienced.

He said nothing to the boy, hoping that as in much of life, it is best to forget and hope afflictions just go away. He had received though a letter from Don Gallo, the local boss, which warned him that these young men were different from the old Mafiosi. They worked for the boss of bosses, in Providence, Rhode Island. Then a month later, he heard the same knock on the door, and he answered it. It was the same thug, only angrier. Grandpa was pushed into his kitchen table where he had a hammer he was using to nail up a picture of Grandma. The thug warned him, "I am here to no longer deal with you. You will now join her."

But Grandpa reached around, grabbed his old rusty hammer and smashed it into the thug's arm, who felt it break, and in fear he dropped his gun. Grandpa reached over and put his bread knife in his hallow of his neck. "If you move, it is you who will join Satan. Now I want from you a promise that you will leave us alone."

"Yes, yes."

"Your word is nothing. Swear by St Michael that if you lie, your dead mother will be received into the hottest circle of hell, where the real devils live, where even Dante is afraid, into the inferno, *the infernum*. A mother's curse is here on a revolting son. Swear it before St. Michael."

And he did and then ominously enough, the statue fell down and cracked in dozen pieces. The hood took it as a sign from God, and he ran out the door.

Actually Grandpa had dragged his foot along and the plastic tablecloth pulled the statute off the corner, and it was destroyed. Grandpa was upset that this was necessary, but he accepted it as a sign of God.

And so that was his sole acquaintance with the Camorra, or then called the System, the new mob whose fathers were the accursed ones in old Naples.

On September 29, months after the distasteful confrontation, Grandpa received a well-wrapped package mailed from Providence, Rhode Island. He pulled out all the paper and straw, and there was a beautiful statue of St. Michael, and in Italian script was the Biblical saying. "Be strong in the Lord and in the strength of his might." Grandpa had won a tiny battle against Satan, and he took St Michael and put it back in the bedroom.

52. THE NEXT GENERATION

Grandpa had two activities he enjoyed in his life as a gardener: picking cherries off his four magnificent trees and the processing of grapes to make wine. But as the years passed, he was too shaky to climb the high ladder to the top of the trees, and also seemed to lack the stamina to hand press all those grapes for wine. He became increasingly reliant on younger men to perform these tasks under his demanding directions. But they lacked the enjoyment of manual labor, the great feeling of hard work well done. Besides some of his grandsons were off to college, trying desperately to break out of blue collar work. Another had gone on to be a priest, a calling not known for its work ethic, especially parish priests. Still another, a good worker, had fallen in love with one of a town's *putanas*, and he snuck around all night to see how unfaithful she was.

Grandpa was forced to rely on his youngest son, who was a hardworking mechanic but did not like garden work. One day, Grandpa watched the cherry trees open up right under his view. If he saw them, his personal foes the black crows would smell them. He rushed to his youngest son and begged him to pick the cherries tonight, this afternoon if he could. But the son was in the middle of rebuilding a transmission, a good paying job, and he promised, "Yeah, yeah, sure, as soon as possible, Pop." He continued to put off the task, and then at dusk the black crows invaded like a plague from the Old Testament called down by Moses.

They came and came and picked the trees apart almost methodically. There were few cherries left, and then to add to the insult they shit all over Grandpa's truck with their purple droppings. The bastards did it deliberately. Grandpa was dismayed, where was his son?

The next day he said nothing but reminded his youngest son that he was going to the Farmers' Market in Newark to buy white and red grapes for the making of wine. The pressing of the grapes should begin as soon as possible. He asked his son again to please take some time, get a group of his young virile friends together for a couple of hours, and take the wine press and carefully feed the grapes basket by basket. Not too hard though, for the blades will cut into the tannin and make the wine bitter. So he explained it, and his son said, "Yeah, I will get to it as soon as I can. Sorry about the cherries, Pop, but I'm try to make a living here, and time just passes by."

But week after week, his son saw what a huge job he had in front of him, and where could he get relatives or even friends to come over to press personally those grapes? Besides he was a mechanic not a man of nature, so he attached a strap to the handle of the press and then hooked it up to a gas-powered motor to run the machine. The wine press began to move the handle faster and faster, and soon the total job was done. The wine was pressed, the gallons filled up and pilled against the walls. He then took the engine away and went back to his real work and real life.

Much later, Grandpa proudly looked at his son's work, let it ferment for a while, and then suddenly decided to try one glass of the new wine. As he sipped it, it was bitter, so he spit it out and tried another gallon. The same. Had he brought bad grapes in Newark, he wondered, but he went to the same farmer year after year, and then he looked at the wine press, maybe it was too old. But soon he realized that the pressing of the grapes was too harsh, too abrupt, and he came to the judgment that his son had ruined his wine somehow.

His son had pressed the grapes, so the tannin mixed with the wonderful fragrance of the outside grape. An angry Grandpa pranced over to his son's garage and asked him what he had done to the wine, and he then was treated to an explanation of the power of technology over nature. But Grandpa called him a lazy fool, said he walked through life *stunad*, and took the gallon and threw it at the garage wall, sending glass and red wine all over the area.

That night he was beside himself. All those years he had worked on the making of wine, people came to drink it, and asked for extra gallons for their friends, and now when he needed a little help everybody, including his sons, vanished. The only person who had ever encouraged him was Grandma, who would tell him, "This is the best wine I have ever tasted, even in Naples." Or "These cherries are so full and ripe, tonight I will make you *two* special cherry pies." But she was long gone. He had tried all those years to live without her, to live by himself independently, but the nights were too long and the days barren.

Then he realized that he would have no wine even for himself. He might as well go to the A&P and buy Manischewitz or some other inferior wine. He suddenly speculated that he could ask his kind brother-in-law, whom everyone called Zio Nada, for some gallons to tide him through the year. He was a gentle, hardworking fellow who had married Grandpa's sister who was a widow with five children. Grandpa had watched him as he gently raised another man's children. And when Zio Nada came to America, Grandpa helped him become a fine American citizen, one of Zio Nada's greatest honors. He raised his family in Madison, took any dependable work he could find, finally retired at 75 and lived quietly with one of his daughters.

Grandpa rode up to North Street and stopped by to see him. He wanted some wine, but he also needed a person to talk to. When he finished Zio Nada offered him four gallons of his prime wine, and said, "I am honored to make such a gift to a person who had done so much for me." But he warned Grandpa to keep the gallons hidden from the rest of the family, which he did. As they gently placed the wine of life in his pickup, Zio Nada remarked, "You know, Raffaele a mother can raise nine children, but nine children cannot take care of a mother. The same is true of a papa."

Grandpa looked up at him, and just responded, "Amen, my friend, so it is."

53. THE CHAMP

Grandpa came home to wash up at the end of the workday and didn't feel like preparing dinner. He had some leftover pasta e fagioli, but he was tired of preparing his usual dinner for one, and disliked eating leftovers. He decided instead to go to the center of Main Street and have a few slices of pizza at Caesar's Pizza Palace which did not have a liquor license. So he grabbed a small bottle of wine and made his way down the front stairs carefully, stopping at his mailbox on the wall near the front door. In those days mail was delivered twice a day, especially in the center of town, and as usual he got bills and more bills.

As he walked slowly up Main Street, he went past the chicken market, where even as a young man, he hated the smells, past the gauche fashion hat store, and the dated drug store with three of its neon letters out. It looked familiar, at times too familiar, like a village in the paese. He ambled into the Pizza Palace, and he saw the bust of Julius Caesar greeting him. The old man thought, *How sad, the great conqueror relegated to a mediocre pizza parlor, the conqueror as a maître d'.*

He went up to Sammy and ordered two slices of plain cheese pizza well done and asked for a glass for his own wine. He quietly sat down and listened to the juke box which was featuring somebody else's selection with Mel Tome singing on and on. As he poured wine into the dirty glass, he looked around the pizzeria and saw the same posters on the wall, especially the one featuring a complete map of Italy, and he always looked with pride to the designation "Napoli." The remnants of today's pizza were reheated, and Sammy gave it to him without a nod. The palace was full that night of undiscriminating customers, quietly chatting about nothing important.

Then in walked in a tall, muscular, good looking black man with short hair. He was trying to locate a seat, and then was going to order, but people leaned their vacant seats toward the table to indicate they were supposedly taken. The black man looked confused, and then realized it was the usual slight. Even in this small cracker town, race was a factor in getting a slice.

But Grandpa, watching the entrance, motioned to the black man and pointed to a seat at his table for two. The stranger came over, nodded gratefully, and sat down. Grandpa simply said, "There is no table service at this place," and he would order for him at the counter. "What do you want, son?"

"Two slices of cheese pizza and an orange drink."

Grandpa thought, *It is true, blacks love orange soda.* He went up to Sammy leaning on the counter, "Two slices and an orange drink."

Sammy replied, "You serving a *moulinyan* now, Ralph?"

The old man hated that expression, "Just give me the slices and the drink. Your pizza ain't nothing to brag about, you should welcome any customers."

Sammy quickly gave him the order right out of the oven and pointed to the cooler for the orange soda, "Hope you guys enjoy the orange soda," he snickered.

Grandpa quickly put the tray down in front of the black man and sat down to finish his own wine. "Thank you, you didn't have to do that. What do I owe you?"

"Don't worry, it's on the house. You're not from here?"

"No, I work over at Myersville, up off Springfield Avenue through New Providence and Summit."

"I know the area, some great farms up there."

"Do you know who I am, mister?"

"No, should I?"

"I am Floyd Patterson, the heavyweight boxing champion of the world, and I am training this year in the old converted farm in Myersville."

"You seem too young to be a boxing champion."

"I was 21, the youngest man ever to win the title."

"At 21, that's incredible."

"I started boxing in the Olympics, but Cus D'Amato, my manager, said it was time to go professional, and when Rocky Marciano retired, I had my big chance."

"I remember Marciano, the 'Rock from Brockton.'"

"Yes, he and Louis were the greatest."

"You train every day?" Grandpa thought as he made small talk, *This guy is tall, handsome and well proportioned. I never looked half that good in my prime.*

"Six days a week, I desired today to get away from all the handlers, the stooges, and the endless grind, and I ended up here, hungry. People think being an athlete is glamorous. It is 90% dirty work."

"Who are you fighting next?"

"A Swedish guy, Johansson. Frankly, the heavyweight champion of the world is fearful of him. Can you believe I know fear so personally?"

The old man looked at Patterson quizzically and remarked philosophically, "I am a lot older than you. We all know fear. I face it every day—fear of the unknown and fear of the known that has hurt me in the past, fear of death and disease, and especially of loneliness... My wife died, you know?"

"I'm sorry, my parents in Oklahoma are both dead already. Cus is like a father to me, a father who takes 20% of my winnings."

"Is he worth it?"

"Oh yeah, he is the best trainer in the country. How else would I be champ at my age? But I fear I will become known as the youngest man ever to lose the crown."

"You are already a champion, no one can take it from you."

"Listen, why don't you come up and watch me train. It's right up the road. I will give them your name and you can come right away. You will be a celebrity on the farm!"

The old man was delighted, and then humbly bussed the plates on the table, and they left.

As they moved by Caesar's bust, Sammy yelled out, "Hey Ralph, how was the orange drink?"

"The same as usual Sammy, everything is the same. Oh, by the way, would you like to meet my friend, Floyd Patterson?"

"Oh, Jesus H. Christ, I did not recognize you. Floyd Patterson, the great boxer, welcome, welcome champ, please come anytime. The food will be free, and so will be the drink," Sammy crowed. And then they exited out the broken wood screen door.

In a week's time, Grandpa made his way to the training camp and was let into the farm by a guard who seemed to know his name. The guard led him to the huge barn which had been turned into a gymnasium. He saw a regular sized ring, young men skipping rope, shadow boxing, and lifting weights. A grizzly old timer screamed at Patterson, "Jesus Christ, Pat, peek a boo, peek a boo, can't you cover your face? Johansson will go for your pretty face, he wants your throne, always dodge and hit him low, be agile, peek a boo."

Then D'Amato looked at Grandpa, "Christ, I hope you ain't today's sparring partner!"

"No, I am just here to see Mr. Patterson. He invited me to visit."

"You don't look like a newspaperman; I don't want the press here. You are a distraction to the champ."

"I am just a gardener. This was once a great farm."

"It will probably go back to that soon if we don't win."

Patterson heard the exchange and just shuddered. He waved to Grandpa in recognition.

So the fight came, Patterson was beaten, and he was hurt in a depressing bout. Grandpa watched the fight on his black and white television, but the next year, 1960, he saw Patterson back as the champion, the only man ever to win back the heavyweight crown. Patterson continued to be a major boxer, and afterwards moved home to New Paltz, New York. He became the head of the New York Boxing Commission, and the high school named a modest field after the great champion. By then he had a falling out with D'Amato and was training his own son to fight professionally. At age 70, he died of complications from Alzheimer's—a penalty that boxers were increasingly seeing as a casualty of a career in the ring.

54. SAN GENNARO

As all Americans know, the U.S. mail is basically monopolized by ads no one wants and solicitations for charitable gifts from organizations you never heard of. Grandpa went down the fourteen front stairs at 81 Main Street to get the afternoon mail, and there he found in the usual junk mail a real letter with a postmark on it from San Francisco. He was surprised, for he knew few people came from that city. He opened the envelope carefully after he threw away the ads from the A&P and the latest request for money from the Diocese of Juneau. The letter was from Susan, his granddaughter, whom he had visited several years ago in California. She was at that time a high-ranking executive with the chocolate factory, Ghirardelli.

In the letter she was informing him that she was being sent by the company to Italy for six months to study Italian confectionary recipes and wondered if they could meet there since they had so much fun in San Francisco. Grandpa thought a bit, and then realized that frankly he was getting tired of the sibling rivalry breaking out lately in his family in Madison and maybe needed, even at his age, a change of scenery. She asked if they could meet at the September 21 feast day of San Gennaro (Januarius) in Naples, not far from where he and Grandma grew up. In fact, Grandma's family was still in Benevento where San Gennaro was once a famed bishop before he was martyred by Emperor Diocletian in the fourth century.

The story was that after he was killed, a pious lady collected some samples of his blood, and her vials are revered by the faithful to this day. The reason was that several times a year, the bishop of Naples, then a cardinal, would bring out the vials and they would suddenly liquefy and then after several days go solid. If they liquefied, then the people would have a good year, if not a tough year was in store for the people of Naples. It was a pious tradition carried over into the New York City and New Jersey area by the Napolitanos; the parade in New York City became immortalized later in Francis Ford Coppola's *Godfather II*.

Grandpa became more excited as he pondered a trip and made reservations on his own with Pan American Airlines from New York to Rome and then a smaller airline to Naples. In those days, people who traveled went in style, not in jeans or in sweatpants. He looked at his only suit and was embarrassed by its age and wear, and so he went up Route 22 to

Robert Hall to get a suit coat with two pants, a famed special of theirs. Still he needed a good hat and he went up to see the Rose City Formal Shop and bought a bowler hat and felt both the suit and hat served him well.

When he finally arrived in Naples, he moved slowly through the gates with his beat-up suitcase and was stopped by a half-dozen taxi drivers who wanted to take this obvious American anywhere he wanted.

"Where are you from?"

"Rotondi," Grandpa responded.

"I am from there too. Jump in and we will visit home. It is only an hour away."

"I don't know the address anymore. My name though is Finelli."

"Finelli, that is my name!"

But even Grandpa was not naive enough to play that game. "Just take me to the cathedral."

"Ah, you here for feast day? It will be crowded. We have to use the back alleys."

So they drove through the narrowest passages that the Roman Empire must have built. In one case, Grandpa thought he could put his hands out the windows and touch the side walls at the same time, but it mattered to few of the drivers. He finally arrived at the side base of the St. John's co-cathedral steps and got out. He gave the driver a fine tip, which is why they like *medigans*.

There was a huge crowd, and Susan had said they should meet at the base of the first step. He looked around and finally their eyes meet, and she ran over to him delighted. There is a strange way that the affections of young women make an old man feel good. She was unmarried, and unfortunately not very attractive, but she had a fine personality and a wonderful view of life.

They talked for a while about her new assignment, and then they walked up the three tiers of marble steps, following the crowd into the cathedral. There on the altar were attendants, turning over the two ampoules, with the blood of the saint liquefying. It would rest there for eight days, re-solidify, and be put away. The blood was viewed several times a year, and this event in September was the one that was most anticipated.

The faithful went up and touched or kissed the ampoules reverently, and afterwards the vials were held up outside to the crowds. Susan and Grandpa paid their respects, and she bought a book in English on the famed story of San Gennaro, and Grandpa purchased a tiny blue rosary which he wanted to put on Grandma's tombstone back in Madison.

As they walked down the steps, Susan miscalculated the last step and fell into the traffic, Grandpa tried to catch her, but she was still hit by a speeding yellow Fiat that was passing a tourist bus from Rome. The Fiat crushed her arm and she collapsed. The driver immediately jumped out of the car, and tried to protect her. He quickly grabbed Grandpa and Susan, and sped off to the nearest hospital. There it was obvious she was in pain, and Grandpa cradled her in his arms getting blood all over his new suit and his hat crushed.

At the hospital, she was bundled up and her arm was set. The driver stayed with her and Grandpa all night, and together they said the "Ave Maria":

"Ave, o Maria, piena di grazia, il Signore è con te. Tu sei benedetta fra le donne de benedetto è il frutto del tuo seno. Gesù Santa Maria, Madre di Dio, prega per noi peccatoti, adesso a nell'ora della nostra morte. Amen."

After two days the Benedictine nuns, who ran the hospital, insisted that Susan had to leave, and could heal at home with the right care. But she lived alone in Rome. The driver, Mario, insisted that she stay with his mother, a countess, on her estate on the island of Capri, and after much discussion she moved there with him and Grandpa.

Grandpa stayed less than a week and decided to go to Benevento; Susan was being taken care of by the countess and her staff better than in the hospital.

When Grandpa was leaving for Naples, he received a tightly wrapped package, and when he opened it there was a marble head of San Gennaro, with a note inside, "I hope this makes up for what I did to your hat. Mario."

At customs in New York, the agent who was obviously an Italian American from Staten Island asked Grandpa what his business was in Rome and Naples.

"No business, just to visit my relatives."

"What is in this bag with the string all around it?"

Grandpa was a great collector of string, and he kept the statue in its original wrappings. "It is a bust of San Gennaro."

The agent roughly opened it up and thought the white bust might be a huge piece of cocaine, and then he read the lettering under the head.

"This is the guy they have the parade for? I go there every year."

"Yes, that is San Gennaro."

The agent looked sarcastically, "Well, I guess one should believe in something in life. Go ahead."

After a year, Grandpa got a letter from Capri, where the countess told him that Mario and Susan had gotten married and were moving to Naples. She had given up her job with Ghirardelli, and he was managing the family's combined assets in the city. Soon she was pregnant, and they had a bouncing big boy, whom of course they named "Gennaro," or "Jerry" as Susan called him.

Every several months the countess in her beautiful Italian handwriting would inform Grandpa of what was happening and especially how the baby was growing into a fine young man. Then in one letter, she wrote, "Raffaele, there is something strange happening. Let us be honest, you and I both know Susan is no Sophia Loren and my son is no Marcello Mastroianni. But together they have produced an incredibly handsome young boy. My friend at the University of Naples calls it recessive genes. At night I look at his face and form, and I think I am looking at a classical god, sprung from our joint blood. It is just like the bust of the young Raphael. I tell the boy the story of how a heroic American from across the ocean saved his mother's life, and he loves the tale better than Jason and the Argonauts or Aeneas' founding Rome. I may make up some details along the way, but that is the grandmother's prerogative. He is so fine and fitting, I think that it is a miracle, another miracle of San Gennaro."

55. COMING HOME
Dedicated to Gilda

As we have seen, after the devotions to San Gennaro, Grandpa and his niece Susan stepped off the sidewalk in front of St. John's subcathedral in Naples; she was distracted and was hit hard on her left arm by a Fiat passing too quickly around a tourist bus from Rome. She fell to the ground in pain, and Grandpa ran over to hold her in his arms. Her young blood splattered all over his new white Arrow shirt and suit, and the people around crushed his bowler hat. The driver quickly jumped out of the Fiat and was upset at his negligence. He took both of them to the nearest Benedictine hospital and together they stayed with her that first night, praying the rosary to the Virgin Mary. After two days, the nuns indicated quietly that she would have to leave for it would be better for her to heal at home. There is no place worse than a hospital when you are sick.

Susan protested that she really had no place to go, but the driver immediately stepped forward and said she and Grandpa could stay at his mother's villa on the nearby Isle of Capri. They accepted, and the countess met them at the port when the boat arrived from Naples. It was the exact spot in fact in Naples where St. Paul was brought as a hostage in 67 A.D.

The countess immediately took charge and treated Susan as if she were her own daughter. When she heard of Grandpa's intervention, she regarded him as an American hero. The villa overlooked the magnificent waterfront, was set up on top of a grassy knoll, and was heavily staffed by the countess's maids and butlers.

For the rest of the week and beyond, Susan was treated as a baby princess, and at night Mario the driver would read to her from Alessandro Manzoni's novel, *The Betrothed*, the greatest Italian novel of the period.

In less than a week, Grandpa felt that she was in good company, and that he could leave his niece in their hands and return home to the United States. In fact, he noticed that when he wasn't supposed to be looking, he could see sparks in the eyes of the couple. He decided though that since he had come so far, he should visit his family in Rotondi and his wife's family in Benevento. So he sent a telegram to each family saying he was in Capri and would like to visit the old families.

He never got a response from the Finellis for the telegraph company was woefully unreliable, but to his surprise he was informed that the Perones would be honored to see him. They would pick him up the next day in front of the hotel in Naples, and their grandson Philip would drive him to their estate. Philip spoke English well since he had spent four years in Bayonne, New Jersey. Grandpa laughed—did the Perones think that he had forgotten his mother tongue!

Right on time, Philip arrived in a red pick-up truck, and Grandpa threw his beat-up suitcase in the back, and off they went home. It was about an hour or more and as they traveled down the paved roads Philip remarked how much the region had changed since the war. Benevento was once a duchy, and then a province of the Papal States, and was now a major agricultural and economic center. The Perones drove fresh produce up the new highways to Germany and southern France, and in the city itself the family owned an apparel factory that did rather well. Grandpa quietly looked down at his stained Arrow shirt and said nothing. *God*, he thought, *they must think I look like a cafone.*

When they arrived the whole extended family was outside waiting for him. They had also called the family's branch up over the hills, and they came running over. It was like when the American army liberated Naples. Grandpa got out of the truck and was greeted by his wife's youngest brother, Andrea, who was now an old man too, and his wife Jenna. They cradled him in their arms, and then introduced him proudly to each member of the family. The house was large and long; whole sections had been added to its salmon-colored main part.

They took him inside in a proud procession, and had Grandpa sit in the major upholstered chair. Immediately they put wine and antipasto in front of him. Then Jenna insisted, "You will not get these types of olives, cheese and tomatoes in America, will you Raffaele?" He laughed and agreed. Then little babies walked over to see and touch him, for they had heard of this special *medigan* who had come one day and married Aunt Luisa.

Jenna was his wife's special cousin and she knew all her secrets. She smiled and said, "Raffaele, I remember the day you came to ask for Luisa's hand. I saw you jump over that stone wall in your gray suit and American pointed shoes. You went right through the front door like you owned the house."

Grandpa laughed, "Yes, Jenna. I still have the suit at home, and the shoes were made in Italy, yet I don't think I can hop over that wall anymore!"

Grandpa knew however the story that ran through the family, on both sides of the ocean, that when he came to court Luisa, she ran to the barn in fright, only to be followed by her favorite cousin Jenna. The story went that she was being wooed by many men and had another man in mind for marriage. But Grandpa convinced her father of her great future in the new world, and eventually she did as she was told. For over a half-century Grandpa had heard the story that he was the second choice, but he never said anything. Once he remarked to his daughter Margaret, "If she didn't want me, the hell with it. I would have found another wife."

But Jenna interrupted him as he laid back in the best chair. "Oh no, Raffaele. She was just scared to go to America and never see Benevento again. All her other suitors were local boys who gave her gold and emeralds, but she was incredibly impressed by you and by your sense of command and the promise of a real future. Women can have dreams too. They gave her gold; you gave her yourself. She loved you more than anyone. Since it was a winter's wedding, we all knitted for her a wedding dress. It was more beautiful than lace."

Grandpa was startled for he had never heard that story before. Suddenly for the first time in fifty years, he felt really good about their quick courtship, and he felt good about himself. Zia Jenna turned to her husband Andrea and said, "My God, what an awful shirt he has on. Give him one of our best shirts from the factory." Grandpa then felt obliged to tell the story of how he rescued Susan at peril to his own life. That made him even more of a *medigan* hero.

Her husband brought Grandpa a new fancy shirt, and Andrea helped him put it on his still muscular body. He proudly related that he had given a shirt just like that to Luigi Pirandello when he visited Naples. The next year the playwright won the Nobel Prize in Literature.

Some of the older ladies looked in awe at the old man, still in shape from his hard, physical work. One said, "I am sure there are many women here who would still like to go back with you to New York City."

Grandpa was always Victorian in his attitude towards sex, and he blushed and remarked, "You beautiful older women do not need an old *medigan*."

Then Zia Jenna enticed him to tell her about Luisa's last years. They had been so separated from her, and Luisa could not write well.

"Well, she enjoyed her children and her grandchildren. The floor above us in the apartment house had a five-year-old boy who came down every day to see his grandma and play with the pieces of wool he pulled out from under our bed, black and white, and she put them in a special drawer just for him. She died soon after."

"Ah, how sad," said Jenna. "What does the boy do now?"

Grandpa responded, "He is in school."

Zia Jenna and six other women prepared a feast that could easily feed the entire family and another one. Women in the Perone family cooked for the pleasure of it, not as in the United States just to get a meal on the table.

In walked a short, tubby monsignor, the family's priest. He had been assigned to a parish in Benevento, but soon he was being chased by a young woman constantly stalking him. The wise bishop sent him to a friend in Rome, and he ended up in the Congregation of the Sacred Office or what used to be called the Inquisition. He was happy and contented and greeted Raffaele with a fierce embrace. He would have been Luisa's nephew.

In Rome he became a rather good curial bureaucrat, and the family admired him, except for Salvatore. Salvatore disliked the Catholic Church and was a follower of the old Risorgimento heroes Garibaldi, Mazzini, and Cavour. Garibaldi hated the papacy so much he named his horse Pius IX or Pio Nino. Salvatore greeted the monsignor, "Hey, what special collection are we to expect from Pius XII this week? Get the Americans to pay their fair share! Peter's Pence is just a cruel remedy to support the pope's miserliness. Look at the Borgias."

Monsignor said, "Ah, the village atheist. Your interests are unchanged."

Then he turned to Grandpa, grabbed a large plate of food and sat down next to him. Grandpa in a sign of respect moved back for him, and the priest asked, "How is America treating Italians?"

Grandpa happily remarked, "Good, good. We are all glad the war is over though."

The monsignor added, "Now, we must be wary of the communists."

Salvatore cut in, "Only the communists can save us from the pope's Christian Democrats. At least they are honest."

The monsignor responded sharply, "So the village atheist is now the village communist. Weren't you a fascist under Mussolini? What ignorance."

As they chatted between courses, Andrea wanted to show Grandpa his fields. They went outside, and Grandpa remarked offhandedly how Grandma would say that she would stand on the little balcony above and see what was going on. But there was no balcony. Perhaps she misremembered. "No, Raffaele, it is down there in the marble pile. Ten years ago, an earthquake hit us, and the structure fell, and we just put it over there in a pile. Maybe someday we will get to fix it."

Grandpa smiled and walked over to the stone wall and gently touched the top of it, remembering earlier days. The ground felt dry and hard. It hadn't rained since the beginning of the year. They went back in, and waves of desserts were on the table replacing the dirty dishes. The monsignor turned to Grandpa, "Raffaele, have you ever met the pope?"

"No, he doesn't make calls to America, especially at his age."

"I can get you into a small audience of twelve people if you want to see him. Will you go?"

"Of course."

Salvatore responded, "Hold your wallet, my dear friend."

Then Grandpa remembered. He had no place to stay. The monsignor quickly responded that he could board at the North American College for American and Canadian seminarians. The college had a reputation for turning out young men who went on to become bishops in their home country. Grandpa laughed, "I am too old to be a bishop, but I would like to stay with them."

For two more hours the family remembered and laughed and constantly picked at olives and cheese, tomatoes and red wine. Then the monsignor tapped Grandpa's arm and said, "If we are to make Rome tonight, we must get going." They left to great dismay and Grandpa looked once more at the balcony pieces. The roads to Rome were reminiscent in some ways of the old causeways that the centurions used 2,000 years ago, and then the government had turned into modern roads and expressways.

They ended up at the North American College on Janiculum Hill, and the monsignor convinced the American rector that Grandpa was a great Catholic benefactor in the United States, and Grandpa ended up in a typical seminarian's room—a simple bed, a bureau, a washbasin, and a crucifix on the wall. He put his suitcase down, profusely thanked the monsignor, and set a meeting time of 6 a.m. to go to the papal apartments. He walked around the spartan structure and went outside to the typical Italian inner portico as darkness came slowly. There were laminated pictures of the classes from each year on a rotating column.

He thought for a moment: Monsignor Dauenhauer had graduated in an early class. He walked over, and he saw him at a very young age. Then Grandpa looked closer at his picture, and he rested on his intense eyes, just as he was looking out off to the future. He was serious and almost contemplative, like he seemed so often sitting on his back porch in the rectory in Madison.

Grandpa could barely sleep that night, and the next morning he fasted, hoping to receive communion before meeting the pope. The monsignor arrived on time, and then they were in the front row, going up the stairs. It seemed the monsignor was known by everybody. Grandpa climbed up the marble stairways, each one headed by more and more hardened looking security men. Finally they arrived with several other couples in a spare waiting room. Grandpa would sit in a pew inside on the left of the modest chapel, but the monsignor would pray with the Holy Father on the right. The chapel had huge golden candlesticks given to Pius from the American bishops. When Pius walked in, he was so thin, almost emaciated, with sharp features and rimless glasses. Then he began the Latin ritual, and at the end, he blessed the group and walked out.

The monsignor had arranged an audience with Pius for Grandpa and some other honored guests. In the reception room, in swept the elderly, thin pope who could speak ten languages. Grandpa suddenly realized he didn't even know what to say. When he met the pope, he didn't want to just say, "Hello, Papa." Pius walked around the circle, smiling and giving a few words of encouragement to each person.

Next to Grandpa was a cute brunette girl, about twelve or thirteen, with her parents, doctors from Philadelphia. When Pius came up to her, she curtseyed and kissed his papal ring. "What is your name my dear?"

"Gilda."

"Ah, what a pretty name. Do you speak Italian?"

"No, I am an American your Holiness." He asked if she obeyed her parents. "Oh yes."

And then he put his palms together, "Dear Gilda, make me a promise. When you go back to America, you will work spreading the Italian language and culture within that great land. I have been to America. I love Americans. Will you promise me that?"

Gilda responded eagerly, "Oh yes, your Holiness."

Then he came to Grandpa and asked him in Italian where he was from. The old man told the pontiff that he was from near New York City. "Oh, yes, I have been there when I was secretary of state."

And Grandpa spoke out unexpectedly, "I want to thank you for saving Rome during the war."

The pope was startled, and then responded rapidly, "I did my best, but I am not Innocent the Great. One night the bombers even hit my family's cemetery, and Montini and I raced out there, and people cried when we arrived. Montini gave out money to the poor. And I prayed with them. Some of the tombstones were overturned, including those in my family's plot. And weeping people with bloody hands and faces came up to hold me. That night my cassock was covered with blood, the blood of the living in a time of the blood of the dead. I could not sleep, my friend. Your pope was hopeless." And then he stopped. "I must not remember too much, for it will haunt me." He gave Grandpa a medal marking his pontificate.

At the end of the session, he walked slowly through the door and out the side. Grandpa was deeply moved, and the monsignor was so impressed by his own ability to get his relative into the apostolic apartments to talk to the pope.

That afternoon Grandpa caught the nonstop plane from Rome to Idyllwild airport. As it slowly took off, he touched for good luck the medallion Pius XII had given him, and then he wondered if the little girl next to him would indeed help promote Italian language and culture. So much gets lost in the immigration process, and then the next generation has its own story to tell.

56. BUON NATALE

The Italian people are quite sure that the beautiful nativity scenes all over the world were due to their favorite saint, Francis of Assisi who made the first one 600 years ago. Churches and houses had such wonderful scenes of the barn or cave that the Savior was born in with his mother and step-father praying on each side of him, and the barn or cave being surrounded by animals that lived in reverent awe of the event that had just occurred. Being true to that tradition, St. Vincent Martyr Church had a beautiful layout done by German workmen some years earlier and brought to the parish by the beloved German American pastor, Father Lambert, in the 1920s. The high point was of course the sight of the baby Jesus who was the center of the tableau.

The priests and nuns would carefully lay out the nativity scene and leave it up through the feast of the Epiphany on January 6. Then it would be taken down, lovingly packed, and placed in the church basement. One year, the nuns decided that the whole scene should be framed in evergreen branches, even though evergreens did not grow in Bethlehem. So the principal, Sister Jude of Divine Affliction, asked Grandpa if he would cut down some fine evergreens and help place them around the scene. As always, he concurred, since she had been so good to him and his family.

As he began his assignment, he heard from the Sodality Society women that someone had come into the church the one night it was open and stolen the baby Jesus. It was an infamy, a sacrilege, no circle in Dante's hell would be hot enough for that person to spend eternity in. Grandpa was unsure what anyone would do just with the baby's carved image with its little diaper on, but apparently there was no limit to the types of craziness some people engaged in, especially as the holidays approached.

Still he had his duties to do, and he went out to the nearby forest area fronting upon the new housing project and cut off four branches. But when leaving, he looked over and saw a young girl dressed in a fine coat with white gloves who was preparing a little bed for what looked like the statue of baby Jesus. He quietly walked over and complimented her on her fine care of the baby and asked if that was the carving of the Church's on Green Village

Road. She quickly admitted it, and responded, "All my life I have wanted one thing to love, to love with all my heart, and now I have it, baby Jesus, who is mine and mine alone." It was cold and Grandpa told her to go inside and leave the baby under the tree in his fine new bed. She turned and went toward one of the large split-level houses.

Then he went into town towards North Street where many of the old Italians lived, most of them retired and bored with the endings of life. He went into the ornate house of an old friend, Angelo Bonaratti, who was a wood carver by trade, and who made all sorts of beautiful works in his cellar. His family was totally uninterested, so he rarely tried to sell any. He even carved a life size figure of his beloved wife which he would gently kiss.

Grandpa arrived with an idea: he wanted Angelo to make for him a carved baby Jesus, but lo and behold he had three in his basement, and Grandpa asked for the one that looked most like the one in the woods. Angelo was delighted to give it to him free, since no one had shown him much interest after he retired. Then Grandpa said that he wondered if Angelo could find a nice gown for the baby since it was cold outside. Did he have a sort of dress like the new Barbie dolls? But Angelo had one even better—he had a gown from an Infant of Prague statue that he had made himself. It had sequins and fake diamonds and made the baby look like the princess of Savoy. Grandpa liked the new look, and he offered to buy the whole package, but Angelo refused, for it was Christmas he said.

Grandpa took the carved statue in the gown back to where the little girl had laid the original baby Jesus from St. Vincent. He put down Angelo's and then took the other one to the church. He matter-of-factly walked in and with some evergreens he covered over the baby Jesus until he could replace it without any attention. Later at the noon Mass, the old ladies of the Sodality saw the carved baby in the crib, and screamed out that it was a miracle, it was sign of the Resurrection. The younger people thought that it was a present from Santa Claus. The pastor said nothing, but just thanked God for His generosity. Grandpa said nothing.

At Christmas Mass at noon, Grandpa caught a view of the little girl from the forest coming in and she saw him. She ran up and showed him her child and told him how beautiful he looked in the daylight in his new clothes. She had always wanted something to love, and now this Christmas she had it.

57. CODICIL

James Patrick Fitzgerald was an astute businessman who owned several successful pharmacies, including one in Madison. In earlier days pharmacists actually made many prescriptions, mixing them by hand and sorting them into dark, glass bottles for distribution. But as medicine progressed, pharmacists became faceless men and a few women who took pills from large bottles and just put them in small labeled bottles made out of cheap plastic. With the growth of the drug industry and the emergence of antibiotics, the numbers of separate remedies nearly overwhelmed the average drug store.

Fitzgerald's empire included a Rexall store in Madison operated by Mr. Michael McGee, who knew everyone in town and their ailments. He was a gentle and humble soul who would go to his store in the middle of the night to fill a prescription for the very sick. He saw himself as a honorable professional, and his drug store didn't sell candy, cigarettes, or toys. He was simply a fine registered pharmacist, and that was why Grandpa patronized him for years.

One day Mr. McGee told Grandpa that Fitz need someone to take care of his lawns and gardens at his beautiful ranch house on Wilmer Street. Fitz and his wife, who had died early in their marriage, had one child, a boy who went west to Wyoming and bought a ranch complete with cattle and other livestock. The son worried about his retired father, for as time passed he lived a lonely life more and more. Grandpa was hired to do the lawns and flowers in a very rich neighborhood in a town with many such neighborhoods. Money can buy that type of company. After he completed his work, Grandpa would be invited by Fitz in for a drink, and soon some conversation. They talked of family, of neighborhood gossip, food, and Fitzgerald's favorite pastime—classical opera. Like Grandpa, on Saturday afternoon Fitz would listen faithfully to the Texaco Metropolitan Opera productions live from the Opera House in New York City.

Grandpa of course favored Verdi and Puccini, Fitz adored Wagner, and so together they covered the landscape of 19th century opera. Fitz especially loved the Wagnerian *Ring* cycle and was fascinated even at an early age by the heroes and heroines of the German classics. Grandpa let Fitz know a family secret he told few others—his family had some roots in Cornwell, near the very spot King Arthur founded his Round Table. In fact, Arthur's father was a Roman, Grandpa proclaimed. And so these older men would dwell in the world of myth and romance, mixing the elixirs of history and legend shamelessly on the weekends of their aging lives.

Fitz wanted to pay Grandpa for his hours of wonderful, manly companionship, but he refused and only took money for the physical work he did outside. Fitz was surprised that such a man could make a living, for the world he lived in was populated by con men, sharpies, exploitive drug companies and avaricious doctors called specialists. *The old man,* he once thought, *lived in a world of noble men and virtuous women—both strange illusions.*

Just before he died, he had Mr. McGee witness a codicil to his will drawn up by his attorney Frank Volpe of Volpe and Volpe. In it, he left $50,000 to Grandpa, a most tidy sum in those days. Then a week later, Grandpa came over that Saturday and couldn't get in. No one answered the door. He came the next day with his oldest son, and again no one answered the door. Fearing the worst, he had his son break the small glass pane near the lock of the back door. They crept in, and there Fitz lay in a pool of his blood, dark red and sitting there almost stagnant. He had put a gun to his head and ended it. His face looked blank and his mouth twisted, with his body in a heap in front of the corduroy sofa. The burdens of life had overcome the wonders of life itself. Grandpa's son turned weak, he had never seen a dead man before, let alone a gunshot suicide. Grandpa quietly and respectfully moved to the phone on the coffee table and called the police. Later at home, he phoned the son in Wyoming. He just told him his father was gone and left out the details.

Two months later, Grandpa was talking with Mr. McGee who abruptly lamented the death of his boss, but said, "I'm glad that he remembered you in his will."

"What do you mean, in his will?"

"He left you $50,000 in a codicil just before his death. I witnessed it, and Volpe was named the administrator." Grandpa had never heard or dreamt of that, and so he went to Volpe and Volpe to ask the lawyer what happened to the bequest.

Frank Volpe, whom the older Italians derisively called "the fox," argued with Grandpa that Mr. McGee must have misunderstood. For wills are difficult things: you have codicils, which really aren't codicils, wills that place great trust in administrators, i.e., lawyers, that Mr. Fitzgerald was very wealthy, but he did not allocate $50,000 for Grandpa. In fact, he wanted the money let out slowly at the administrator's discretion. The old man knew Volpe for years, and he could see through his slanted eyes. "Fitz was pretty clear about the bequest, and I was a witness to it."

"No, see he misunderstood what Fitzgerald was talking about, how he would like to leave money to honorable men like you. But he never did. You know that you can trust me, Raffaele."

Grandpa left his oozing offices and went home to discuss the matter with his son, and they agreed that he should go see Andrew Falcone, another local lawyer whom Grandpa had dealt with before. Andrew welcomed the old man but was fearful he was getting caught in pro bono work again. He hated pro bono, it was an illegal tax on lawyers, he concluded. But when Grandpa mentioned the $50,000, his eyes lit up for in those days that was a lot of money. But as the old man went on, Andrew realized the fragility of the case's evidence. He candidly said to Grandpa, "Look, Ralph the only witness to the codicil is the druggist, and under cross examination he will crumble. Verbal agreements are not worth the paper they are not written on. You need a copy of the codicil. Any lawyer taking your case will expect 40% of the judgment, and there is a good chance you will lose and have to pay costs. I could take your money, but even I know a bad set up when I see it."

"But the law is for giving people justice. This is very wrong."

"Ralph, yes, it is, but only rich people get what they can buy. And you are not a rich man to wage a crusade for justice. Courts favor administrators without a written agreement to the contrary. I am sorry to say this to you."

Grandpa left dejected. He wondered if Falcone was just afraid of Volpe, afraid to do battle with the devil. He ruminated on it for weeks, and then he heard from his son the unexpected news that Volpe had suffered a severe stroke. He couldn't say anything but "Mama, Mama" to his hired caregiver from the Dominican Republic.

In several months, one of his partners wanted to take Falcone's corner office, overlooking Main Street, and remove his collection of West Law Books. No one wanted to buy them, so they called in a used book dealer from Morristown who stored books inside a huge waterproof barn.

Soon the farmer realized that he had taken more than he could ever sell, and so he put them way up on the top shelves alongside *The Great Books of the Western World,* 60 volumes of obscure philosophy or whatever. One afternoon a young man came in to buy a used law school textbook, and he noticed the West collection. He shyly asked the farmer-book dealer, "How much you want for the whole West collection?"

"A hundred bucks, they are in prime condition, used to be owned by Supreme Court Justice William Brennan of New Jersey. You can have them all for $80 on one condition. You take all of them today."

And so a deal was struck, the second year law student pulled into the barn floor with his old Ford Fairlane, and piled them in the trunk, back seat, and the right side of the front.

The farmer asked the kid, "You going to be a lawyer or something?"

"Yes, I am a second-year law student at Seton Hall Law School."

"What type of law you in? A lot of money in some of those companies."

"I intend to be public advocacy lawyer, representing the poor."

"The poor…what the hell do they need a lawyer for. You can't make any money that way. The courts are for the rich, ain't you heard?"

58. THE THIRTEENTH APOSTLE

Grandpa sat easily in his armchair and decided to read his *Book of Solomon*. The family knew he had such a volume, written in Italian and sold to him years ago by a fortuneteller in Naples. He was pondering the admonitions about the nature of good and evil, the primordial questions of life. It seems when God created Adam and Eve a speck of evil crept into them through their nostrils, and as they and we understood more about bad acts or indulged in bad dreams, the forces of evil grew stronger as if feeding on their souls. Grandpa didn't know if he believed in the devil or Satan or Lucifer, but he was a product of the brutal twentieth century, and he knew he believed in the evil of man.

He re-read the passages in his mind's eye, and for some reason he wondered if what men learned as boys was so much out of date or no longer useful or true. Grandpa finally thought back to his childhood and how often he had to run to another farm for assistance. It was too close to saddle up the horse and too far to walk comfortably. Now he had a truck and a telephone, the latter sitting proudly in the corner nook of his kitchen wall on a wooden triangular shelf. From there he could call all over town, even to Morristown, and on rare occasions to Italy. Much of what he had heard about time and distance was obsolete. He wished he had learned how to change his truck's oil, for example, like his younger son who could do it with such ease.

Now Grandpa's family doctor in the early days was Myron Shapiro, whom he rarely visited, but his family adored. Penicillin was just coming into popular use and Shapiro was seen as a miracle man. Then after the war, a new, young personable doctor, John Adams, opened a practice in town, just above the pharmacy, a rather convenient place. One day in the store Grandpa was buying a newspaper and met the new physician he had heard about. They introduced each other and immediately hit it off. Grandpa thought he looked like a bright fellow who probably was up on the latest medical advances, and he looked to the doctor as a wise, Italian gentleman who was polite and respected in town, where people were often cold and clannish. When Grandpa's oldest daughter had a family feast, Grandpa invited the doctor, his wife, and son to meet everyone and hopefully to win them over from Shapiro.

The most interesting part of the year in New Jersey is the end of autumn which so colors the roads with its beautiful maple and elm trees. But soon the trees become sticks and shadows. It was too cold to really work and make any money, and Grandpa noticed as he aged the cold seemed to settle inside his bones, in his feet, in his hands, and even down the crease in his backbone. People said that was normal, for old age comes on slowly but irrevocably like a thief in the night.

On the edge of the town, more near Morris Plains than Madison, there was also a newly transplanted Rev. Jacob Archer, a born-again evangelist who claimed to be the last apostle, the thirteenth, of Jesus Christ. The Savior appeared to him regularly in his nights of ecstasy in the dense forests and told him the secrets of the universe. The Lord ordered him, the last apostle, to bring the special gospel, the secret gospel, "the gnosis," to people. The goal was to be transmitted beyond the time of the followers, to the larger world. The apostle knew facts and stories about Christ that no one else had fathomed. Matthew, Mark, Luke and John were fine, but only he knew the total truth of salvation. No one else knew the why of salvation, the true story of the fall of Adam and Eve, and the exact hour and day of the second coming of Christ.

And so the apostle, after forty days in the woods, emerged to take his place as the great prophet. Not far from his rough cabin in a clearing, he set up a huge canvas tent that he had found in a junk yard. The word got out in town, especially among the bored, that there was a man claiming to be the last apostle of Jesus, a blessed man who had eaten and sat and talked and listened to the Savior as He walked the shores of the Galilean Sea. There were rumors of healings and of visions and of terrible physical battles on stage with Satan himself. The apostle always prevailed. People with sick minds and troubled souls flocked to him and left with hope and optimism. The organized religions in town tried to ignore him, and the monsignor warned Catholics that the Bible itself spoke of a reign of false prophets coming before the Last Judgment. It was this way that Grandpa first heard of the apostle. But he was a confirmed Catholic, and the Church had so many rules and regulations that he could barely keep up with. The last thing he needed was to fall under the influence of a self-proclaimed prophet.

As time passed, the apostle looked for a woman to take on the domestic duties while he focused on his great ministry. The relationship would be strictly business of course. But he chose a comely lass who came to his services enthusiastically again and again. He offered her the job and even provided a bed for her in his disjointed cabin, but soon he too knew the pleasures of young flesh and she got pregnant.

She was afraid of what was happening to her, and the apostle took her to the new doctor who informed her of her condition and how she would deliver around Christmas. How wonderfully appropriate the apostle pronounced. When they got home, he ordered her to nail up aluminum foil to the ceilings so the devil would not be able to land and come in, and she obediently did so.

A terrific snowstorm hit Jersey in late December and the roads were closed in and out of Madison, and with cars stranded along Main Street, the town couldn't plow the thoroughfare. Grandpa watched as they tried heroically until a second ice storm hit the area and covered the snow. *Thank God, I have enough canned food inside*, he thought. But not everyone was so fortunate.

The apostle's woman went into early labor and there was no way to reach the doctor, to even talk to him, let alone visit him. Since they had no phone, the apostle walked three miles to the nearest house and humbly explained the situation. They let him use their phone, and he called the doctor's emergency number. He explained the frightening condition, and Dr. Adams realized that the woman was facing complications from what sounded like a breech birth. But he couldn't get out there, even down his own street. The apostle went hysterical and started to curse God Himself. The doctor cut him off and told him that he should go home immediately and be at her side. The doctor would do his best to come.

Deeply upset, he looked out to the partially plowed Main Street and saw his car totally buried. He looked down the street and saw only one figure, Grandpa, shoveling the snow in front of his apartment house. Why he was doing that was anyone's guess, for nobody could get down on either side of the walk past his place. Probably he was just bored. The physician ran down as best he could, tromping on the snow and ice, leaving his footprints along the way.

He needed somebody to talk to at least, and he told Grandpa the total story quickly. Grandpa looked helplessly around and said, "Honestly, you'd have to be Santa Claus to get through this stuff." And then it suddenly hit him. The town had a Santa Claus coming into town in several days to ride around to amuse the children and probably the adults. The horse and sled were being housed in one of the stalls in Mantone's Garage across the street from Grandpa. Grandpa grabbed the doctor by the arm and went over to the gas station where Mantone, also bored, was working in another bay on a transmission just to kill time and make some money.

Grandpa had known him for years. Indeed Mantone had graciously taught his youngest son the car maintenance business. He quickly explained the problem, and Mantone looked over at the horse and the sled which were both decorated with bells and wreaths. "Ralph, look. I am a car man. I don't know how to even hook him up. I just feed him and clean the crap away." The physician's heart sank.

But Grandpa replied, "I know how to hook him up and to drive it. I did it for years as a boy in Avellino."

Mantone shrugged his shoulders and said, "Go ahead and do your thing."

Expertly Grandpa braced the horse in, took the whip in hand, and told the doctor to jump in. On down Main Street the bells rang as people looked in wonderment, and Grandpa drove the sturdy horse like it was indeed a reindeer. The physician was scared for his life as the sled slid and pushed in the snow and on to the ice layer. After an interminable length of time, they arrived at the cabin, close enough to hear the woman screaming and the apostle's cursing the Almighty.

As Grandpa steadied the horse, the physician jumped out and ran inside. It was a difficult birth for all, but finally the world saw a reddish boy in good health. The apostle was ecstatic. "It was God's blessing at the end of a long trial," he said. The mother was totally exhausted but happy. The apostle then named the baby Judas, after the disciple who had betrayed Jesus and then committed suicide. The apostle regarded him as an instrument of God's Will who made possible the death and final resurrection of Christ. Christ knew what he was up to for He knew everything. And Jesus made Judas in fact the agent of His greatest work on earth. Thus this new Judas would be dedicated to the crucifixion. On and on he went, even as he preached to his crowds later.

Grandpa drove home more slowly, too slowly for the physician for he was frozen from his own sweat. Grandpa had never heard of a child named for Judas, and the apostle seemed to him a false prophet, a frail man who should not be teaching others about frailties.

At Mantone's he unhooked the loyal steed and dried him off carefully for he was crusted with snow and ice. Grandpa gave him hay and water and patted his head. "Good boy, sometimes the old ways are the best ways."

Years later Judas changed his name to Jude.

59. LENI LANAPE

Over the years, Grandpa worked for many rich people, and while they admired and trusted him, few became friends. He did his work, and they paid him and that was that. One family was the Tildens, a brother and a sister who lived alone in a beautiful Victorian house off Woodland Road. They were the grandchildren of the famous and fabulously wealthy Samuel J. Tilden, who had actually won the 1876 presidential election, but was cheated out of it by unscrupulous Republican bosses. The electoral vote was a tie with some other votes in dispute for months. Finally the Democrats agreed that they would support the Republican candidate if the Republicans agreed that they would pull out the remaining Union troops from the South. Only General Grant, honoring the Lincoln legacy, refused, but it happened, and the Republican nominee labeled angrily by Tilden supporters RutherFRAUD B. Hayes, consummated the bargain. Tilden never ran again but compiled a huge fortune in New York City. Two generations later his grandchildren decided to leave the city and move out on the train line to Madison.

Grandpa took care of the Victorian inside and out, but after seven years, both Tildens decided they wished to enjoy more the city and its culture, and they moved to a magnificent mansion on Fifth Avenue. They sold the Victorian house quickly, but they also owned 33 acres on the outskirts of the borough which had been given to Samuel Tilden years ago by someone who people said was the only Democrat in town. In a magnanimous gesture, they called Grandpa in and told him that those acres were his severance pay. He could do whatever he wanted with them.

The acreage was overwhelmed with weeds and hilly, but to Grandpa it was an incredible addition to his empire. He could now grow corn, which he never could elsewhere, and new brands of tomatoes, and of course, in a patch in the front facing the road, his beloved pansies. It was too much for him to turn over all that dirt, and so he hired a nearby farmer to plow up the soil and level the knolls. But what would he do with the crops? His own family preferred to buy corn and tomatoes at the A&P, so they could make only one trip for groceries to the store.

Then Grandpa built a wooden stand, and had the farmer put up a rudely painted sign, "Free vegetables, take what you need. Leave some for others." And every other day, he picked the crops and placed them in pyramids on his stand. One day he found under a tomato, a five dollar bill. Another day a prayer card to St. Benedict, the patron saint of farm workers.

The second year, he hired the same farmer who plowed up the acreage. Grandpa loved to walk the trenches and smell the fresh soil. The earth looked like a beautiful woman opening herself to a fertile young lover. But one day he glanced down and saw a group of arrow heads, some hard beads, and a long spear. Those were obviously remnants from the old Indian tribes who were supposed to have hunted near there eons ago. Grandpa wondered how they sold their lands to the white man, for he had only a bill of sale from the Tildens.

The more he thought about it, the more he felt uncomfortable with the ownership of the land, and after much hesitation he decided to go to the Falcone law firm to do a legal search. After some research, the younger Falcone told Grandpa that he had gone back to the royal grant from King Charles I in 1715 to Lord Calvert giving him tracts of land. "But who gave them to the king? What right did he have to seize Indian lands?" Grandpa asked naively.

"Look Ralph, he had the right of conquest. The red coats beat the red men. It is like how the Romans stole the seven hills from the Etruscans. It is called the right of conquest."

Grandpa left disturbed, for he had never taken or stolen anything in his life, why start now? When he left Falcone he walked up to the library and asked to talk to someone who knew about Indian life in the area. The director was an anthropologist and knew all about the Indians who migrated in northern New Jersey. She explained, "They were called the Leni Lanapes and were mainly hunting tribes. They migrated from here all the way to what is now New Providence. That area was actually called 'Turkey', until the English Congregationalists built a church with a choir loft. During services, the loft collapsed, but no one was hurt, so they called the area 'God's Providence,' thus New Providence." And on and on she went, but then she mentioned that the descendants of the old Lenapes would hold their monthly meeting at the local Elks Club next Tuesday at 8 p.m. She gave Grandpa the chairman's number and said to call him and go talk to the tribe members.

So he did and arrived to their surprise. The meeting was a mixture of older men in traditional Indian garb and younger guys in business suits who looked like they just got off the train from their jobs in tech companies and investment houses. Grandpa was politely introduced by the chief who remarked simply that "This gentleman has sought us out and asked to speak briefly to us as the last descendants of the great Leni Lenape."

With that august introduction, Grandpa simply remarked that he had inherited 33 acres outside of town and found some relics which he brought with him. They nodded but said nothing. Another guy with arrowheads. He then plaintively said he had farmed the land for two years and given away the crops each year. But he did not understand how the king of England could give away their lands, and so he wished to talk to them on the matter directly, man to man.

They stared at the old Italian, without saying a word. Finally the chief broke the silence, "You must pardon us, sir, we are not used to a white man asking our permission to use our land. May we meet for a brief time and discuss it together. Please, we appreciate your being here." Grandpa politely exited.

For a half an hour, they heatedly discussed what to do. Some older members actually believed that Grandpa was a ghost of an ancestor sent to test their allegiance to the traditions of the tribe, traditions long forgotten by the ambitious young. But after half an hour, they called Grandpa back in, and with deep respect the chief announced that he could do what he wanted with the land, but at his death, the land should be deeded back to the Leni Lanape Council sitting in that room. They profusely thanked him for respecting the land, respecting the traditions, and respecting them. White men have not been so honest or gracious, they agreed. The chief then told Grandpa that some thought he was sent by their forbears to remind them of their glorious hunting days, when they gracefully and in freedom roamed the land. "May you go in peace, great man, and live as long as the rivers run, and the mountains reach the sky."

So Grandpa left; later he had a codicil drawn up in his will for the disposal of the 33 acres. And when he died in 1969, the lawyer informed the tribal council of their legacy. They met and prayed to the spirits to take up the soul of the Great White Farmer so that on the summer nights it would float like gentle mists above their tribal lands. Soon though the leadership of the council changed, and the fate of the land came up. No one wanted to farm it for they were now living in an upper middle class suburb. They decided to sell it to a developer who built expensive split levels on its acreage. The only concession they made to the Indians' tradition was that they named the street cutting though the property, Leni Lanape Lane.

60. FINDING BABY JESUS
(for Mark)

Just before Christmas, I visited Grandpa in his dated apartment at 81 Main Street. Despite his many children and grandchildren, he was often alone, staring out his back door and looking at the garden that was fallow and covered with frost. I greeted him, and he reached over and gave me his traditional present, a two dollar bill in an envelope with an opening showing the portrait of Thomas Jefferson. I sat down and noticed he had a small nativity scene on his table, one he had undoubtedly purchased at the drug store on Main Street in the center of town. I acknowledged the scene and asked him if they had those in Italy.

He laughed, "It was St. Francis of Assisi who in the thirteenth century created the first nativity scene, complete with real animals." Grandpa reminded me that years ago he had given my mother a fine German nativity creche, which in turn had been presented to his family by the pastor at St. Vincent's, Rev. John Lambert, who was a German by birth but who had studied at the University of Genoa. When my Uncle Sadie got polio at age 13, he laid in bed, while a physical therapist from Berkeley Heights who came three times a week performed exercises and placed warm compresses on his inert legs. She and Grandma prayed together at the end of each session, and at times Lambert came over to the house to join them. Years later, after Grandma died, the old man gave the crèche to my mother, and after my father died, she gave it to me. Somehow decorating for Christmas was shortened after the death of a loved one.

I asked him about the Lambert nativity scene, and he told me once again the story of Uncle Sadie, and how after a year he fully recovered. Then he smiled in a quizzically way, and added, "Did I ever tell you about the problem of baby Jesus?"

"No, all I know is about the crèche we have."

"Of course, you would not know. It began when I was 15, and very much wanted to see the world outside of Rotondi. I worked for the farmer next to us and helped him cut wood which he sold to the rich who had elegant fireplaces in their huge apartments in Naples. All I knew was that the city had nearly a million people, and seemed to be exciting—or so, I was told.

"When I insisted to my mother and father that I was going to spend a weekend in Naples, I was accused of having *voglia di girovagare*, what you would call wanderlust, and they were perhaps right. My mother feared the reputation of Naples as being a place of pickpockets, thieves, drunken sailors, and *putanas*, and worried about my uninformed virtue. But I reassured her that it was only a weekend, and surely even the devil could not act that quickly.

"Then a farmer had a full load of firewood, and I asked if I could join him going into the city, and he was glad for the company. The roads were terrible, full of holes and rocks, but we finally made it after travelling 60 kilometers or so. We stopped at the terminal in the heart of the city, and he let me out. 'If you are here on Saturday at five, you can return home with me.'

"Since I had no money for transportation, I profusely thanked him and said I would be there on that very spot. He kindly gave me a sandwich of peppers and sausage, and a bottle of light wine for the rest of the day, and off I went. There at the terminal, a weary looking professor of classics who said he was from the University of Naples was leading a disjointed tour. I did not have the fee, but stayed in the back of the crowd listening, and nodding. He took us on a broken down wagon to Mount Vesuvius, and when I hesitated since I did not belong, he chastised me, 'Hurry, I do not have all day.'

"So I became part of the group. We first saw the great fiery Mount Vesuvius, and then he pointed the way to Pompeii, where common people had suddenly been frozen in time for all eternity. We moved on to the Royal Palace, and then to Castel Nova, built in 1219—a magnificent sight. The large wagon drifted down to the Mergellina Port, a great site of incredible blues. Up on the hilltop, horse-drawn carriages were parked with newspapers tucked into the windows, which allowed amorous couples to make up for the lack of privacy in Italian homes.

"The good professor went on to tell us about his university, the oldest one in Europe, founded by Frederick II in 1124. We stopped in town to see the Naples National Archeological Museum with a magnificent collection of Roman statues and mosaics. I could not imagine that these artists lived before Christ. I had many questions but was afraid to ask any since I was an unpaying guest. Then the tour stopped at the Duomo di San Gennaro, where several times a year the solid blood of the saint liquefied if a good year was coming up. I was fascinated by the story and sat in the pew and listened to the tales of the patron saint of Naples and those of us who lived in the area. I said a prayer for my family, and then thought of my poor Momma who was making tomato soup with hard bread for Christmas. She desperately tried to give each of us a holiday stocking with three pieces of candy, and an apple, just to show that Jesus did not forget the poor from where he came. She had gone to an auction and bid on a nativity scene which no one else wanted since it lacked a baby Jesus. So for years, she put out the crèche, but she tied some wool together in a figure and placed it in the manger.

"I spent the night at a Catholic house for German and American students and slept quietly and quickly so no one could ask me for my fee. The next morning I had a free cup of coffee and a biscotti and left to explore more of the city. I asked one carabinieri where was a good place for a visitor to roam around and sightsee. He remarked, 'You can see the nativity scenes, engraved statues, and endless prayer cards, down the long street to the right.' It was a long walk, but I finally saw the street so jammed one could not easily move around, and you could smell the different odors of the people milling around, for every family has its own scent. I wondered what I smelled like, if they realized I did not belong as they did.

"Finally, I went into one side street, which had hosts of nativity scenes, and also separate little statues. There was a small carving of baby Jesus in a manger. I knew I had to have it for Mama, and so I decided to buy it. I was short six lira and tried to get the owner to sell it for what I had in my poor pocket. For some reason, maybe the joy of the season, maybe my sad look, he agreed, and I walked away with a baby Jesus wrapped in brown paper and tied it with heavy twine. For the rest of my life, I collected twine and string, even in the New World.

"I caught my ride home, and then went into the barn and hid my package. Momma embraced me, for she never got over her fear of big cities. At Christmas Eve, she laid out her pathetic soup and hard bread. Then we all checked our stockings and went to sleep happy. But at midnight, I slipped out into the barn, and pulled out the package, and put the baby Jesus statue in place in our kitchen. When the daylight came, Momma was down at the stove, and saw the baby Jesus. She started screaming, 'Look, look all. It is miracle, it is a miracle. *Miracolo*. Baby Jesus has really come. Look papa, my prayers have been answered.'

"So that Christmas was important and special to her. The next year, papa and I emigrated to America to get some work and then went back after six months. I returned years later by myself and came back several times. People called us 'birds of passage.' When Momma and Papa died, none of my brothers or sisters knew what happened to baby Jesus. He just disappeared, as strangely as he came."

"So that is why you smiled when I mentioned the nativity scene?"

"Yes, that is why. At my age, all you have are memories, and some are very good ones."

"Have you ever thought at your age of going back once again to visit Italy?"

He got very somber. "Why the hell should I? Not all memories are good ones."

So it was on that day that I understood that Grandpa was a man of sentiment, but not sentimental, that he was a man who wished to let parts of his past be buried, and that he was once a young boy devoted to his Momma's heart.

61. ONE IS THE LONELIEST NUMBER

As Grandpa reached for a cup of espresso, the black phone in the corner rang belligerently. He hated phone calls in the early morning or late at night, for they only brought bad news. He picked up the heavy receiver, for he had refused to get a princess phone, and heard the voice of Frank Volpe, the attorney uptown, "Raffaele, can we get together sometime today?"

"Some problem, Frank?"

"Yes, mine not yours."

"I'll come up right after breakfast. Is that okay?"

"That is great. Thanks a lot, Raffaele."

Grandpa walked up to the office and sat down in the old leather chair Volpe had had since the last war.

"Raffaele, I trust you and admire you, as you are aware. I am going to tell you a family secret. As you know, my brother Al died two weeks ago."

"I know, I am so sorry."

"The whole family appreciated you showing up for both the wake and the Mass. It was so sad."

"Heart attack?"

"No, I can say this only to you—it was a suicide. We didn't tell the priest. He could not have been buried in sacred ground. So we kept the casket closed. He shot his face off. This is not unusual for my family; our father killed himself by hanging on the crossbeams of a barn, and a cousin in Italy poisoned herself. We have what is called congenital depression. Frankly, I feel at times depressed for no reason, it is in our blood."

"I am sorry, Frank, I did not know. You always seem so happy. I knew Al and worked with him on the Dodge estate. He was quiet but never depressed. I guess I never knew."

"We knew, and there was not anything we could do for him. Medication, shock therapy, high priced psychologists. Nothing prevented the final atrocity. I had to bury papa and now him. I can't do it anymore, Raffaele. He was a rich man, after his wife died. He had his fortune and hers, and it didn't matter. But I have called you here to help our *famiglia*. Please."

Grandpa deeply nodded, "Of course, anything Frank."

"Al left a son, who goes to the Catholic high school, Bailey-Ellard. Frankly we fear that it is in his blood—he is so quiet, a sad boy who just looked at his father's closed coffin and didn't say anything, He is living with me, but I can't deal with his problems, it is in our blood. We need a steady role model, a man who is honest and caring, with his head screwed on right. Life has paralyzed us all; we need somebody who can bring the light. I have been asked by the *famiglia* to please have you become the boy's guardian for a year."

Grandpa was startled, "Thank you, but I am too old to be much of model to a young teenager."

"Yes, we have discussed that, but we feel that you are so respected and decent, and you knew Al, if only in passing in the early years, so that you could contain the boy, dilute his cursed blood, teach him to enjoy life. Please, Raffaele, please for me and the boy."

"I knew him only in passing."

"He is in the care of a psychologist in Morristown, Elisabeth Gerro. Go talk to her, please."

Grandpa was never good at saying no, and reluctantly agreed. But his family had no suicides in Italy. He wasn't even sure about what the warning signs were, and why people took their own lives. After all, he believed that life was gift from the Creator to be taken only by Him. For it is written, we know neither the hour nor the day.

He went up to see Dr. Gerro and was given permission from Frank to talk about the boy. Grandpa was a little tired and reserved at first, but Dr. Gerro was open and expressive.

"Mario is a good boy overall, but the death of his mother from cancer hit him hard. She was the only person who could talk to him, and he said she was the only person in life who was always nice to him."

"So sad, " said the old man, "that he has the malady too. Frank said it is the blood."

"No, it has nothing to do with his blood. Sometimes Frank is an idiot. No, there is indeed a propensity in some families toward suicide, look at the famous painter, Vincent van Gogh. And he had it all. Somehow this boy has to see people contented and doing meaningful work, with meaningful relationships. The only girlfriend he had left him to date the Bailey-Ellard quarterback, and he never dated again."

"What can I do? I am totally ignorant of his sort of illness...except it did occur with my brother's widow and daughter at Greystone. I just can't imagine welcoming suicide, death is so final, it is unnatural."

"For some it is a quick end to a sad life, a termination to a terminal disease."

"But I am an old man. My child rearing days are over."

"I think the family feels that Mario needs some balance. He needs a man who is respected that he can talk to. They don't think he has a peer who is a good influence, and the family is in shambles."

"But I am an old man, I can't relate to an energetic and troubled teenager."

"People feel you should be yourself, and it will help the boy."

"What is this suicide? What causes it?"

"Frankly we have speculations, but not a cause. All we know is that the occurrence is going up in America."

"I will help of course, but what can I do exactly?"

"Be yourself. Let him see a strong, honest man."

And so Grandpa left and was as unknowledgeable as when he came. That night he met Mario for dinner at his apartment. Frank brought over his suitcase, and quickly left, to Grandpa's chagrin.

"Please sit down Mario. Want a coke? I'm making a quick dinner for us."

"No."

"How about a glass of my wine."

"You would give wine to a minor!"

"You can give wine to guests in your own home."

"I am a guest. You mean you're my paid guardian."

"Paid, by whom?"

"You are getting a $500 a month for keeping me."

"I am getting nothing. Your father was an early friend of mine. We worked together for the Dodge people. I don't charge friends."

Mario was a bit embarrassed and apologized.

Then Grandpa put down two plates of pasta, poured two goblets of wine and began:

"Tell me, was your father so depressed? Was it the loss of Maria?"

"Yes, in part, he loved her dearly. The death stayed with him day after day. But I guess you know about my grandfather and how he ended his life. Who knows why?'

"Yes, I have heard."

"And your job is easy—it is to make sure I don't make it three in a row."

"You must want it, make sure you do. I will help, but it is your decision in the end."

The old man said little, then finished off the meatballs but just pushed his pasta around. "Look, I cannot stop you from doing anything. But I can show you the beauties of nature which is a good part of the joy of being. You may see or not. There is nothing more attractive than a little girl picking pansies…"

Mario just listened and finally said, "That is all meaningless, a child who will die, a flower that will wilt."

Grandpa was not a man of tough love. You got his message, or you didn't. "Here is the way it will be for the next year, my son. You will go to high school five days a week, on Saturdays and holidays, you will work with me gardening at different sites in town."

"I hate gardening."

"I don't care. This is how you will earn your keep."

"So, you are not getting the $500 a month after all."

"I already told you. Your papa and I came over here and worked together."

Mario looked at Grandpa's dated apartment and his threadbare furniture. "It looks like he did a hell of a lot better making money."

"Yes, in terms of possessions he certainly did. But I have five living children and a host of grandchildren. I am rich beyond compare, my son."

Mario said nothing, pushed the spaghetti around and finally said, "You know it is in my blood, and no psychologist or priest or even a wise old man can stop it from overturning me."

"I am an old man, whether I am a wise man or not, I don't know. But I do know life is so brutal and so short, you want to fight to hold on to it. You will feel better than you even knew after a good day's work. Yes, I know your family's sad history, and I will pray for you."

"Forget prayers, I have done that routine. I have read in school Dylan Thomas's definition of life—cruelty, doubt and, confusion. I live in that world."

Grandpa responded as if pricked by a pin, "I do not know Thomas, but I agree we are drowning in all that. But we have beauty, joy, and the rising sun. They remind us of life in its entire splendor, Mario."

"You are an optimist."

"No I am just an old man who has seen a lot. You are right. I can't do what psychologists and priests do, or your papa couldn't help. But tomorrow, we begin early. It is a new day in your whole life."

They finished dinner, Mario was put up in the guest bedroom and he vanished till morn.

It was Saturday, and they began early. Grandpa had promised the town he would update the rundown James Park, dedicated to Madison veterans who had died in the wars. Mario jumped into his Ford pickup truck. He didn't realize the morning could start on the weekends before the cartoon, "Mighty Mouse."

Grandpa showed him how to trim the evergreens and put across a string so he could do it straight. To Mario's surprise, the old man used a manual pair of shears not an electric one. But for a new recruit, he did a good job, as Grandpa put assorted flowers in front of each memorial tree. He called Mario over, "See, this is to remember my nephew Nicholas. He died at Iwo Jima on the first day. He was a Marine. He was 19."

Mario looked silently and thought, *What a waste.*

Grandpa seemed to work harder as the sun got hotter as he wished to finish up the work before dinnertime. Then they put his rusted tools back into the truck, and Grandpa offered to take Mario to Rocco's down off Main Street.

It was a good day's work, and Mario did feel that he had accomplished something. "Tell me, do you ever think of Nick and his sacrifice?'

"Yes, many days. He was your age almost, and a good quiet boy."

"He died in a meaningless war, Pop."

"No, it was a war that needed to be won, but that doesn't mean we don't weep. Before he went over, he told me one night he did not expect to return."

"Doubt and confusion."

"He was a good boy, and a real gentleman. But his family never got over it. Death is so final."

Rocco was playing the collected songs of Mario Lanza, the Philadelphia tenor who was at times truly magnificent. His "Be My Love" was on the top ten list of popular music for six months. Grandpa, who had met Caruso twice, said that Lanza was as close to Caruso as one can get, but he still was not the Great Caruso, although he played him in the movie.

"I wonder how any man can hit that high note," Mario asked.

"Ah, he is the master of the high C's," Grandpa laughed.

"Uncle Frank tells me you a widower."

"Yes, my wife died before she was 60. I loved her, I think, more than she loved me. But who knows the human heart's feelings."

"Tell me, have you ever thought of suicide?"

Grandpa stopped and then responded, "I have known deep depression and terrible sadness, but not a thought of suicide. It is also against the Church's law I imagine you have?"

"I live with it, and my father's death made it so graphic and so normal."

"No, man should not have a say in when he will leave any more than he had a say when he began. Did Al tell you that he was thinking of it?"

"No, never. I know he was depressed, but not suicidal. But the death of mother made him deeply sad, he rarely spoke after that. Except one day he saw you in the green truck, and said, "There is a great man, I knew him once but no more.""

"I didn't realize he would remember me!"

"Yes, he remembered everybody and every slight that he had ever experienced. He lived with those demons, you could see it in his face, especially at night They would get a hold of his soul, and sometimes he could barely shake it. More and more he used alcohol to drive them away."

Grandpa listened quietly and wished he had visited Al more in those years, especially when his wife was alive.

"Whiskey is bad for you, Mario, it leaves you *stunad* in the morning and you cannot do anything until noon."

"I don't drink. I don't like the bitter taste. But it does chase the demons away. They just get bigger and then pop."

Grandpa sipped his cream soda waiting for his veal parmigiana and the boy's pizza slices.

"Stay away from the hard stuff. It is what killed Alexander the Great."

"What?" the boy asked.

"Yes, the great conqueror died at 32, leaving no more worlds to conquer. He used to salute himself every night with the hard stuff. So it is said that he cut his wine with a sort of soda."

"How do you know about the death of Alexander?"

"I saw it on a television show. He conquered the world, and then insisted his soldiers marry native girls wherever he was. That way there would be only one race."

"Interesting. My uncle said I must live with you until I graduate. He insists you are the most decent man in Madison. What did you do to earn that title?"

"I do not know. There are many fine men in Madison, more decent and more successful. I am just an old man who lives according to the *tradizione*, the old way of life. Tell the truth even if it hurts; give a man a handshake as your word; respect women and care for children; do one good deed a day; take care of the poor and the maimed; acknowledge God even when He does bad things to you; enjoy the little things in life; promote friendships; treat strangers as friends; embrace the sun, fear the moon, await the change of the seasons; and smile every morning. Every day when I wake up in the morning I say, '*Grazie a Dio sono vivo*' (Thank God I am alive). There are many other codes that will make you more money, give you pretty girls to seduce, provide wealth, but in the end, life is measured by its simple triumphs not by its world successes. Do well the ordinary duties of the day. For much passes away, except a man's reputation. I am pleased that Uncle Frank gave you to me as your guardian, if only for a year. It is a great honor."

Mario was quiet for the longest time. He realized that this old working man lived by a real code of behavior. He was not just a *cafone*, but a person who had thought about life with the depths of a Plato. But still he would not let go. "Your code is admirable, but it is out of date. A man like you could have been richer, with large estates not a decrepit apartment in the center of Madison. You're a good man, why not go for it. Go for the brass ring."

"Ah, my boy, look around you at the sadness. The brass ring soon tarnishes and what do you have left?"

Then they went home in silence after the meal. Sunday Grandpa was up early to go to church. He was surprised when Mario was waiting for him in the kitchen.

"Mind if I go, pa?"

"No, no, we can make the seven o'clock mass if we hurry."

Finally the boy graduated from Bailey-Ellard—in the middle of his class.

Still Grandpa insisted on a party and had his daughters prepare a feast, for such occasions deserved recognition. The girls outdid themselves, all insisted, and the old men played bocce. Before the game, Grandpa asked the other guys to let Mario win once. And the balls suddenly went short, or long, and he came close to the little ball or *pallino*. It was a great game which Grandpa insisted the centurions played while wailing for Caesar to decide to cross the Rubicon.

The next week Frank Volpe called Mario and Grandpa to his office to inform them that as the executor of the family will, he had taken the liberty to invest Mario's inheritance in a stock called IBM. Al and his wife had a considerable amount of money, a house, a cottage at Asbury Park, and some land in north Jersey in the cities overlooking New York City. Overall Mario's net worth was $2 million. Grandpa was startled. Mario was quiet.

Afterward, Mario offered to split the bequest up with Grandpa, but he knew the old man's answer.

Mario went out in Grandpa's truck and brought a beautiful black Corvette and then visited a realtor. He wanted to buy a horse ranch in nearly Florham Park and breed horses. How he became interested in that occupation was a total surprise.

But he opened up the ranch, hired a considerable number of staff and lived like a squire. Finally when it was painted and repaired, he invited Grandpa.

The old man came and was impressed by the beautiful stately mansion. In the back was a long warehouse three times the size of his.

Grandpa remarked, "Ah, Mario, you have a fine wine pressing operation here."

"I do, I do, more than yours I bet. I hope the wine is as good."

"Let us see."

"No, pa, this is the same, really,"

"Oh, let me see." And he pushed open the door and saw a beautiful new wine press. He saw bottles filled up to the roof. But in the corner, he saw two guns—an M16 and a Luger. Above them was the scapula of Our Lady of Mount Carmel that the old man had given Mario one tough night.

"Are there suddenly lot of wolves and bears in Florham Park. I never remember them."

"No, pa, they are there for the nightmares."

"You still have them?"

"No, but you know. Nothing is forever."

Grandpa fixed his eyes on Al's old service pistol. "Mario, be careful, some things are forever."

62. WEEDS

The women in the Sodality of the Blessed Virgin Mary at St. Vincent Martyr were weary of seeing the gardens of the church look so overrun and totally disheveled, and they had read about Grandpa's work at Princeton University as a "consultant." So they decided to ask their co-religionist to help his own parish. Never prone to say no, he agreed, and of course it turned out to be a more extensive job than he expected, and unlike at the university he refused to take compensation. He asked only that priests say a series of Gregorian Masses in Grandma's memory for thirty days straight. He decided to divide the space up into sections that featured pansies, tulips, and the saddest flowers of all, lilies, the symbol of death.

As he worked though he noticed a stream of older boys coming out of the rectory, some with looks of guilt on their young and innocent faces. *What is going on?* he thought. After seven days of this traffic, he began to get suspicious, and he approached his grandson, an altar boy, and bluntly asked him what was happening at the rectory that made it so attractive. He had always found it a dark and dated place, full of overstuffed furniture and old sofas.

His grandson hemmed and hawed, but as Grandpa became clearly annoyed, he told the old man, "This new pastor acts weird with boys."

"Weird, how, son?"

"Weird as always taking them to strange places. He touches you and invites the boys to pool parties or house parties. He and another priest have a fenced in house on Sherman Avenue."

"What do the neighbors say?"

"Nothing I know. I hear this from other altar boys."

"Have you gone with him?"

"No, I don't trust him."

Grandpa nodded, but he didn't believe his grandson. Boys at that age are preoccupied with sex and talk of nothing else. But the next several weeks in the summer, he saw the same occurrences, and one day a group of boys scantily clad in bathing suits piled into the car of the priest and swiftly left with him. For some reason, he decided to follow them. They went up to the lake; the priest's parish car was parked at the edge of the tree line, and

Grandpa parked a bit away, and quietly trod like a breeze on leaves to see what was happening. There on the ground were piles of clothes, towels, and a Roman collar. The group stripped down to skinny dip, yelling, screaming, horsing around, and slapping ass. And the most active was the priest. It looked to Grandpa like some kind of pagan holiday, and he stayed only long enough to bear witness to the transgressions.

Back home, he came face to face with what he saw. Should he tell the bishop of Paterson, but he had transferred the priest from the hard labor of that Passaic city to the comforts of the quiet suburbs. He could think of no one to confide in.

Then it struck him—Sister Agatha, the hard, rugged principal who made a virtue out of meanness. The other nuns hated her, the children feared her, the priests tried to ignore her. But over the years, she had become the school principal and ran a tight ship indeed. At the end of the day, he approached her and asked to speak to her in private. She figured it was another complaint about how she treated the children, but she knew the old man from his many children and grandchildren who had been her students at the elementary school.

Once in her office, Grandpa told her bluntly what he had seen, and as he went on, he felt that she knew these matters from her own sources. She squinted at him, "I too have had suspicions. He is too friendly to be a proper priest, but I insisted to myself that I have to trust the bishop's judgment in visiting him on us. But something is going on, I did not believe it is as bad as you say."

Grandpa asked, "Should we tell the bishop our suspicions?"

"No, he is either naive or dishonest, another Vatican mistake."

Then she pondered, "One of my students is now the police chief, Jimmy Fitzgerald, and I will go with you and ask him how to deal with such talk. They surely have seen this elsewhere."

The next afternoon, they went to the chief who still lived in intimidation of Sister Agatha. She told the story that she and Grandpa had agreed on. And to her surprise, the chief did not blink but pulled out a thick file. Apparently, the Madison police force had its own documents and was aware of the group on Sherman Avenue. They were ready to move on the priest "orgy", as the chief called it, if it became more apparent.

"What should we do?" asked Grandpa.

Fitzgerald answered, "Let me propose a letter for him that is notarized for the bishop and then get the pastor to sign it. I will release it to the newspapers and the bishop at the same time. The Morristown paper loves scandals. Sister, please make an appointment for the three of us to visit the pastor, make it at three in the afternoon, just before the newspaper deadlines."

So they went up in unison to see the priest, who figured it was another nuisance visit about some damage the kids had done. Instead he was confronted immediately by a resolute police chief. "We all know of your activities with young boys, and of your record elsewhere. [The other two never knew of that.] This is a letter of resignation to the bishop in which you are leaving the priesthood forever and asking to be laicized by the Vatican. The bishop will never give you a letter of reference as he would be open to civil damages. Do you understand? Actually you have no rights, this is the worst crime against the young. Our juries don't like that stuff in this area. May God forgive your rotten soul."

A shaken priest signed the document, and the three of them abruptly left the grim rectory. Outside the chief said that he had to go to the editor and then to the weak-kneed bishop. (On Sunday a new Filipino priest was in place of the bright young pastor.) Off the chief went in a hurry, and the principal and Grandpa looked closely at each other.

Sister Agatha watched the old man, and saw he was clearly upset.

"What is it, Raffaele, surely you don't feel sorry for that sinner?"

"No, I don't. We have protected our own children, but what of the others he has violated? Do they think they are the ones guilty in some way of this terrible crime, that they led him on? Do they have difficulties with women and living with their wives in a normal relationship because of their memories? How many innocent souls were lost because he was their ideal of a priest?"

But Sister Agatha was a principal, and she was not going to let him go home feeling that way, "Now you listen to me, you are a gardener and know how the most beautiful garden has ugly weeds. We must pull them out. We cannot pull them up in every garden in the world, for God has given us just a few years to live. But today we have protected *our* garden. We have done good. Now I must go in the church and say my beads, for I must pray for my soul; surely no one else in this parish will."

And she turned on her heels, pulled out her rosary, and climbed up the side of the stairs to the church entrance.

63. THE LOSS OF INNOCENCE

St. Vincent Martyr in Madison was one of the oldest Catholic churches in the state, and the new ambitious pastor decided to publish a special history of the congregation. While people were researching the major parts of the volume, there was talk of the disappearance of the famed statue of the Virgin Mary. On the right side of the altar of the church was a full-sized reproduction of Mary, and for some reason her eyes seemed to follow you as you walked by. It was like the smile of the Mona Lisa. But when the new brand of ecclesiastical vandals after Vatican II decided to rearrange the whole inside, they ripped the marble altar apart, placed the choir on the left of the floor, abandoned the loft in the upper back, and made the pews into uncomfortable chairs throughout the old church. And the ancient statue of Mary was gone. The priests claimed they did not touch it in their crude redecoration.

The story was that one night a group of *goombahs* under their mothers' orders put the statue in a pickup truck and hustled it off to the house of a devout Italian admirer of the Virgin who reverently placed it in the basement of her home surrounding it with flowers every day. No neophyte priests were going to destroy the statue the way they had cut up the marble altar. One of his grandsons went to Grandpa and told him about the history, and he was proud of the efforts because of all the money the Italians had given for the church and the school. But when he was asked if he knew where the statue was, he gave off a nondescript response.

"Perhaps."

"Well, can you tell us at least where the statue went?"

"No, I can't."

"You don't know, or you don't want to talk about it?"

"Perhaps, yes."

So thus was the mystery of the missing Madonna.

The same pastor, who asked for a commemorative volume, also decided that he would begin "a mission back to Jesus" for the somnolent church. He would bring Jesuits to run a nine day novena, to hear confessions all day, and to say a special Mass every morning. The Italian people were confused for they thought that the mission to Jesus was what they had been doing every

Sunday. But out of respect, they went along with the new pastor, an Irishman named Joseph Patrick O'Brien.

O'Brien began his mission by putting the golden monstrance with the Sacred Host in the middle of the church altar and leaving the church open all day and night. It was, he said, a sign of the openness of Christ to us sinners. But on the second day, the monstrance and the host vanished; it had been stolen! The priest was angry and terribly distraught; if the bishop heard of this he would be shipped out of the highly regarded affluent parish into the harsh lands of Paterson.

He needed help, but it had to be discrete help, effective but quiet. He needed the assistance of respected members of the community, and he decided to visit Grandpa since he had heard of an article about him and Einstein working together, it was said, on a piece of property at Princeton University. So early before lunch he climbed the back steps of the old man's apartment to see Grandpa who was just having a piece of provolone and salami and a glass of watered down wine.

At the tap on the screen door, Grandpa looked up. He had not seen a priest in his place since the saintly Father Lambert came to visit his son when he had polio. "Good day, father."

"Ah, my friend, may I come in."

"Surely, let us have a glass of wine in your honor."

"Good, but don't dilute it. I can take it straight." *He was an Irishman, of course*, Grandpa thought.

He got down to business quickly, almost in a panic. "My friend, I have come on a serious moral problem and I need your help." And he went to explain his great mission for Christ, and how the monstrance and the Sacred Host were stolen.

"That is a sacrilege, father, a gross sacrilege. I am sorry."

"I know, and I want you to help me. I need to know the names of the people who stole them, and I can only get the names if I know a person in the right place."

Grandpa frowned, *was the priest asking him for the name of mobsters who could assist him?* "Look, father, I have all of my life stayed away from the mob, the Mafia, La Cosa Nostra, whatever they are calling them this week."

The priest immediately knew he had hit the wrong note. "Oh no, your reputation is well known and respected by all, especially your pastor. But you are a man who surely has known a lot over the years; can you at least give me the name of the local don here in town. I will talk to him one Catholic to another."

"What, one Catholic to another? These men are mobsters, rapists, extortionists, who prey on Italians more than anyone."

"I know that, of course. It is terrible. I condemn the Mafia as the popes have. They will go straight to hell. But I just wish to know where the don lives. I have not come to praise him."

Grandpa just wanted to get the confused priest out of his house. "Try Archie Gallo, he lives next to the Knights of Columbus Hall. He sits there all summer on a chair reading Dante's *Inferno*."

"Dante's *Inferno?*"

"Yes. I guess he wants to know what it will be like when he gets there. For surely he won't be meeting Beatrice."

The priest ignored the humor and grabbed the full glass of wine, gulped it down, and responded, "Thank you, my friend."

"Yes, and my prayers too, good to finally meet you, padre."

Father O'Brien drove up quickly to the Knights of Columbus Hall on North Street, and there he saw Don Gallo. He stopped in front of the dumpy Cape Cod with a statue of the Sacred Heart of Jesus in the front. He called over to Gallo, "Mr. Gallo, may I come over to see you?"

The don was startled, but he had an Old World sense of hospitality and rose up to greet the priest.

"I am Father O'Brien, the new pastor."

"Yes, I know."

"How do you know already?"

"I am paid to know. Last week a pretty girl came by, and I stopped her and asked how Yemen was. She was surprised I knew that she was sent by the State Department to sing jazz to those barbarians. I am paid to know everything in this neighborhood."

"Well, then let me tell you about the terrible robbery your church has had, Mr. Gallo."

And he went on to relate to him, the mission, the Jesuits, and the loss of the monstrance and the Sacred Host.

The don listened closely, and remarked at one point, "You sure the Jesuits did not steal it? They are a bad lot, especially in Europe."

"No, no, it is a neighborhood job."

"Father, I am very sick. I don't know if I have the stamina to help."

"Please, Mr. Gallo, please Don Gallo, you are my only hope."

"All right, you will have the gold monstrance in two days."

"Two days?"

"Maybe three."

So the word in the neighborhood went out. Someone had brought disgrace on the region and on our religion. In two days, the sacred vessel must be placed on the steps of the church or a mother will be wailing and wearing black for seven years. The next night, the monstrance was on the steps undisturbed.

Three months later, Don Archie Gallo died of stomach cancer, and his family wanted him to be buried in consecrated ground after a full funeral Mass. He especially wanted them to play Aquinas' hymn *Tantum ergo* which he first heard as a boy in Italy. The busybodies of the parish demanded that the pastor not allow the scandal. He was a mobster, a murderer, a pimp. But Father O'Brien ordered a full funeral and an orthodox burial. Immediately, the bishop called. He loved to chastise his priests for offenses, real and imagined.

"You have violated canon law. This man Gallo is a scandal to the Church. You cannot give him a Mass and a burial."

But O'Brien explained rapidly, "I was there when he died. His family called me, and I gave him the last rites, and then heard his final confession. Boy, did he have lots of mortal sins. I wish I could just tell you a few of them. Before the end I gave him absolution, and he died in my arms and in the bosom of Holy Mother Church."

The bishop did not know what to say. "Well, father, you acted appropriately, just like a good priest. I support you. May God bless you, father. I am so glad I put you in that parish. Goodbye."

And he abruptly hung up. Father O'Brien aimlessly played with the colored buttons on his phone, and thought, *I wonder what type of sin it is to lie to one's bishop.*

64. IT'S ELEMENTARY

Some days are just more wearying than others. Grandpa once speculated that in the morning you feel two types of pain: the old ones due to age and the new ones arriving that day. *It is a great life if you don't weaken,* he would consistently think. He sat down slowly, put on the radio, and waited until *Amos and Andy*, a comedy featuring the Kingfish, came on the radio. It was a group of black actors in neighborhood situations which showed the stupidity of people we all live with. Most of the old immigrants did not know the main actors were supposed to be black, but they were really white. In fact, when the *Goldbergs* came on most of the Italians thought the mother was not Jewish, but one of theirs. It was the craziness of offensive Depression era American humor.

Grandpa laughed at the hijinks of the Kingfish, and then turned the radio off at the end of the show. He preferred his old black and white television, and often dozed off watching his favorite shows: *Perry Mason* and *Gunsmoke. It was too bad someone doesn't invent a way to keep the shows in the television and then one can go back later and watch*, he speculated.

Nothing very good was on that night, and so he turned to Channel 9, the old movie channel. Grandpa had seen *Casablanca* six times and *Gone with the Wind* four times. There was a very limited array of films in their repertoire then. But that night they had a Sherlock Holmes film, *The Hound of the Baskervilles*, starring the indomitable Basil Rathbone and his sidekick Nigel Bruce. Grandpa settled in his chair and began to observe the Great Observer. More than the story, he was fascinated by the techniques that Holmes used in his work: acute perception; identifying physical markings; extracting clues from the common stuff of life. It was a difficult way of thinking for him. *How much of life have I personally seen over the years, and not really seen at all?* He was just not observant enough. He overlooked clues too often and found his eyes normally did not see what was in front of them.

And the next days and weeks, he went back to work with no real fervor. One of his clients was Mrs. Joan Freidman, a rich socialite who had married a physician, Herbert Freidman, a gynecologist. She married for love, or at least affection. He married for money. They constantly argued, and when the windows were open any passerby could hear the vulgar language used by the doctor.

"You rich bitch, if you think I am going to kiss your ass, you're are wrong, my dearest. I am a respected doctor and I don't need your low level approval. Go back to your finishing school, you bitch."

She responded, "Just because you look at women's crotches all day, doesn't mean you have to play house with them."

"If you were not such an ice cube, I'd be in your bed more, although I doubt I would enjoy it."

Grandpa had never heard married couples talk that way. And it continued day after day. One afternoon in sympathy, he brought Mrs. Freidman two bottles of his finest red wine as a gift for her graciousness to him. She invited him in, and they talked of the lawn and the gardens and their children and grandchildren. She was German by background and was reading the poet Goethe in the original. Grandpa didn't know Goethe, but he respected what poets did, and talked to her in a haphazard way how he had learned in school about Petrarch and his beloved Laura.

"Oh, to have a Petrarch, to be a Laura," she exclaimed and then seemed to become so lonely-looking.

They met several times and talked briefly after he finished his work, and she greatly admired their companionship. Apparently, she secretly visited her lawyer at Volpe and Volpe in Madison, and had Grandpa be the heir to $1,500. He didn't know, but her husband found out from the lawyers. *Was this just the beginning of her breaking up her fortune,* the doctor wondered.

Then one afternoon, her husband came home early and found his wife dead. She had been drinking some of Grandpa's wine and eating several biscuits. The police chief immediately arrived, and ordered the body brought to the funeral home of Thomas Chanconne where an autopsy was ordered. Her husband said that in his professional opinion, she probably died of a heart attack, for she was a worrying sort. Grandpa heard the news right away, and all he could remember were the angry conversations of the good doctor.

The chief did a cursory exam, but the medical examiner judged from a preliminary autopsy that it was conclusive: she had been poisoned. And all she had taken in that day were a few biscuits and a glass of red wine. The chief asked Grandpa to join him with the doctor at the house for some questioning about the strange death. The chief began, "My friends, it appears that our beloved Mrs. Freidman did not die of natural causes."

"What?" the doctor muttered.

"She was poisoned with a fairly strong dose. We have examined her stomach and the biscuits. She was poisoned from the wine. Ralph, was that your wine?"

Grandpa trembled, "Yes, yes it was. It was the best of my stock that year. My friends and I have been drinking it with no problems."

The chief just responded, "Well, this was a real problem and she is lying in Tommy Chanconne's to prove it. Did she open it herself, doctor?"

"Of course, I don't drink, and I am sure that the dago red was to blame."

Grandpa was startled. The chief went on, "Did a maid or you open it for her before you left for the day?"

"No, I left early, and the maid was visiting her daughter in Morristown."

The chief went on, "The corkscrew has no evidence of poison on it, but the bottom of the cork and the bottle are contaminated. She apparently opened the new bottle, and drank it immediately, and soon died. Do you understand my comments, Ralph?"

"No, it is a good wine. It was bottled pure, and I gave it to her as a sign of friendship."

The doctor snarled, "You gave it to her because you couldn't wait for your $1,500 from the will. You guineas are all alike, like Sacco and Vanzetti. They used a gun, you used poison, like the old d'Medicis in Florence." And on and on he rambled as Grandpa stood frozen.

"It cannot be, I don't even know about $1,500, what is it for?"

"Well it ain't for murder. You'll get nothing now," screamed the doctor.

The chief stepped in, "Ralph this is very serious, I will not release the autopsy until it is replicated by the more professional FBI lab in Newark. You won't be arrested, but you are not to leave Madison. Doctor, I am sorry about your wife's demise, but now I must go through her possessions. Ralph go home, count yourself lucky so far. You had better get a lawyer to protect yourself."

Grandpa left in a daze and went back to his apartment. He could not understand what had just happened. The first thing he did was go to his warehouse and systemically drink a half glass of his wine from six different bottles. All was good. He looked at the bottles he had used for three years, and the corks were brand new.

For two nights he paced the floor. Somehow this had happened. It had been a good deed, a present, and now a nightmare. Once the autopsy got in from Newark, his reputation would be destroyed even if they later found him innocent. He would be forever the guy with the poison wine.

He should have not talked to her, sat down with her and chattered about Petrarch and the German poets. *But it seemed so innocent, so pleasant. How did it happen? The chief had made up his mind, even though he has known me for many years, and he had played with my kids. Now he thinks me capable of murder! Good God what have I done to deserve this,* he thought.

He must pull himself together and defend himself alone for no one will help. Then he thought of Sherlock Holmes. He was an expert on poisons and types of cigar ashes. Grandpa decided to adopt his teachings—he must be more observant. The next day he quietly went to the scene of the crime again and looked first for strange footprints on the outside near the windows. All he found were his own—a truly bad sign. Then he retraced his steps from his truck to the backdoor, and how Mrs. Freidman took the bottles from him and thanked him. She didn't open them or lay them aside. Then how was she poisoned—not by the crackers, but by his wine? He went back to his own warehouse and looked again at the wine bottles. Could the glass have turned rancid, and poisoned the wine? "No, glass doesn't turn and these are only three years old," he muttered. Grandpa had purchased new corks and even swallowed pieces of them and could not find a problem. *Good God, what would Sherlock Holmes do?* At this point, he would settle even for Doctor Watson. Then he had a sudden insight, too crazy to be true, but perhaps like Holmes you have to discount one by one alternative explanations.

Three days later the chief called Grandpa and the physician together at the scene of the crime. He was going to arrest Grandpa for first degree premeditated murder. *He was just doing his job,* he reasoned.

At the house, he surveyed what they knew of the terrible crime, and then he turned to Grandpa and concluded, "You have admitted you gave the two bottles of red wine to Mrs. Freidman, did you not?"

"Yes, I did."

"We know that she was poisoned from one of them."

Grandpa then unexpectedly said to the physician, "Yes, from one of them, but how about the other bottle, why don't you have a drink?"

The physician responded, "It doesn't matter, you have poisoned my poor wife."

Then Grandpa abruptly turned to the chief and presented him with the second bottle of wine after he looked at it clearly. "Chief, drink this one, but be careful. It is also poisoned!"

"Ralph, what the hell are you saying?"

"The open bottle and this other one were tampered with. Look at the cork. I bought these new corks this year, but this has a pin prick in the middle. If you could piece together the first cork, it too will have a pin prick."

"What the hell, I didn't look at the second one, damn it."

"This is total nonsense, he had admitted he poisoned both bottles, arrest him for Christ sake, chief. I want to see the little dago electrocuted in my lifetime," the physician protested.

"No, I do not have needles, only doctors do. You injected poison in both bottles, to kill your wife, didn't you doctor?" The chief grabbed the doctor's bag and looked for some needles. They were thinner than the usual ones and fit perfectly in the cork hole.

The chief angrily looked at the husband, "You bastard, of course you did it. You killed your wife. Since when does an Italian gardener have access to these types of needles and this clear liquid poison? You did it!"

The physician went silent and was handcuffed and went away in the squad car. The chief sheepishly turned to Grandpa, "Great detective work. I should have you on my squad." Later the physician got twenty years in Rahway State Prison, a facility that did not believe in rehabilitation, but only good old fashioned retribution.

Mrs. Freidman was very wealthy, and her estate went to her two hippie children who lived in Berkeley, California, except for $1,500 that was reserved for Grandpa. One afternoon, the attorney Volpe, "the fox" the old Italians called him, came over to visit Grandpa. He had been the trustee of her will and gave him $1,500 in one hundred dollar bills; he said that way Grandpa wouldn't have to pay taxes. The last time he had come to Grandpa's place, he wanted him to sign a petition to force a gay man out of town. Grandpa had tossed him out. Now he figured he would be in Grandpa's good graces, but the old man told Volpe it was *denaro sporco*, dirty money. But Volpe wisely insisted that all money was dirty money one way or another, for that is why God said we cannot take it with us when we go. He dropped the bills on the kitchen table, bowed and left.

Grandpa looked at them and replayed in his mind the whole story of how close he had come to having his reputation sullied and a murderer go free. In the end in a hostile world, one cannot count on others to protect you, you must be yourself alert and observant. Then he had an idea, he called up the Goethe-Institut in Manhattan and told them he wished to contribute a bequest in Mrs. Freidman's name and was sending by certified mail a letter with a cashier's check in it. What was their address? "On Irving Place? Ok." And so, the $1,500 went to the study of the German language and its greatest poet. Three weeks later in gratitude, the Institut sent him a bilingual copy of Goethe's finest work *Faust,* which told the story of a man who sold his soul to the devil for more things of this world.

65. THE WHITE FATHERS

The family knew the story of the courtship of Grandpa and Grandma which is related earlier. He arrived from America dressed in a fine new linen suit and good shoes and visited her father on the Perone farm. He had come determined to take a wife, and he had in mind their lovely daughter Luisa. He made overtures to the family, and they liked the idea of their favorite daughter marrying a rich *medigan*. But she ran away and hid in the barn, and finally she was convinced by her cousin that it would be a good marriage and she would get to see the land of milk and honey and live a life of ease. So they got married in the winter, honeymooned in Capri, and took the boat *Celtic* to the New World. Everybody knew the story of her reticence, and Grandpa got tired of hearing them repeat it. Once he said to his daughter, "If she didn't want to go, the hell with it." He would move on he had decided, but he did not.

They lived a full life, but some thought that he loved her more than she loved him. If so, nobody said so, for in those days people knew discretion. When before the age 60, she contracted an incurable disease and died, he was inconsolable. For months, he did not touch anything that she had placed around the apartment, including her clothes. Then one day, he decided that enough was enough. He started sorting through her possessions, and surprisingly he found a great deal of gold jewelry that she had squirreled away in her cases in her bureau. He had never seen her wear them, and some were quite beautiful, if not loving. Then he realized that these trinkets and chains had been given to her by her former boyfriends, and his anger and jealousy emerged. *She should have never even smiled at another boy until she met him.*

The next day, he took them all to the Rose City Jewelers and asked how much they would give him for all the gold. The jeweler, who had known Grandpa for years, remarked that this was "Italian gold," and was unalloyed with other metals. It was worth more than one thought—some $1,500 or so. "I could try to sell them, and give you the returns, as each piece would be purchased by individuals."

But Grandpa did not want to see people walking around Madison with the jewelry around their necks or on their wrists, and asked, "What else can we do with this gold?"

The jeweler indicated that since it was so pure, "I could melt it down into a bar of gold which would be worth $1,500 according to the most recent price on the open market." He expected a 10% fee for all his troubles, but Grandpa would still get a very nice piece of change. He agreed and came back a week later to take home his bar of gold. Now what was he going to do with it?

At this same time, the pastor of St. Vincent Martyr had announced that there would be a seven day retreat for men, run by the White Fathers. The Italians had heard of the Jesuits, the Dominicans, the Franciscans, and a dozen other orders, but the White Fathers? Apparently, they were missionaries to the poorest areas of the Third World, and they roamed vast distances in small airplanes providing the sacraments and also food and medicine for the poorest of the poor. Because of the airplane aspect of their mission, they became romantic heroes to many American Catholic boys. They were sort of Eddie Rickenbackers in white cassocks.

They came into the parish like an African desert storm, and the men flocked to their retreats since they seemed so virile and manly in a world run by widows, spinsters, and nuns. The men, especially the Italian American men and the Knights of Columbus members, filled the church. Men from even Berkeley Heights and its William Paca Italian club also made the trip for the full nine days. One of the priests told the story of imperialism in Africa, and how he was assigned to a former Italian colony in Addis Ababa, Ethiopia. Grandpa didn't even know the Italian government had a colony there. *Damn Mussolini, international thug,* he ruminated in his pew. The priests told stories of the incredible poverty, the malnutrition that the people endured, the death of infants, and the low life expectancy of children. They even showed heart-wrenching blown up pictures of stick children dying in their crying mothers' arms. Grandpa, a great lover of children, was deeply moved by the graphic stories of the White Fathers. At the end of the evening's retreat, each of the men received Holy Communion and prayed for the poor of the world, which thank God did not include them or their relatives in the old country.

The White Fathers asked modestly for some money for their work after each session, and people gave with respect. The last night Grandpa came with a different objective. When the collection plate came around, he did not give any cash. Usher Gerry Gerro looked at him with the evil eye, but the old man glanced away. Then after the service, he went into the sacristy, and talked to one of the White Fathers, saying he wanted to give him a special package. The Father looked at a brown box wrapped in an A&P bag and opened it in front of Grandpa. Grandpa was a great collector of old bags and used string for any occasion. There inside the bag was the golden bar. Being a man of the world, the priest knew exactly what it was, and thanked Grandpa profusely, "This will buy a lot of medicine for poor children in Ethiopia, sir."

"Yes, I know, please tell the children that not all Italians are *fascista*." Then he went over to the statue of the Virgin Mother which had the eyes that followed you, and lit a candle for Grandma, and walked away. He could swear the Virgin statue was smiling at him as he progressed out, but he did not turn around fearing that he would end up like Lot's wife—a figure of salt.

66. ONE LIFE TO LIVE

Just as he was on his way out the screen door, the telephone rang, and Grandpa heard the girlish voice of his granddaughter, Anna. Over the weekend, she had her new infant daughter baptized at St. Vincent Martyr Church in Madison, N.J. In the excitement of the ceremony and the adoring glances at the angelic baby, they had forgotten to get a copy of the little one's baptismal certificate. Could Grandpa stop on his way home and get a copy for their permanent records? In the Catholic Church, one could not receive communion, confirmation or marriage without the first document. Baptism opened the door to all the other sacraments. Grandpa obligingly said he would get a copy, and then hung up. "Good God," he murmured. "Am I the only one who knows where the rectory is located?"

At 4 p.m., he drove his old green Ford pick-up truck to the rectory and rang the multi-bell front door. It sounded like a Gregorian chant. Grandpa expected to see the housekeeper, a small, quiet Irish lady, who even the priests called "Mrs. O'Toole." She had been a widow for a decade, was a haphazard housekeeper, but a superb cook—which meant more to the bachelor priests.

But instead, the new curate, John Field, appeared in a black shirt and pants, but no Roman collar. He was part of the new wave of young priests, and he had been assigned to help the aging Monsignor Dauenhauer, a long-time friend of Grandpa and his family. *He is so young*, Grandpa thought. He explained briefly why he had come, and the priest warmly welcomed him. Grandpa asked him how the monsignor was doing, and the priest simply said, "He has his good days." The priest took Grandpa into his small study with a beautiful statue of the Infant of Prague. He motioned for Grandpa to sit down, but the old man was reluctant since he was "dirty" from a day's work in the gardens. "No, sit. It is an honest work. Before I went to the seminary, I worked with my grandfather who was on the staff at Mrs. Twomey's estate."

"Ah, a beautiful home and garden," Grandpa admiringly observed. "I used to work the rose gardens there when I first came to America."

"Ah, a rose man. Indeed."

"No, I love pansies more, and I am making new hybrids of the most exciting colors, Father."

The priest passed him a copy of the baptismal certificate and offered Grandpa a glass of white wine, which of course they enjoyed, for the sun was beginning to set after the three o'clock high mark.

The priest talked strangely of how he missed working with his grandfather, and then suddenly asked if he could work with Grandpa gardening, especially in the rose and pansy sections. Grandpa was a little surprised, but he of course concurred. In those days no one ever said no to the clergy or the sisters. He thought it was just a gesture of hospitality, but then the priest remarked, "I am off on Thursdays. Can we meet in the afternoons to garden together? It will mean a lot to me. It is God's work." So, over the years, he religiously showed up and enjoyed his companionship with the old man. He was a model priest they said, a priest's priest. He played basketball with the kids, organized a Girl Scout troop with even a Brownie contingent, set up Tuesday bingo to support the threadbare school, and heard confessions, even late into the evening. He forgave in God's name acts of near adultery, impure thoughts, dirty language, and the deepest fear for the very old that God did not even exist.

But after seven years, he left the priesthood quietly, and married a pretty Irish nurse from Overlook Hospital. He worked for the building and trades union and became a singular voice for civil rights for blacks. At night he would sit in his Adirondack chair in his backyard and watch a bald eagle flying over the gardens. He still retained his friendship with Grandpa, and neither spoke of his exit from the priesthood.

Then one day he was carelessly driving his black Volkswagen, hit a side bar, and crashed into an immovable tree. He broke five ribs and was temporarily paralyzed. He was rescued by an off-duty firefighter who pulled him out of his car, and then took him immediately to Overlook Hospital. They quickly looked for internal injuries, but in the process the x-rays found he was suffering from a form of amyloidosis, a disease that meant at best several months of life. He suffered incredible pain, especially in his legs, and it was more at times then he could even endure. And then he decided to celebrate his life and the gift of death. Grandpa promised to take care of his gardens and placed beautiful bright pansies in flowerpots. Other parishioners couldn't deal with the marriage of priests, but Grandpa was incredibly loyal to friends. Deep down he never knew how a vibrant man could retain vows of celibacy. Anyhow, in the backyard he sorted out the weeds and raked away the planted shrubs under a stone Buddha and a cement seat under the ferns. Here Mr. Field mediated twice a day, sometimes actually falling into the rituals of St. Ignatius of Loyola, the Jesuit founder.

He decided that he wished to rent out the hospitality room at the local Swiss chalet. His last supper would be the low budget feast he enjoyed as a young priest—rotisserie chicken legs with gravy. Then he would die swiftly and gracefully by lethal injection administered by a Canadian doctor friend. He would end his time on his terms before his voice totally gave way. He would be surrounded by his loved ones, not by machines and wires.

His message was not one of pain but of redemption. And in the process, he had come to preach when he was a priest messages of salvation to women who had abortions. He wrote a book of his experiences, *The Priest Who Sought the Pursuit of Cosmic Spirituality*, and he studied gestalt and was fascinated by the Jesuit theologian Pierre Teilhard de Chardin.

Every Wednesday his wife and children would light the dining room candles and put out the newest pottery. His family created pots of daffodils from Grandpa's stock.

The family doctor tried Lidocaine, a powerful local anesthesia used often by dentists and sought to free him from some of the pain. Finally he said to his family and friends, "I don't want to suffer anymore." His family and friends met together, including Grandpa, and his wife put a white khata, a Buddhist prayer shawl, around his shoulders. She quietly said to him, "I offer the blessings of a courageous heart." His union friends sang an old Celtic folk song, "But since it falls last my lot that I should rise, and you should not, I'll be quiet, I'll gently reserve, softly call, goodnight and joy with your all."

Field would doze off, saying, "We hear the blossoms pour forth into the night. We hear the silence of the bees. We hear the brushing of the wind in the trees. I will see you later. I will see you later," he concluded. And the doctor gave him Propofol, and then a paralytic drug called Rocuronium. Grandpa shuddered. He had never thought that assisted suicide would last so long. He thought life was hard, but that death would come easy. Since Field couldn't go into the garden, the family set up a garden in his room, an altar with green boughs and strong eagle feathers, a small candle, and a tiny bell. His wife told him to recite the names of his Irish father and Irish mother to help him come on the journey. And he recited the words of the Persian poet Rumi as well. They then began to sing the Gershwin song, "Who Could Ask for Any Thing More?" The others joined singing, "I've got daisies in green pastures, and who could ask for anything more?" Oddly he asked for a recitation of the prayer of St. Francis of Assisi:

> Where there is hatred, let me sow love.
> Where there is injury, pardon.
> Where there is doubt, faith.
> Where there is despair, hope.

Grandpa thought that he was still deep down viewing a traditional Catholic funeral. That evening Field's body was covered by a purple sheet, and then a thick brown blanket, and his body was cremated and stored in an urn below the statue of Buddha.

Grandpa felt that all this was strange, especially for a boy raised in the Latin rite. Two weeks later he walked quietly into the backyard and sat down on the marble bench, and began to pray for Field, and then reached into his pocket where he had his favorite possession, a rosary given to him years ago by Monsignor Dauenhauer who had had originally received it from his friend Eugenio Pacelli, Pius XII. Grandpa rose up and placed the rosary over the head of the Buddha, and then sat down.

But no, not this way. He rose, took off the rosary and then left. Field had made his choice, and it would be a sacrilege to seek to undo it now.

See: "The Life and Death of John Shield," *New York Times,* May 28, 2017.

67. THE BALLOON MAN

Ever since Grandpa was young, he would seek circuses and fairs to frequent. He especially liked clowns who seemed to tantalize people with their weird colored costumes. When he came to the U.S., he retained his affection, for even as adults we hold fondly onto our childhood sentiments. In Madison, he made friends with a new doctor and his family and would go with them to the local circus which usually set up shop in nearby Florham Park.

His favorite was an elderly clown called Benjy dressed in a red wig, an American flag, and large floppy shoes. His carried balloons of all sorts of colors and shapes most of the time. Some younger kids were frightened of him, but many went up to him to buy balloons. The older kids often received extra gifts, but he said nothing to scare them.

Circuses are as old as European fairs, but in America they were beginning to be phased out. The costs had grown prohibitive to maintain the animals and opposition has increased to incarcerating animals for human amusement. But that point of view was one that never crossed most people's minds. Finally after a couple of lean years, the circus closed, the elephants were put in zoos, and the fine specimens of young men and women drifted off to other jobs and places.

The balloon man stayed in the Madison area and rented a cheap room, was hired for birthday parties, and barely made ends meet. He was a regular at Catholic services, but he really was not a member of the faith. He just enjoyed the pomp and circumstances of High Masses, especially the vestments which for some strange reason reminded him of his old clown suits. He really wished though that he could rent a suit like the bishop of Paterson wore.

So he went to the library and learned about the more flamboyant saints, and came across the young St. Theresa of Lisieux, France, the so-called "Little Flower." She wanted to enter the Carmelite order at fifteen years of age, but she was blocked by different authorities. She finally appealed to Pope Leo XIII who seemed a little wary but left it in God's hands. Theresa was told she was to do His will not hers. She prayed, hoping her commitment to be a "victim soul" would lead to her sainthood, to being with God for all eternity.

Benjy learned that a victim soul was one who deliberately sought more pain and disappointment in life in order to bind more closely with Jesus in His suffering and crucifixion. Such saints prayed for more and more heartaches to offer up their hurt for the souls in purgatory. Some saints like St. Francis and St. Padre Pio actually experienced the stigmata in their bodies. The victim soul concept was a topic that men and women of faith dared to debate, for it seemed to question the inscrutable mind of the Almighty. Benjy was not sure he understood the whole idea and why it was desirable to the holy way of life.

Benjy did not want a life of more problems and suffering. His business was to make people laugh, enjoy themselves, and teach the little ones to relish his silliness. Man was created to mimic himself and other creatures. He had been told that there were several caves in France with pictures of primitive men hunting and fishing. Man knew what he was doing by enjoying himself. It was primitive man at play.

Suddenly he began to develop his own theology of joy, very different from that the Church. Man was created to enjoy the fruits of the earth and to mold his own creations. The pastor hired a Dominican priest to conduct a novena for the parish. He was an incredibly learned and articulate preacher. But he seemed to disagree with Benjy's view right away. For he insisted that man, like Adam and Eve, was not meant to enjoy the earth but to sweat under its burdens, to teach children not to be happy, but to be serious and sorrowful, for they had been expelled from the Garden of Eden. Life is short, and its ways are brutish. Name one man who has lived a life of total joy, he questioned.

Benjy was not a theologian, but he did enjoy the joys of life, especially making people laugh. Why can't people offer up joys as easily as heartaches to God, he pondered. But in a private conversation, the preacher insisted that Benjy wanted people to live lives of cotton candy and conduct high wire acts and never fall.

The balloon man could not deny that he was excited by happiness. And when the novena was over, he did not go to confession after all. He gave up the theology of victimhood. He must do what he liked best—selling balloons. He would wait on the sidewalks in front of the church with balloons of different colors. For weddings, he used white balloons, for graduation yellow like his gloves, and finally for funerals all black. But he told the children that they should let the balloons at funerals go up to heaven for their beloved to enjoy.

The pastor was not delighted to have a clown in front of the church, But Benjy stayed on the public sidewalk and could not be bothered. He appeared at event after event, making balloons symbols of his philosophy of life. Some young parishioners thought that was something to emphasize day by day.

Others stayed with familiar drugs and casual sex. One Sunday the bishop visited St. Vincent's parish, and he specifically blessed Benjy, having heard about his strange theology. It was heresy, but it was a harmless one, he told the pastor.

One afternoon after a funeral of a young girl, Benjy the balloon man walked up to the cemetery on Noe Avenue, sat down with a collection of balloons and laid in the circle of priests under the granite altar. The altar was engraved with "They were priests according to the rite of Melchizedek," the famed priest who blessed Abraham and El Elyon or "God on High" in Genesis.

He did not feel a victim, but just the last act in a slow-moving circus. Soon he expired. Grandpa was busy planting pansies on Grandma's gravesite when he saw the clown sloped over. He ran up to him under the altar and saw that he was indeed dead. He quietly cut the strings on his wrist and let the balloons float on upward into the sky.

68. A MIRROR SELF

The monsignor looked out of the dirty back windows of the rectory and saw the aging parochial school. "They are," he mused, "the future of the Church, the second generation after the immigrants who brought the faith with them in their hearts." He wondered what he personally could do to accentuate his commitment to these families. He could not help but notice that as the families grew up, the members separated from each other—even going to different Masses on Sunday. He wanted to provide some association that would, at least for an hour a week, embrace every person in the family, even if only to talk about common problems like illnesses, money difficulties, and unruly children. He eventually decided to give it a special name, "The Confraternity of the Holy Family."

He was proud of his own idea, and the next Sunday he formally announced it at each of the six Masses that day. As he was explaining it at the 6 a.m. Mass, Grandpa thought to himself that he had had a full life with a wife and five children, who were now all gone from his apartment. Frankly he welcomed the quiet sometimes; yes, it often melted into loneliness. As he left Mass the monsignor pulled him aside, "Ralph, I need you especially to help me make this idea work. You knew the cycles of life; please tell me you will come."

Grandpa was not going, but he could never say no to the beloved monsignor. So when next Wednesday came, he arrived and so did 75 other people. He was surprised at the turnout, but he figured men got out of the house to smoke their stogies in peace and listen to others talk. The women welcomed being together so they could chatter and gossip about endless mundane things. But he was wrong. There really was a need for an association to bring each side together. That night they talked of the children, the cost of college, and the endless problems of mothers-in-law.

Sitting near Grandpa were the Russo sisters who had just lost their father, Eduardo, who had come over to America on the same boat from Naples as Grandpa, *The Celtic*. He had died of complications from diabetes, and the "girls" were in their 60s and both were widows.

Rosa and Maria Russo were two years apart but went everywhere and did everything together. They came to be dependent on each other, shared the same doctors, and made the church the center of their social lives. They ate together often, vacationed together, and even shopped together.

One day Rosa wanted to buy a new shawl at Bamberger's in Morristown, and Maria drove them both from Madison. Rosa decided to also buy a new slip and vanished into a dressing room, leaving Maria in the piles of stockings and shoes. Maria was startled, for among the hazy garment piles she saw a man passing who looked like a younger version of their papa.

She followed him around the carousels, and then walked over to talk to him. He was pleasant, thoughtful, and was waiting for his daughter to come out of dressing room #2. They talked of the sales at this time of year, of the increasing prices of clothes, and of the tightening policy on returns. Then the man smiled and and remarked, "It is a great life if you don't weaken." Maria was startled, the distracted man had given an admonition that no one ever used except her father. It was not a common expression among old Italian men who were not given to truisms. She asked him his name and where he lived. He too was from Madison but lived in the Green Village Road area near the golf course. He played every day he remarked with pride. Then Maria couldn't help saying, "May I say, you are the very image of my father in his younger years."

Then the man, named Arthur, said he really did not know his birth parents, he was adopted and grew up in Madison, went to trade school, and was a master carpenter. He could be anyone's child, he quietly noted.

Maria waited until Rosa appeared, and indeed Rosa was even more struck by the similarities, and so they decided to get together on Saturday. Arthur was obliging, and they met at the Nautilus Diner on Main Street. And they again realized that this adopted son who looked so like their father must be one of his earlier offspring.

Maria belonged to the genealogy society of the Madison Historical Association in the library, and she asked him if he would join and they could compare ancestors. But Arthur demurred politely. His current family knew only who he was now. He had no need to know his biological father, or even if they were his living sisters. He lived a good life and wanted no surprises at the very end. They tried to convince him, but he gracefully dropped a $10 bill for coffee for them all and bid a fond farewell.

But Maria and Rosa, being Italian princesses all their lives and having things their way, insisted on pursuing it. They invited him over to Maria's house on Green Avenue for a lunch of lasagna. In their conversation, they insisted that the old man had an obligation to tell his children of his sisters and of the life of his supposed father. They thought all would be pleased by such a discovery. But he disagreed, and said it was best to leave things alone.

They decided to show up at the next Confraternity meeting and sidelined the oldest man there—Grandpa—to ascertain his advice on their newly found brother. He really did not want to get involved. They insisted that Arthur was probably an illegitimate child of their father, and they wanted to know if Grandpa was aware of that liaison. He just quietly and noncommittally said, "No child is illegitimate, he is just a love child. If this man wishes to be left alone, let him be. He has right to privacy, and he respects his family's peace and quiet. He is afraid they will think less of him. But let him be, ladies, for he has lived according to God's laws and wishes to die that way." And so they went off unhappy, and never came back to the Confraternity of the Holy Family again. As he looked at their vacant chairs, Grandpa thought, *Sometimes the ties of family can bind you too tightly.*

69. A POLISH NUN

The biggest problem about being a landscape gardener was that Madison was a leafy community, and Grandpa was expected to work for his clients on trimming the increasingly tall trees. The elms had all died due to Dutch disease, but the maples continued on, and he had to work harder on climbing up to get a few clips off them. Finally, he decided he could not do tree work, so he looked around to hire a younger man to do just the high parts. He had heard of a Polish fellow, Stan Pilsudski, who was young and agile, and after a brief meeting he delegated those chores to him for a modest sum.

Pilsudski was an immigrant from Poland who had left the turns and screws of Communism to come to America. His family had almost all been killed in various wars and police actions against the Polish people. When he was young, he had associated with a fellow Pole named Karol Wojtyla, who was an amateur actor. Wojtyla stayed and became a priest, Stan left and went to Buffalo, New York, where there were many other Poles. Later he left for New York City, and headed toward Madison, New Jersey where he happily married an Irish lass.

Grandpa watched in amazement as he swung across the branches and artfully cut and trimmed. His work was better than nature itself. At lunch they would sit with their bags and talk of the old countries. Grandpa told him of the beauties of Italy, and Stan would talk of his beloved Krakow. He would recount the historic piety of the Polish people, and how a famed uncle of his had stopped the military advances of the Bolsheviks right after the Great War. Grandpa countered with stories of the famous saints of Italy, from St. Francis to St. Rocco, and recounted the tale of the vial of San Gennaro's blood in the Naples cathedral which liquified several times a year. One day, Stan brought Grandpa a pamphlet in English with an account of the sayings and teachings of a young nun, Sister Faustina Kowalska, from near Krakow, who recorded the incredible mercy of Jesus in her *Diary*. She emphasized not God's justice, but His boundless mercy, for while we all want justice for the others, we want unbridled mercy for ourselves. She lived only 33 years and died of tuberculosis, but she left her *Diary*, her set of special prayers called "The Chaplet," and a picture of Christ she had ordered painted based on her apparitions of the Lord.

For some reason, her teachings spread throughout Poland in her young life, and Poles going off to war brought the picture and the Chaplet with them to the Eastern front. After the war and in Communist captivity, Polish veterans and later priests spread the word of her teachings across Europe and even into the eastern United States. She was not a saint then, but her work got her intense negative scrutiny in the Vatican, and a more sympathetic view among the faithful. Stan became a devotee of the concept of Divine Mercy. The idea that Jesus was less concerned about the "thou shall nots" and more concerned with love and mercy resonated with him, especially after seeing the harsh world around him. When he came to America, he brought no money, few clothes, but he did bring Faustina's ideas.

As he told Grandpa the whole story with such fervor, the old man was taken with it, but he had to admit that Italy had so many saints that it was hard to honor them all. Stan said to him, "Just recite every morning, 'Jesus I trust in you.'" Now Grandpa began the day with a simple evocation, "*Grazie a Dio*," thanks be to God I am still alive. So he could not see any harm saying this special saying in the early morning. Stan gave him a prayer card and on one side was the picture of Sister Faustina with the portrait of Jesus in the background, and then the prayer on the back, but it was in Polish. Grandpa took it reverently, and put it in his old wallet, and thanked Stan, paying him generously for his work on the trees on Mrs. Sanford's property.

One day, Mrs. Starleze came to see him. She was an aged woman who lived off Green Village Road and who had lost her husband to cancer years earlier. She mainly lived for the church and its activities. She was a member of the Sodality. After she haltingly walked up his front steps, she told Grandpa that she was a part of a prayer group that was holding a vigil for the Paterno family, whose eight-year-old girl was apparently dying of the complications of whooping cough. Grandpa knew nothing of the story, but she asked if he would come next Tuesday night to the prayer vigil for the child, to pray for her recovery. The doctors had said they did all they could do, and her parents should let her die in peace. Grandpa angrily remembered when a doctor told his wife that his baby daughter, Margaret, should be left to die in peace. So he said that he would indeed show up, but he was unsure if he could have much more of an impact than they all would, for they were such righteous women in the eyes of God. "No, no, everyone counts," said Mrs. Starleze, for she believed in the healing power of prayer.

When Tuesday came, Grandpa was totally exhausted and fell asleep at his own kitchen table. When he woke, he realized he had nearly missed the prayer vigil, and angry at himself, moved quickly to his truck, and drove up to the church. There he saw them finishing up, and Grandpa was so embarrassed and disappointed. Then for some incredible reason, he went up to Mrs. Paterno and apologized. She was in a fog, and her husband in deep grief, just acknowledged Grandpa's presence. He then asked if he could personally lead a prayer for their child. She just nodded.

Grandpa was not an orator and was rather reserved in general. At Mass he sat in the back and fingered his beads and took communion. But he rarely participated in any meaningful way, for in those days the laity was supposed to pay, pray and obey. But now he stood in front of the fifty or so people of the Sodality and began, "I am sorry I am late, but I wanted to add my prayers to yours this evening." He pulled out the prayer card of Sister Faustina, and related, "This is the sister of Divine Mercy, who promised us that God would grant through her any wish we had if it was right for us. God, this wish of mine is simple: let this girl live and prosper. Chase away the whopping cough, and let her come forward to us, to pray and to serve you. I ask this in the name of Jesus. Jesus, I trust in you."

People stared at the working man in coveralls, what was he talking about? They had never heard of Faustina or of Divine Mercy. It sounded like the Sacred Heart of Jesus, but more merciful. He walked over to Mrs. Paterno and gave her the worn prayer card, pressing it into her hands, saying, "She will be well in two days." Why he said that no one knew, it was so unlike him to show any demonstrable emotion or to dare to anticipate God. But he did, and people saw it and swore that it happened. In two days, the young girl was back playing and laughing. The old ladies in the Sodality said it was a miracle, but Grandpa refused to talk about it, for it was bad luck, he insisted.

Years later, the young girl grew up, went to medical school and worked with Pfizer on a successful whopping cough vaccine. She had made a difference in the lives of humankind. One solitary night, she told her husband, years after they were married, about her recovery. He was an English professor, who was an agnostic, which is an atheist without convictions. He was also an anarchist, who hated all governments, but was happy when he received his monthly paycheck from Kean State College in Union, N.J. He laughed at his wife, "Come on, you are a woman of science, you know that penicillin is a better cure than all the prayers in the world."

She nodded to keep him quiet, and he went back to watching the Knicks lose once again to the Celtics. A month later, she took off early from work, and went to the St. Vincent cemetery; she had called beforehand and gotten the exact location of the gravesite she wanted. It was Grandpa's, lying next to his wife. She took a laminated prayer card with Sister Faustina on it and placed it on top of Grandpa's tomb stone. The only difference was this one had the prayer written in English. Later in 1978, Karol Wojtyla became Pope John Paul II, and he insisted that Sister Faustina become the first saint of the twenty-first century.

70. INTERVENTION

As he looked out of the back screen door, Grandpa noticed it was drizzling, and that the old wooden door was peeling again. Louis had charged $500 to paint the door and the back steps gray and had done a lousy job, the old man concluded. From the porch, he could see the branches of the rose bush he had planted years ago in the center of his garden to memorialize his daughter Anna, who had died at only 26 from some internal problem he never fully understood.

He was waiting for his three other daughters who were coming to talk to him about what they said was something important. He wasn't sure what they wanted, and they rarely came over to see him anyhow. But when they arrived, they ran out of the drizzle, and he could not help but notice how much weight each had put on since they got married.

They ran up the back stairs, and he embraced each one perfunctorily as they went into his kitchen almost as in a race. He offered them a little wine, but they each said "no" abruptly. Marie started talking almost immediately. She had taken a course in intervention therapy at Morris County Community College and considered herself an authority on family psychology. Intervention was when the family saw a problem with one of its own and would meet with him to provide solutions. Obviously, the intervention target was not happy about such an interference. With her were Rose, a telephone operator, and Amelia, a part time clerk and housewife.

Marie began, "Pop, you know how much we love you, but we're worried about your living alone, especially after your recent car accident."

Grandpa defensively responded, "I just grazed the parking sign in the Chinese restaurant. He made such a big deal. I ended up giving him $25, but he decided everyone in town had to know about it. His food is lousy anyhow..."

Marie moved on, "One day Louise came in and you had left the gas on the stove on. You could have blown up the whole place."

The old man said nothing.

Marie continued, "You have already given up your license, we know, but still you are here alone at night and could just collapse and no one would here for days."

Louise added, "We love you, but don't feel you can live alone anymore."

Grandpa was unaware of what was being said. "I have three girls and three boys, surely one can take care of their old man."

Marie snapped back, "We all have our own lives and jobs and families to take care of."

Rose responded, "Most of us don't even have an extra room anymore. We have TVs in them or save them for when the grandchildren come in the summer."

They knew what he was thinking—the Old Italian proverb, "A mother can raise eight children, but eight children cannot raise one mother or father."

Marie was ready. "The times have changed. You now need the kind of care that professionals can give you. You need more medical attention than Dr. Felepa can provide when you choose to go. Nowadays people demand specialists, tests, emergency patient care. We don't have the time to leave our jobs and take care of your appointments."

Grandpa responded quietly, "I never realized I would be such burden when I got to this age."

Rose argued that it was not that he was a burden, but that he demanded special care.

Grandpa nodded slowly at the three of them, "What do you have in mind?"

Marie had studied the whole question, "Across from the church is a new assisted living care village. You could have your own room, three meals a day, and a day full of activities, more than here. They have a medical care unit off the dining room, and they are linked up to each resident by a buzzer that allows them to know where you are and if there are any problems. It is around your neck."

"Around my neck?"

"Yes, it will protect you day and night."

"What do I do with my things here?"

"Most will have to go," said Marie.

"Who will take care of them when I am not here? I am worried mostly about Mama's hope chest that she was saving for Anna."

Marie responded sharply, "Look, Pop, that stuff means a lot to you, but we have our own stuff. This means nothing to us, frankly."

Grandpa just nodded again, "When do I have to be out of here?'

They responded together, "The end of the month. The place is called Saturn. Like the planet."

Grandpa just nodded, and they quickly got up and left.

He watched them go down the stairs and run to Marie's Toyota for which papa had given her the down payment. He watched how big their asses were.

One of his sons-in-law said it looked like the backfield of the New York Giants.

He was taken back and walked through each room wondering what he was going to take. Here, in this very plain apartment, he had laid out his wife and his first daughter. As the news washed over him, he stopped and thought for some reason that he needed outside advice. Where were his sons? He had so favored them, where were they? They surely knew of this meeting and didn't care to come, he assumed. None of them had ever been strong men, he concluded a long time ago. Then he called his lawyer, Frank Volpe, and explained what was being proposed to him. Volpe said he did not know Grandpa's physical condition, but, "Do not sign any papers, give anything away, or make anybody your agent or give anyone your power of attorney. They will ask you for a will that gives them the right to stop treatment on what they assume is your death bed."

"But only God knows my time and place."

"Just sign nothing, make believe you don't understand English in your dotage."

When the day came Grandpa carried off a few pictures, the Infant of Prague statue, his books on Goethe and on Petrarch, Grandma's Bible and the picture of them at the Isle of Capri on their honeymoon. That night he was so anxious he rearranged over and over again the few possessions he had.

The room had a bed, a small TV, and a tiny refrigerator. It was barren of pictures, not even a calendar. The residents found the Saturn was a clean, smoothly run, controlled institution with about 100 inhabitants. It was like clockwork, but Grandpa hated the food which made few concessions to the large number of Italians in the area and in the institution.

When he was a child and was naughty, his mother would threaten to put him in a "home," but she never did. Now she had her way, he mused. Once a week, they had religious services, but frequently they were not Catholic. The church sent an ancient Sister of Charity to distribute communion to Catholics, but he did not even hear her prayer. *Hoc est corpus meum.* He remembered those prayers in the old Latin when he was an altar boy in Rotondi; before school he would serve the 7 a.m. mass and learned the Latin by heart. It is funny how those things stay with you, even in your elder years. He went to the other services, but they were flaccid. Like most of Protestantism, they could not even count as true heresies.

He tried to be part of the afternoon games, but he thought Bingo was boring, although he constantly won, to the annoyance of the old ladies. He went to musical events, especially being impressed by an old piano player from Carnegie Hall in New York who loved Italian opera; Grandpa sat alone and cheered him on.

He had no real friends there. He got to know a local florist, but he vanished in an ambulance, and soon they cleaned out his room. He became fairly close with a proper gentleman who had been a vice president for Goldman Sachs, and he told Grandpa what stocks to play, and for a while they both made money. But in a month or so, he was gone too. Grandpa met an old woman who was still lithe and used only a cane. She had been in the first class of the Rockettes in Radio City Music Hall; Grandpa told her he had gone with his grandchildren and especially loved the nativity scene.

Frequently he went out in the sun and watched the flowers spring up. The planting was uneven, and Grandpa wanted to make changes, but he was told the center had a hard and fast contract with a group of landscape gardeners from Chatham, but Grandpa knew they were not really landscape gardeners. So he kept his tongue and watched the flowers dry up.

At night when he watched television in his room alone, as did all the others, he was forced to use the bad Comcast menu. He sat there, but he did not enjoy the channels anyway.

His daughters had promised him visitors galore. But they rarely came once a month, and he watched as some other inhabitants had their grandchildren and great grandchildren come and talk to their grandpa. He had no one come, and since he did nothing, he had no pictures. People who rarely did visit wanted to talk about their ailments, and Grandpa listened respectfully. After a month, nobody came to see him or even call him on the phone. They said he had nothing to talk about. Once the head of the family, he was a lone dog at Saturn.

The food remained poor, and he decided to see what was wrong with the kitchen. He came upon a nice stainless steel setup that was manned by illegal immigrants whose dietary needs were not his own.

He asked Marie to bring him some provolone and wine from the warehouse, but she would not do it. "It violates the rules, because the cheese gives you gout and raises your blood pressure. The attendants are very strict, Pop."

He nodded and remembered all the problems she had gotten into with boys over her teenage age years and how he had covered up for her so as not to shock Mama.

One strange day he walked by the dining room that had been decorated during the off hours of 2 to 3 p.m., and there was a proper, gentle, pretty, old lady surrounded by children, grandchildren and great grandchildren like he should have been. They were celebrating her birthday; she was encased in a wheelchair with plastic tubes tied to mobile air tanks. She waved wearily at her people, listened courteously to the pastor's prayer, and was glad she was there. It was a landmark she never thought she would reach. Grandpa had seen her before, sitting at a table for four, as she carefully cut the meat for a woman who was obviously approaching dementia. She had bright eyes, a kind of concern for others, and sounded like his wife Luisa. It was so long ago, he could be mistaken.

As he passed by the dining hall entrance, she called out to him, "Raffaele, *vieni qui*." He looked up at her and recognized her for some reason. "*Si*."

"Come here, join my family. There is always plenty in an Italian family!" And she handed him a big piece of birthday cake.

"What is the occasion?"

"I am 100 this month."

"Good God, I hope I live to be 100 and be in your shape."

"I hope so too, and may I be there with you."

She smiled shyly, and he went on to test some real Italian food from the caterers. Actually, the family had ordered only enough food to feed the immediate relatives. But the guest of honor constantly added to the number by inviting the people of Saturn. Luckily the caterers were Italian too, and there was enough food to feed everybody—invited or not invited—and there were leftovers. It was like the parable of the loaves and fishes.

Grandpa had watched the great-grandchildren, and it reminded him of his own whose parents never brought them to him anymore. He stopped and could not even remember their names. All he knew was that every Christmas he gave each of them a $2 bill. He graciously thanked the guest of honor, wished her another century of good luck, and left feeling good about himself and her. She made him feel like family, as if he had known her all his life.

One day, he was watching a rerun of *Gunsmoke*, and he wearily wished that Marshal Dillon was still courting Miss Kitty while she was running the brothel. So he walked out of the room for a stroll, past the dining hall kitchen, and saw out of the corner of his eye a fire moving along, embracing the ovens. The staff panicked in a dozen languages no one understood. Grandpa ran out to the dining room and saw two frightened ladies in wheelchairs. He suddenly grabbed them both and pushed them down the hallway and outside to the manicured lawns.

By the time he finished that, he heard the fire engines from Madison, Chatham, and Florham Park. In the library, he found two confused women with canes. He led them down the halls and outside as well. The firemen abruptly pulled Grandpa over and told him to stand by the fire truck in all the chaos. The driver was Jimmy Fitz, a friend of Grandpa's for years. He yelled, "Ralph, you are a hero today." They were totally successful, and the old ladies outside treated Grandpa as if he were Douglas MacArthur in the Philippines. In ancient Rome, he would have had a triumphant parade on a white steed.

Instead Jimmy gave him a ride back to Main Street, and Grandpa did what he always wanted to do, he rode in the front passenger seat of the fire engine with the sirens and lights on. When he arrived at 81 Main Street, he jumped off.

Grandpa walked quickly up the first flight of stairs to his apartment, and for the first time in a while he had a spring in his steps. He opened his door with the spare key under the mat, and rushed in. The apartment never looked better. Even old furniture seemed to sparkle like Park Avenue. He was home again.

The very next day he called Frank Volpe to see if he had to do something about returning. A chipper Volpe pronounced, "Return? First, much of the structure was damaged, and second no one is going to capture a hero and return him where he doesn't want to be."

"A hero, what hero?"

"Did you not see this morning's *Star Ledger*. The first page talks of your heroic behavior, and you are standing in a picture next to a fire engine from Madison in your old flannel shirt. Great job. No one will ever bother you again. You are king of the mountain. By the way, I never signed any power of attorney forms for you. You are your own man, Raffaele, Congratulations, hero!"

Grandpa thanked him profusely and went into the kitchen to make lunch. He was starving. He desperately wanted fusilli and twisted open a bottle of Ragu sauce. He never liked Ragu, it tasted metallic and too acidic, but it was better than what he was getting at Saturn. So he started boiling water for the pasta and heating up the sauce at the same time. See, he could still do it without causing a fire, girls.

While he was carefully watching both pots, there was a rapping on his back door. It was Marie who had heard about the fire and Grandpa's extraordinary feats. The *Madison Eagle* ran a special edition with Grandpa's *Star Ledger* photo on the front page.

Marie exclaimed, "Are you okay? I just heard. How terrible it must have been for you. You must be in a state of shock. We should go see Dr. Felepa. We need to find another place for you. Oh, you must be scared, Papa."

Grandpa pushed the screen door closed as she stood there, "*Va via*, Marie, *va via*."

71. MARGHERITA PIZZA
(For Madison)

One of Grandpa's daughters lived on Long Island and had just gotten divorced. Grandpa hated Long Island, saying once that it was a large potato farm cut up into lots for overpriced split levels. But this time he had his first experience with the Long Island Railroad and ended up in Bellmore and was greeted by his daughter and her cute daughter, Madison. She was named apparently after the family's hometown that was so different from the Long Island enclaves where life totally revolved around the schools.

This week the parents were to attend an event in which they would sit in their children's chairs and hear about their curriculum. Madison was in the fourth grade and was a lively student who had a great sense of fairness and charity. *Such kids are rare*, Grandpa thought. In any case, they both went with Madison to her class, and sat in uncomfortable chairs too low for most adults. Madison had taken a transfer student from Hempstead under her wing. Darrell was a shy, slight black boy whose mother worked hard to get him a better education.

When the game of musical chairs ended, Grandpa and his daughter stood with Madison, and the other parents, usually mothers, sat with their children, except for Darrell who had nobody. He sat there stoically, but finally he put his head inside his shirt and started to cry. He was once again alone. Grandpa and his daughter watched as Madison tried to make it all better, but he sobbed and sobbed. Finally, Grandpa went over to him and sat with him, asking, "May I be your partner. I am called Grandpa, and I am sure your mother would approve of me."

Darrell stopped crying and welcomed his new visitor. The program went on and on. The crayon masterpieces were pointed out, as was the sheet of paper identifying what words fourth graders should know. Darrell did all right, but Madison was really superb. Still Grandpa treated the work as if it belonged to Leonardo himself. And then the kids got together and sang the songs of Thanksgiving, nice flaccid songs that did not offend any ethnic group in heterogeneous Bellmore.

At the end the teachers said the kids could go home with their parents or guardians, but those alone must stay for the early bus. Poor Darrell felt again like an outsider, but this time Grandpa put his hand on his shoulder. The old man turned to his daughter, "Why don't we all go for pizza?" The kids were delighted to accept his unexpected invitation. Grandpa walked with Darrell across the street, saying to him that there was an important story connected with pizza, and Darrell was delighted to hear it from his new friend. Madison watched them with a smile, proud of her Grandfather.

Of course, they all ordered pizza of different varieties, pepperoni, sausage, pineapple, anchovies, but Grandpa insisted that they also get a Margherita pizza. "Darrell, do you know where they got that name, Margherita?"

"No, Grandpa, where?"

They sat down and Grandpa began to sip on his orange soda; everyone else had ordered Coke. "Well it started when King Umberto died and his widow, Margherita of Savoy, became beloved by the people of the new Italy. The pizza has three colors: white, red, and green, or the pie, the sauce and green basil on it. They are the colors of the Italian Revolution, the so-called Risorgimento. As a boy I once saw them in a parade when they visited Naples before Umberto was assassinated."

"He was killed? Did you ever talk to him?

"No, no, in Italy no one ever talked to the king or queen. But here in America I once talked to President Roosevelt. That is the difference between the United States and Italy. In any case I named one of my daughters after Margherita, or Margaret. Everything has a history, Darrell, and now only you in your class knows the true story. You might want to tell them the story during some exercises someday."

Darrell felt that he had been let in on a cosmic secret and was wondering when he could spring it on the whole class. First, he went over to whisper it his friend, Madison.

Later, his daughter took Darrell home and Grandpa to the train station. Luckily the escalator was working, and he stood in the wind, overlooking the medical facilities stores. When the LIRR came, he sat in the newer seats, and thought about Darrell. A tear came to his eye, but the teachers had to realize the world was changing. Both parents had to work in the daytime, and his daughter told him Darrell's mother held down three jobs to pay for a modest dwelling in Bellmore so he could get a better education. Her not being there was really a sign of devotion. Her husband had died in Vietnam.

As for Darrell he had not wanted to go to school that day, but his mother insisted. He had made a nice friend. He told Madison on the way home, "I will never order any type of pizza except Margherita pies in honor of the queen and the Italian people."

72. SONS OF ABRAHAM

Grandpa grew up in a province east of the port of Naples, and there were two types of people: Catholics and others. After they were expelled from Naples, the Jews went north to a more tolerant Rome, and only the Rothchilds had a major presence in the former city, leaving behind a synagogue they built in Naples. There were some random Jewish peddlers and merchants, but they were isolated. When he arrived and moved to New Jersey, Grandpa met other Jewish figures, but had few dealings with them.

But he watched in horror as the thug Mussolini embraced the Nazis and passed a range of anti-Semitic laws and then rounded up Jews for deportation. The Italian convents and monasteries and even the pope's summer residence at Castel Gandolfo hid Jewish families. The Italian police looked the other way and were less than scrupulous about arresting peaceful fellow citizens. Only later, watching a television series on World War II did Grandpa and most of America see for the first time the gruesome footage of the death camps. *The men looked so worn,* he thought, *the women so ragged, the children so sad. Thank God this was not the world he lived in, that was not America.*

Grandpa owned a three story apartment building near the center of town. The first floor embraced two stores: a radio repair shop, and on the right a confectionary shop. Grandpa lived above the first floor and across the way from him was another renter, who had decided to leave to buy a small house. At about that time, Grandpa was approached by the owner of the Bottle Hill Restaurant who wanted to find a convenient place for her new hire, an ice cream and cake man named Isaac. Grandpa welcomed the business, met the shy slight man who always wore long sleeve shirts, and shook hands sealing the deal. He was not a believer in contracts.

That Friday night three of his oldest friends from North Street arrived to play cards. As they began, Ernesto blurted out, "Hey, why you rent to a Jew?"

The old man surprisingly looked up, "What?"

"Yeah, that Isaac is a Jew, one who even goes to temple on the weekends."

Edoardo joined in, "Okay, be careful my friend. They love to cheat us Americans, and they capture Catholic children and use their blood."

Grandpa sharply responded, "Use the blood for what?"

Edoardo insisted, "For making their Jewish bread."

Grandpa was incredulous, "How do you make bread from blood?"

Edoardo insisted, "They do, and they have a secret book on how to take over the world. They are kikes and Communists. All of these are Jews, be careful, they are the killers of Christ. Lord have mercy on us."

Grandpa was at first silent, and then ordered, "The same people who call them kikes, call us wops. *Basta*, play the cards."

They finally left for the night. Then he thought, *Who would kill children, that is nonsense. And if they rule the world, how could they allow the death camps that had been on television. It is all nonsense, old folks' tales. As for Jesus being crucified, it was by our people, the Romans, and Jesus and all his apostles were Jews. Wasn't the Mass Jesus' Passover. This is all crazy nonsense. I am not a learned man but even I can see foolishness. Why did I waste my wine on those cafoni.*

So Isaac lived across from Grandpa, and often saw the old man playing with his grandchildren. Then one day after work, he visited Grandpa and shyly asked him if he would like to be his guest at the services at the local synagogue. Grandpa had never been at any religious services but Catholic ones, still he could not bring himself to say no. So when the next Sabbath came, the two of them walked up to the synagogue. The faithful seemed to nod when he walked in, and he recognized some of the people there, whom he did not know were Jews.

Grandpa quietly watched the services; in some ways it reminded him of the low Mass in the Catholic Church. He listened intently to the Kaddish prayer, and the blessings from God, the Almighty One. He noted that this rabbi said a special prayer for the victims of the Shoah, the Holocaust. Later he learned that nearly every person there lost someone in their family in the death camps.

At one point, the rabbi passed round the sacred scrolls of the Torah and each person reverently kissed it, and when it came to Grandpa, the old man kissed it as well.

When the service was over, the rabbi walked toward Grandpa and gave him a silver goblet to mark his visit. The old man took it gingerly into his hands, fearing he might drop it. On the way home, Isaac turned to Grandpa and remarked, "People were not sure you would kiss our scrolls." Grandpa holding tightly the cup, simply responded, "I figured if it was good enough for Jesus to do, it was good enough for me."

At home, they parted amiably, and the old man took the silver goblet, and placed it near his statue of baby Jesus, dressed in a sparkly garb of the Infant of Prague. He thought they looked good together.

Soon Holy Week and Passover occurred in the same week, and Grandpa went to Good Friday services, and listened more intently than usual as the priest recited a litany of prayers: May God bless all Christians outside the true

Church, bless atheists and agnostics, bless government officials...and then he said, "bless the perfidious Jews." Grandpa had never heard the expression before, and he turned to his daughter and whispered, "What is perfidious." She simply responded, "Untrustworthy, sly." The old man was genuinely startled; he had never heard that word before. Maybe it was new or maybe he had just become more sensitive to the Jews after his dispute over renting to poor Isaac. At the end of the service, he stayed as if he were still praying, and when the priest came out to snuff the candles, Grandpa uncharacteristically went up to him, and bluntly asked, "Why do you call the Jews perfidious?" The priest was surprised, "They are perfidious, they killed Jesus, and now we are graciously asking for mercy for them and their conversions."

"Ask for mercy for them, and for all of us who sin. That would include the descendants of the Roman soldiers too? Are you going to say that in this Italian parish?"

"Look, the Church gives us this script to say all over the world. I don't make this up. Write the bishop or the pope."

The old man left angry and despondent. And when Easter came in two days, he refused to contribute any money, the first time in memory. He later notified Isaac that he was dropping his rent by $10 a month. It was then he noticed that Isaac had his left sleeve rolled up, and on it were tattooed numbers. The marks of the Holocaust had come home, here in his own apartments.

In 1958 the Sacred College of Cardinals elected the elderly patriarch of Venice, the rotund Angelo Roncalli. He became known as John XXIII; he was to be an interim pope before the next strong and younger one would succeed him. But he had other plans, and among the reforms he accomplished he eliminated the reference to the "perfidious Jews" in the Good Friday ritual.

When in 1960, one old Italian cardinal insisted on using the expression at Mass in front of John XXIII, the pope screamed out in the middle of service, "NO, NO, say it the new way."

73. THE RUTGERS TOMATO

Of the many things Grandpa enjoyed in life, ice cream was one of them. As a young boy he had been introduced to the delicacy at a festival honoring St. Gennaro, whose vial of blood liquefied several times a year at the great cathedral in Naples. No one knew why or how that happened; scientists from Cambridge and Heidelberg said there was no natural reason for this change in substance to occur, and so the Church properly labeled it a "miracle." It soon became a special Neapolitan observance, letting the poor people forget for a few days the woes of their lives and the devastating plagues that so beleaguered that port city. It was there in Naples, in September, that Grandpa's father introduced him to gelato, a stronger relative to the common American ice cream.

Once in the U.S., Grandpa never brought ice cream home, but always ate it in the Carvel ice cream store. Every day in the summer, he would walk alone to the center of town and sit in Carvel's with a cone of vanilla and chocolate mixed elegantly in a twisted pyramid. He would stare at the posters of ice cream cakes, shakes, and malts, but he stuck loyally with the perennial ice cream cone. One day though, he noticed that the proprietor had a certificate from Rutgers, the State University of New Jersey, stapled to the wall. It announced clearly that Francisco Delato had successfully completed the ice cream decorating course offered by the university's School of Agriculture's Extension Service.

"Hey, Francesco, how did you get this paper here?"

"I completed a course on ice cream design at the extension school, you know where it is, near the Catholic cemetery."

"And for that the university gave you this? How wonderful."

"Yes, I am very proud, and my family thinks now that I am a college man."

Grandpa smiled and went home. His adventures in the U.S. in education had consisted only of several months at the night program in the high school so as to master English. But he claimed that the teacher—an Irish lass with flaming red hair—had made improper advances to him, and he quit in a Puritan huff. Later he heard that she had been divorced, which explained everything.

This certificate was not from a night school, but the big university, and so he gathered up his courage to go to the Extension Center. He drove his beat-up Ford pickup and went to Saint Vincent Martyr Cemetery where Grandma and some of his children were already buried. He hated cemeteries and the thought of being covered with cold hard dirt with people visiting who did not even remember your face, your laugh, your touch. God, he missed Grandma so.

He easily found the Extension building nearby on empty land with large greenhouses covering acres of experimental crops. He timidly went in, and asked about the extension courses. The attendant was dressed in a white smock and had a very Midwestern smile of welcome. Grandpa immediately knew this was not the flaming red-head.

He explained his thoughts about taking a course in what was listed as horticulture, and on the list, he saw "Flowers." He immediately signed up for it, saying that he worked for years on strains of pansies. His family had facetiously called him "the Luther Burbank of pansies"—a reference to the great scientist whose work revolved around potatoes.

The attendant liked the idea of enrolling older students in flowers, since he taught the course and was paid by the number of students he serviced. So every Tuesday afternoon, he and ten younger students would learn the principles of horticulture, but Grandpa quietly began to realize that these lessons were ones he had mastered on his own in his boyhood, and now in his backyard garden.

Somehow, he had figured out how to cross-breed pansies, and he arrived at the most startlingly attractive flowers in hues no one had ever imagined. When the instructor asked the students to bring some samples of their current work to class, Grandpa filled his pickup with pallets of pansies, and he threw in some of his tomato plants that he had worked on. The class loved the pansies and praised him to the heights over the fullness and imaginative color schemes. The instructor even put them out on the counters for people to see, and lackadaisically pushed the tomato plants in the back of the counter.

At the end of the week, the plants thrived in the controlled environment, and the instructor proudly exhibited them as if he had somehow inspired them. Then one night, he was making a sandwich and reached for one of Grandpa's tomatoes and sliced it quickly. He was startled at the sugary taste, and it lacked the mealy center that usually so marred the vegetable. He took a second one, and then showed the third to a colleague who was working on new tomato strains for Jersey farmers. What had the old man hit upon, they wondered?

They waited for the next class, and the two of them told Grandpa that they loved his pansies, but they wanted to know more about how he came upon the tomato brand. He carefully explained in broken English the techniques and the components he worked on, and they knew that what he had produced was a winner, better than the School of Agriculture had come up with in all its controlled experiments. Remember, this was before the popularization of DNA.

Several days later, they honestly admitted their discovery to the dean who immediately notified the various bureaucratic layers of Rutgers. They were honest or prudent enough to realize they needed to acquire the patent from the old man, for Italians are a contentious people. The president of the university was almost a Hollywood cast college president, Mason W. Gross, who was a Cambridge graduate, a lecturer on Spinoza the incomprehensible Jewish pantheistic philosopher, and the scholarly authority on the TV show, *The Answer Man*. When he was confidentially considered for the open presidency of Harvard, he promptly said he would never leave Rutgers and became a state hero overnight. The dean had decided to bring in the big guns: Gross, his haughty treasurer, and the instructor to visit Grandpa in his backyard. They greeted him, surprising the old man at work. Grandpa had recognized his instructor of course, and also Gross from the newspapers, but still they swooped around him with the tall Gross looking down, smiling his best college administrator grin at Grandpa.

They explained in simple terms that people loved his tomatoes, and they wanted to make them commercially available. Grandpa would get 15% of all the net profits, the university would get the rest, for God knows what. They were talking millions. The old man listened politely, but he said, "No." Gross and his treasurer offered him 25%, but again he demurred, and finally said succinctly, "I have no right to these tomatoes, they are a part of God's world, and I just rearranged them. I cannot take money for His work." Gross knew of God, but not of a personal deity who cared what people did. For he believed in Spinoza, whose God was some vague life force. He had forgotten his early courses at Cambridge.

But they persisted that this was the way things are done in America— money and contracts, not handshakes. What could they give Grandpa in place of money? What conditions could they add to the contract?

The old man replied—two things. "One, no tomatoes are to be used by the Pope Company." Generosa Pope was a supporter of the Fascist thug Mussolini, and had used his newspaper, *Il Progresso,* to support him until the Allies won the war. Gross simply nodded, for he knew nothing about Italian-American life. And then Grandpa wanted a diploma just like Francisco had. Gross was confused, but the instructor knew exactly what he meant—a certificate of accomplishment. Gross was startled since he did not even know his university gave such meager honors.

But all agreed, and the old man took Gross's gold Cross pen and signed his name in the most beautiful old Italian script to the contract. Except when he saw the 15% royalty, he crossed it out and wrote in 0%.

A week later, the certificate arrived in the mail in a hard case like the academic degrees came in. Grandpa took the certificate, framed it, put it in plastic to protect it from the harsh New Jersey rains, and nailed it to his shed door. There under it was a prayer card to San Gennaro.

He had gotten what he wanted, and proudly showed it to his grandchildren—recognition, he said, from the great state university. And then the university began a major advertising campaign of its newest agricultural triumph, "the Rutgers Jersey tomato."

74. SAVING A SOUL, ONE AT A TIME

Grandpa realized how critical the right fertilizer was for his crops, and he would only buy it from one nursery up in Darlington, New Jersey. Near there was the Immaculate Conception Seminary which trained young men to be Catholic priests. One of his grandsons was studying there, and the boy decided one weekend to hitch a ride back to Madison with the old man.

Grandpa drove at his usual speed, as his grandson talked and talked. He became a conscientious member of the Church, but like most Italian men Grandpa distrusted priests and especially bishops. He was not a great advocate of celibacy for everyone. St. Peter had been married and lived with his mother-in-law, why can't a priest have a wife too?

His grandson wanted to be driven only to St. Vincent's rectory, and there he paid a courtesy call on the pastor, and then phoned his other grandfather to take him to his place. Grandpa was not an admirer of Joseph Saldito. He considered him a loud blowhard. Besides he grew up in the same village as Lercara Friddi, Lucky Luciano, the boss of bosses in the United States. But he could not say, "Don't visit him!" Besides one of his daughters had married one of the Saldito boys, and he was a decent, God fearing, honest husband.

So the grandson left Grandpa's truck and went into the rectory where the pastor greeted him as a long lost relative, for he was so honored that one of his was in training at the seminary. The candidate asked to use the parish phone to call his other grandfather to pick him up and sat down with the pastor. They talked about their days there at different times and ran over the faculty who bored or inspired both of them. Finally, Joe Saldito arrived at the rectory door, and he cautiously greeted Father O'Brien whom he had avoided for years. O'Brien asked him in and graciously offered him a glass of wine as a sign of hospitality and praised the great progress his grandson was making to the priesthood.

Saldito was bursting with pride and did indeed sit down. It was a fine dry wine, and the pastor and his guest finished off the bottle quickly. The grandson had made a vow of abstinence from wine in honor of the Virgin Mary, who probably in real life drank wine. O'Brien was a known lover of alcohol and in the rectory basement he had a real bar and called the floor

"O'Brien's Tavern." There other priests would congregate and gossip about the sanctimonious bishop who just made their difficult jobs harder. They especially hated his arbitrary personnel changes.

When the bottle was drained dry, Saldito thanked the priest, and then told him bluntly, "I do not go to church anymore."

"I know Joe," O'Brien responded.

"I no go because at my wedding day, the priest up in Morristown made us wait over an hour and a half while he ate and took a short nap. There we were outside the locked church waiting with our families and friends. When he finally came, he did a quick ceremony, no Mass, blessed everybody, and went back to the rectory. I told my bride to go to the reception, and I would be a little late. I had a revolver in the glove compartment of my car and was going to kill the bastard. But my wife screamed, 'You are not going to ruin my wedding day, I beg you this.' And so I went with her, and he lived to defame the Church. He is dead now and will be with a harsher judge. Now I just stay home on Sunday, read the newspapers, and visit my grandchildren for lunch. But I never forget."

O'Brien listened intently, and the seminarian shuddered. Saldito had told the story before, but never in a rectory to a priest. O'Brien read people well, and rather than being defensive, he quietly said, "Joe, you are right; I would have killed him too. The Church would have one fewer bad priest. On second thought, I would not kill him but go to the church on Saturday and face him and punch him so he would have a black eye for Sunday services. Yes, that is what I would do!"

"A good idea, I like you. This wine is not as good as mine. Come over to my house on Tuesday afternoon, and I can return your hospitality."

"Good, see you then."

And so Mr. Saldito and his grandson walked out. O'Brien had his shortcomings, but he did not get to be pastor of one of the biggest money parishes in the diocese for being naive.

The following Sunday, Grandpa was at the 6 a.m. Mass, and as he received the host, Father O'Brien leaned over to Grandpa's left ear, and quietly said, "See me at the end of Mass today." As the other parishioners filed out to go home and make tomato sauce, he sat in the pew. Finally Grandpa was alone, and Father O'Brien came out, and sat by him.

"It is good to see you again."

"Yes, you too."

"I need your help. You know Mr. Saldito very well."

"His son is married to my daughter."

"And we have talked about his feelings against the Church."

"He does not go, that I know."

"Yes, and I need to find out more about him, what makes him tick. What does he prize most in life?"

Grandpa thought for a while, and said bluntly, "He is a man totally controlled by pride. He is not just proud but governed by demons. And he is an unhappy man, who is given to alcohol, not just wine but the hard stuff." Then he went quiet, saying more than he intended.

"Saving a soul is a hard business."

And they bade farewell before the next Mass began.

One Tuesday followed another, and Father O'Brien showed up for hospitality regularly. Then on one afternoon, he said to Mr. Saldito, "I feel sorry for you, Joe."

"Why? I have money, family, and some friends."

"Yes, and I hope I am one of them. But soon your grandson will be ordained and say his first Mass, and you, his grandfather, cannot even receive communion at his hands. All the town will be talking about it."

"That is not fair."

"That is the Church's policy. I just don't want you to lose out, to stand out in church in front of all. Those women gossip."

"Yes, gossips—they come to Mass and funerals. That is their barren lives. What do I do, do I have to go to confession? I have not confessed in years. I can't stand in line with all those sinners."

"Yes, well we can do it now right here, Joe." And O'Brien leaned over and began, "Bless me father, for I have sinned."

So Joe went to confession for the first time in 60 years. He then took two glasses of wine and saluted the priest. On Sundays, he began to arrive at Mass; first standing up by the back wall, and then sitting in the back pew. And he finally observed his grandson's first Mass; after all it was a matter of pride.

Not too much later he died and was buried in the church cemetery. Father O'Brien stood there; next to him was Grandpa. The priest smiled as the body was lowered into the cold, hard earth next to his late wife. Father O'Brien turned to Grandpa who was paying his final respects for the sake of his daughter.

"It is rare that a priest knows he has definitely saved a soul. Joe is going to end up in heaven. He may have to spend a couple centuries in purgatory, but he will end up in heaven, and you helped me to save that soul."

Grandpa was embarrassed, and responded, "No, it was the Virgin Mary." And then he turned on his heels and started walking down the hill to Grandma's grave. His head was spinning with talk of mercy, justice, heaven, purgatory. As he moved down the ill-kempt lawn, he mused, "It is a tale best told in winter."

75. THE MISSING HOST

Deep in central Newark, N.J., there was a group of neighborhood thugs who insisted that they were devil-worshippers. They grandly announced that they intended to have a "Black Mass" dedicated to Satan and held at the local high school auditorium. In the Mass, they would spit on a consecrated host and then the minister of the august group would call from hell the curses of the dead and step on and crush the host under his booted heel. The announcement caused great consternation in the Catholic community, especially in the Italian North Ward. For Catholics believed that the white host was not just symbolic but was the Real Presence of the body of the Savior. Soon a group of young, virile Italian boys bought Louisville Slugger bats and threatened to break up the Black Mass and save the host. It was going to be a first class riot. The police, of course, were bound to protect the First Amendment rights of the organizers of the Mass, but they were Irish Catholics and were more on the side of the Italians. Even Father Divine and his Divine Angels, a hero in the black community, denounced the sacrilege. So the police hierarchy did what they did best—they banned the rally due to the vague criteria that it constituted a violation of the regulations of the fire department.

The strange Mass of sacrilege did not go on, and the organizers promised another site, but not outside for they feared it would become an opportunity for the bat swinging opponents to break up their sacred gathering. It was with such a background that this story took place.

Like older Italian people, Grandpa on Sunday went to the 6 a.m. Mass. People went that early so as to get home to make sauce, get the kids ready for the children's Mass at 9 a.m., and perform the tasks of even the day of rest. One early morning, Grandpa walked up the center aisle, and passed the fifth pew. There he strangely saw Mrs. Winehouse sitting with a clean Kleenex open on her lap, and there was a host that she had just received. She had taken it out of her mouth and was splitting it in half. She ate a piece, and then carefully wrapped the other half in the Kleenex and put it in her pocketbook.

Grandpa knew that this should not be done and wondered all the way home what was happening. He had known her for decades, and she was not likely to be a Black Mass type. Still he believed in minding his own business and forgot about it. Then the next weekend he saw the same transaction. Finally he felt bold enough to visit her at her home on Maple Avenue, a tiny Cape Cod where she lived with her husband, a banker who has contracted Lou Gehrig's disease.

Grandpa rang the doorbell and offered to help her, for she went out so infrequently, and she surely needed groceries at least. She appeared timid and welcomed him in. In the conversation, he offered to shop for her, and she was frankly relieved. Then he carefully said he could not help but "notice that you took a piece of the host with you on Sundays."

She blushed and just said at first, "Yes, yes I do." She then took Grandpa to the back bedroom and there her suffering husband was, all hooked to medical devices and machines. "He is totally incapacitated now, he is dying, Ralph." Then she admitted that she gave him communion, "half of mine when I get home."

"Well, why don't you tell the priests, they will come to the house?"

"No, they say the parish is getting too old, and they would be doing nothing but giving out hosts to the old and infirmed. 'Tell him to just pray,' they insisted. So I have done this on my own."

Grandpa was genuinely embarrassed, for he had violated his own first rule—leave people alone. Backpedaling, he asked plaintively if she would give him a list of groceries, he would go to the A&P and get them. Indeed she did, and off he went somewhat humbled. When she had listed one can of something, he brought two, for they were not likely to spoil. Finally he arrived back on Maple Avenue and brought the bags to her house. He just told her that he had nearly doubled the order, since they had a two for one sale. She was delighted and asked what she owed him. Grandpa said the receipt was in one of bags somewhere, and she would find it. But as for now, he had to run for he had many errands he had to attend that afternoon. She could pay him later.

On the way home, he pulled out the receipt, crumpled it, and then threw it out the window. Main Street was dirty enough anyhow. Then three months later, he learned that Mr. Winehouse had passed away, and Grandpa attended his funeral. At the end of the services, the wife went to him, "Ralph, my husband died after he received Communion."

"Did the priest come out and give it to him"

"No, I gave it to him. Ralph, my husband died after he received Communion with a big smile on his face. I think he saw his guardian angel."

Grandpa nodded, "Perhaps, he did."

76. THE CHAIRMAN OF THE BOARD

Some of Grandpa's grandchildren thought he ought to see at least one Atlantic City show in his life, and one of them had "contacts" to see Frank Sinatra and his friends in the Rat Pack in performance. The tickets were scarce, but the contacts were "connected." Grandpa was not a big admirer of modern popular music, but he had heard some on the radio. Besides at his age, the opportunities for new adventures were few, so he went. The trip to Atlantic City from Madison was long and boring, and he was surprised to see how varied the state's landscape was.

At the city, they went to the Crystal Palace, a garish front cover on a cement block structure surrounded by cheap stands, stores in various stages of disrepair, and rundown dwellings. But in bright lights, the Palace was featuring "Frank Sinatra and his Friends." The visitors ended up sitting in the middle front row, a true gift from the "contact." Grandpa enjoyed the show, for Sinatra was a consummate performer. His voice was not as strong as Caruso's of course, but he was subtle, emotional, and personal in interpreting lyrics. He once said he made love to the microphone like it was a "broad." He sang for an hour and a half with no break.

At the end of the show, Grandpa was asked by his grandson if he wanted to go backstage and meet Sinatra. He nodded, figuring they would never get in. But they did, and Sinatra was surrounded by scantily clad chorus girls, who gave a new definition to the term "tootsie." Sinatra cavalierly waved them out and began to take off his make up when he saw the crowd from Madison who had introduced themselves as if they belonged there. Sinatra was distracted, but polite, and he made a special notice of Grandpa who was standing quietly by. "This is our grandfather, Raffaele, Mr. Sinatra."

"Glad to meet you, I'm Frank, Francis Albert from Hoboken."

Grandpa laughed, "I have some cousins in Hoboken, off Washington Avenue."

Sinatra responded, "I was from Monroe Avenue."

Then an idea suddenly struck Grandpa, for in life spontaneity is sometimes better than well-wrought plans. He had been named chairman of the CYO banquet to raise funds for young people's activities. Everything costs money. He could not say no since he had so many children and grandchildren who had gone to St. Vincent's Elementary School. So he agreed; he would have Gerry Gerro sing a bit and then serve the people spaghetti and meatballs at $5.00 a head. Italian people hate to pay for anything, and even $5.00 for dinner and some entertainment raised hackles.

Why not Sinatra instead of Gerro? he wondered. So he simply blurted out, "Mr. Sinatra, we have a CYO dinner in Madison, New Jersey. If you could come and just sing one number it would be a sellout for the Catholic Youth Organization."

Immediately Sinatra's agents intervened rudely, cutting off Grandpa, "He is booked for that day."

Grandpa quizzically responded, "I didn't even say the day."

"Well, he is totally booked here and in Vegas."

Sinatra quietly intervened, "What day is it?"

"October 2nd in Madison."

"The last time I sang in my Hoboken, the bastards booed me in front of my father."

Grandpa reassured him, "Believe me, no one boos the great Sinatra in Madison."

Sinatra turned to his entourage, "Am I booked that day?"

"Yes, here, starting at 9 p.m."

"You hold yourself like my father, Marty, a quiet decent guy who was a fireman. My mom was loud and bitchy, an abortionist who went to church regularly, and was a precinct leader of the Democrat party. Well, I will sing at your CYO dinner at 6 p.m. and leave for here soon after. By the way who is your favorite singer?"

Grandpa honestly responded, "Caruso, I saw him sing once."

Sinatra laughed, "Well, I am not in that league, but at least you didn't say Crosby! Jim, call the Jersey governor and see if he can have a New Jersey trooper lead us from the benefit to AC."

Grandpa was overwhelmed with his answer and his own boldness. *He has such blue eyes,* he thought. They gave his agent the particulars and bid farewell to the chairman of the board.

On the way back, the grandchildren just sat silently as the night shadows passed by. What had just happened? They were successful men: accountants, insurance agents, builders, and Grandpa did not even have a high school degree? What they forgot was neither did Sinatra.

So back home, Grandpa decided to go for broke. He raised the price of tickets to $25 and moved it from the dimly lighted cafeteria with its cement block walls to the new gymnasium. He had posters made announcing "Sinatra!" with the date on it. And then he had them nailed all over the telephone poles on Main Street from the YMCA way down to the high school. The police seeing him nailing them, just waved, for they loved the audacity. Was he really coming? Did he just say that to get an old geezer out of his dressing room? Grandpa talked to Gerro, but he wasn't offended. He would be known forever as the man who was replaced by Old Blue Eyes! Grandpa even gave him a free ticket.

On October 2, the gymnasium was filled to over-capacity, people waited in the parking lot and just hoped to see the star. The rectory was overwhelmed with calls from Catholics who only came to church on Christmas and Easter, demanding tickets.

Then at 5:55, a series of black limos arrived in line, backed by two blinking state trooper cars. Out emerged Frank Sinatra in a tuxedo, and he waived to the cheering crowds near the old church. Reverently he bowed his head and grabbed Grandpa's hand.

"Ah, my good friend, I am here!"

In the gymnasium, Sinatra was overwhelmed with the cheers, the overtures, and the applause. *This is no Hoboken,* he thought. Grandpa sensitive to the time constraints grabbed the microphone and called for order. "On behalf of the CYO and the parish, I am glad to welcome a fellow paesano from Hoboken, Frank Sinatra."

Sinatra rose, went to the microphone, took it off the stand, introduced himself to J. J. Roselli, a young local piano player, and had him play, "It was a very good year," his famous rendition of the ages of man. Then he sang in honor of his host, the "Isle of Capri," for someone had told him that Grandpa and Grandma had honeymooned there. A nice touch indeed. The old man quietly grew misty. Members of the audience cried, and Sinatra held them in the palms of his hands from then on.

He could have left, but he had just begun. For a full half an hour he went through the Great American Songbook of Berlin, Porter, and the Gershwins. He had the crowd conclude with him, "O Solo Mio." Everybody knew it, and they sang in gusto along with Sinatra. He then stopped, bowed, and thanked Grandpa for the invitation and the "great piano player," J. J. Rosselli. But rather than slink out, he sat down to eat. Initially he had a plate of spaghetti and meatballs. While he ate with one hand, he signed autographs with the other. And he still talked to his host Grandpa.

But he did not talk of Hollywood, or of Vegas, or his friendship with politicians. He talked of his modest father, Marty of Hoboken, how the singer was arrested as a kid, and how some bastard on Broadway had Sinatra's mug shot blow up into a poster. He talked of where he started, the club owner at the Rustic Cabin, and how he said he was okay, but had to change the last name, it was too Italian. He asked for another meatball and grabbed it up with hard bread. Grandpa knew that Sinatra was on a tight schedule, but he did not seem to care. People paid to hear him after all.

Then he said a modest goodbye and gave Grandpa a wrapped long-playing record. Grandpa accepted it gratefully, "Is this from one of your movies?"

"No, it is Mario Lanza in *The Great Caruso*. You will love them both. I wish I could sing like Lanza. I know I owe you $25 for the dinner. I don't carry cash, so take this check."

"Oh, no, no," Grandpa responded.

"Yeah, give it to the kids."

Then he got up and began to leave, but the crowd yelled, "Encore, encore." And Frank Sinatra saw in a blur for a brief moment the old neighborhood on its feet. He walked over to the mike, called Roselli to the piano and spoke.

"My friends, when it seemed my career was over, my wife Ava Gardner got me a part in a movie, *From Here to Eternity*, and I won an Academy Award." The crowd cheered wildly, and he then announced, "This was the first song I made after my throat problem and my long recovery." Sitting on a stool, he leaned back, lit up a cigarette, and began:

"Set them up, Joe" And then he started, "It's one for my baby and one more for the road." Like all of us Sinatra had known depression and failure, for he was the bard of America's moods. When he finished, he disappeared out the back, with the limos waiting, and down to AC to make some money. Grandpa sat down and for some reason opened up the check. It was for $2,500.

A week later playing cards with his old buddies, Grandpa was bluntly told, "You are foolish. *Cafone*, you worked so hard on that Sinatra dinner and got nothing in return."

The old man looked nonchalantly, "Didn't I tell you that he gave me a record of *The Great Caruso*, and he also whispered to me that I was now an honorary member of his Rat Pack." And then he laughed and laughed at them. In the end, they both did it their way.

77. MALOCCHIO

For our freshman year, the university required us to take an elective on different cultures and customs, and I enrolled in a course on folk customs. I expected we would be taking a comparative survey, but the professor asked us to examine our own backgrounds. A Jewish friend of mine wrote extensively about the shtetls of Eastern Europe by reading the short stories of the great Isaac B. Singer; another looked at the folk tales of Irish fairies and ancient warriors; and I decided to examine the concept of the Italian malocchio, the evil eye. I had frequently heard that this person or that one in the neighborhood had the evil eye, and she used it especially on vulnerable people, such as pregnant women with blue eyes. It was prescribed that people so afflicted pass a dish of water with olive oil over one's head and make the sign of the cross to chase it away.

I had never met a carrier of the evil eye, and I decided to make contact with such a possessed person. I went up the gray, creaking backstairs on Saturday morning to visit Grandpa who was plaintively smoking his pipe and reading *Il Progresso*. When I was young, he complained I ran down the stars so fast he had to repair them twice. He saw me climbing up and welcomed me wholeheartedly. One of the problems of growing old is that no one casually visits you. He pronounced, "Ah, *come stai*, Marcus?"

I sat by him and asked, "Anything in the paper?"

"No, Giuseppe Pope is still that right wing editor his father was when Mussolini was in power."

"Never learned his lesson?"

"No, never learned. But toward the end of World War II he vigorously supported Roosevelt and the Allies."

"Grandpa, I wonder if you can help me in one of my university courses." I had asked him previously for help on my Sacco and Vanzetti paper.

Again he said, "I am not a learned man, son. But I respect greatly the university since we worked together on the Jersey tomato."

"Well, this is a little different. I am writing a study of people who have the evil eye."

He turned a bit pale and put down his paper on the bench. "Why don't you look at Garibaldi or one of our heroes in America like Joe DiMaggio?"

"But the idea of the evil eye and witches is more interesting to me. And more people believe in it. People all over the world, not just in Italy."

"Let it be, leave the evil eye alone. It is better not to get involved with evil in any way, my son. We don't even know what it means and who has it. In Italy, some religious believed that even Pope Pius IX had the eye. That is a frightening mix: evil and the vicar of Christ. No wonder he lived so long and brought so much woe on the Church."

"I am not interested in popes or misguided saints, but in local women who have the gift of the evil eye."

"It is no gift. It is a curse on the community."

I responded, "You have lived here since the 1890s. I can't believe that you do not know a woman who possesses the evil eye."

Grandpa got a little huffy, "I know, I know of course such people, but I tell you to leave it alone. People do not respect the voyager, look at what happened to poor Cristoforo Columbo."

"Let me try, if I don't find anything, you will be the first to know."

"And if you do find out, who will know then?"

"I want to impress my professor that I can do original research on my own town."

Then he stopped, "All right, the lady you want is across the street in the Saldino Chicken Market. She works in the back of the building. She is rarely seen by anyone. She cuts the heads off of the chickens—cuts or twists with quick motions."

"I have never seen her."

"That is why she is kept in the back room. I only know because old man Saldino and I were drinking heavily one night, and he spilled his guts out to me. I think he only hired her because he was afraid of her."

"Oh, I see...how do I meet her?"

"If you are crazy enough, go through the back door and just look for her. Ask for Mrs. Gallo. I would not go if I were you."

But I did not take his advice and went across the street to the chicken market. I always hated the smell of that place when I was a little kid sent over to get some chicken parts for dinner. One afternoon, I jumped in front of a car to get there quickly and was nearly killed. Bad sign. When you are young, you are immortal.

I moved over to the cinder block building and entered through the wooden screen door which was ajar. I called out a bit frightened, "Mrs. Gallo, are you there?"

"Where else would I be...in heaven?"

I gave her my name, mentioned my grandfather, and asked if I could fully enter. She greeted me glumly and came toward me in a bloody apron.

I wasn't sure how to address her. I couldn't say, "Hey, I hear you have the evil eye and I am trying to find out more." Or, "My professor wants me to talk to a possessed woman like you."

I hesitated and started slowly, "I am a college student at Rutgers, and I am taking a course on folk notions and contributions, and some people have told me that you are most knowledgeable in that area. My fellow students are doing Irish fairies and Jewish settlements in Czarist Russia. Can you give me some information about Italian practices?"

She squinted at me, and remarked, "You mean you have been told I have the gift of the evil eye, and you want to know how I do it? Huh? You are a courageous boy. Yes, I indeed have that gift, but someone not in the tradition cannot pass it on, if that is on your mind. The evil eye exists in much of the world. We Italians call it *malocchio*, but people call it by different names and use different amulets to fight it. The best one I have heard about is from the Turks, they are strong believers—that is why no one can ever defeat them in battle. A friend tells me that even their greatest leader, Ataturk, wore six amulets to protect him from his own people."

"Yes."

"Come and visit me tonight. I don't get many people to talk to. I am finished here at six. I have twenty more necks to twist, and I will meet you at my house at 32 Melrose. Wait for me on the porch, and we can resurrect the old myths. Are you sure you want to do this? You will get answers you have not expected in many cases. You know, your grandfather is afraid of me. He even goes to the 6 a.m. Mass because he knows I go to the 8 a.m.! Well, at least you have the courage he lacks. See you soon. Leave the apron here. It is stained with blood."

I walked six blocks to Melrose and the tiny house was covered over with weeds and branches with a giant tree on the front lawn. The roughly painted white house had a small porch with two aluminum chairs in the front and between them was a rusted metal table with a small thick candle on it. I slowly sat down on the right, since I had heard the right was good luck. I looked at the front lawn and saw a variety of equally tiny homes, all the way up from the street. I guess nobody wanted to have a bigger house than she did and stayed with the original plans.

It was a strange neighborhood. No flowers grew up between the foliage, and no birds sang in the high trees. Very different from Grandpa's garden. Then down the street came Mrs. Gallo, slowly but firmly until she reached her house.

"Ah, you found it all right. Most of these houses look alike. I think they were all built the same right after World War II."

"It was easy to find."

"Nothing is easy to find in life, boy." I nodded in agreement. "So you want to know about Italian folklore...and there is so much even in this country. Suppose I just focus on the evil eye which we have talked about.

You know the evil eye is even found in the Old Testament. Yahweh warned the Hebrews about it. He calls it Baal, the powerful one. Note that in the Ten Commandments, He says, 'Thou shall have no other gods before me'—not that there are no other ones already, but there should not be any in front of Him.

"The Apostles feared the powers of the women with evil eyes, and they told Jesus they did, but he cast them aside. He turned the evil ones into pigs and threw them over the cliffs."

"When did the evil eye began after that?"

"Probably in the Turkish area of the Middle East, for there Christianity first came as a foreign religion. Somehow, some men had the special gift of the evil eye, just like some had the gift of speaking in foreign tongues or curing the lame. St. Paul talks of it somewhere. Women were more likely to suffer the evil eye, and women were more likely to get a talisman to protect themselves and their families."

"Why do so many evil eyed women go to church and religious services?"

"People fear their power and at church they let down their guard. There we get them as they start to pray. Then they go home and complain they have a terrible headache...and it must be from us. They fear that we will come over and say how beautiful the new baby is—'bel bambino'—and the children are up all night with stomach pains."

"But what pleasure do you get from giving people, especially women and children, the evil eye?"

"Pain and pleasure are the same thing. They are only heightened emotions. They pull us from the humdrum of life through a special porous wall to the other side."

"But there is so much hatred and pain on this earth already. Why increase it?" I insisted.

"We bring that pain on individuals not on whole tribes of people."

"How can that be? There is so much suffering for so many people."

"How can it be otherwise? You and I are children of the awful 20th century. We are all witnesses to mass murders, holocausts, earthquakes, plagues. For us, that is all of creation, like Cain, the mark of our times. Stop and think, which is worse? Our terrible wars and God-made terrorism? Or our tiny pinpricks of annoyance. Look at our wars in terms of our time on earth. Yes, women and men are giving you the evil eye. And if you are able to do away with it, why haven't you."

"We try, you all are afraid of holy water."

"Really! You pass holy water over your heads, say few prayers, drop in oil, and make the sign of the cross. And so you think our evil eye passes by? If so, why do you baptize your young children, the very essence of innocence, asking them to give up the glamour of the world, swear off the enchanted devil and all his ways, forsake sin in all its delights? Why are you so fearful for your own children?"

"That is a myth."

"Be careful what you say. You think the evil eye is just an old lady's tale. But there are too many who suffer in your world. And then they ramble on—this is the reason special women are granted the power of suffering and redemption. Yet you believe the Holy Woman alone knows the blessings to forgive you, to give you mercy, to temper the anger of the Almighty One."

"Yes, but you encourage miscarriages for women."

"And you provide abortions for all reasons by the millions. You call it 'freedom to choose.'"

"But you do the work of the evil one, in all forms with no apology."

"And if there were no evil, you would not recognize good. For in a world of good and happiness, there is no adventure. Think of such a world—more pompous people, grand gestures, endless hope in a so-called just world. It is true that we bring evil, but it is only by that measure, son, you can appreciate the rest."

"We should be happy for you bringing us the evil eye?"

She reached over and lit the candle. "Wait, it is getting dark outside, although I do love the dark hours."

I noticed she looked more wizened than before, thinner, more capable of remorse, with fiercely colored eyes that gave me a bit of a headache. "So I should say in my college paper that evil is good so we can appreciate goodness. And that you transmit the evil eye, so strong people can feel the forces of a negative power and become humble."

"You can put it no better way. It doesn't matter what you believe, evil is a part of your universe and will be a part of your grandchildren's. Remember you are a child of the world of atrocities. Even I am frightened sometimes by your people. It is your generation who proclaimed, 'God is Dead.' He is not dead but lives quietly in the world you created. Here pick up the candle so you can see as you walk home. I understand the darkness, and I will see you as you slowly disappear."

And so I left with the candle, walking farther and farther away. I never told Grandpa about my conversation. I never wrote in class about my conversation. Instead I did a paper on "La Befana," the Italian female equivalent of Santa Claus who comes on January 6. But that is another story.

78. FAUX FESTIVAL

"The world is a beautiful place to be born into, if you don't mind happiness not always being so much fun." Poet Lawrence Ferlinghetti

Late one night, Grandpa got a phone call from a cousin, a stonemason, who unlike him had retired and moved to Clearwater, Florida. After much friendly chatter, he invited Grandpa to leave the snows of New Jersey for the 75° weather and go with him to the feast in honor of San Gennaro in nearby Safety Harbor. Grandpa responded that the feast wasn't until September. "It is now February," he said.

"No, no, they decided that with the hurricane season they would change the date since the festival was run by LIADO, dedicated women of Italian American roots, and no priests dared to complain to them about the change in date."

Grandpa thought it would be interesting, but he realized that he was a little too old. He did ask, "Could the invitation could be extended to one of my grandsons?"

"Of course, of course. The dates are February 17 and 18, and at Safety Harbor near the spa and resort at the beautiful beach discovered by Ponce de Leon as 'the Fountain of Youth'."

"Ah," Grandpa said, "I would love to go. All I enjoy in life—food, warmth, music, and a prayer to a famous saint from Napoli. It is my idea of a good time."

And so Grandpa thought which grandson he could send, and he came upon Marcus, then a junior at Rutgers College. Grandpa met with him and outlined the program and convinced him it quickly would be great to leave New Jersey, even for a week, in the winter. Soon Marcus was convinced, and in English class he asked a beautiful statuesque blonde if she would like to go to Florida for an Italian festival. "Nobody does it better than the Italians."

She was every Italian American boy's dream: thin, long blonde hair, rounded hips, upturned breasts, and a beautiful face with blue, sparkling eyes. Marcus once observed that at every Italian festival that he went to, he saw Italian men with widow's peaks holding on to dyed blondes. It was in their

DNA.

And so Marcus and his friend went down to the Tampa airport. He rented an expensive car and drove out to Safety Harbor's beautiful spa and resort right along the lovely bay. Between the water and the hotel, the Italian Americans had set up their booths and created an outdoor auditorium for their festivities. The program included a talent show, the Da Vinci Brothers comedy opera company, Santa Semolina—a life-size puppet—and a singer, Dominic Del Monte. It would start with a long procession headed by a priest and a Knights of Columbus delegation carrying the statue of San Gennaro.

Marcus had made reservations at the hotel, and with his girl by his side he asked for two keys for one room. She said nothing—he thought, *home free*. Then upstairs he opened the door, and she paraded in. He tried to lock the door, but she quickly pulled down his pants, ripped off his oxford buttoned shirt and threw him on the double bed. And then she also undressed quickly and jumped on top. She was like a tigress protecting her cubs. He felt her fingernails dig into his back and buttocks, and then they continued for hours. She soon fell asleep, but he laid awake. Maybe he had gotten more than he could handle.

In the early morning they went to the park, and the events began with another religious procession headed by three elegantly dressed Knights of Columbus men with colorful plumes and Father Tom, a traditional Italian priest dressed in the white cassock of his Spanish order.

They began with the United States' national anthem, and then sang the beautiful national anthem of Italy which Marcus had never heard. "*Il Canto degli Italiani*" was written by Michele Novaro with lyrics by Goffredo Marneli in 1847.

Fratelli d'Italia,
l'Italia s'è desta,
dell'elmo di Scipio
s'è cinta la testa.
Dov'è la Vittoria?
Le porga la chioma,
ché schiava di Roma
Iddio la creò.

[Brothers of Italy,
Italy has woken,
Bound Scipio's helmet
Upon her head.
Where is Victory?
Let her bow down,
For God created her

Slave of Rome.]

It was beautiful, almost like a Verdi opera, and Marcus enjoyed the vigor of the people who knew it, but his girlfriend couldn't care less. The priest in Italian and English warned the audience that God only spoke Italian, so that if they expected to go to heaven, they better practice their language skills. Then the festival began, featuring its singers.

The girl looked at Marcus and perked up. "God, what a handsome man. He looks like Vic Damone." Marcus just squinted at her. The tenor was indeed good, but not that good. And after his act was over, Marcus went over and introduced himself and told him that he was friends with the family that owned the Claridge Hotel in Las Vegas. They were always looking for opening acts before the eternal Tony Bennett went on. Bennett was especially pleasant to young, new singers, for he remembered when he was one a hundred years ago.

Dom was delighted and gave Marcus his card, while his girlfriend looked on in rapture. The sun beat heavily that day, reaching nearly 90° and there were no trees on that strip except for some thin palm trees. Marcus wanted to explore each and every booth, while his girlfriend went back to the hotel to get out of the heat.

He was stopped by two old ladies who made rosaries, and they wanted to know the real story of San Gennaro, so he told them at length how he had been beheaded in 305 A.D. by Emperor Diocletian. He was the bishop of the important province of Benevento where Marcus's grandmother was born. At Gennaro's death, some pious woman soaked up his blood and put it into several vials. Every year since then the blood frequently liquified for reasons no scientist even today knows. If it liquifies at all, it will be a good year for Naples. If it doesn't, it will be a year of peril. The ladies loved the story about the brave and courageous bishop, and Marcus went on to get an Italian ice and then a sausage sandwich.

Finally, moving out of the heat, he decided to go back to the hotel, and as he went up to the room, he began to hear animal noises. He quietly opened the door with his electronic key, and he saw Dom, the singer, on top of his girl who was in full pleasure.

He walked in the room, threw his suitcase together and quietly left. As he moved, Dom heard the sounds of the door being closed. Marcus looked at the two naked lovers, took Dom's card and threw it at him. "Goodbye to Tony Bennett, my friend." He then took the elevator down to the front desk, and there he threw the key at the clerk, "I will not pay for this room."

"Why sir?"

"It has rats in it."

"My God, please be quiet. There are guests nearby. I will credit your credit card immediately, sir."

"Good, have the room cleaned now."

Marcus walked out, got in his car, caught an early plane back to Newark airport. The next day, he went to see Grandpa to finish the bizarre circle he was in, but Grandpa was so excited, he only wanted to hear the details of the San Gennaro festival. And his grandson told him that they even played the Italian anthem, and Grandpa lit up. He hummed the chorus with its famed ending:

> *Stringiamci a coorte,*
> *siam pronti alla morte.*
> *Siam pronti alla morte,*
> *l'Italia chiamò.*
> *Sì!*

> [Let us join in a cohort,
> We are ready to die.
> We are ready to die,
> Italy has called.
> Sì!]

It brought out good memories to Grandpa when he was young in better days. And then he proudly turned to his grandson, "You see, Marcus, sometimes we must forget the depravity and the sins of the world and turn to spiritual matters. Do you agree my son?"

"Yes, yes, I do, Grandpa."

79. A LESSON TO BE LEARNED

Marcus was not a very good liar, or even a very good qualifier, so two weeks later he saw Grandpa after his Florida trip. He felt he had to talk to him with the full truth of the trip. He had chosen Marcus, of all his grandsons, to represent him at the San Gennaro Festival at Safety Harbor, and even paid for his plane fare from Newark to Tampa and back again. He told him the full story of the festival, but Grandpa ended up singing the beautiful Italian anthem. He loved it for he remembered walking to that elegant aria as if it were written by Verdi himself. In fact, the anthem was written by two young men in the Risorgimento.

So on Saturday next Marcus walked into the backyard and saw him sitting aimlessly on his aluminum chair with a stained maple bench next to him. He looked up and welcomed him heartily, for the elderly get few young people as visitors in their life as they go on. *"Comé stai Marcus Aurelius?"*

"Great, Grandpa. Beautiful day."

"Indeed."

"So, Grandpa, I wanted to talk to you about the Florida trip."

"Oh, I was so proud of your visit. My cousin in fact just wrote me a letter yesterday about how impressive you were—like a banker, he commented. He said the young girls were most impressed. Too bad that we are cousins. You don't want to be like Aunt Maria and Uncle Vincent and marry your cousin. We had to go through craziness with the Vatican to get that dispensation!"

"No, no. I didn't want to tell you, I took this beautiful blonde from my English class with me, and we registered for only one room at the spa."

Grandpa looked up and then curled his lip and said, "And? One bed, huh? The reason they call it Ponce de Leon's fountain of youth!" And then he laughed self-consciously. "I need those waters not for you, but for me!"

"Well, not quite." And Marcus told him while he was watching the San Gennaro festival, his blonde girlfriend vanished into the cool air-conditioning of the hotel and spa, that he walked into the room quietly not to wake her.

There she was with the singer, like naked jaybirds, screaming in an impassionate embrace. "I then told the clerk I wouldn't pay for the room, that it had rats, and he should immediately fumigate them out. I got into my rental car and left her stranded and looked for an earlier flight back to Newark. The next day I changed course sections in English and took another one without her."

The old man philosophically mused, "You are not a Neapolitan. You are more of a Sicilian. Revenge served cold. Have you seen her again?"

"No."

"Eh, that is probably best. I had something happen like that to me when I was a little older than you. I enrolled in night school at Madison to learn English, and the teacher, a divorced woman, tried to seduce me. She had tasted of the forbidden fruit and believed the stories of macho Italian boys. I got out of the class and bought a small black Philco radio and learned American English from it."

"But I thought we might have had something really going. She was so beautiful. I could have easily loved her."

"She loved you, huh? Son, women, even the good ones, are different from us men. Under the shyness, the reserve, the modesty, is a thick layer of animal passion—*animale*—which when touched becomes almost crazy. If you ever notice that after sex that we feel it once, and they enjoy it three or four times and more intensely?"

Marcus was startled, for all said that the old man was the last remnant of the Victorian Italian era. He had six kids or so, but never talked about sex or even womanhood.

"They think that they are doing us a favor, but it is the opposite. We are Rotor Rooter men with wallets," he unexpectedly remarked. "I was married a long time and had four daughters and never understood them or their mother. They live in their own world. It is narrowly focused and goes up and down like a piano player. In the morning they are quiet, in the evening moody, and in between, who knows? You can give them fruits and flowers and candies, and you never know how the evening will turn out."

"I didn't expect that the dago singer would be in my bed," Marcus ruminated.

"Eh. She was just attracted to him, but you didn't get serious, for she would end up your *putana* rather than your young wife. We have one *putana* in the family already."

"I think we Italians are mesmerized by blondes."

"Yes, opposites attract, but you were attracted to her for what she gave away so easily to others, because they all have a layer of the *animale* under the soft skin and cheap makeup. We think that's the real person."

"How could she have done that in our very bed?"

"This is why they change the sheets after every guest!" Marcus had rarely heard Grandpa talk like that. "It is much easier to control this in Italy than in America. In Italia they have large families, chaperones, nosy aunts to watch virtue. Soon they get married and are overwhelmed with children. Then they must worry about their own daughters' virtue. But I bet they have dreams and fantasies in which many a neighborhood man plays the part of Valentino. My friend Padre Pio told me once that in confession the sins of women are more graphic than those of men and more frequent. He can't say so to his superiors. He told me he had them recite more acts of penance, and pray especially to the Virgin Mary."

"But Grandpa, she was my soulmate!"

"Soulmate... What is that?"

"Two people bound together forever by the force of destiny!"

"Ahh, *la forza del destino*... Remember it is Verdi's tragedy, not a romance, Marcus."

"There is only one woman per man, Grandpa."

"Nonsense, there are many couples that marry, are unmarried, live in loneliness, endure in misery. Your true love will come along."

"I want to give you back the money for the air trip to Tampa," Marcus said.

"Oh no, you represented the family well. Forget about the rest. Go. Go in peace."

Marcus left the old man, and as he walked down the driveway, Grandpa called back. "Hey, hey Marcus... Women are like buses—miss one, catch another." Marcus had never heard him laugh, but he roared as if he had discovered an immutable truth from God.

80. A DIALOGUE ON FRIENDSHIP

"God chooses those whom the world considers weak and foolish to confuse the strong and the wise." 1 Corinthians 1:27.

Every Saturday night, except on holy feasts of obligation, when Don Giovanni could not be a part of the game since he had to say Mass, the six Italians gathered to play cards at Grandpa's apartment. Before the game, which lasted until one or two in the morning, the players ate antipasto and drank wine usually diluted with cream soda. Grandma carefully put out all the refreshments, and some plates and forks with six goblets. Then she wisely vanished. The last thing she wanted after a long day was hours of male gossip and shouting as they slapped down the cards in triumph.

The game they played, known everywhere, is called *Bristola*, an extremely popular card game that uses 36 cards (not 52), and which contains pictures of coins, cups, clubs, batons, and swords in the pack on the other side of the numbers. They played with six people on two teams. One could play even with just two people. Most of the cards had a point value. The total value of the cards in the deck added up to 129 points. The player or leader would end up with 61 points. The winners would yell "*caprotto*," and scream the word to confirm victory. Most expressive players threw the cards down with vigor and volume. Grandma slept in the farthest away bedroom, seeking only peace and quiet.

As a good Mediterranean host, Grandpa welcomed the other five players: Don Giovanni, Alphonso, Uncle Nick, and Rocco. Fiore who had gotten sick was replaced by Grandpa's grandson Marcus. They hastily sat down, and he poured wine into each goblet and put the antipasto in the center of the table. One could keep quiet in the game, or give signals to partners, but mainly their game was punctuated by gossip and was replete with rumors of the goings on in the town. The men liked to make fun of women and their small talk, but the men were far and away the major carriers of common news.

Grandpa cut the cards, and they began:

Rocco: Raffaele, how are things at the Dodge estates?

Raffaele: They are good. I hear they are hiring two more gardeners for the back of the estate's planting.

Rocco: Can I tell my two cousins; they just came over from Rotondi?

Raffaele: Of course, tell them to go to the hiring office. You go with them, so they can give the right answers. The director there is a *stronzo*.

Rocco: I think they are illegals, my friend...

Raffaele: Don't tell anyone; just get them on the payroll and paying taxes. That is all the employers want.

Don Giovanni: You are a good friend.

Raffaele: Just trying to help; you can't be a friend to a person you don't know.

Alfonso: No, friendship is the rarest gift of all. I can count on my fingers the number of friends I have. My wife says no one will be at my wake. Don Giovanni, do they give a wake if no one comes?

Don Giovanni: Of course, you have at least one friend,
The Father Almighty,
He is with you.
And He will never leave you.
In the end, He will be there.

Alphonso: I worry about that a lot.

Raffaele: Play the game.

Don Giovanni: You know Cicero
Says friendship is the marriage of two noble souls.
You must be loyal to each other in peril,
Share the good times without envy,
Is that not so, Marcus?

Marcus: (surprised) Yes, Cicero says that
Friendship is forever,
But after childhood, friends vanish.
Keep what you have—

Treasure it, hold on tightly.
If a person asks for a favor,
Do it happily…

Don Giovanni: Not if is immoral,
Or violates the Church's laws.

Marcus: Yes, of course, but friends
Don't ask immoral things, do they?

Alphonso: But if it is easy and necessary,
What do you need a friend for?
I need a friend to do
What others shy away from:
To help me avoid the police,
Or flee from my in-laws.
Still friendship, except in one's family,
Is the highest gift of all, it is true.

Raffaele: Play the damn cards.
Pass the wine.

Nick: Some friend you are—
I am closer than a friend,
I am your brother, yet you give me this cheap wine.
You know I want real whiskey.
You hold me away from my desires.
You are a lousy friend,
A lousy brother.

Raffaele: Nick, you don't need the hard stuff,
I held it back out of concern for you.

Nick: I do not need your love.

Don Giovanni: No, no let us remember friends.
This is what Jesus shared with his apostles,
They were fearful, but he forgave all.

Nick: He gave them real wine at the Last Supper.

Rocco: No friend in this world,
Can be a friend except

In bad times, for without that
Who needs a friend?

Raffaele: We are all friends here,
Bound together by a common language
And a common culture,
Let us enjoy each other's company.

Rocco: But we haven't defined friendship.
We are like the old Greeks, we talk
Too much, but never give
To each other a definition
That one can live by.

Marcus: Good friends,
It is clear, friendship is a second self,
So friendship improves happiness and abates sadness.

Don Giovanni: *Non nobis solum nati sumus,*
Not for ourselves alone are we born,

Marcus: Exactly, no life is soothing without friends.

Don Giovanni: Friendship and truth are sacred
Endowments of the human mind.

Raffaele: You two seem to have defined the term.

Marcus: Loyalty is what we seek in friendship.

Nick: And who is so loyal here?
It is better to live like a hermit in the woods,
Like the shadow man who roams in Chester.

Raffaele: What are you talking about?

Alphonso: It is said that some people have seen the last hermit in New
Jersey.

Don: I have heard of it in confession. I don't believe in it myself.
But who knows?

Raffaele: We should see for ourselves. How can a man live without company? Such a man is an *animale*.

> Rocco: So much for your notion of friendship, Marcus.
> This hermit lives alone
> In the middle of nowhere.

And as the long game ended at 1:30 a.m., the men who had worked hard all week got up and left having grown weary and their minds confused. Grandpa took the paper plates and cleaned up. He placed the antipasto remnants in the refrigerator. He even washed the six goblets, so Grandma wouldn't face a dirty sink in the morning.

As he washed out the goblets, he mused over what had gone on. In this most common game, they had discussed at length a philosophical question which they never did before, for working men do not engage in such scholarly dialogue. What is friendship? What brought that about? Soon they will be discussing what is justice, then what is truth. Even Pontius Pilate didn't know. They talked about the rumor that some goombah had seen a hermit in the woods in Chester. The neighbors called him "the last hermit in New Jersey."

A couple of weeks later, on August 15, the whole family rented a DeCamp bus to visit the relatives in Mechanicsville, a suburb of Albany, New York, to attend the feast of the Assumption which was more ornate than the event in the Madison area. They even had fireworks. It was a long bus ride, and Grandpa passed it up. So he stayed behind and, was in the end lonely and bored.

But he decided that he would visit the Chester area and see where the so-called hermit lived. And he drove all the way up the byways through Morristown to the rural and near deserted areas of Chester. There was really nothing to see except a few vacation homes boarded up, and endless acres of white pines and shrubs.

He saw nothing, it was another New Jersey myth like the blue-eyed devil of the Pinelands. Grandpa, a bit superstitious, believed in the myths and legends of here and in Italy. Then he found footprints and openings in the ferns. He moved toward the openings, and saw a rundown cabin, and inside it a disheveled young man sorting through the cabinets. The intruder spotted Grandpa through the dirty windowpane, and yelled out, "Stop, who are you?"

"Who are you? Are you a renter or a visitor?"

"No, I am what you call a hermit. I live alone and see no one."

"Ah, YOU are the last hermit in New Jersey?"

"The last hermit in New Jersey, I like that title."

"So, who are you then?"

"I am who I am."

"How can you live alone as a hermit? How do you deal with the winter cold, having no food, getting sick, how do you survive?"

"I eat what I find in these cabins, people are so wasteful, and I come and go with no one seeing me. I sleep in caves and under the blankets I find around. Since I come in contact with no one, I contract no diseases."

"Why do you do this?"

"I live alone like at Walden Pond. It is a good life. No aggravation, no bosses, no orders, and it is so beautiful, don't you agree?

"Yes, I love nature, but it is too cold to live in nature all seasons, and you speak to no one, how can you do that?"

"It has worked well for five years or so, so I can't complain."

"Aren't you lonely? How can you not talk to people?"

"I am happy to contemplate nature. Here, sit down old timer."

Grandpa sat on a rustic kitchen chair. The hermit sprawled out like he owned the cabin. Grandpa continued, "I think even at my age one must have some time for thought and admiring nature. But I cannot live without friendship, without anyone to talk to, to laugh with, and to share our fears. Do you not end up talking to yourself during the long days?"

"Yes, and it is an interesting conversation, better than to talk with idiots at work or at cocktail parties."

"But if you talk to no one, you will never learn anything new. All you hear is the sound of your own voice. Life becomes an echo. You need to think new ideas."

"I am satisfied with my own thoughts. Why are you so surprised? Do you really take into account the ideas of others in your behavior? If you did so, you would not believe anything for more than a single day. Please, my good man, leave me be. I am happy with my life. How many can say that? Can you?"

Grandpa tried to be more practical. "Sooner or later the Morris County police will track you down. You need a place of your own, even if you wish to live outside. I hear there is a rich man who is going to donate 18 acres up here to the Catholic Church, for some purpose. Perhaps you can get a place there alone."

"That is for a monastery. To be a monk you must believe in God, the Church, the Virgin, and practice poverty, chastity and obedience. I am not a believer in any of those. Can you live with those fantasies all your life?"

And so the strange meeting ended. Grandpa and the hermit bid an almost courtly farewell. Still he worried about the lonely man. After they parted, Grandpa would appear monthly at the same tree groupings and leave foodstuffs and wine for the next two years, but then stopped when no one picked them up. The hermit had vanished.

Grandpa was somewhat annoyed. Was he being made a fool of by this supposed hermit? Was it all a guise? Italians are a generous but not a trusting people. In any case, he forgot about him and went back to his normal life. He had promised the pastor he would trim the church hedges, and he showed up on Sunday, and began working although it was the Sabbath. There he met Eugene, a young, thin ascetic-looking deacon who was going to be ordained a priest at St. John the Baptist Cathedral in the fall. He knew him well and decided to tell him the story of the vanishing hermit. The deacon noted that as a young boy he would go into the woods and pray and contemplate the glories of God's creations. Grandpa sourly responded, "Yes, but this guy doesn't believe in anything."

The deacon responded quietly, "No one who loves nature can be an atheist."

Grandpa, like everyone in the parish, liked Eugene, and he had known his parents, Pasquale and Anna Romano, for decades. The boy, Eugene, called GeeGee, was the eighth of nine children and was a devoted follower of the faith. Italians love nicknames. Grandpa wanted more children than he had, but Grandma almost died after the last one, and so they stopped, much to his sadness. Perhaps if they continued, they would have ended up with a priest like GeeGee.

GeeGee was very contemplative and could be seen often on his knees on the bare marble floor in the inside entrance praying in front of the statues of St. Therese of Liseux and the Neapolitan author and confessor St. Alphononus of Ligori. More fascinating was a side altar which featured a statue of Mary of the Immaculate Conception. The old statue had a strange look—its eyes followed you as you walked by. Grandpa called it "the parish's Mona Lisa." But GeeGee adored the statute, and he became even more committed to the contemplation of Mary and her tribulations. He even wondered about becoming a Trappist monk, like his hero, Thomas Merton, and not a parish priest.

Nearly all the parish thought he was already a saint, and they followed his family and career as if he were a gift given in their midst. One night when Grandpa went to a Monday night novena, his grandson, Marcus, lit the tall candles, but the wick was too long, and a fire started at the base of the candelabra. Eugene quickly grabbed a stepstool, put out the candles, and said nothing to the boy. Grandpa remembered that act of kindness more than anything else.

After 11 years as a priest in three different local parishes in the diocese, he felt he had a special vocation. After several years of prolonged conferences with two timid bishops, his was given permission to establish a secluded ministry if he could get the donations. He created a dining hall, a fine small chapel, and about a dozen tiny huts for the monks. The community was called a "Laura," a compound of monks dedicated to silence, prayer, and contemplation. He called on all the contacts his huge family had and acquired the support of Italian American craftsmen: carpenters, electricians, plumbers, cement layers, and genuine artists who sought to do what the D'Medicis did, build a church that was so elegant that it would guarantee them a final place in heaven. But Grandpa was not there; he had died a decade before the project was completed.

Father Romano adopted the rules of the third century Desert Fathers, the Catholic hermits who literally disappeared into the deserts of the Middle East and Egypt. As he interviewed candidates to be residents in the Laura, he came upon the hermit of New Jersey. The cops had indeed instructed the cabin owners how to nail up their dwellings so no one could get in and how they should dispose of any food left over from the summer. It became almost impossible for a hermit to live in those new conditions. He hated to admit it, but he needed some support structure to continue his solitude. He had heard that Abbot Romano was interviewing candidates for admission to the Laura. He showed up one morning, and immediately impressed Eugene. The abbot thought that he had extensive experience in solitary living and the intense contemplation of nature. He soon admitted him, and the hermit did take the vows in a perfunctory way. What he believed was unclear even to him. Surprisingly, it worked well. The other monks respected his absolute solitude.

One day the abbot asked each monk to put on the paten on the altar a slip of paper with the name of the closest friend they had before coming to the monastery. It was, he said, time to pray for their souls, and for their good deeds.

The hermit left the chapel without putting in a name and went back to his sterile cottage. There he looked at the cross above the bed and the dim bulb that barely allowed you to read the Scriptures, and finally had a sense of what he wanted to say. He went back through the torrential rains and wrote down, "the old Italian man who brought me food." And as he dropped the paper on the paten, the lightning outside crackled, and it hit the chapel directly. There were no lightning rods in the compound. The main support beam dropped, downed the huge crucifix above the altar, and hit the hermit directly as he wrapped his white cloak around his head. The damage to the hermitage was extensive. The hermitage began to rebuild, but without its most famed hermit.

See: Marcus Tullius Cicero, *On Friendship;* Eugene L. Romano, *A Way of Desert Spirituality* (rev.) New Yorker: Alba House, 1998.

81. SACCO AND VANZETTI

One college course I was taking was constitutional law, where we were assigned to write an in-depth paper on one major case in American history. One person took the Dred Scott decision, another the Scopes "monkey" case, and I chose the Sacco and Vanzetti trial. I had heard it mentioned in oblique ways in the family, but never in any way that made much sense, for they knew the particulars and spoke about it in a code. Most of us knew that they were Italian anarchists who were found guilty in a much contested trial in Massachusetts on charges of murder and burglary.

I decided to go visit the patriarch of the family, Grandpa, who that April day was sitting on the bench on his own porch, overlooking the garden and grape boughs that had yet to come to full bloom. He was quietly puffing on his pipe and waved to me to come up. He inquired how I was doing in college, for he was especially proud of Rutgers University that had once given him a certificate of accomplishment for his work on tomato strains. I told him that I had this special assignment and needed his help. He modestly responded that he was not a well-educated person and was not sure he could be of much assistance. "What is it about?"

"I am doing a long paper on the Sacco-Vanzetti trial. Was the trial fair? Was one or both guilty?"

He suddenly became sullen and asked plaintively, "Why are you doing that? It is best to leave the trial alone. It has been too many years."

I responded, "Yes, but people still want to know if justice was served."

"Justice, son, is for the rich. Most of us just try to stay away from courts and lawyers if we can. "

"Would you please give me some help on this, Grandpa?"

He put down his pipe and suddenly went into a different mode of behavior. It was like my Jewish friends remembering the meaning of Passover. It was the voice of a family's legacy reaching across the generations, hoping to tell truths that the young should have, but do not care about.

He started, "In 1917, your grandmother had a baby girl, your mother, and she wanted to show her to her family in East Boston. They were the Perones and were very comfortable in Italy, and I think they had reservations about me marrying their lovely daughter. But by then, I was an American, and they thought I must be very rich and a good catch. People in Italy in those days believed that in the United States, milk and butter were delivered right to your door. Nobody told them you had to pay for them at the end of the month. Others said that the roads were paved with gold, nobody was honest and told them that many of the streets were not even paved, and that they brought Italians and Chinese over to do that hard work.

"But it was her family, and we traveled by train to Boston's South Station, and her people picked us up. We went to their two family house in East Boston that overlooked the Boston bay. It was a quiet place, where people got along together, and the Perones operated a bakery in the larger city of Boston. They were good to us and were so delighted to see your grandmother and the baby, and I walked around the area looking at the New England houses and their gardens. There was an Irish tavern there owned by Patrick Kennedy, the grandfather of Senator John F. Kennedy.

"But one day, one of the neighbors asked if I would like to visit Boston and hear the famous speaker from Italy, Luigi Galleani, at the Park Street Church. He was the unofficial head of the anarchist movement, and the anarchists were all over the world. One had killed King Umberto in Italy, one had killed President McKinley, and several had bombed President Wilson's attorney general's home. And many of them were Italian and Slovak.

"I went to the Park Street Church, and it was packed. Most people there were foreigners, and vendors sold pictures of J. P. Morgan and John D. Rockefeller with black ribbons on the edges. I went in, took a pew seat and waited for Galleani to speak. He proclaimed the anarchist gospel to all: no government, no institutions, no oppression, but freedom for all. He pointed to the anarchist violence in the Midwest, and in Europe as well. He swelled with pride and gave his speech in a mixture of Italian and English which at times I found confusing.

"Then he sat down in triumph and asked for questions. One person jumped up and asked if he approved of violence and murder. Galleani said, 'It is what it is.'

"Another asked him what of the Church? He responded defiantly that it was worse than the government, it left people stupid and the Virgin was 'a Roman whore.' I was startled by his language. Finally, I got up and said I had come to America for a better life, brought a wife here, and had five children at that time. 'Are you telling me I made mistakes, that I need to overthrow America?'

"Immediately his followers started to swear at me in Italian, and one leader, Nicholas Sacco, pointed to me and said to the crowd, 'He is a plant of the capitalist class!' I sat down and feared for my life. When it was over, I quickly got out the front door onto Park Street but was stopped by an amiable man with a handlebar mustache in an oversized overcoat who smelled of fish.

"'Stop, please I am sorry my friend Sacco gets angry at all this. Your question was a good one. My name is Bartolomeo Vanzetti. I too came here for a better life, but I just sell fish as I did back in the Piedmont area. I would rather leave this capitalist hellhole. Your question was a good one, here take some of our pamphlets and read what we have to say. Come back and I will introduce you to Galleani myself, and I will pay for a good lunch in the North End with me and Sacco.'

"I grabbed the pamphlets and headed to the water taxi back to East Boston. As I boarded the boat, I took the pamphlets and threw them in the garbage can at the pier. The last thing Boston needed was another Italian anarchist!"

"So you knew Sacco and Vanzetti?"

"Only Vanzetti, I never went back."

Jumping the gun, I asked, "People say Sacco was guilty, but Vanzetti was not."

"I don't know. But everyone believed Vanzetti was the smarter of the two. Who knows?"

He went on, "Then in 1920, there was a bloody robbery in South Braintree. Two or three bandits took the payroll at a shoe factory and killed the paymaster and a guard. The guard was an Italian.

"The trial was held in a country that was fearful of anarchists, especially foreign born ones. They claimed that the two anarchists were not only preaching against the corrupt system but planned a robbery to help pay for an attack on buildings on Wall Street in New York City. In this trial, nearly 200 witnesses were called, and they disagreed with each other. The Italian consul who had been in Boston testified by mail that Sacco was getting his passport renewed at the time of the robbery. The bullets did not fit the gun that was supposed to be Sacco's, and a cop at the scene of the murder said the cap they found did not even fit him. Sacco had worked in that factory sometime, and at first nobody said they recognized him. As for Vanzetti, he claimed he was selling fish for the holidays, and people who saw him came into court. For some reason, the defense attorneys had them admit that they were draft dodgers during the war, and that they had fled to Mexico. They also admitted they were anarchists. The judge said to a friend that he would get those 'anarchistic bastards.' On the stand, neither Vanzetti nor Sacco spoke English well enough to avoid the trick questions. With all that evidence to review, the jury made its decision after only three hours of debate. The governor appointed a special commission to re-examine the case after protests came in from all over the world. The head of this committee was the president of Harvard, and they upheld the verdict. Then in 1925, after years of appeals and protests, a known robber named Madeiros said he was a part of the murder and Sacco and Vanzetti were not there. One newspaper man tired of the long process told people it was just the story of 'two wops in a jam.' The Boston people hated the Irish, but they hated the Italians even more." And then he abruptly stopped short.

I asked Grandpa what he thought: "Was the trial fair, and were Sacco and Vanzetti guilty?" He got up and went inside his apartment and soon emerged with a brown manila envelope and gave it to me. Inside were articles on the arrest, the trial, the appeal, the Lawrence Commission, the execution, and the worldwide reaction. I looked carefully through them as he returned to his pipe and started puffing again. Inside was a copy in English of the famed Vanzetti defense at the end of his life, one that would ring around the world.

"If it had not been for these things, I might have lived out my life talking at street corners to scorning men. I might have died, unmarked, unknown, a failure. Now we are not a failure. This is our career and our triumph. Never in our full life could we hope to do such work for tolerance, for justice, for man's understanding of man as now we do by accident. Our words—our lives—our pain—nothing! The taking of our lives—lives of a good shoemaker and a poor fish-peddler—all! That last moment belongs to us, that agony is our triumph."

I put down the materials and asked him again: "Do you think they got a fair trial?"

"No one believes any more that they did."

"Do you think that they were convicted because they were foreigners and looked so foreign?"

"Most of us believed that they were anarchists who did not get a fair trial, some believed because they were Italian anarchists."

"Do you think they were guilty in spite of an unfair trial?"

"I don't know if either Sacco or Vanzetti were guilty. But here is the history, maybe you can add to it."

I politely thanked him. He took the manila envelope back and re-sealed it. I argued in my paper that the trial was unfair and a farce in American legal history. But I was in doubt if one or more of them were guilty or not. Could a simple shoemaker and a humble fisher peddler commit such atrocities against working men? Italian Americans stopped talking about it.

Grandpa died in 1969, but in 1977, Massachusetts Governor Michael Dukakis issued a proclamation declaring that they were "unfairly convicted" and that "any disgrace should be forever removed from their names." No one though called the families of the victims ahead of time. The proclamation was issued both in English and Italian.

82. ITALIAN GALA

Retirement revolves around boredom and television, and television at least induces sleep since most of it is so mediocre. Early one night, Grandpa was watching channel 9, the movie channel, which once again was featuring *It Happened One Night*, with Clark Gable and Claudette Colbert. He had seen it so often that he knew most of the dialogue; suddenly the phone in the kitchen alcove rang loudly, and he got up to answer it. People rarely called him anymore, not even solicitors and politicians running for office. He answered it, and on the other end was a familiar voice, "Hello, this is Jim Stafford the Third, do you remember me?"

"Of course, you were kind enough to get me the consultant job at Princeton University. A great place, and I enjoyed it immensely."

"Well, people still talk about you and Dr. Einstein. You apparently were the only person who could relate to him on a human level! In any case, I am calling you to ask another favor. I am a major donor to a variety of causes: the United Jewish Appeal, Boy Scouts, Catholic Charities, Sons of Hibernia, and the Italian American Educational Foundation. The last group is having its gigantic fund raiser at the Waldorf Astoria Hotel in New York City, and I will out of town making money in Germany so I can continue to be a philanthropist. In any case, I have given the foundation a very major gift for scholarships, which Lehman Company matched, and the hosts want me to be on the dais with the honorary guest this year. I would have sat right near her, but I cannot go. You really are the only Italian I know who doesn't want anything from me or isn't trying to get me to invest in their harebrained scheme. Will you go?"

Grandpa was startled; he surely had no scheduling conflict with his boring retirement. But he could not take the place of a millionaire whom he had barely met over the years. But still, it was for a good cause, scholarships for Italian American kids to go to college, an experience he never had. So on a lark, he answered, "I would be honored to go in your place, but I cannot sit on the dais with the guests and the major patrons. That would not be honest."

"No, no, you will be representing me, and it is my contribution that got me that close to the main honoree. By the way, the honoree that night will be Sophia Loren, do you know her name?"

"What? Of course, we all know her name. I rarely go to the movies, but even I have seen her in some of her great films. Sitting next to Sophia Loren, that is really a remarkable turn of events."

"The only thing is that this gala is very formal, and you must go in a full tuxedo."

"Of course."

"Good, I know it is quite a trip to New York City and the Waldorf. I will send my chauffeur to pick you up and wait to return you home. He will be at 81 Main Street, at 5:30 pm, next Tuesday. Is that ok?"

"Perfect. Thank you."

"No, no, thank you, have a good time. Say hello to Sophia from me!"

Grandpa looked at the telephone which he gently held onto. *What was happening in life? He was a retired old man, a working man, now he was eating with the rich in the most extravagant city in the world, more than Rome, more than Naples. It was New York City, the city of the very wealthy and the very poor, and I am going to the Waldorf for dinner.* The only person he ever heard of at that great hotel was the famed general, Douglas MacArthur, who lived there for the rest of his post-war life. *And my dinner companion, Sophia Loren, this must be some Italian joke, something Puccinello would dream up. But Mr. Stafford was not a man of practical jokes.*

Then he began to worry—he had no tuxedo. Even for his children's weddings, he had worn his one good suit, but not a tuxedo. How would he get one in a week? Then he remembered, of course, Angelo Albino's son ran the Rose City Formal Shop, and people rented tuxedos all the time. Angelo's father had come over on the boat with Grandpa and had actually worked for Grandpa in the early days. He was not a gardener, but by trade a tailor, and so he opened up a small shop right by the old YMCA. Business was good, and he gave it to his son who was proud of the tradition.

Grandpa went the very next morning up the hill to the Rose City Formal Shop and was greeted with genuine affection by Angelo Junior. Grandpa told him the incredible story, and the young tailor believed it without hesitation. He pulled out his best tuxedos and took one in to fit the old man perfectly, and then gave him a bowler hat to top it off. Grandpa looked at himself, *I look like a Milanese banker.* And indeed he did. Angelo was patient and caring with his stitches, making sure that they were invisible but strongly woven.

He stepped back and proudly proclaimed, "Ah, papa would be proud of my work. Go and meet Sophia with confidence, my friend. Our family goes with you."

Grandpa took out his wallet to pay, but the tailor insisted, "It is a present from the family that you have done so much for over the years. I do not charge old friends. Just make sure you bring it back the next day."

And so on Tuesday, a fully dressed Grandpa with his bowler hat stood in front of 81 Main Street waiting for his limo. It was only five o'clock, but he did not want to be late. People looked at him from across the road as they entered and exited the chicken market. Was this some advertising for a new store, or what? Right on time, the limo came, the chauffeur ran out and opened the door, and welcomed Grandpa in. They moved through the ugly industrial areas of northern New Jersey, though the tunnel, and then past the stately Rockefeller Center and on to Park Avenue which was beautifully decorated this time of year. There in front was the Waldorf Astoria in gold trim. Grandpa got out, and the driver said he would wait until the whole gala was done.

Somewhat reserved, Grandpa walked in and was immediately greeted by a host wearing an Italian American Foundation button. He looked like one of those ambitious lawyers trying to make it on Wall Street. "Hello, how are you? Good to see you again, please go over to the left banquet hall."

Obediently, Grandpa went left and entered the lavish banquet hall with the gigantic logo of the foundation behind the dais. As he walked in, they asked him the name he was sitting under, and he said "Stafford."

"Oh, Mr. Stafford, how good to finally meet you. You know you are sitting on the dais, on the left side of the guest of honor tonight. Lucky you!"

A hostess led Grandpa to the dais, and there were the usual wealthy Italian American types with fancy suits cut to make them look thinner and who lived in the world on a shoeshine and a smile. He was quiet and deferential, but they took that as the standards by which the very rich carried themselves. Thus this humble man fit in to the world of the falsely humble. They brought him the very best cocktail which he only sipped, and a full plate of hor d'oeuvres, meant just for him. His seat was heavily padded while the audience had regular seats in tightly packed tables. There was more silver on the table than in the U.S. Mint, and it would take a college course to figure out which fork to use when. They insisted on talking to Grandpa about the future of the wheat markets in Australia, and the oil deposits of Saudi Arabia. He listened intently, as if he knew what they were asking about, and then they assumed that he had some secrets that they should know if only he would trust them with them.

The chairman of the foundation was Marco Galena, who greeted Grandpa with a big hug, and told him how excited he was at this year's turnout. They were honoring Sophia Loren, of course, and also the Yankee shortstop Phil Rizzuto, and Joseph Albanese, an old associate of the legendary mayor, Fiorella La Guardia. "It will be a royal night," he pledged.

Then it happened, from the side door in walked Sophia Loren in a sparkling black dress, with her head erect, on high heels that made her look even taller than her 5'9". She had a long stately nose, rich red lips, and her black dress was cut seductively low so her ample bosom peeked out on top. She was more beautiful in person than in the movies.

She slowly made her way to the dais, signed autographs and had her picture taken with every man who could make it to the reception line. When she reached her seat, only Grandpa had the good manners to hold her chair for her, Old World manners that she recognized and appreciated immediately.

She gave him a fixating smile, and wondered, *My God, how much money did he give for this honor? He looks like a Milanese banker.* She never cared for those types of people and let her husband, Carlo Ponti, deal with them. But when she started talking with him, she heard the familiar sounds of a Neapolitan dialect. And she lapsed into Italian and began a conversation with him, ignoring most of the fawning men running up to her and taking pictures.

"I think from your accent, you must be from Naples. Did you know that during that awful war my family and I lived in Pozzuoli, near Naples, and once the Allies bombed the munitions plant there in Pozzuoli and I was struck by shrapnel and wounded in the chin?" She then turned her beautiful face toward Grandpa and showed him her tiny scar. Grandpa was totally fixated by her beauty and tried not to look below her neck. "Are you from Naples, or an outlying province?"

"I am from Avellino."

She sipped a glass of red wine and quietly pronounced, "This wine is terrible."

"Yes," said Grandpa, "it is from the bottom of the barrel."

Then she responded, "You know you have a very fine white wine from Avellino, Villa Raiano Wines?"

Grandpa told her he knew the wine. In fact as a boy, he had worked in the vineyards there and helped in the pressing of the grapes.

She smiled at him with her wide lips, and then when on, "We moved to Naples, but after the war our family returned to Pozzuoli and opened up a pub in our living room, selling homemade cherry liquor. I waited on tables and washed dishes, and the pub was popular with American GIs. Then when I was 14, I entered the Miss Italia 1950 beauty pageant, and was not selected."

Good God if she was not selected, what was the winner like?, the old man wondered to himself.

"I still love Rome more. Did you see me in *Yesterday, Today, and Tomorrow* with Marcello Mastroianni?" Grandpa lied and nodded yes. "Up in the Piazza Novona on the left as you walk in is a second story apartment, and there I played Mara. I came to love the Piazza and almost wanted to buy that apartment."

"I saw the Piazza when I was young. It is where Julius Caesar was murdered, not the Forum."

"Yes, yes, you are right. It was like Lincoln; Caesar was leaving the theatre when they killed him. 'Et tu Brute.' I always wanted to play Calpurnia in

Shakespeare's play."

On and on they continued, and then the chairman abruptly called order, and began to give out the awards to the bright Italian American students chosen last year. As they were introduced, they stood up, and Grandpa could not help but notice that more than half of them were girls. It was then that he felt somewhat ashamed, for he had always forbidden his own daughters to go to college. Women should get married young. But this was a different world in front of him...and beside him.

The chairman then introduced the guest of honor, and Sophia Loren rose up and in the lights the sequins on her black dress glowed as she tilted her head and began, "I want to thank the foundation for this great honor, for I was a child of the terrible war and never had a chance to have much learning, Now these boys and girls are going to college, thanks to the generosity of people, like my good friend Raffaele, sitting next to me."

The old man almost crawled under the table.

She praised the leadership of the foundation, and their support for the productions of her husband, Carlo Ponti. She talked about how she had wanted to interrupt her career for Carlo and then come back into the movie business. She stopped and remarked, "Then in the middle of my career, my critics said I was just another 'Italian mama mia' and would never come back to the film industry. I guess they were wrong. Whatever you see here is due to spaghetti."

The audience hooted and cheered and rose almost as one in a standing ovation. She was an accomplished actress and knew when it was time to exit. She then sat down. It was a very short speech, like the Gettysburg Address. But the guests came that night not to hear her remarks, but to say they had seen her, and there she stood luminous in the shaky, bright lights.

The chairman continued on with other awards and recognitions. But who really cared? Sophia turned to Grandpa and said, "Here is my address and phone number in Rome, Villa Ponti, when you come to do business there, call me and Carlo, and we will take you to the Piazza Novana. Right there at the entrance is the best gelato store in the city. He just loves good gelato." She wrote the information on the program and gave it to him with a smile. Then she was overwhelmed with fans and sycophants. Grandpa left as a group of sponsors were coming up to ask him to fund the next Christopher Columbus parade in October. He caught his limo and then retraced the way back to Jersey.

The next day he brought the tuxedo back, for the romance was over. He simply left it with an assistant and walked home. As he was getting very old, he knew he could never take a long trip back to Rome. And surprisingly he told no one of his experience, for who would believe it, even in his own family. One night, he decided to try the new ice cream store near his apartment house, Luchene, which was patterned on the Café Greco near the

Spanish steps, where the great poet Goethe used to eat. It had beautiful mahogany molding and endless mirrors. Grandpa liked the mirrors, for he would look in one and then that reflection of his looking would appear in another mirror which in turn was captured in another mirror, and which became a tiny reflection of the mirrors and of him alone. He once thought crazily that this is what God must be like.

One afternoon, he went in and ordered gelato, *limone* of course, and sat down to eat it. He began to doze off somewhat, and then he saw eating with him Sophia and her husband who also order *limone*. Behind them, he could vividly see the *Fontano dei Quattro Fiumi*, Bernini's fountain of the waters of the four rivers, with children playing and splashing and lovers holding hands.

83. A ROOM OF HER OWN

When his saintly mother died, a thin, diffident Aristo decided to leave his *paese* and go to America. He had heard it was a land of dreams with streets of gold and homes where delivery men early in the morning brought free milk and bread for breakfast. He has been friendly with Raffaele Finelli back in Catholic grammar school, and he shyly approached him once when he returned back home about sponsoring him in the New World. Grandpa as always agreed, and Aristo came over with Grandpa. A year later, Aristo had worked so hard that he had accumulated enough money to go back and take a bride. He knew few young women, and he put himself in the hands of a skilled and expensive marriage broker who arranged an *a'mbasciata*. He did not even know the bride on their wedding night; she was the oldest girl in a family of five who took care of everyone after her mother died. She loved her family and siblings but grew weary year after year of the duties that were both hers and those she inherited from her mother. Aristo seemed to her to be a gift from God.

They married, moved to Madison, New Jersey, and he went to work long hours to support both of them. He labored hard at the Dodge estates, sometimes even asking for overtime to make more money on top of his penurious salary, and she took in crocheting and piecework for a local clothing factory They scrimped and saved, and finally got together a down payment for a Cape Cod house on North Street. She soon had two children and stopped making money, so the burdens on him became even heavier. But he never complained. When he grew exhausted, he thought how much harder it had been working in Campania.

As the years passed, the marriage demands from her became more extensive. She wanted better clothes, more jewelry, trips to New York City to see shows and museums. He worked harder to fulfill her fondest dreams, but he rarely had time to take her, and so she went with other woman from the affluent parts of Madison. But she was always unhappy, with a sourpuss that became a prominent part of her lined face. Finally she was so discontented that Aristo asked, "What do you want?"

With much thought, she responded, "I want to be wooed again!" They had been married for two decades, and he stopped and enumerated what he had given her since the time they had left Italy. How could he woo her and work twenty hours a day to meet her demands?

She read more feminist literature which her best friend gave her, for every discontented woman has such a "special friend" who teaches her how to be even more unhappy, a sisterhood of misery. One day, right after her older daughter got married, she informed Aristo that she wanted to take that bedroom, install a new Yale lock, and have a "room of my own." And so he redecorated, replaced the bed with a chaise lounge, and built bookshelves for her new feminist bibles. All times of the day, she would vanish into the room of her own, and he really never knew a decent meal at night after work.

Aristo was a gentle soul, and so he put up with these demands—these were stops on the train of American marriage, he thought. Still he was not a learned man and did not know what her unhappiness was due to. Women in America lived longer than men, controlled the family money, received the inheritance, did what they wanted whenever they wanted, and firmly expressed their discontents about all sorts of things to everybody.

Meanwhile she took up art and worked in a poetry workshop at the local library; other colleagues encouraged her mediocre efforts. She and her friends met weekly and chronicled their unfulfilled dreams. She believed that whenever she went to the A & P grocery store, she was ogled and that was another sign of male dominance.

She attended a variety of events and especially began to self-publish her poetry which she had read at various university conferences in Madison in the summertime. She felt the need to express herself and saw herself as a part of a new national movement of female minds that had been oppressed for too long by men. Once she even called poor Aristo "her oppressor." He was startled, he had just given her two high priced tickets to the hit show *The Odd Couple* for her birthday. She chose to take her special friend and not her husband with her.

Confused and depressed, Aristo went to see his oldest friend, Grandpa, and explained in careful and slow syllables what was happening in his life. When he got to the demand for "a room of her own," the old man looked up, "A room of her own? Isn't she a married woman?"

"She calls herself a feminist."

"You mean a suffragette."

"No, they won that battle. Now they call themselves feminists."

"Do you have a room of your own without her?"

"No, we just have a small black and white TV in the living room where I watch the Yankees on Sundays. What can I do? I love her, but I'm losing her."

"She wishes to be lost. She is caught up in misery, and there is little you can do." Grandpa explained, "Women aren't like men. One day they are happy, another day sad. They can't stay happy for too long. It is the ugly side of boredom. They wake up in morning with gloom, resent making breakfast, wait until you leave, do a little dusting, and call that work while you are laying bricks and lifting cement. When you come home exhausted, she is weary from the world and its long day. Then at night she wants to tell you how awful her life is, and then she sleeps, and it begins again.

"What can I do Raffaele?"

"Take up bowling. Join the Knights of Columbus at the church. Come over here and play cards with us."

"But I will leave her three nights a week!"

"Yes and try to find things to do on the weekends. If I were you, I'd go to the movies. It is a good escape. Invite her to the movies, even if she doesn't like them, and then ask her to have pizza at Russo's."

"She doesn't like the sauce at Russo's."

"Of course...tell your daughter that one night a week she must invite her mother over to see the baby."

"She likes the baby."

"They all like the *bambinos*. A *bambino* can charm the sourest Italian woman."

"Are all women like this—the Irish, the Jews, the Polish?"

"Yes, surely, God wouldn't curse just us. I heard that poor Jewish men have it worse. Give them all a room of their own," Grandpa pronounced grandly.

"Where did they get this idea of a room of their own, Raffaele?"

"Ah, my grandson at Rutgers took a literature course, and he said she was a rich, unhappy author who ended up committing suicide in England by drowning herself."

"May God have mercy on her soul and all the souls she influenced," Aristo sadly noted

84. AMERICA'S BISHOP

Sometime after the gala, Grandpa received a phone call from the office of the new principal, Sister Jude of Divine Affliction, to come and see her at the end of the school day. He figured that after the splendid success of the Sinatra dinner, she was going to thank him for his efforts and for the incredibly generous amount of money he had single-handedly raised for the CYO. When he arrived, she waved him in and closed the door.

"You have done a marvelous job on the annual gala for the CYO, and we have raised more money than in the last five years combined."

Grandpa bowed his head at her gratitude, but then she went on, "You know of course that Mr. Sinatra is not exactly a role model for the Catholic youth in this parish. He has been married and divorced multiple times, he drinks and carouses in Las Vegas, he is connected to the Mafia, and his mother was an abortionist in Hoboken." *Thank God she doesn't know she was also a Roosevelt Democrat,* thought Grandpa. "We must have another event that is more Catholic, more religious, more in tune with our social teachings."

Grandpa simply responded, "I am sure you can find someone to do that."

But Sister Jude of Divine Affliction had a different idea. 'You were so successful in getting Mr. Sinatra, I would like to put you in charge of this noble task."

Grandpa shuddered, "Perhaps it would be better for you or the pastor to get someone. How about the bishop, we rarely see him here?"

"I love our bishop, but let us be honest among friends, no one in his right mind will come to listen to him speak."

That was true, at the last confirmation Grandpa went to, he almost fell asleep as the bishop droned on, but that was the problem with Catholic priests in general, they cannot preach. Sister Jude of Divine Affliction wanted Grandpa alone to mastermind her plan: she wanted to have a large communion breakfast, really a brunch after a late Mass, and have as a speaker Bishop Fulton J. Sheen. Grandpa looked at her and just pronounced, "I have seen him on television and heard him on radio, but I don't know him."

"Yes, but you can write him and tell him that St. Vincent is the second oldest parish in the state, and that it was in the care of the beloved

Monsignor John J. Daunenhauer. They knew each other well in Rome many years ago. I have taken the liberty of actually writing the letter, all you have to do is sign it as head of the CYO fund raising committee."

"But I am not the head of it anymore."

"Just a formality, just a formality."

Then Grandpa, a bit annoyed, inquired, "Why do we have to apologize for Sinatra?"

"You don't know the pressure I am under in this job."

"Do these people expect the pope to give back the corrupt money that built St. Peter's Basilica?"

"Now, now, you and I are simply servants of God."

"Sinatra gave us a check for $2,500. I guess we have to send it back?"

"Oh, no, I am sure he meant it as restitution for his sins. Besides I cashed it the next day." So Grandpa signed the letter, figuring Bishop Sheen wouldn't come anyhow, why belabor the issue?

But three weeks later, Grandpa got a letter delivered to the parish office from the Society for the Propagation of the Faith in New York City. Under Sheen's leadership it had raised millions of dollars for the poor of the world, which only added to his prestige. Bishop Sheen answered that he would be honored to come to the communion breakfast, and said he remembered with great affection his late friend Monsignor Dauenhauer. He would come by train from Manhattan to Madison, and he gave them dates he would be available.

Grandpa assumed that the priests and Sister Jude of Divine Affliction would take care of the visit from there on, but she insisted that he take control of the matter. He wrote back and offered Sheen a limousine to pick him up at his office and then drive to Madison, but Sheen for some reason said he would rather take the train, and that he could be recognized at the station with a clothes bag in his hand. Grandpa was startled. *Of course he would be recognized, some 30 million people watched him every week. He even beat Uncle Milton Berle for an Emmy award. Sheen modestly explained he had better writers: Matthew, Mark, Luke, and John!*

Grandpa borrowed a good looking car to take him from the station, and up the short hill to the school auditorium where the sermon was to be given. First he would stop at the nearby rectory and give the pastor a chance to say hello as a courtesy. Fulton Sheen arrived as he said. He surprised Grandpa for he had intense eyes, swept back hair, and was rather short. On television he looked over six feet tall. His smile was magnetic, and he greeted Grandpa with a sincere embrace. Grandpa tried to take his clothing bag, but Sheen demurred saying it was part of his need to be humbler—whatever that meant for the best known Catholic speaker in America.

At the rectory, the priests and Sister Jude lined up to greet him, and he was pleasant if not jovial. The pastor offered to walk the bishop over to the school, but Sheen simply said he should go with Grandpa so people knew who he was. They awkwardly laughed, except for the old man. Sheen vanished into the rectory and emerged with his familiar red cape, red cummerbund, a cassock with red piping, and a beautiful silver cross which he tended to finger as he spoke on television.

Of course nobody needed to be told who he was, and the entire audience rose in respect and applause. He smiled broadly and sat at the main table with Grandpa, the pastor, and Sister Jude. She quietly handed Grandpa a piece of paper with remarks introducing Bishop Sheen. He was surprised he was doing that too, but he had gone too far to turn back.

He rose to the microphone and read, "Bishop Sheen, we are pleased to honor you at this communion breakfast and recognize the fine work you are doing spreading the gospel and helping the poor. We know that we are in the midst of a holy man, a man some of us may see declared a saint in our lifetime. Ladies and gentlemen, the star of *Life Is Worth Living*—Bishop Fulton J. Sheen."

Sheen was a master at speaking whether it was in the university, on radio, television, or at endless communion breakfasts and retreats. He was from Illinois, but years in Europe had given him an Irish-Oxford lilt to his diction, and he was a master of the pregnant pause. He touched all the bases of Catholic orthodoxy, and then reminded them that the Eucharist, communion, was the very center of the faith. The Mass was simply the Eucharist with some readings, just like the earliest Christians recited in the Roman catacombs. He stressed that without the Cross, there could be no Resurrection. They too had to learn to bear their crosses in the ordinary duties of the day. He recalled that they had the real Bread of Life, but there were some people who were so poor in the world they did not even have money to buy mundane bread. He held forth that the Church must be especially concerned with the poor of the world, not the rich, for it is easier for a camel to go through the eye of a needle than for the rich to get into heaven. He recalled that it was Jesus not he who said that. He then gave all a blessing and stepped away.

This was a hometown audience, and they loved the celebrity bishop who made them feel good about being Catholics, about being special, about having a real mission in life beyond Sunday Mass. If only their own priests could resonate that way with them.

As the event concluded, he moved away, but an old Italian lady came up to him, crying that God had taken her husband of fifty years away that month. Grandpa feared this, for Sheen would miss the train back if he stopped to hear too many people. But he did and told the woman that God had called her husband so he could prepare for her a fitting place in heaven. She stopped crying and kissed his hands, and then others came forth for his autograph on his books, to bless their babies, and thank him.

He changed his clothes back in the rectory and returned in a black suit with a simple Roman collar. Grandpa had the car waiting, but Sheen insisted that he walk back to the station at the bottom of the hill. "Time is ticking, Bishop."

"I know but I need to decompress. I should walk, it is good for humility."

And so they both went down the short hill to the station and just as Grandpa feared, the train pulled in and pulled out as they crossed the street. Sheen just nodded, "Time and tide wait for no man." They both went up to the station waiting room, and sat down. It was totally empty, for everyone who wanted to get the train did.

Grandpa simply apologized, "We should have allowed more time, I am sorry."

"For what? I am so happy to be here. It is good to be wanted at times in a man's life, you surely feel that."

"Yes, I do, too often, "Grandpa mused. He realized that Sheen had had little to drink, and he went over to a vending machine and bought him a Coke.

The bishop smiled, and then asked seriously, "Why did you say I was going to be made a saint?"

Grandpa honestly replied, "The good sister wrote the introduction. I just listen to you on television. But I think she is right. It is most wonderful to be here sitting with a possible saint."

Sheen became flustered, "I will never be declared a saint. I commit often the first sin, pride, and that is enough to keep me away. When I raised millions for the poor, I thought of the poor, but I was personally proud I had accomplished what had not been done before. I beat Uncle Miltie, and I was proud not just of people listening to the Gospel message, but that I personally had won. I was proud, that is why I refused your kind offer of a limousine. I need to go through life carrying my own suitcases."

"I do not wish to debate you on sin, that is your business. But it is good to be proud, for wasn't God proud on the sixth day after His creation."

"You know more Scriptures than I do! In any case I will soon be off the air, so people will not even recognize me in a year "

"How can they take you off with 30 million viewers?"

"I will tell you a story which must be confidential between two old men. One time I found that Cardinal Spellman was trying to charge millions for powdered milk given to the Congregation, and I refused to pay. He had gotten it for free. He insisted and insisted since he was my superior. I went to the pope, and Pius ordered him to stop, and Spellman swore he would get me. Moving me off television is just the beginning. But it is God's will to teach me humility."

Grandpa just muttered, "We cannot blame God for all the evil our friends do."

Then the train came, and a very tired Sheen got up and began to board the train. As he took his bag with him, he reached into his pocket and gave Grandpa a rosary with each decade in a different color. It was a gift from his Congregation, and each decade represented the five major continents where there was poverty and work to do. He went inside the train and sat down near the window. As it pulled away, Grandpa watched as Sheen closed his eyes, looked upward, and his fingertips met. Standing on the platform, Grandpa wondered, *Maybe this good man was right. I have never seen a rich man in a limousine praying. There are five continents, let's see: Europe, North America, South America, Africa, Asia. A lot of people to worry about, a lot of souls to convert.*

85. DEATH OF A DON

Don Archibald Gallo was stringing Christmas lights when he felt a sharp pain in his chest, keeled over, and crumpled to the ground. His wife screamed but had the presence of mind to call the Madison Ambulance Squad. They rushed to North Street in front of his Cape Cod, helped him on to a stretcher, and brought the Don and his wife to Morristown Memorial Hospital.

His arteries were as hard as the lava rock of his home, Palermo, and only one artery was partially open. The doctors put a stent in it but told his wife that he needed bypass surgery. His chest would have to be cut open, his sternum broken, and arteries from either his chest or legs were to be grafted.

Gallo refused and wanted to go home and waste away and die. He knew the consequences of his decision. At home, he asked his son Carmine to go over to St. Vincent rectory and get a priest to give him the last rites and hear a long confession.

The priest who opened the door was a new curate and refused to go to Gallo, knowing already his long history as a mobster. He should instead say an act of perfect contrition, the priest counseled, and leave it in God's hands. When Carmine told his father, the old man refused to believe it. He told him to go see Grandpa, tell him that he had once done him a favor, and now the time of reckoning had come.

Carmine did as he was told, but Grandpa was not happy to see him and listened to Gallo's demand. What favor had the Don ever done for him? Carmine offered to take the Grandpa up to North Street and begged him to come quickly.

Grandpa very reluctantly went up to the house and saw the Christmas decorations scattered on the sidewalk. He went in, paid his respects to the wife, and entered the bedroom of the Don. Gallo was honored to see him, but Grandpa insisted, "And what do I owe you?"

The Don reminded him of his beautiful granddaughter who was being sexually harassed at work by her producer boss, a real pig. Then she said that it suddenly stopped. "I had my boys pay him a visit, and he came to respect her virtue. She even invited me to her wedding."

Grandpa realized that when she came to see him, his only advice was that she use the system to report his advances. That was not a good answer in the new world they lived in. He had let his granddaughter down, and so she went to another with more persuasive methods. "What do you want of me, Don Gallo?"

"I wish to die in the arms of the church, with the last rites and confession. I can't get a priest to come and perform the sacraments. They say it would be a scandal to the Church."

Grandpa could not believe it, saying "The Church deals in mercy not justice."

"I thought so too since I was little boy. Now I must get ready for my death. My family cannot have me buried in consecrated ground."

Grandpa reluctantly said, "I will talk to the monsignor. We have been friends for a few years." And so, Carmine drove Grandpa to the rectory, and he rang the bell and out came the young curate. Grandpa told him he wanted to speak with the monsignor, but the curate insisted he needed his rest. Grandpa simply walked by the young curate and called out loudly for the monsignor. He emerged, laughing and was pleased to talk to a friend.

Grandpa refused his kind offer of a glass of fine wine, and got down to the business of Don Gallo, "a member of your parish."

"Raffaele, to give him the sacraments would bring on the Church great scandal. It would be unheard of for that man to be buried near your saintly wife and daughter. He has shown no contrition all his life. I have never seen him at the altar rail all the years I have been pastor."

"Monsignor, of course, you are right. In the scales of justice, it is much tilted away from him. But he is asking the Church, the Church of sinners, for mercy, now at the end. Like the thief nailed to the cross by Jesus, he wishes to be let into the kingdom. His sins are powerful, he needs a priest of your caliber and holiness to get him out of hell."

"Oh, my friend I am too weary to save rotting souls."

"No, no, you are a priest forever. Go to him"

The monsignor got his black stole with its red piping, picked up the sacred oils and a consecrated host from the chapel, and departed with Grandpa and Carmine.

At the Don's house, the neighbors saw their beloved monsignor visiting this mobster as an act of mercy. He blessed the wife, and went into Don Gallo's room, and the priest without solicitations, put the sacred oils on his hands, feet, mouth and forehead. These were the Church's last rites. Then he sat down and abruptly said, "Please leave my friends, I understand that you wish to confess your sins, Archibald."

"Yes, father, yes." And all left including Grandpa, and for 45 minutes an exhausted and somewhat shaken priest emerged and after giving him communion, was ready to leave. Apparently, Gallo decided to tell the holy man everything, his transgressions from murder to extortion to prostitution to loan sharking. And on and on he had gone, purging his immortal soul.

The monsignor blessed his wife again, and with Grandpa and poor Carmine they went back across Main Street to the rectory on Green Village Road. There was no talking in the car. As the monsignor got out of the car, he turned to Grandpa, "Raffaele, you owe me a big favor."

"Yes, monsignor, please don't call it in too soon."

Two weeks later, Gallo died, and a Mass was quietly said for him, and he was buried the same morning in consecrated ground. Outside of the immediate family, only Grandpa attended the funeral. All his aides, allies, and so called friends had already forgotten the Don.

At the cemetery, his wife came over and thanked Grandpa profusely, kissing his hands

"Now he is buried in the same ground as your lovely wife, Luisa." Grandpa nodded, and then felt a shudder go down his spine, for the ways of God Almighty are strange and inscrutable indeed.

86. A FREE CITIZEN

At the age of 82, Grandpa pretty much knew he was reaching the end of the line. He had parked his faithful pickup truck in one of the decrepit garages in the back, and carefully placed his tools in the shed that he used to make wine and store utensils. It is ironic that as one acquires advanced knowledge in life you end up lacking the energy to keep the machine going. His children had moved away, and he rarely saw the next generation. He had no one willing to listen to his stories, tales of how he had met the great Caruso, ate with Sinatra, or counseled Bishop Sheen. Those adventures would die with him. He wished that he could write a memoir like Caesar did: "All Gaul is divided into three parts." But he forgot the next lines, *damn memory*.

He looked out at his prize possession, his garden, and in the middle was a sturdy rose bush, which he had planted nearly thirty years ago in honor of his young daughter who had died suddenly in her 20s. Around it were healthy patches of pansies, growing as they should—orderly and nestled together.

Grandpa could see the warehouse and noticed from afar that the Yale lock was missing. He had been slothful, leaving it broken and not buying a new one—tomorrow, tomorrow he would do it. He tried to space out his errands, to give him something to do each day. But he thought the old lock was just broken, it would not close, it must have fallen to the ground. With a sense of tidiness, he went down to check it out. The lock was placed on the side, not tossed on the ground.

He went in and surveyed the dark warehouse and turned on the overhead light. And then he saw in the corner with the burlap bags, four frightened people huddled together—a man, a thin woman and two sleepy children. The man immediately jumped up, begging him not to call the police. Grandpa didn't even know what the police were doing dealing with foreigners, and said simply, "Yes, Yes." He spoke fairly good English, and Grandpa was suspicious what was happening here, "What are you doing in my warehouse?"

"We jumped on the train, and the first time they checked for tickets, I took all the family off at the Madison stop. I looked down the hill and came upon the back of this building and saw the open warehouse with no lock. We stayed here last night too."

Grandpa was a bit taken back. He hadn't seen anybody in his own backyard. "What do you want? You can't stay in this shed forever. Who are you?"

"I am Juan Martinez, this is my wife Angela, and my children, Jose and Maria. We are from Honduras, the city of Tegucigalpa, the murder capital of the world. We have traveled through Mexico into the United States, and then I decided to go north for a better way of life."

Grandpa realized that they were illegal immigrants, and that the politicians were continually talking about kicking them out of the country. This attitude toward foreigners wasn't new. In 1920, the United States closed the door to Italians among others. But so much had changed since he first came. Now they were even arresting children. Grandpa listened quietly as Juan told him the story of his life and that of his family. He had gone back to Honduras twice to take his bride and had one child there. A second was born in Texas. The poverty and violence in Honduras were no place to raise children, and so they engaged in an incredible journey through Mexico and decided that they wanted to go away from the border and ended up in New Jersey. He knew no one in the state, and did all sorts of odd jobs to pay for their upkeep. The police had become more prone to pick up illegal immigrants in the state, and they moved around to avoid detention. He took the train from New York City west into the state, away from the big cities and away from other immigrants as well. Now he was here—but they were destitute.

Grandpa was a law-abiding person, but he saw in the young Juan and his wife, the faces of another frightened immigrant couple who came to Madison many years before. The children looked so terrified, and the old man first asked, "When was the last time you all ate?"

"We have run out of what we brought. I took some of your vegetables in the garden, and at night we drank water from the hose. I am sorry I stole from you."

Grandpa just responded, "It is God's bounty," and then he insisted that they all should come upstairs with him for a meal. The wife did not want to leave the safety of the warehouse, but Grandpa insisted that the children needed food. So they traipsed up the stairs in the dark and sat uncomfortably at his kitchen table. He began to make eggs, sausage, coffee, toast and put out a variety of Italian cookies which the two children devoured. *Kids are all alike,* he thought.

Then he offered them his back room for a while, but again the wife insisted they stay in the warehouse where no one could see them. They left, but first Grandpa swore he would help tomorrow, and indeed he got up early to do so. He went up to visit the Catholic pastor and asked for assistance, for surely these people were Catholic. But the priest was wary, saying he didn't want his parish involved in this "immigrant thing." Undeterred, he visited the principal, Sister Jude of Divine Affliction, and spoke eloquently in broken English of the need to enroll two new school children at St. Vincent's where he had sent his children and grandchildren who had been so fortunate. The principal did not want any more nonpaying students, but Grandpa had come off the hugely successful Sinatra banquet that brought in more money than any event. She finally agreed, and then gave him several green and white uniforms for the children.

Having accomplished that, he went down Waverly Avenue to see Joseph Pearson, who owned the furniture moving business and also ran the row houses in Pearson Lane. Pearson was having some difficulties hiring movers for his low paying company, and Grandpa presented him with the offer of a strong young Hispanic who could work in the company. Pearson was skeptical, "I don't know, I am really staying with Negroes. They get stinking drunk at times, but they sure can lift." Grandpa ignored the comment and went on, "But more and more people using your trucking services will be Spanish speaking; you need a guy who knows the language."

Pearson thought, "Yes, you may be right. Bring the boy in tomorrow. But Ralph, he better not be one of those crazy type Mexicans."

Grandpa reassured him, "No, no, he is a good boy from Honduras."

"Where the hell is that?"

"South of Mexico."

"They probably are even lazier than the Mexicans are."

Grandpa undeterred asked Pearson if he had a vacant house on the Lane and could Juan and his family move in there?"

"Yes, but he pays $40 a month, and I don't expect a whole dozen spics inside."

"Can you give him an advance, Joe?"

"Jesus Christ, Ralph, what am I, the United Way! Ok, two weeks, and he better earn it. Ralph, please go home, you're killing me financially."

Grandpa had two successes, but he needed to get the family citizenship, so they didn't live in a legal shadow, for the country was getting harsher on illegals, as they called them. He did not know the law, but he knew several lawyers: Volpe and Andrew Falcone Jr. He had come to the U.S. with Volpe's old man. He had used Falcone before to get Carmelita out of Oak Ridge, but in those days he had money. Now he was retired and lived on a shoe string. Falcone was a sleaze and did not do free work for anybody. Grandpa had no real money, but he had memories.

He went up to Falcone's paneled offices and slipped by the secretaries into Andrew's office. There he was working on a real estate deal that would make money for everyone, despite the zoning regulations. Falcone knew he was in trouble already.

Grandpa explained the need for immigration help, and Falcone said he had friends who owed him a favor at the Newark office, but such work was very time consuming, and it was expensive.

Grandpa remarked again, "Andrew I know well your grandfather and also your saintly late grandmother. She was the best friend of my Luisa. But when she came to this country, she never became a citizen. She figured that if she was in America and didn't get in trouble, she was an American. One day she told my Luisa that she was not a citizen, her husband had never dealt with the matter since he was so busy building up this great law practice. She cried to Luisa that as she was getting older, they would find out and deport her like she was Lucky Luciano. She especially wanted to stay with you, her favorite grandchild. But my wife told her not to worry, she didn't vote, did not pay taxes since she was married, and rarely talked to anyone outside of the family. So, she was content and finally died in peace. She was so proud of you, especially I remember how satisfied she felt when you graduated from Seton Hall Law School."

By the time Grandpa settled back, Anthony was in tears, and said he would take the case "pro bono," for the good of all. And so Juan and his family settled into Pearson's Lane; Grandpa agreed to open an account for him at Frank's Meat Market which at first the old man covered, and Juan and his wife scrimped and saved and bought a little cape cod in Green Village. The kids loved the school.

Then Juan's number came up almost magically, and he and his whole family were to be naturalized, except for his child born in Texas who was already a citizen by birth. Before he and his wife were made citizens, they knew more government and civics than a college freshman. He invited Grandpa to his swearing in ceremony, and the old man took the Public Service bus #70 from Main Street to the Morristown courthouse where the whole family became Americans. As they were leaving, Juan gave Grandpa a present of thanks, and he gratefully accepted it.

On the bus back he opened it. It was a small American flag on a black stick, made by the kids. Grandpa placed the flag in the cup the Jewish community had given him, next to the statue of the Infant of Prague. He then pulled open his file drawer and laid out his own Americanization papers in which the judge signed that he was "a free citizen of the United States of America." He folded it up, and pondered, *How good it is to be a free citizen.*

87. THE CATTANO CONTROVERSY

Behind Grandpa's three story apartment house was an asphalt lot on the left and his beloved garden with his long, yellow warehouse on the right; and still a little behind them was the grape arbor and the cherry trees, that led into another lot in front of a large set of broken down garages. His grandkids liked to play basketball there, but the basketball space lacked the critical essential of a net. So they approached the old man and plaintively asked if they could nail up a back board with a rim on the dilapidated garage above the doors. Grandpa said "Fine, as long as no hit the cherry trees."

They quickly accomplished their task and played poorly but diligently endless contests of pickup basketball, run and gun. At twilight when they went home for dinner, Grandpa looked out from his porch and saw a tall, thin black man shooting hoops with a very different style. He recognized him, for he lived behind the garages in Pearson Lane, a collection of ticky tacky row houses where the African-American workers for Pearson's Moving Company were quietly housed and socialized among themselves. The player was Danny Wilson, once the finest center in the history of the Madison High School basketball team and a Suburban Conference All-Star. He was then a phenomenal six feet tall and was nicknamed "Jumping Danny." Now broken by age, very hard work, and occasional illness, at times he still looked lithe and graceful as he hit one basket after another. He didn't play run and gun, but had a beautiful hook shot that seemed to emerge from nowhere. After ten minutes he would stop and vanish. Then one day he saw the kids play, and he walked over to show them some other ways of dribbling and shooting. Still their team in the CYO went 0-15.

Grandpa one day went down and pulled Danny aside, and asked if he and a friend would soon pluck the cherries before his perennial enemies, the big crows, attacked the crop. They could strip a tree in a day, so timing was of the essence. Danny and he agreed on a figure and a few bowls of cherries.

Grandpa did not know it, but unlike most Americans he lived in a racially mixed neighborhood according to the U.S. census. But he kept to his plot of land, and other people kept to theirs. Nobody stole his tomatoes or cut his mint, or ever destroyed his grape arbor, so life was good.

One day he went to the Rosedale Pharmacy where one of his granddaughters worked and for some reason bought the *Newark Star Ledger*, the Democrat-oriented paper that mainly served the city populations. He came home, sat under his proverbial fig tree, and read avidly that his fellow immigrant, Peter Cattano, had created another controversy in town. This time Pete decided that despite New Jersey laws, he would not cut the hair of black folk. "They ruin my scissors and my clippers with their crinkly hair," he pointed out to the reporters on the sidewalk on Main Street. "Besides Negroes have their own barbers, let them stay with their own." Unfortunately he had made his simple statement two days before Dr. Martin Luther King's "I Have a Dream" speech in Washington D.C. in 1963. King had given his speech before the Lincoln Memorial; Pete gave his comments before Bruno's Sub Shop. In America, most of life is optics.

The local Methodist seminary students from Drew University had announced a protest in front of Pete's establishment the next day, and Grandpa was delighted. He genuinely hated Cattano for two reasons: one, when his daughter left for nursing school, Pete told his gullible customers that Ralph's self-righteous family had sent her away because she was pregnant. And then Grandpa disliked the whole idea that a black father could be embarrassed in front of his son if he went to Cattano's shop. It was wrong.

Uncharacteristically, he abruptly decided to join the young men on the picket line, very much out of sorts for an immigrant turned citizen who had supported the Republicans since Teddy Roosevelt. The next day with his arthritis, he walked up toward the top of the center of town and saw the students. He watched as they chanted and waved pickets and walked in a circle. Pete had suddenly decided to put the stars and stripes up over the door of what he called the "Salon Elite." He had never put that flag up before; he said that was because he hated Franklin D. Roosevelt so much.

As Grandpa approached the group, a seminarian gave him a sign saying "Pete must go," So he took it, agreed with the sentiment, and walked in the circle for 15 minutes or so. He was the only old person there, certainly the only old Italian. Meanwhile Bruno's was doing a stupendous business that day. As Grandpa walked around, the organizer came and whispered, "Glad to see you, old timer." Grandpa continued and began to see the customers cheering Pete on. Many of those guys he knew. He smiled and murmured, "*Cafoni.*"

Then he stopped, his arthritis got the best of him, and he handed the sign to the organizer and moved slowly home. Three days later, the *Star Ledger* announced that the state bureau that licensed barbershops and beauty salons ruled that discrimination in state regulated places was forbidden, and if anyone violated the order, they would lose his or her license. When the seminarians sent in a black student, Pete sullenly gave him a lousy haircut, which he gave to whites as well. He was both a racist and a crappy barber. But the story was carried all over the nation.

Grandpa was delighted. "Justice wins out," he proclaimed to his daughters who were somewhat embarrassed because he was on the front page of the newspaper with his picket sign. He cut the picture out and put it next to his postcard of Garibaldi. He also knew that for genuine Italians the sweetest nectar is revenge served cold. A week later he went up to clean the family cemetery plot. The Cattano family had bought a space for all its members, including Pete when it was time. The plot was right near his own. The old man shook his head, "Just my bad fortune, I have to spend eternity next to that *stronzo.*"

88. BAIL MONEY

The summer was scorching hot, and the lawns and garden were parched dry, and Grandpa meticulously watered his garden to keep it alive. But after one month of heat, when New Jersey seemed like Manila in the summer, the governor declared a water emergency and limited showers and banned watering. Even the lawn in front of the Dodge Town Hall looked like an African desert. Grandpa could not let that happen to his garden. "Whoever heard of Italians without gardens," he proclaimed to his daughters. So every day, he drove up to a small stream in Prospect Park and filled five gallons of water and drove back and sprinkled the water on his plants at their roots. It was, he argued, the best he could do.

Then one afternoon God had decided to hear his prayers, and the heavens opened up so suddenly he had to run under the porch. Ever since he was a kid, he loved the rain, for in the daytime he could carefully study its effects, and at night he felt calm and cozy sleeping in the loft of a tin covered roof of the home where the drops seem to play a powerful set of drums. One night unfortunately he left his schoolbook in the eaves of the roof, and it got wet and warped. The next day he had to appear at school and explain the soggy condition of his tattered book. The angry teacher, Andre Silvano Tedesco de Maria, took the useless volume and gave him an even more tattered one, "You must pay the school for the one you inconsiderately destroyed. One week of hard labor before and after classes. Do you understand?"

But even with that episode, he still loved the rain, the nursemaid of nature's bounty. Besides at night, he could rarely get a full night's sleep. Later as an old man, his mind played and replayed his worries, as it does for all of us. He thought of his children and their children's problems, and at times he still reached over to touch Grandma, but she was long since gone. He was never to know true love again.

So he would pace his apartment alone and in thought at night. But one night he appeared at the porch door and saw the rain bouncing off pools right in front of his garden. Even the grape bower and the cherry trees seemed to be pleased by the buckets of rain thrown in their faces. But then he saw a thin, young black man moving toward his shed where he kept his tools and wine, and easily break the rusty lock.

Grandpa was startled, he was being violated. This assault on his life had never happened before. It must be like what a woman feels who is being raped by a stranger. He reached over to call the local police department, but then he saw a cop come out of the porch overhang, enter the shed, and grab the intruder. The Madison police had begun foot patrols a year before to learn the central neighborhoods better, and a cop would frequently walk into Grandpa's backyard in the middle of the night. Down the porch steps, Grandpa walked to confront the robber, but while the cop held him and put on the cuffs, Grandpa saw a frightened black teenage kid who was shaking as the rain came down on all of them.

"I will take him away. He'll go to jail. This is the judge's new policy. Zero crime in this county. Keep watch, you may want to see him on trial and sent to jail."

Soaking wet, Grandpa made his way back up the stairs and tossed off his drenched slippers. *Trial, jail, he deserved all that,* he convinced himself.

But as the trial date came up, Grandpa spent hours watching one of his favorite shows, *Perry Mason*. He wished one of his progeny would be a fine lawyer like Mason. He knew the judge for Morris County, Nicholas Falcone, whose cousin also had been a lawyer and who took illiterate immigrants' money to write a simple letter back home to Italy. Sometimes Grandpa volunteered to write the letter in his beautiful Italian script for free, thus cutting into Falcone's income. Nicholas got to know Republican WASP leaders and was characterized as a good law and order judge, who would keep the white suburbs safe from Newark and Morristown. Grandpa frankly thought that the kid would get a stern warning and let go. Grandpa had nothing of great worth in the shed—old tools and barrels of wine. When he told that to the cop, the Irishman responded, "Yeah, he wanted to steal the tools to buy drugs, that is what them boys live for."

The day of the trial came, scheduled at ten in the morning in Morris County courthouse, and Grandpa arrived early. The formal courtroom was indeed like the one *Perry Mason* was in, and Grandpa felt comfortable. The judge arrived, and all rose, and he obviously wanted to dispose of the case. The black kid was indicted by the bench, not a grand jury, and told to plead. He stood silent. The judge intervened, "If you don't plead, I must enter a plea for you of not guilty under the law, but I must tell you that this act involves the word of a highly decorated policeman against a street savvy kid from out of town, and it is not hard to decide. He looks pretty guilty to me. Where is his lawyer, Mr. Prosecutor?"

"He does not want a lawyer. He says he is embarrassed."

"Where is his father or mother?"

"He doesn't know his father, and his mother died of a cocaine overdose."

The judge simply responded, "The apple doesn't fall far from the tree, huh."

Grandpa was shocked, this was not the way *Perry Mason* worked. There was no defense, no jury, no fair judge, no Perry as in the show, no witnesses called. The judge continued, "I have a full calendar. So let's go on with this. You are obviously guilty. Three months in jail, or a $500 fine. If you could get a sponsor for community service you could go, but no one here is going to offer that option, Frankly who would want a street kid who steals to work for them? Looks like you will enjoy the hospitality of the county for three months, boy."

The frightened kid said nothing, But then to the surprise of all, the victim in the case, Grandpa, popped up and offered a check for $500 as bail, and said the kid could work for him for three months. The judge knew Grandpa and always felt he was a strange man, but he voted as a dependable Republican, and the old Italian people liked him, and the judge was faithful to all the Italian friends of his own family who came over with Grandpa from Naples on the *Celtic*. He stared down on the old man and simply said, "So ordered. Take the kid."

Grandpa grabbed the boy's arm and did not have to write out a check since the convict was in his charge, and he was a long respected member of the community—the victim in this case. The clerk simply gave him a receipt for the human being. And the two strange fellows left.

Finally the kid asked, "Why did you do that? I was guilty, and you were to be the person I stole from."

Grandpa quietly responded, "Yes, you did. It was very wrong. But this judge and his *medigan* prosecutor were going to send you to jail, lock you up like an *animale*. Man is not an *animale*, but a son of God. When I came to Ellis Island, I was in fact a boy younger than you, and the authorities looked at me and locked me in a cell, a hospital room with bars. I could look out and see the Statue of Liberty. I only had pink eye, but they left me in a cell for a month. A month in jail with black rusty bars. I cried every day and prayed to the Virgin, and then was let go.

"Come with me I will find a place for you to stay—a good friend of mine, and a great basketball player, lives behind me in Pearson's Lane. We must find you a place to stay." And they arrived at the poor old row houses, and Grandpa found Danny, and inquired about a place for his new worker, Calvin Cleveland Roosevelt. Danny knew of a place with one room at the end of the hall, but also knew Pearson would want some rent in advance, for he hated to give anything away for free, especially to Negroes. It was a bad precedent. So Grandpa accepted the terms and peeled off some bills, "This should please him, and will you see the boy gets meals?" Grandpa shook Danny's hand and went back home. They both had hands with hard calluses and understood each other as working men do.

For weeks CC worked for Grandpa. After a day, the old man brought two sandwiches, one for him and one for CC. He wondered if black people liked sausage and peppers like they liked chicken. But chicken bones bothered his false teeth. CC watched as Grandpa conscientiously worked on other people's property, especially how tightly he wound the lawnmowers' blades because it gave a nicer cut. Grandpa's brother Nicholas worked for him for two weeks, and he abruptly quit. He said that Grandpa wound the screws "tighter than a bull's ass." And Grandpa would not use a power mower, for it sliced away at the grass. CC simply followed Grandpa's directions and watched intently as the old man lovingly cared for his flowers around the back of the house.

After three months, CC had done his service, and Grandpa had to remind him that his time was up. But CC did not want to go home for he had none. Grandpa had talked to Danny about a job in the moving company, but CC surprised him.

"Sir, I'd rather continue doing gardening with you."

"But the work doesn't pay much, and it's continually hard work."

"I am young and strong and want to see nature grow. I wish to be a gardener, not a mover."

Grandpa, who was not an arguer, said he would loan CC money for a truck, and would give him some spare tools to use, the same tools he was trying to steal that rainy night.

And so CC became a gardener, with his own paneled truck—a truck with his name on it and worked the local area. Frequently Grandpa threw some business his way as he got older. One late Friday night he was drinking with his buddies, playing endless hands of cards, perhaps too many. Gennaro complained in an alcoholic haze, "I hear they call you the patron saint of the *moulinyan*," a crude reference to blacks that Grandpa never used in his house.

He looked up surprisingly, "Look, the boy's a good worker, you shouldn't care about his skin, look at this."

And he pulled up his shirt, and the skin on his belly was as white as a baby's butt, but next to it was his dark garbled hand. "See that color, it from the sun after all these years. Which is the real me? The great thing about Americans, we judge a man by his work, not his color. Isn't that right, my colored Italian friends?" Then he poured another glass of wine. "You know, Alexander the Great used to cut his wine with a sort of cream soda. He was a great conqueror, greater than even our Julius Caesar. Caesar's second wife, Cleopatra, was black, I read, a beautiful black woman."

89. PUNCHINELLO

Sometimes, one falls so early in love with May and its handmaidens. On Saturday, Grandpa was mixing hybrids of pansies together and trying to make new strains. He was placing a finer assembly of creations that showed a strong display of abundance with Mother Nature. Around him were azaleas that were drooping over the driveway. He had created a half dozen palm crosses for placement on the headstones of family members in the cemetery. People walking in and seeing all this thought they were viewing the work of Merlin the magician.

Grandpa was weaving wood branches of old boxwoods, honoring again the reproductive possibilities of nature. As he sorted out the work, he stopped and heard his favorite grandson who was ambling down the driveway and into the gardens. He was quieter than usual, dressed in casual clothes and a new pair of expensive boots.

"*Come stai*, Marcus Aurelius?"

"Hello, Grandpa, I was hoping you would be celebrating May."

"Ah, my son, come here, and I will be show you what I am doing, so you can focus on these miracles and for a day let the law sleep."

"I have done just that today."

Marcus was a graduate of Rutgers and had law degree from Columbia University Law School. He lived a charmed life. In New York City, he had lived on the west side of upper Manhattan, was well connected to members of the Law School, and one of his colleagues had introduced him to his sister, Adele, who was a yoga instructor and even had a public television show on the City channel. Marcus was startled when he first saw her. His friend had been blunt, "She is a real honeybun, isn't she?

Marcus agreed right away but said nothing. He welcomed an introduction, and he felt that she was a true gift from God. Suddenly they talked about yoga, and in a month's time she was explaining to him the secrets of a young taut body.

After law school, he was offered a fine position in the governor's office in Trenton, and she moved in with Marcus, but they lived near her parents' house in the most elegant neighborhood of Short Hills, some fifty miles away. That way she could have an easy commute to Manhattan, but he had a longer one to the AG's office in Trenton. They were fascinated with each other's successes and soon had a little girl who was a truly delightful child.

But as time went by, the couple had more arguments and after ten years of marriage they came to a near separation. They stayed together for the child, but the girl, Maddy, had a difficult time and sat in her room with towels under the door to cut the noise of arguing across the hall. Sometimes she even went to nearby grandma's house, where she had to go when she wanted to get away, a lonely child without friends.

Marcus somehow wanted to see if his grandparents had such experiences, such nastiness and bitterness after their very long life. How did he even know what his grandfather experienced? He assumed that people showed him respect.

Marcus finally blurted out that day, "Tell me, Grandpa, did you and grandma fight often, not giving in an inch." Finally he looked sadly at the old man and saw tears in his eyes. He just nodded and said how happy he they had been.

"We were married over thirty years, had a host of children and made do with what we had. Yes, we had elements of sadness and deep anger. At nights we often went to the same bed without talking to each other. Grandma rarely mentioned it the next day. But when the days are over, you realized you wasted so much time arguing and pouting.

"Are you having problems, Marcus? Are you ok financially? I have a little money."

"Oh no, we are fine, too fine. She had a great deal of money and we live in a wealthy neighborhood near where she grew up."

"And you?"

"I am fine. The governor wants me to be appointed Attorney General, and he will make that appointment after the election. I am going up the Democratic ladder of success. Hurrah."

"So you have it all but very little to enjoy. We had our difficult times, but I think we knew love was important. Probably I loved her more than she loved me. Perhaps not. Who can know. The doctors said she had some form of neurological condition, but she was gone before 60. And soon I was 70 and alone. Do you want those years to go away, Marcus. "

"I do not even know what love is."

"I am not sure if after all these years I do either."

"We have definitions, but who knows. When I was young, the useless Italian government put a high speed train through the farms. The people had never known how they worked or where they went. Then one day my mother got up early and was hit by one. She died under a speeding train and was mangled beyond recognition. A month later my father, always in good shape, died. The doctor said it was of a broken heart. He had no doubt that love was involved. And we all were sure that this was so. I put a picture of the Virgin Mary in her casket. I said nothing. Soon I left for America again, and several years later I came here to arrange to marry your Grandmother. As I said to you, I had always felt that I loved her more than she did me. What can you do? She accepted a husband. I took a lovely wife. People in those days were different than now. What could I do? It is what it is. Do not find yourself in such a strait. For the night is long, and the miles are so far.

Marcus expected that Grandpa would tell him what he should do, but the old man changed the subject, or maybe he did not. "How is Adele doing?"

"She tells me that she is fine. Perhaps the stress of life is too much for her and for me. I am lonely."

"How is Maddy? She is so cute. They are wonderful at that age. Enjoy her, son."

"Yes, indeed. She is so wonderful for me."

"I wish I saw her more. But I know her. Give her my regards."

"I am sorry, Pop, that we live so far away."

The old man said little, but he stared at his garden. *How long will this last after I am gone. I just want to see the June planting.*

Marcus smiled and kissed Grandpa and then dragged himself out. Grandpa wished he could help, but he knew he could not intervene in the heart more than he had.

Another month later Maddy was crossing Short Hills Avenue by St. Rose of Lima Catholic church, hit by a car. and tossed over to the side. The police called both parents immediately, and the child ended up at Overlook Hospital in Summit.

Her hip and arm were crushed, but the breaks were clean, and her parents and mother's mother gathered around her while they set the fractures.

That night Marcus went over to Madison and immediately told Grandpa the terrible account. He was so upset for the child; they drove over to the hospital. They went to the third floor and Grandpa walked in, and he was taken aback by a smiling modest-sized man, Governor Richard J. Hughes who greeted Marcus. Marcus's mother was embarrassed by the working clothes that Grandpa was still in. But Hughes grabbed his arm and introduced himself to the old man and started charming the girl—saying that he was fortunate to have two families, one from his wife who was a widow and his own from his widower status. He had altogether nine children and told the child to come and visit them at the mansion in Trenton. "I have kids of all ages and sizes; you can choose which one you want to play with." And he laughed and left.

Adele's mother had come before the governor, and she brought a beautiful Madame Alexander doll—dressed up like the young Queen Elizabeth II. She was sitting on the side near her mother.

Again, the girl welcomed Grandpa and he talked to her quietly and then looked at her injuries. Grandpa promised that he would come again with a special gift if he could find it at home. He nodded and then left with Marcus.

Like some many of the incapacitated, she began to want to leave quickly and go home. But she stayed for four weeks. At home, Grandpa went through the old hope chest he had in the spare room. It had originally belonged to his second daughter, Anna, who was his favorite child. The hope chest was two feet by four, made of pretty mahogany, and inside it was covered with cedar to protect the treasures. As he looked inside, he saw delicate articles of lace, some of which went back to Grandma's wedding, woolen coverings, and a small baby blanket. But he could not find what he wanted. He searched the bottom layer, and there it was. A puppet of Punchinello, a small hooked-nose character representing the fool or clown who supposedly lived in the neighborhood of Aversa. He was an old Neapolitan, was a bit soiled and had been handed down since God knew when through the family. Grandpa was not even sure if it was originally from his family or from his wealthier wife's family. It had a gray hat, white smock, trousers, masked face, and a distorted body that could do all sorts of comic routines. It was based on a country clown, with a shrill voice, cowardly appearance, boastful demeanor, was usually stupid, and given to tricks and stunts. Children of all ages loved it, and Grandpa was intent on carrying it over to the hospital. Would Maddy appreciate this foreign clown?

The next day, Grandpa arrived with the puppet and produced it with a sense of flourish to the girl. He began making up dialogue from plays that he had seen years ago as a boy, and soon other members in the hospital room joined it, including the doctors. Even his in-laws acted along, and Maddy insisted that she hold and play with the puppet. Later even his daughter-in-law told him that she enjoyed Punchinello more than any of the other dolls she received.

"Do I have to give back Punchinello back to Grandpa?'

Immediately the old man cut in, "No, no, it is yours. Give it someday to your children when they are sick. Just teach them to love him. Remember whatever I have is yours."

So a month later she was hobbling with Punchinello in her hand and decided to visit the old man in his blossoming garden. The girl looked at his incredible red tomatoes and asked if she could take some with her, and of course he agreed.

"Perhaps you can come over on this Sunday for lunch," his grandson's wife asked. "I'll cook and use your tomatoes." But Adele seemed a bit uncomfortable. She had never had him over in all the years of their marriage.

"Wait, take some mint too, too."

Adele looked down and quietly said, "I understand you like fusilli. I'll make it just for you. My mother could help. Did I ever tell you that her mother was from Italy?"

"Where?"

"Calabria." Grandpa laughed but said nothing.

"I know you people say they are the people with the hard heads."

So Maddy left with Punchinello in one hand, a bag of tomatoes in the other, and said, "See you Sunday, Pop-pop."

90. SENATOR FUSILLI

America is a great country if you have enough money to enjoy it. As Grandpa got older, it was tougher making ends meet. He lived on a modest Social Security pension, some savings, and his work. He refused to raise rents in his apartment house, even though the cost of oil went up yearly, and he still charged renters a meager $40 a month. He could increase his number of jobs, but he got more easily tired as the years passed by. With all his children and grandchildren, none had ever asked if he needed any money, but he wouldn't have taken it anyhow.

Then out of the clear blue sky, he received a phone call from the Madison Borough Hall. It was from the secretary for the first Italian American U.S. senator in New Jersey history, and one of the few in the collection of senatorial wind bags. The senator, whom Grandpa had never met, wanted to see him in his branch office at the Dodge Borough Hall in Madison. Grandpa was so startled he never asked, "About what?"

He went uptown in his best suit, an Arrow white shirt, and a red checkered tie. The office was on the second floor, and as he modestly introduced himself, the secretary told him to take a seat by the door. The black chair had the Rutgers University logo on it, and on the wall was the so-called unfinished portrait of Franklin D. Roosevelt painted in large part just before his death in April 1945. Grandpa looked at it, and remembered him in 1936, when he had shaken the hand of the great president, and they compared fedora hats. Grandpa, a lifelong Republican, had voted for Roosevelt in 1936, 1940, and 1944. But for the rest of the ticket he chose Republicans and hadn't even voted for this senator.

Then the senator came out and waived him in, "Ah, my friend, come in. Come e stat?" Whatever that meant. Then he erupted in laughter, "Is it not good to have a senator who can speak Italian?" Frankly, he knew as much Italian as Grandpa knew Mandarin.

The senator, whose father's family had been named Tortellini, after the circular, ricotta filled pasta, had been in the House of Representatives for six years, and then made a bold move to take the Senate seat just vacated. He was short, with slicked-back hair to cover over his partially bald spot, and wore pointed brown Italian shoes, and a blue shirt with cufflinks given him by the president of the United States. Actually, he had gotten the cufflinks in a pawn shop off Dupont Circle in Washington, D.C. He talked fast, almost in a caricature pattern, but basically Grandpa figured he was telling him all about the great things he had done for the people of the northern part of the state, especially for those on the railroad lines to New York City.

Grandpa listened intently as best he could, and appreciably nodded as the senator put his brown Florsheim shoe on the coffee table edge. *He thought he had the world by the coglioni,* Grandpa mused. Then Senator Fusilli came to the crux of the meeting, he was going to run for re-election and after that for the U.S. presidency. *Nice ambition,* Grandpa pondered. The senator was somewhat weak among the voters in the Morris County region and needed a good man who was well-respected in the Madison community, and could handle what he called "constituent services." Tortellini quickly saw Grandpa did not know the expression, so he explained, "a person who will listen to people's problems and try to help them."

Grandpa honestly responded that he was not educated enough to know the huge federal government, and how to get assistance for people. The senator waved him off and blunted explained, "Look if they are just regular people, call the agencies in this book and say I am calling. Don't worry about them getting answers. If they are rich people, you immediately call my office in Washington D.C., and I will handle it myself. An easy job, right?"

"Seems so."

"You can do it for three days a week, if you want," and then the senator laid out the salary that floored the old man. "Plus you get very generous health benefits. You know that they are good, for Congress has them. People can't expect us to go from the Senate to crappy Social Security, right?"

Grandpa just sat there. "Look, people like you. The old timers still talk of your victory gardens years ago, and how you worked on some damn thing with Albert Einstein. I do not quite understand it, but you are a folk hero! Richard Tortellini needs a folk hero! Take a week, think it over and come back. Come tomorrow to my press conference, here outside the Borough Hall. I should get some great national publicity."

Grandpa thanked him profusely, without realizing he had gotten the usual ten minute Tortellini treatment.

He went down to the Town Barbershop on Waverly Avenue for a haircut, since he had years ago boycotted the one on Main Street. Carlo Delguidice greeted him warmly for he rarely saw him, and he kidded, "Hey, pop, you got your good suit on, did you go to a funeral?"

"No, no, just a meeting at the Borough Hall."

As Carlo cut his hair and talked about everything, Grandpa interrupted him and said, "Tell me Carlo, what about this Senator Tortellini?"

"Oh, Christ Jesus, Ralph, he is as crooked as they come. I would not be surprised if he were not mobbed up. Last month an agent came from the FBI asking me about him."

"What did you say, Carlo, if I may ask?"

"Sure, in confidence, I told him the word on the street was he was getting kickbacks from cement contractors because he sponsored the new roads bill. Tortellini is a total tool of the county bosses and of the building trades unions. He has no one in his pay here in town. His name should be Senator Fusilli not Tortellini, for he is as crooked as a corkscrew."

"Oh, are you sure?"

"As sure as anyone can be. He is not very discrete. He was on TV bragging he was dating some Hollywood starlet. What a weird match!" And then Carlo started laughing so hard, he nearly cut off Grandpa's left ear.

The next day, Grandpa showed up quietly for Senator Tortellini's press conference on the lawn of the Dodge building. The senator came out dressed smartly in a silk suit, black wing tipped shoes, and a pale pink shirt. He began dramatically dragging out the picture of FDR from his office and announced:

"My friends, this great man gave us Social Security. I am committed to it. My mother is on it and her mother was on it. No one will take it away; that is why you have a number and card of your own. I want you people here to know that I, your senator, Richard Tortellini, will not only work to save it, but I will fight for a 6% cost of living adjustment. Yes, 6%, so you all can get ahead of inflation."

Now no one in the crowd knew that Social Security was being threatened, but they loved the idea of a 6% COLA. So they cheered, and when he raised high the picture of FDR, they cheered even louder.

"The greatest compliment that can be paid to me is that I am a son of Franklin Delano Roosevelt and a son of yours." Then he concluded, "Avery deer chi," and went inside. Grandpa has seen him at his best. He went home and considered seriously Tortellini's offer. He knew that Carlo was right for he was well plugged in—the senator was too slick, too calculating, and too ambitious to be honest. But the money was so good, he could live his life in dignity and independence. All night he tossed and turned, knowing it was his old morals and new opportunities that were clashing. He had always wanted to live and die as a noble Roman with honor and respecting the values of truth and honesty. Now he would be working, would be the public face, of a man who was on the shady side of the law. But good God he needed the money so much, and the temptation was almost overwhelming.

He prayed to the Virgin, but she said nothing to him. The days were ticking away, and at home he spotted on the shelf the leather bound volume of Goethe's *Faust* which the Institut had given him. It was the story of a man who sold his soul to the devil, and now Grandpa faced that choice. He consulted his oldest son who told him to take the money and run, but make sure he kept copies of all paper records for later.

He needed the money more than he ever realized. He was weary from giving the rich a fair day's work for so little. *Maybe,* he considered, *he could do this job for a year and then save up the money and quit.* He had tried to save even to the extent of not buying the newspaper every day, and when he was out purchasing only one not two slices of pizza. Small things count, but they really don't add up the way a big infusion of money would. He didn't want to spend his last years in the county poor house. He tossed and worried.

Then two days before he was going to see the senator about his final answer, he stopped at the drug store and bought a copy of the *Newark Star Ledger.* The headlines jumped out at him, "Senator Tortellini to resign. Senator accused of influence peddling with a North Korean contractor; Pay for Play charges raised by FBI in Newark."

My God, how quickly the powerful fall in this country. My decision was made for me by another, Grandpa thought. *Perhaps that is why the Virgin Mother never answered me.* So he went home and rested. But he was ashamed, reflecting on whether he would have accepted the position after all. *Why is it in life one is never tempted by the good people,* he wondered?

91. WILDWOOD

Two of Grandpa's granddaughters were going on a holiday for nine days to Wildwood, at the very tip of New Jersey. It had nice beaches and a huge boardwalk with games and eateries. They were somewhat shy girls, and they insisted on wearing a one piece bathing suit instead of the normal bikini. Phyllis loved to watch the bare chested lifeguards with their strong arms, broad shoulders, and muscular chests. *What girlfriends they must have,* she mused. Anna enjoyed sitting on the benches at night and viewing the young men in Spandex who looked so endowed as they paraded the boardwalk. Little did she know that half of the guys had stuffed a sock in their bathing trunks to give a more imposing impression. Life is so much illusion.

They enjoyed the beach and the roasting sun, and soon became bored and decided to play the various games on the boardwalk. They were supposed to be games of chance, but of course they were fixed or otherwise there would be no prizes left. The two girls, young and hopeful, tried their skills on a variety of spinning wheels to win all sorts of great prizes they would go home with. Unfortunately, after two days, they lost 80% of their money at one game of chance because they wanted to win a sewing machine. The game of course was fixed, as everybody who had been around knew. They had not been around. Phyllis tried to call her mother; they had no money and needed help. But she could not get her on the phone, so she called Grandpa to find out where she was. He responded that she was at an all-day shower in Belleville and would not be back until late. As he heard her sigh and then cry, he asked what the problem was. She told him everything, and he simply asked what the name of the game was, where it was located, and where the girls were housed. He promised to come down and help.

He hated the idea of driving to Wildwood, so he enlisted his grandson Alphonso, telling him his cousins needed him. Alphonso's gallant spirit was touched and he offered his services. Since Alphonso was unemployed as usual, Grandpa knew he had time to kill and promised him that he would pay for the gas. When Alphonso came to pick up the old man, he was changing into his one good suit, a conservative gray double breasted with a matching tie. He then reached into his bureau drawer and came up with a calling card from Volpe and Volpe, attorneys at law in Madison. They had handled the will of Bernardo which gave part of his considerable estate just to Grandma which she in turn donated to a shelter for unwed mothers.

The trip was excruciatingly long. New Jersey may be one of the most densely populated states in the union, but it has vast expanses of vacant land, pine barrens, and ticky-tacky houses and motor courts. When they arrived in Wildwood, Grandpa went to see the distraught girls and then promised to meet them in a half an hour. He was dressed to the hilt and went in to see the owner of the "Merry Gifts of Chance" on the boardwalk near the seafood restaurants. He went in and mentioned the girls' losses, gave the sleazy owner the card "Volpe and Volpe," and simply said, "I talked to the county public attorney and he said I should see only you and that he was sure you would take care of this matter personally."

The owner looked at the card and at Grandpa, and asked, "How much did those ditzy girls lose?"

"One hundred and eighty dollars."

The owner simply peeled off nine twenty dollar bills and huffed, "Tell them never to come in here again. This is the boardwalk, not the community chest."

Grandpa quickly took the money and returned to the cheap motel the girls had rented, and they were gleeful. They embraced him, quickly got into their bathing suits, grabbed towels, and headed for the beach. "Be careful," the old man warned. They did not even notice poor Alphonso there. And they did not ask them to lunch or to have a drink. Such is the gratitude of the young.

Grandpa felt guilty and asked Alphonso if he would like lunch, and of course he knew the answer. They went across the street to Dough Rollers, an Italian McDonald's, which was having a special "all you could eat for $4.95." Grandpa and Alphonso finished off the first round, and the old man was full. But Alphonso stayed for two more helpings of spaghetti and meatballs and was content when it was over.

Alphonso stopped on the way up the boardwalk at the stalls where he could win a stuffed dinosaur if he could knock down three milk bottle pyramids in a row. He aimed back and decimated the first two, and then Grandpa gave him a dollar to pay for the third which he knocked down. So for three dollars they got an animal that cost 40 cents to make in Taiwan. They now were the proud owners of a stuffed green dinosaur which stayed obligingly in the back seat.

On the way home Grandpa took off his coat, loosened his tie and relaxed after a good day's work. Once again good had triumphed over evil. Then he reached into his pocket and found the calling card. Ah, now he was the second Volpe. He wondered if he had outfoxed the owner, or if the owner knew Volpe and had feared him. Could Volpe's reputation have traveled down by word of mouth from Madison to the shores at Wildwood? It did not matter, so he tucked the card in his shirt pocket, just in case. Life is so much illusion.

92. A PRINCE OF A MAN

Grandpa died of a heart attack in May 1969. He was laid out at Burroughs Funeral Home, only a stone's throw from his apartment on Main Street. According to the Italian custom, the funeral wake lasted three days, two shifts in the first two days, the final closing of the coffin on the third day, and shipment to St. Vincent's Church for the funeral Mass. On the first day of the wake, the funeral home was full of old Italians who had come over with him to the new land. There were children and grandchildren, and their friends. After two hours in the evening, the door was closed as the priest entered and began saying the rosary. Suddenly, in the middle of the prayers, there was a pronounced banging on the door, a noise that scared even the most stalwart of men and women. The banging continued on and got louder, as if it were the Grim Reaper himself trying to enter. Finally someone had the sense to open the locked door, and in walked a large black woman dressed in her Sunday best to pay her final respects to the man she called simply "Ralph."

Nobody could figure out who she was and what attachment she had had to Grandpa in life. Maybe she was just one of those professional mourners— women who went from one funeral to another just to be in attendance at wakes, often of strangers. For generations, women of all ages dressed in black for years, and as one family member after another died, they seemed to wear black all their adult lives.

As the wake began to end, she wept and began to wail, crying out, "God, take him now into your bosom, let him enter the valley of Jericho, let him cross over the Jordan River to be with You. Oh, Lord let it happen now." She continued crying and dabbling her eyes. The daughters looked at each other and could not figure out who that woman in the back was, and even the nosiest of them were ignorant.

The coffin was carried to the church the day of the funeral Mass, and the pastor rose and praised Grandpa for his allegiance to his family and to the church. He talked of his good works for the school, and how he raised more money for student activities than anyone before or since. He did not mention the role that Frank Sinatra played in all that. He reminded people that those who believe in Christ Jesus will never die, and that Grandpa believed. As he was working up to a crescendo, the same black woman entered the church, sat in the very back pew and screamed out, "He was a prince of a man, a true prince. Great Jesus take him into your arms and remind us that once there was such a man. Oh, Lord, who will give us flowers in the spring now?" The pastor realized he had been upstaged, and simply stepped down from the marble pulpit and continued the Mass. The family was a bit embarrassed, for people rarely grieved that publicly anymore, even at Italian funerals.

When the Mass was over and people went to their cars, one of the sisters who had gone to school with "Jumping" Danny Wilson, who also attended the Mass, stopped him and asked who she was, for he was taking her home. The woman's name was Rachel Allen. Danny said that Grandpa had helped her out over the years with getting firewood for her stove and would occasionally provide her food and with a pallet of flowers which she loved.

But the story was more complicated than that as he knew. For years Danny had dated Joe Pearson's part-time secretary who told him a detailed tale some of which the daughters knew, but most of which they were ignorant of: Grandpa lived behind Pearson's Lane, a string of houses that was owned by the local moving company and which housed the black men who were hired by his business. Danny relayed, "Mrs. Adams' husband was a mover, and they lived in one of those dwellings. They had a son, a wonderful, bright, good natured boy, named Elroy, who turned into a fine teenager whom I taught how to play basketball, and who excelled in Madison High School. Upon graduation he joined the army to get the GI Bill of Rights and later go on to college. Six months later, right out of basic training, he was killed in the Korean War. The president said it was not a war, but a 'police action.' But he was dead. Mr. Adams took up drink and abandoned his mourning wife, as if he were guilty of sending his only child to war and to his death. Soon he passed away in despair. His widow was still allowed by Joe Pearson to live in the apartment, but she had to provide rent and her own fuel.

"Sometime later, Grandpa was playing solitaire, and I showed up at his back door. We knew each other well, and he asked me to come in. Grandpa was delighted for the company and welcomed me profusely and offered me a glass of wine. I had come to Grandpa for a favor on behalf of the families of Pearson Lane. They were tired of looking at the mess the Lane was in with the weeds, cars parked every which way, no driveways, and a situation that was perilous to the little children on their rusty tricycles. Could Grandpa help them clear up the place, and make the kids proud of where they lived? When he heard the words kids and peril, Grandpa was immediately won over. He said down with a piece of lined paper and drew out the plot as he saw it from his back porch. He would need to go and walk off the measurements, but he planned the elimination of the weeds and random trees, a new driveway with some pavement on it, and a cordoned off area for the children. Behind the houses he would plant a community garden so the inhabitants could raise their own vegetables. By the time he got finished, it looked like a New Deal planned community from Roosevelt, New Jersey!

"I was a bit overwhelmed, but Grandpa went over to the Lane and walked off the size of the plot and talked to the men and women wondering what he was doing. He asked the children where they would like to play, and they pointed to the left side near the movies. Grandpa had walked many times through the Lane on the way home; pass the men and waving good-naturedly to the children. Other Madison residents feared to go into a 'Negro area,' but Grandpa regarded it as just another neighborhood, and all the world was his neighborhood. The residents would wave back at the old man, for by then he was a bit of a celebrity. Some remembered when he took a black youngster who had tried to steal from him and turned him into a gardener, and how he had helped the Martinez family from Honduras whose father worked for a while with the company and lived in the Lane. From such small kindnesses, one builds a reputation in the black community.

"Grandpa warned me that he needed Joe Pearson's permission to do all this, for it was his land. But he knew Joe and would talk to him in the morning. Joe's secretary told me, on Wednesday, Grandpa went up to see Pearson and explained his plans. Pearson looked quizzically at him, and said, 'What is in this for you?'

"Grandpa was a bit taken back, and then said, 'If this area is fixed up, my property values go up, and so do yours.'

'Yeah, where you going to get the rocks for a driveway? That stuff is expensive.'

"Grandpa quickly responded, 'Your friend Mantone is moving his garage and has a lot of junk to bring up to his new Main Street location. You move it for him free, and he will give you a truck load of crushed rock, just right for a new driveway.'

'And why would Mantone, whom I hate, do that for me?'

'Because you will move him free of charge, and in return he will get crushed rock from God knows where.'

'And who is going to pay your little black friends to work on Mantone's move? He has a whole lot of crap there. They don't do anything for nothing. Live in the real world, will you Ralph?'

'I will get them to give up a Saturday morning to do it for you for free, and will explain what we have agreed to.'

'Christ, you talk better to those darkies than I do. Ok, it is a deal.'

'When you talk to Mr. Mantone, get him to throw in five gallons of white paint and some brushes.'

'Why would I want to do that, Ralph?'

'Because those houses have not been painted since Jesus walked the earth. They will look nice, the workers and their wives will be happy, and the kids will be proud to come home.'

'How am I to get Mantone to do that?'

'I will talk to him, he used to play with my boys. He is a good man, and I will tell him of your extremely generous offer to move him free.'

'He is not a good man, he is a shit, but if you can do, do it. You tell your friends on the Lane that if they get the paint, I want the whole thing done at once. I don't want them to do half and lay around drinking and listening to Dodger games and rooting for that damn Jackie Robinson.'

'No problem, Joe, no problem. One other thing. How about some playground equipment for the kids? It will raise the retail value of your houses.'

'Jesus H. Christ, Ralph, whenever you come in here, I end up poor. Please go home.'

'But Joe, I already have a sign carved free by Angelo Bonaratti that says, "Joseph Pearson Park," it is so beautiful, and the kids will remember your name forever.'

'All right, all right, do it. Buy it at a cheap store on Route 22. And don't call it 'Pearson *Memorial* Park.'

"And so Grandpa left, and it happened as he planned. First, he cleaned out all the rubbish and the weeds, and then he laid out the driveway, and the rocks came like clockwork. It looked beautiful, and then as Grandpa laid out the children's park and the gardens, we worked quickly to repaint the whole complex in two days. It looked like a suburban development, and we were so proud, and our wives and children were happy at life's turn of events. They took up a collection to pay Grandpa for his work, but he said, 'Use it to put a fence around the children's park so no cars ever will go there.'

"Three months later, he was told that he was being honored at the Central Avenue Bethel AME black church. He really felt embarrassed, but he did not want to hurt anyone's feelings, and so he went up to Central Avenue. There the minister, Dr. Ernest Lyons, took him to the very altar, and had him sit near him.

"The choir was dressed in beautiful red robes, with blue shawls, and they came strolling down the aisle sideways to the choir section. The music was upbeat and truly magnificent; it was hard for even Grandpa not to tap his feet, and the little boys and girls in the choir waved to him unashamedly. He smiled back, as the minister began:

'It is the Lord's Day, it is the Lord's year, and we are here in his glorious presence. St. Paul tells us that at the end of the world we must say that we have fought the good fight, have finished the race, and have kept the faith. And that is us here at Bethel. With us is a stranger to this church, but not a stranger to this neighborhood. This man singlehanded helped our brothers and sisters refurbish Pearson's Lane. He led those people like Moses into the Promised Land, and now we are so proud to live there and near those apartments. Whenever I go to the train station or to the movies, I think of Brother Ralph, for he alone did God's work. Brother, come here and speak to us—he originally spoke Italian, which I know was one of the languages heard at Pentecost.'

"Grandpa seemed embarrassed for he was not a speaker, but he got up, and simply remarked, 'I listened to you sing, and if God doesn't hear you then it is His problem!'

"They laughed for only a white man could speak so arrogantly to the Lord. Then he went on, 'I ask only God's blessing on our work and on our lives. Amen.' Then he sat down and muttered, *I have not made a fool of myself.*

"The preacher praised him more fulsomely, but stopped periodically, 'You know he is a sinner, Lord, yes, like all of us he is a sinner. But today in the Lord's Day in the Lord's year this man has earned salvation, and we are glad at Bethel to bear witness, for he is good in God's eyes.'

"After the service, Grandpa was invited to lunch in the basement, and the food prepared by the women of the parish was extraordinary: ham, turkey, roast beef, macaroni and cheese, baked bread, croissants, cakes and pies. We all thought the feast was truly worthy of a king. And as he ate, the children performed in his honor, dances and ballets, in the most beautiful ways. When he finished three hours later, he left drenched with sweat; he said he had not had such an emotional moment since the birth of his last child. As he was leaving a woman came up to him, and politely asked if he had any sticks of wood left from his work on the houses. He said a few pieces, but what did she need? She told him that she had no firewood for her home and that she lived by the fireplace in the cold Jersey winters. Grandpa took down her address and said he would help...and thus began his monthly donations of wood to Mrs. Rachel Allen, which lasted for years until some of the Pearson Lane people heard of his donations and embarrassed began to take up the slack themselves. When he died, she came to his wake and funeral. She was the mystery woman you saw.

"It was that work that the Klan burned down in 1959, and the old man stubbornly got us all to rebuild even nicer. The AME church yesterday had a special service for Grandpa, but no white person came."

Then Danny got unfamiliarly philosophical, "You know it is strange, is it not, how many secrets of goodness, generosity and tenderness are never known to even the closest of friends? Sometimes it is the stranger who knows most. But somewhere there is a tally of such charity that is kept, and that is why people believe in heaven.

93. FINALE

May for all of us is the most beautiful month of the year, as we see the beginnings of a springtime of growth, of beauty, and of love. But it was a sad month, for it was in May Grandpa died. He was sitting in an easy chair surrounded by the small children of his youngest son and experienced a pain in his chest, and then he felt the Italian sun hitting his face, like it did when he worked the fields at home in Rotondi, as it did when he came back to propose, as it did when he visited Nuzo's grave one afternoon. He had had heart problems for a while, and he passed away at the age of 85, the age the gypsy had told him he would live to when he first met her in Naples.

He was buried according to the new rites of the Church, and then laid next to Grandma. Now who would take care of her gravesite? He left to his sons his apartment house and asked that they give each of the other children $2,000 from the proceeds. They sold it, and the developer cut up most of the apartments and paved over the richest soil around to put black top for parking. Before the building passed on, the brothers asked members of the family to come and see if they wanted any memorabilia that he had.

It was then that I saw the serving platter of Marilyn Monroe sprawled out nude. Actually I really went for the *Book of Solomon,* but it was nowhere to be found. It was as if Grandpa seeing the end, simply discarded it forever.

However, I did see the manila envelope which had the Sacco-Vanzetti material in it, and as I opened it out fell two items that were not originally there: a $2 bill which was a common gift to his grandchildren and a browning picture card with ragged edges like it had been in a wallet for years. I did not at first recognize the woman in the photo, but then realized it was a very young Grandma. On the back of the photo, he had written in his very stylized Italian script a notation: Paradiso, xxx, lines 28-39. I went home and reached for my Ciardi translation of the *Divine Comedy,* and found the following citation:

> *Dal primo giorno ch'I' il suo viso*
> *in questa vita, infino a questa vista,*
> *nonn'e il sequire al mio cantar preciso;*

ma or convien che mio sequir desista
Pio dietro a sua bellozza, poetando,
Coma a l'ultimo suo ciascuno artista.

Cotal quell io lascio a maggior bando
chequel de la mia tuba, che deduce
L'ard a sua matera termindado
Con atto e voce di spedito duce
ricomincio: "Noi siamo usciti fore
del maggior corpo al chel ch'e puro luce.

From the first day I looked upon her face
in this life, to this present sight of her,
my song has followed her to sing her praise.
But here I must no longer even try
to walk behind her beauty. Every artist,
his utmost done, must put his brushes by.
So do I leave her to a clarion
of greater note than mine, which starts to draw
its long and arduous theme to a conclusion.
She, like a guide who has his goal insight
began to speak again, "We have ascended
from the greatest sphere to the heaven of pure light."

He had chosen to give me a sign in the form of a two dollar bill that this message was for me, to be kept alive even by a person who did not speak the author's language. So I got an Italian copy and read the lines again, they were more harmonious, for Italian has more rhymes possible than English. And they were more uplifting, more ethereal, more spiritual, and more swept up in sweet, sweet love.

ABOUT THE AUTHOR

MICHAEL P. RICCARDS is the author of numerous books and verse plays. He has compiled four books of short stories in "The Rose City Series," in addition to his autobiography, *A Hero in My Own Times*. Grandpa was his maternal grandfather whom he knew and at times worked with.

Dr. Riccards has been a college president at three different institutions, a public policy scholar at the College Board, and the founding head of the Hall Institute of Public Policy. He has been a Fulbright Fellow to Japan and a National Endowment for the Humanities Fellow at Princeton University. Dr. Riccards is married with three children and five grandchildren.

His editor is Ms. Cheryl Flagg, previously at the Council of Graduate Schools in Washington, DC. She is co-author of *Wilson as Commander in Chief*. These short stories were critiqued by the Writing Seminar at Hamilton Public Library under the aegis of Rodney Richards.

The author is a former political science scholar, but above all he is a man in love with the English language.

He can be contacted at mriccards@gmail.com.

Made in the USA
Middletown, DE
16 November 2019